FORCE NINE

CHRIS H. STEVENSON

FORCE NINE

ISBN: 979-8-88653-468-9

Melange Books, LLC
White Bear Lake, MN 55110
www.melange-books.com

Published in the United States of America.

Cover Design by Ashley Redbird Designs

This book is dedicated to Susan Weiner, a loving friend and colleague, along with the United States of America, for its Constitution and pursuit of Democracy for all!

1

Agent Gene took two strides and joined Diane Nine on the other side of the window. He peeked around the frame, fisting a rifle in one hand. "I see two so far. One is standing by the passenger door and looking this way. The other is stepping off the porch across the street and heading for the vehicle, but he has his eyes on this building."

"The locals ratted us out," she said. "We can take two."

Gene made a throaty noise. "The windows on the SUV are blacked out. There could be more in the vehicle. But that's not the worst of it. They're wearing flak jackets. I can't get a clean headshot from here without endangering bystanders." He paused for a beat. "Okay...the passenger just cornered the vehicle to meet up with the other one. Now they're both out of my sight."

Diane tore the baggy clothes off, exposing the combat exoskeleton and snapped the helmet and utility belt into place. The utility belt held a pouch with a dozen circular saw blades.

Gene glanced at the waist pouch. "What the heck are those?"

"Weapons of mass destruction. Stay here. I'll guard the hall."

"Take an AK-47 with you. All you have to do is spray and pray."

"Yeah, but I'm all thumbs when it's time to reload." She showed him her pincer-like claws.

He saw the multi-mode finger control on the combat suit. "Then use it with your off-hand and bring it back when it's empty."

Picking the rifle up and jacking the slide was easy.

"I can't let them get on the radio set," he said, and jumped in front of the window and yanked the rifle up. The gun belched on full auto. Window shield glass splintered. Bullets pinged off metal.

Diane brushed through the door and jogged down the hall, arriving at the head of the stairs. Screams of dismay came from the lobby below. Several hotel patrons ran up the stairs in a crush and headed for unoccupied rooms. After the last person cleared the stairs, Diane ran down fast, the servos in her legs squealing. Too fast. The robotic legs jerked out of sync. She pitched forward, landing on her chest, and belly-slid toboggan-style down the landing, her helmet chin plate striking the steps. She crashed headfirst into the lobby counter. After shaking off the fall, she staggered to her feet.

An armed man leapt onto the porch, heading for the entrance door. She heaved the rifle up and sprayed the front window, taking it out with an explosion of shards. The hotel manager ducked under the counter, screaming her lungs hoarse.

At first, it looked like the advancing man was hit since he'd disappeared after her burst. Then a rifle barrel rose over the lip of the porch. He had dropped down for cover or had been blown down. His gun barked with an orange flash. Bullets whistled inside the lobby striking the walls and staircase. Diane ducked behind the edge of the counter and heard a barrage of fire coming from the second story and knew it was Gene having his own gun battle. His shots were answered by return fire coming from the street near the SUV.

Diane stepped out, sent a burst into the planks of the porch, tearing up chunks of wood. The man's rifle barrel suddenly dropped. She trotted across the lobby, skidding on broken glass, firing single shots at the porch. Reaching the shattered entrance door, she aimed down, fully aware that the terrorist had scooted under the porch to hide. She pumped her last bullets into the planks. The rapid fire was answered with a moan. Fifty feet away, the rear passenger door on the SUV swung open. A man jumped out, firing from the hip. *Reinforcements.*

Diane felt sharp thumps against her torso. The body armor had taken several high-powered rounds, including the face shield, which nearly tore her helmet off. She turned to run, a hail of bullets chasing her, several of which struck her back armor. After making it to the staircase, she half-crawled, half-ran up it. She knew she had been hit when she reached the top landing. The warmth of blood coursed down her back. After reaching the hotel room, she found Bibi and Gene, bobbing and taking shots out the window. She threw the empty rifle on the mattress and called out, "I got one under the porch!"

Gene glanced at her. "Move over here—take this. I just reloaded it."

She took his position at the window while he reloaded her empty weapon. Bibi hobbled across the room, snatched up an extra clip and disappeared around the door. The large woman's heavy steps faded down the hall.

"Bibi, you get back here!" Diane yelled.

"Never mind that," said Gene. "Give me some cover fire —keep them pinned behind the vehicle."

Diane fired short bursts, biding time for Gene who now had one of his makeshift hand grenades loaded in the sling pouch. He approached the window on his knees and lit the fuse. When he had the slingshot pulled back to its limit, he rose up and let it fly. The grenade sailed through the air with a wobbly sizzle and struck the inside wheel well of the SUV. It exploded with a concussion that rocked the vehicle off the ground. Shredded rubber flew like a cannon shot, sending the two men behind the hood sprawling flat. Just as the men groped to their feet, Diane aimed for their faces and pulled the trigger several times. Missed. The men dove for cover behind the vehicle again.

Gene sent another grenade missile out the window. It went long, erupting on the porch behind the men in an explosion of wood chunks and nails.

Firing from the first floor, Diane could see Bibi's shots hit the side panels of the SUV, piercing the metal, breaking the windows and taking chunks out of the upholstery.

The return fire halted. The enemy disappeared. Gene sent another mini bomb out the window. This time it landed on the hood, blowing out the SUV's front windshield.

Diane strained to see any combatants left. "You think we got 'em? Where'd they go?"

Gene eased up to peer around the window. "They might be under the vehicle. No, wait. I can see the rear passenger door opening on the other side. I can't get a bead on him. Okay, now I think he's crawling around to the rear of the..."

A man stepped away from the back of the SUV and knelt. He flipped up a long tube-like object atop his shoulder.

"RPG!" screamed Gene and shoved Diane toward the door. She made it inside the hallway just as her feet left the floor. Then came the sensation of somersaulting in the air in slow motion like she was caught in a vat of molasses. The next thing she remembered was spitting plaster dust and trying to shake the ringing from her ears. It seemed the whole hallway wall had collapsed inward from both sides, burying her.

Strong hands lifted Diane up from the wreckage. Gene pulled her down the hallway, carrying both rifles in the other hand, while she had to work the servo legs. He turned his head to speak but she couldn't hear the words. When they arrived at the top of the stairs, they saw Bibi at the bottom, crouched behind the lobby counter, exactly where Diane had been moments before.

Consumed with an infuriating rage, Diane broke from Gene's embrace and stomped down the stairs, holding onto the rail for support. After reaching the lobby, the terrorist who had fired the RPG had another rocket readied for loading. She clicked her finger control for a dead run, passed through the entrance and launched over the porch. She hit the man in the midriff with a flying body-block, sending both of them thumping to the ground. She scrambled to her knees and caught the man around the ankle just as he got to his feet. Activating the mechanical pincher fingers, she broke his leg. The man howled then crumpled to the ground. Two thundering punches to the face knocked him out. The suit controls gave off electronic snaps and shorted out. She lay on her side and waved for help.

Gene got to her a moment later and tried to stand her up. Failing that, he dragged her to the porch and sat her upright. He rushed to the SUV, checked the interior and then moved around to the other side in a stalking crouch. He reappeared and then gathered up the terrorist's weapons with a full armload.

Gene palmed the sweat from his forehead and said, "There were four of them. The one on the other side of the vehicle has the back of his head filled with wood and the other lay under the porch, where you got him. That makes two dead, two unconscious."

Bibi limped out of the hotel and collapsed on the porch, clutching a breast. "That bastard shot my nipple clean off! I hope this shit's over."

Diane pulled her helmet off, letting it clunk onto the porch. "Girlfriend, I'd love to help you right now, but I've been hit. I think a bullet crept up the seam of my suit when I was crawling up the stairs." A pool of blood had collected on the porch next to her right buttock.

Gene pulled her vest back and peered down inside. "Okay, hang on. I can take care of this."

Bibi gripped her girlfriend's wrist. "Oh, baby, we've got ya!"

Diane had the sensation of being lifted into the air and then floating. Disjointed voices and the sound of muffled footsteps came from far off in the distance. Her eyesight phased in and out of focus.

Then her mind wandered. *I wonder if this is what it feels like when you're going to heaven. I'm dying. Angels will show up at any minute. I'm ready.* They didn't come. Then, before blacking out, she wondered how in the hell she'd ever gotten into this mess. The answer was simple. She had only wanted to walk again. That was it. Was it too much to ask for a dream to come true?

2

Diane adjusted the pocket scope, allowing the image to come into view. The next runner looked promising. Michelangelo had chiseled this one out—broad shoulders, rippling quads and abs like crop rows. He had a nice golden tan, but his face was pointed down, obscured from view.

You can jog without looking at your feet. Just flash me a little face. He did when he rose to straighten his back. He was as handsome as a new car.

With the flip of her hair, she stashed the scope in the side pocket. Forget hot, this guy was incendiary!

Diane nudged the joystick, bringing the wheelchair up to the fringe of the jogging trail. Mr. Stud Cake made the S-turn on the path like a standard bred pacer on the homestretch at Woodbine. She pulled the charcoal sketchpad up and set it on her lap. Just as the young man approached, she let the pad fall to the grass. The handsome runner stopped, panting. He retrieved the pad from the grass and stepped up to the wheelchair. They stared at each other for a brief moment before his eyes panned down to her legs.

He extended the sketchpad. "Looks like you dropped this."

She studied his eyes, looking for that inner light of recognition—that certain spark. It took a microsecond to make the determination. Nobody was home. He was okay as first impressions went, like a trendy piece of clothing pulled off the rack. But once donned, it itched and felt clunky.

She grasped her sketchpad, knowing he hadn't looked at it. "Thanks for getting that for me. It was a clumsy slip."

"Name's Mac," he said. "They call me Mac Attack." He waited for a reaction.

The response came a moment later. "Diane Nine," she said, pleasantly enough. He sounded like something off a McDonald's menu.

He shook his head, his eyes grave. "It's a real shame you had to end up like that. Can't be much fun for you, stuck in a wheelchair when the rest of us are out here puttin' rubber to the road."

"Oh, I get my rubber to the road all right." *Now you can burn your rubber out of here.*

"Yeah, but what do you do about...you know...." His eyes lowered again. He seemed to be in a quandary or hurry. Maybe both. "...About feeling things down there," he went on. "I mean, doesn't it stop you from partying down?"

"What do you mean, partying down?"

"Well, gettin' gigged—laid."

This interview was over. "Look, I have enough parts to party down with. Okay? Sorry I cooled your run. See ya."

He backed away and resumed his position on the path. With a swagger, he crouched and kicked off. He jogged around the bend, giving her the backward finger.

The Huntington Beach Library was the best bet. It held one of the largest literary collections in Southern California and it sat on the crest of the hill overlooking a picturesque lake. Many of its visitors, including the recreational joggers, were intellectually competent men. Most of them were college students. Some of the nicest guys browsed the book aisles—particularly the art and history stacks. Diane longed for a great repartee with someone who stimulated her mind as well as her eyes. Friends made fun of her for loitering and trapping unsuspecting men with the old dropped sketch pad routine. But what was so wrong about being proactive in searching for a potential mate? These were pleasant dates with stimulating conversation. Not blunt force trauma sex.

Today was a day of adventure, opting for the sun and the breeze. If all else failed, a bag of popcorn was reserved for the ducks. She brought the scope to her face again, eying the trail.

The next prospect was a distant speck. Clearly, he was moving and sucking oxygen. Always a good sign. He wore an enormous full-sleeved jogging suit. His arms flapped, kind of like a wounded pterodactyl trying to get airborne. His stride was crazy-legged; he ran as much sideways as forward. She nearly laughed out loud but thought better of it. Instead, she felt somewhat sorry for him. It might have been his first jogging experience. Diane was no stranger to barbs or insults. Even with a slung gut and knocked knees, wasn't Seabiscuit hard on the eyes but chock-full of speed and heart?

Diane perched the sketchpad on her knee. The runner's face didn't show well; his hair kept fouling the view. When he hove into view, his height became obvious. He was more than gangly. Not that it was a deterrent. Everyone towered over her.

She waited a few seconds more and then dropped the pad. But the scope left her grip and landed on the grass at her feet. Frantic that the small telescope would be discovered, she twisted in the chair and reached down. Having forgotten to cinch the lap belt, she nosed over and fell from the chair.

Holding her hands out did little to absorb the impact. Her upper chest struck the ground, and she rolled on her side, facing away from the jogging path. "Holy Christ!"

"Oh! Hold on there," said a male voice to her backside.

"Oh, it's really nothing." She spat out a few blades of grass. "Happens quite often." Which was an outright lie. She always buckled up. Except for *this* time.

He said, "You'll just have to forgive the hands."

She felt fork-truck-sized arms slide under her torso, followed by the sensation of being lifted. Settling upright in the man's arms like a sack of potatoes, their faces were inches apart. He had root beer-brown eyes and a strong cleft chin. His panting breath, smelling of coffee creamer, washed over her--*French vanilla*. He had a pleasant smile, showing a crack of teeth.

"Now if I were to grade you on that dive," he said, "I would have given you a nine-point-five. Only because you threw a little twist into it."

She almost erupted in laughter, averting her eyes. But his face was magnetic. There was something in his eyes—something indescribable that drew her into their depths. Intriguing depths, maybe even a little dangerous. He was strong, steady in his embrace. And it was nice to be in a strange man's arms this far off the ground without a lifting harness. All of her observations were processed in ten seconds.

"I really don't make a habit of getting picked up this way," she said, giving him a timid blush. "Figuratively or literally."

"I wouldn't think you'd have to try." He pulled her tighter into his chest.

"Uh, that's really swee...kind." It almost came out a gobble. "I hope I'm not a burden, and it was nice of you to—"

"No problem. I needed an excuse to stop. I was slaughtering the blacktop."

He bent over, gently placing her into the chair. Then he drew her seat belt taut and snapped it. He backpedaled and picked up the sketchpad and scope, momentarily studying the charcoal rendering of the hills and landscape.

"Looks a little bit like *Autumn* by Lena Kurovska," he said. "I like the way you captured the eucalyptus in the background."

"Oh, you have the appreciation? I was more influenced by Hilary Burnett, especially some of her earlier work. But I'm splitting hairs." She paused a beat, watched his reaction. He wasn't poised for flight. That was a good sign. This might go around the bases. "I'd offer you a chair but the only one around here is occupied."

He handed the scope to her. She told him she used it to pick up extra landscape definition. He bought the explanation and then sat on the grass at the foot of the chair. He cuffed a dollop of sweat from his forehead.

"I didn't mean to break your rhythm," she said. "It looked like you had a good draft going."

"Don't kid yourself. It's a wonder I didn't blow a hamstring. Truth be told, it's my second time out. I'll need to find another activity to boost my cardio, because this is downright hazardous to my health."

"You couldn't think of a more beautiful place to blow it."

"I love the library grounds and couldn't think of any other trail to run." He looked out across the lake. "It's always been one of my favorite spots."

"It's my favorite place, too." Why was she agreeing with him, almost finishing his sentences? "I have no choice but to stay put unless I want to putt-putt around the trail, but I'd only get in the way of the runners." Now she was babbling.

First thing first; the preliminaries were missing. Like, uh, introductions.

"I'm Diane Nine," she said. "I'm a Huntington resident and I cruise this place like a stalker. Lots of free time lately." *I'm getting a word in edgewise. Why is this any different from the others?*

He extended his hand. "Chet Strauss. Huntington, also. So how does a nine-to-five allow you out to enjoy the ambrosia of a day like this?"

She took the hand and flinched. It was cold, but very life-like. Funny, it was never noticeable before. *His right arm and hand are prosthetic. Talk about being caught off guard.*

She smoothed her hair down. "I only work three days, knocking out enough panels to keep the editors stocked for the next issue. It has its liberties."

"You're an artist by profession?"

"Comics. I work for Majestic, responsible for my own issue. The Aurora series, featuring Endura."

His face brightened. "You're syndicated! I've seen the series and read your strip. You're all over the place. Endura of Futura, from the planet behind the sun. Nice work! How'd you manage that?"

"Pretty easy. I went to Majestic Comics ten years ago with an armload of story ideas, panels and samples. I laid down a heavy-duty pitch. I got a call a week later for a trial run in a single issue. It got some great reviews and tagged some extra sales. So, they featured me in the next issue; ran a profile-bio with photos, which led to my first stint as a comic book artist. I'm beginning to think that cartoon graphics and comics are in my blood since I have frequent bubble thoughts." She giggled.

"I'm impressed. A fine arts vocation is a tough gig."

"It pays the bills. Sometimes I feel a little guilty about the size of the checks. Then there are permissions and subsidy rights sales, but William Morris takes care of all that now. We've been in talks with Hasbro about an Endura action figure. I can't wait to accessorize her."

"Looks like Majestic knew a good thing when they saw it."

"I couldn't stop hyperventilating after I signed the contract. It was a real paper bag moment. And you?" Her eyes landed on his hand. "Sorry, I noticed that—"

"Not to worry. It was an industrial accident five years ago. I lost it from the elbow down. I designed the replacement—the internal framework, actuators, sensors, and the dermal sensiflesh."

"No way!"

"Way."

"Are you a doctor or something?"

"Mechanical engineer, MIT. Picked up a PHD in physics while at Cambridge. Spent some time designing at NASA for the last two Rover missions. I've contributed to some breakthrough technology in biomechanics and robotic telepresence. To date, I hold forty-one patents—but it's the lecture circuit that pays. All I need is fingers for calculator buttons." He screwed up his face. "Gak. I just barfed up my whole resume."

Diane cocked her head. "You sound like MacGyver, that guy who could make a light saber out of a paper clip. Don't worry. You're intriguing me. Is there anything you haven't done?"

"I haven't won the Nobel Prize yet. It's on my serious hit list. I find enough applications for my inventions to keep me more than busy. For instance..." He stood up and walked a slow circuit around her wheelchair. He ducked once to look at the undercarriage.

She turned in her chair, finding him at her side. "Is there something wrong?"

"Nope...I could change out those batteries and replace them with some high-output cads, then tweak that drive motor to put out some more torque. The suspension could use a retrofit. There's a lot of wasted space in the frame." He paused, jiggled one of the wheels. "It's just a matter of improving on what's been done. I love to tinker."

He moved around to the rear of the chair. She could almost feel his eyes on the back of her head. She couldn't turn that far around and hoped that he was admiring her hair. She'd had compliments on her platinum locks. He didn't disappoint.

"You've got hair like moonshine," he said. "Nice. Stop the presses. What's this bulky bag apparatus on the back of your wheelchair?"

"That's just my papoose carryall. It's four Sierra packs sewn together that I use for hauling everything. There's a joke that I transport illegal aliens across the border in it. It'll hold a hundred pounds of stuff."

She watched him reappear in front of her, but he did not sit down. His eyes fell to her legs for the first time. She felt the slightest crimp in her heart. Somehow, she knew it wouldn't last, this attention, this profound sincerity. She brought her emotions to heel, expecting the worst. But he surprised her again when he took a small tape measure and pocket calculator out of his baggy pants.

"Forgive me," he said, then ran the tape from the crown of her head to the outside of her hip, then the crook of her leg, and then down to her toes. He measured her shoulder breadth, stabbed some buttons on the little Casio.

"You tape out at about five-four. Do both your pinky fingers work?"

"Uh, yes. But what does that—"

"Look, I don't normally do this, but I've been working on a prototype for the military. It's a full combat military exoskeleton, titanium chassis with telepresence servos and motivators."

"Oh?"

"With some modifications, we could fit you in the bottom half of the torso chassis. I could rig up the sensors to pull commands off the upper body nerve or muscle track. It's just a matter of where to plug in." He stepped back, worked his jaw. "Yep, I think it could work. Now, from what point does the nerve damage begin?"

"Well, from about the bellybutton on down—it was a lumbar fracture. I don't understand. What are you trying to say?"

"It's really simple. How long has it been since you've walked?"

"About twenty-three years. Um, why?"

"How would like to walk again? Unassisted. Even run."

"You're kidding. You're blowing smoke up my...rear."

"No, not at all. With a little luck and pluck, we should have you blowing a smoke trail behind your sneakers. It'll take some time, though. That's unless you don't feel like—"

"No, wait. First, I have to know what's going on."

He looked over his shoulder, giving the jogging path a nervous glance and then brought his eyes around again. "Let's hammer out the details over dinner. What say, tomorrow night at seven? Pick your restaurant. Give me your address and I'll call to verify before picking you up. Don't worry about transport. I have a utility van with a lift gate."

"I don't know...it's kind of sudden." She thought about it for another ten seconds. "Okay. This should be interesting. I wouldn't mind hearing what you just told me in layman's terms." She pulled her purse from a side pouch and gave him a business card. "I'm in Huntington Harbor. Come in through the gate from the Pacific Coast Highway side and show that to the guard. It's already initialed, so he'll allow access."

He took her hand again and gave it a quick kiss. "I'm looking forward to it, Diane. It's been a pleasant visit, short drive-by that it was, but nice nevertheless."

"Thanks, Chet. Yep, interesting. I guess I'll see you."

"You will." He gave her a meek smile and then turned around. He rocked back and forth a few times, building up momentum. He launched. His legs flailed wildly, while the body seemed to fly along by default. She watched him in awe, hoping he would not tangle up and go down. He had a near miss and stumbled just before he made it around the bend. She let out the breath she had been holding. Wow. Was that an exchange with an eligible, professional bachelor? Chet Strauss was a give me this and let's do that type of guy. Anything he had to say was quick, painless. Nothing lost in translation. She hoped she hadn't stepped in a pile by accepting his invitation.

The decibel-busting voice of her personal assistant came from behind her. "Dang, girl, you're awful close to the lake. You ought to back that buggy up so you don't end up with the ducks."

Bibi appeared at her side with an armload of takeout. The large woman set the bags on the ground then flopped down next to them. She stretched her muumuu over her knees, fashioning a small fabric table, then began to organize the food items. She handed Diane a small tub of salad, a napkin, and plastic fork. Then she lined up several hockey puck-sized burgers at her side.

"Chef salad with bacon bits," said Bibi. "You can eat yourself gut-sick and not gain an ounce of fat. You had cottage cheese with pineapple yesterday, so I figured you're due for a good bowel movement today. As for me, I need fries and burgers cruising through my blood."

"You should be a nutritionist," Diane mocked, looking at the woman who had the Whoopi Goldberg mouth and Nell Carter body. "Seriously, one of these days a piece of French fry is going to hang up in one of your arteries. Then ping! They'll have to call the fire department to pick your grand piano-sized ass up off the deck then rush you to the hospital."

"Just so they send a gaggle of hard-bodied hunks." She stripped a sandwich wrapper and cleaved a small burger in two with one bite. She pounded her breastbone, swallowing. "Down, boy! Down!" She looked around. "Now, how'd the shopping go? Find anyone interesting?"

Diane speared a small wad of salad. "Since you've been gone, two more losers. The last loser wanted to gig me, I think. I gave him the exit sign. Oh, and two autographs. A couple of kids recognized me."

"Good on you for giving the losers the boot. They need to be playing with your mind first. So, you haven't done any buying off the rack today?"

"Buying off the rack" was Bibi's interpretation of potential dates. "I wouldn't exactly say that. I kind of put one on layaway. An engineer named Chet Strauss. He seemed pretty decent. He wants to take me out tomorrow night. I dunno, Bibi. Everything went right. Almost too right...and *fast*."

Bibi stabbed a straw into a Styrofoam cup. "What's the problem with that? You're pushing twenty-nine, way past the Hugh Hefner league. You have to get your priorities straight when you meet Mr. Right. Then you can count your blessings." She took a long pull on her cola. "But don't forget to count the little digits in his balance book."

Diane looked wistfully out over the lake past the eucalyptus trees. A large cumulus cloud threw some rolling hills in a dark shadow. She drew in a sharp breath, exhaled slowly. "Bibi, I just hope you're right. I'm damaged goods, like a dented can at the supermarket. I just need a guy who sees the value of the contents and overlooks the packaging. If he has something to offer in the deal, well, good on me. But I'm not ready to kick up my heels just yet. Pardon the irony."

Bibi slapped at a fly on her cheek then took another burger from the assembly line. "All depends on what this Chad has to offer. What's he bringing to the table?"

"Chet. His name is Chet. He's got a sense of humor, and he's a real brainy guy. Loves art, too. But what he told me almost seemed impossible. I still can't believe it."

Bibi spoke around a bite. "Yeah, that he's lost royalty or something...like he's the Duke of Windsor and he told you to keep it to yourself." She laughed, the crumbs falling from her heaving breasts.

"No, it wasn't anything like that, Bibi." She leveled her eyes at the large woman. "He said, well, he said that he could make me *walk* again. Even run if I wanted to!"

Bibi blew a geyser of cola from her mouth, spraying her lap. "That no good honky bitch!"

3

She couldn't quite tell where his hands were unless they were north of the small of her back. He sure was spending a lot of time down there. He really shoved because the hardboard support above her mattress was abrading her bottom or her rib cage.

"Are you kneading my butt again, Ollie?" asked Diane. "Because you're spending a lot of time down there. I'm having serious doubts about your gayness. You wouldn't be having any straight thoughts lately, would you?" She giggled.

"Nope. Not going over to the dark side anytime soon."

He gave her a few butt smacks—his cue that he was finished. She felt the towel buffing down the length of her back, removing the excess oil.

"Got to keep the junk off the trunk," said Ollie. "Prepare to capsize."

"Aye, Cap'n."

He rolled her over onto her back. Ollie swiped the towel from her breasts to her toes, threw it in a hamper, then stood back to admire the results of his massage. "Mighty fine work if I do say so. You've still got great muscle definition, and you're all blushed up nice and pink for your date. Too bad he won't see it. Unless you get lucky." He gave her an exaggerated wink.

"He's not going to get lucky. It's not that kind of a date."

"I just don't see the sense in getting all pimped out if it isn't going to be appreciated. It's like hanging a masterpiece in a gallery and putting a dust cover over it. You have to let that baby hang out there for all eyes to ogle."

"I'm not looking to hang things out. I'm not interested in getting gigged."

Ollie put his hands on his hips. His eyes turned to slits. "Now where did you pick up a word like that? Isn't that something southerners do to frogs?"

"Never mind. It's not important."

"I'll have to use that sometime." Ollie scratched his jaw. "Sidle up to some big bear and ask him if he wants to get the gig on." He put his hand over his mouth to stifle a laugh.

Diane chuckled. Ollie had been her live-in massage therapist and physical trainer for the past six years. He weighed all of 135 pounds, most of it knuckles and forearms. Upon their first meeting, she wondered about his health since he unashamedly confessed to being gay. He was 'clean' he told her, just underweight and unappreciated. She gave him one of the downstairs bedrooms, where he could play his classical music at full volume and entertain friends whenever the need arose. Sometimes his gerbils would stink up the lower half of the house, prompting them to open all the windows to flush the odor out. But he always kept her in stitches with some delightful barb, usually directed at Bibi. That alone earned his keep.

Diane pushed herself up against the headboard. "Where's Bibi?"

"She's downstairs running the lint brush over your gown. I take that back. The house is shimmying. That means she's on her way up the ramp."

"Don't let her hear you."

"What's she gonna do? Give me another black eye?"

Bibi brushed through the doorway, holding a black satin evening gown high enough off the floor so it didn't trail. She hooked it onto the fringe of the canopy bed frame and then went to Diane's chest of drawers. She laid out undergarments: slip, panties and hose. "You checking out Di again?" she asked Ollie over her shoulder. "You should take your ass down to your room and run the air filter machine. Those rats are starting to stink up the place something awful. You'll have our guest pinching his nose in disgust."

"They're gerbils," said Ollie. "And I was just finished with the treatment. So, if she won't need me anymore...."

"Thanks, Ollie," said Diane. "It was wonderful, as usual."

Ollie walked to the door and then turned around. "I hope you knock him dead, princess. Don't let him get away with anything and make sure he picks up the tab. You tell him that if he doesn't bring you home at a decent hour hell will come knocking." He curtsied to Bibi. "As for you, you pallet load of preponderancy you go off and get gigged."

Bibi blew out a sigh. "Git, you little hedonist. We've got work to do." She carried the clothes to the bed and laid them out. She held up a pair of panties. "How about we do the Brazilian Tango tonight? No? Okay, the thong."

"Briefs are fine, Bibi. I'll wear a bra, too. No advertising tonight."

"All right, then. The boy panties and boulder holders it is, but I think you're missing out." She worked Diane's legs into the panties, pulled them up and then inched a slip up to her hips. A lace brassiere followed.

"I don't even know if I trust this dude," said Bibi. "I mean, he's coming off telling you he's going to make you walk, or maybe even run a marathon. I still think I should go with you. You said he had a chopped-off hand. Maybe he put that hand some place where it didn't belong. This man gives me the creeps, if you don't mind my saying so. You just tell him you always have a chaperone to come along because—"

"It's going to be okay, Bibi. Really. I just have a feeling he's not the dangerous type, aside from his fashion sense. There's something about him, and I can't explain it. I think he's too tied up with his own thoughts to be an evil planner. He's also kind of clumsy, in a masculine sort of way. Harmless, but not defenseless."

Bibi wiggled Diane into the gown and fastened it. Once she hefted her onto the wheelchair, Diane rolled to her vanity mirror. She began applying her makeup. Bibi fastened small diamond studs to Diane's ears and then used a brush to tease her hair.

Diane looked at her watch. She was running a tad late, owed to Ollie's extended massage. She quickened her pace, finishing the makeup, adding a shot of perfume to her cleavage and neck. Bibi draped a light, white summer sweater over her shoulders and then stepped back.

"Hooray! That's mighty fine, Ms. Nine. I think you're set to bust a move."

The front doorbell chimed from the upstairs speaker.

Bibi slapped her forehead then strode out of the room. "Dude's early!"

Bibi's frenzied steps thundered down the ramp. Diane motored out of the bedroom and down the spiral ramp, circumnavigating the sunken living room, then pulled into the entrance foyer just as Bibi swung open the door.

Chet Strauss stood on the porch stoop as stiff as a chess piece, holding a bouquet of white roses. He wore a dark blue, three-piece suit, brown oxfords and a black bow tie. He looked pensive, thought Diane. Or totally frightened out of his mind. The image of Bibi standing in front of him with her hands on her hips did not help matters. She nudged Bibi gently from behind. The large woman took the bouquet and headed for the kitchen in search of a vase, mumbling under her breath.

"Would you like to come in for a minute?" asked Diane.

"We might not have time if you've made reservations."

She could tell he was poised to go. "I haven't yet, but we can get into the wind." She rolled through the doorway just as Bibi reappeared at the door.

"Now no funny business," said Bibi and introduced herself as Diane's personal assistant. "That happens to be one prime time lady, and I don't stand for anything under the table. I wouldn't push things past the midnight hour because she needs her beauty sleep. You hear all that?"

"I did, baby, I did." He gave her a curt bow.

"It's *Bibi.*" She slammed the door.

Chet escorted Diane around to the rear of his utility van, which sat parked on her frontage driveway. He pushed a button on the side panel. A lift gate lowered from the rear, exhausting a pneumatic hiss. He tried to assist her in, but she propelled herself easily onto the ramp and inside.

"You'll have to forgive Bibi," said Diane. "She's very protective."

"Already forgiven." He raised the platform.

Chet entered through the side door and began tie-strapping the chair mid-center to the floorboard eye hooks. Once in his seat, he fired up the engine and they drove off.

"Noel's Seafood is my favorite restaurant," she said. "It's on Pacific Coast Highway. They have chair access there—any of the tables will accommodate me."

"Ah, I know it well. That's a great choice. Spitting distance, too. You look very lovely tonight."

"Thanks for that. I need a small army to get prepped, so I can't take all the credit."

Chet drove past the guard station and made a squealing

right turn onto the highway. He punched the accelerator hard while whipping his head from side to side, checking both rear view and side mirrors. He merged instantly into the fast lane, increasing the speed. Yanking the wheel hard, he passed a car on the right that was doing the speed limit and then he swerved back into the fast lane. Diane braced against the dizzying maneuvers, wondering why he felt the need to rush. He swerved again, nearly missing a slower vehicle.

"The speed limit is forty-five here," Diane warned. "We don't have a reservation. It's first come, first served. You can relax."

He did not relax but kept his head pivoting. His suit jacket rode up his back as he fought with the wheel. For a moment, Diane thought she could see a small stream of sweat on the side of his temple. She had no idea what had aroused him to peel down the highway at such breakneck speeds, but she could only hold on and remain quiet. Distracting him, pulling his attention away from the forward view, might cause an accident.

After five minutes, the van lurched again then side-skidded into the restaurant parking lot, nearly taking out a decorative planter. Chet butted the van up against a parking stop and shut the engine off. "Well, we're here," he said.

"I can see that," she gushed. "We couldn't have gotten here any faster if we'd taken the concord. Do you always drive like that?"

He exited the vehicle and dropped the lifting ramp before answering, "Well, I don't like to dally. I can't abide transits unless they're swift." He unfastened her tie straps and helped to guide her onto the ramp. Once on the ground, she gave him a few stern words about his driving skills.

"I suppose you're right," he said, keeping pace next to her on the way to the entrance. "Maybe I owe you an explanation."

They entered the restaurant, a rustic, wood-paneled abode with a low ceiling. Large fishing nets filled with dried starfish, conch shells and sea urchins, hung from the rafters. Sharks' jaws adorned the walls, and within each mouth a photo-bio of an historic sea captain was displayed. The tables were adorned with decorative candles fashioned in the shape of small lighthouses.

A male host, with menus in hand, met them on the fringe of the dining room. He bowed curtly when he recognized Diane.

"So wonderful of you to join us this evening, Ms. Nine! We do have an open table for you. If you would follow me?"

They were led down a carpeted thoroughfare to a private booth at the back of the restaurant. Diane pulled to the outside of the table and nudged against it. Chet refrained from sliding into his seat and, instead, pulled her wheelchair back and lifted her into the booth seat opposite him. He then took a seat directly across from her. It had happened so fast, she had no time to protest.

"Sorry, I prefer the head-on view. Hope you don't mind."

"It's actually a better perspective," she said, once again surprised. This man did not ask. He took charge and did whatever he damn well felt like doing.

They both ordered fillet of sole, with baked potato and coleslaw. An opening salvo of bread sticks and clam chowder arrived a moment later. Diane dipped her bread stick, trying to relax, but her eyes did not leave Chet Strauss. He was either wonderfully bold and confident, or a few cherry slices away from a full fruitcake. She couldn't decide which. She hoped she hadn't made a mistake.

A small girl made her way down the aisle, her face flushed rosy pink. When she reached the table, she looked shyly at Diane then produced a napkin and a writing pen. The child stammered at first but finally got it out.

"I wish Endura would write her name for me so I can remember her for always," said the girl.

Diane looked down the aisle. She saw a mother with an apologetic look on her face standing next to a booth.

Diane took the napkin. "Oh, you bet. Endura is glad you came to see her." She made a small freehand sketch of the cartoon figure on the napkin. "What's your name, dear?"

"I'm Stacy."

Diane finished the autograph with a dramatic swirl and handed it back. "Now Endura will always be with you."

"She sure will!" The girl skipped down the aisle, waving the napkin at her mother.

Diane noticed her dinner guest had taken it all in. *No revulsion to children.*

"So where do you park your engineering self, Chet?"

"I live off Talbert Avenue. I have some property in the abandoned oil fields up on the hill. Granddad got in on the early Orange County land rush when he bought several encyclopedia lots in 1920. As you probably know, investors were reluctant to build up there in the gullies until oil was discovered. Granddad built a warehouse and small bungalow on the property. He used the warehouse for a tractor repair business. My dad inherited the property and business, until it languished and fell into disrepair. When dad passed, I was bequeathed the property and structures."

"Sounds like quite a project."

"Took me awhile to renovate the place for my needs when I fashioned the main building into a workshop. I also moved into the shack to save on rent. So, I guess you could say that I am the little hermit who lives up on the hill. The only access is a dirt road. I have an open view of the coastline, even the pier. I've got jackrabbits and sidewinders for neighbors."

"Sounds reclusive." She hadn't noticed it before, but his good hand was a roadmap of nicks, scratches, chips and cuts.

Most of the wounds were old, but a few were recent. Definitely the hands of a mechanic or technician.

"I don't move around much and prefer it that way," he went on. "My residence is one-point-seven miles from the library, four miles from the pier and nine miles from my old high school, Marina. I live and work within that sphere. It's my little bubble."

She waggled a bread stick at him. "It's a good thing I live in your bubble. Sounds like everything else is foreign territory to you. Have you been driving long? Hate to harp on it again, but you have a peculiar way of getting from one place to another."

He gave her a sheepish smile. "I've been driving for 30 years. I'm not as reckless as you might think. It's only in the past couple of years that I've resorted to moving around quickly, watching my back. I can assure you there's a reason for it. I'm sorry if I frightened you."

"I just wondered if you had a glove box full of speeding tickets."

"I've had my fair share," he said, as he sipped some chowder, dabbed his mouth. "I don't know whether it's a blessing or a curse. Most of my projects have involved high security, 'eyes only' access. A lot of it has been government research projects—top-secret, level. I still have a valid clearance for one military department that's associated with the project I'm involved with. But my association with such work has become known to questionable outside factions."

It took him a long way around the mountain to say that he thought he was being followed, thought Diane.

"I guess that stigma goes with the territory," she said. "Did you ever think that your paranoia might be unfounded? I don't mean to insult or pry, but many scientists and politicians throughout history were delusional or disconnected from reality. You know, the monsters under the bed— things that go bump in the night feelings."

"It's not a question of an overactive imagination. I *know* I'm being followed—watched. I do know that it's not my own government. The department put some men on my case to check it out. But the mystery spies cooled off and never showed themselves. The minute my spotters were pulled from surveillance, the ghosts showed up again."

"This has something to do with your current project?"

"The past two years of it. The stalking has increased in the last three months."

"Do you think they know where you live?"

"No question of it. They've never followed me onto the property, having always turned off before I hit the 'dirty, dirt' road, as I like to call it. I've been picked up on the way out, though. It's always a different vehicle. I've seen Hispanics, Caucasians, Asians and African-Americans at different times, different places."

"I'm surprised they haven't stormed your property and robbed you."

"It's too heavily fortified. Motion detectors, screech alarms and lasers are just a few of the traps. I'm hardwired to two security outfits, so any unauthorized breach is transmitted to law enforcement."

When the food arrived, Diane nibbled, preoccupied with what she was hearing. Swallowing all of this espionage drama, she wondered if she would have room for dinner.

"Do you think they're actually looking to harm you, or trying to prevent you from completing your work?"

He diced up his fish steak and drenched it with lemon juice. "I think it might be more serious than that. A kidnapping would solve a lot of their problems. Getting a few prototype blueprints from me would be a boon."

"You think this combat skeleton is what they're after? Why would they want it?"

"*Military* combat exoskeleton. It's really a miracle of technological evolution—a foot soldier's dream. It's a form-fitting, adjustable titanium alloy chassis connected to a power source that feeds telepresence sensors, which in turn motivate the servomotors. Simply put, it's a covering of synthetic tendons and muscles. Only it possesses much greater torque and load pressure. It gives the wearer some superhuman qualities. It has snap-on, carbon-carbon pads, which cover the vital organ groups—a bulletproof armor. The tactical helmet is projectile resistant and equipped with infrared, night vision, telescopic and laser range-finding com links and interior systems and data array."

She took her first bite, chewing quickly. There was a lot to take in. "You're describing something like a robotic suit that's impervious to damage. Sounds like my Colonel Chaos character in the Aurora Series."

"Not nearly as clumsy. Extremely lightweight and non-intrusive. Minus the helmet and armor padding, you could wear it under a double-X jogging suit without detection. Dry-weight is forty-eight pounds, including the power pack. The implications are staggering; particularly to a military complex that supports a large infantry."

"Hmm...how is that significant?"

"The advantages would be optimal in guerrilla and urban warfare. Imagine an infantry wearing such super suits. They would expend less energy, carry more ammo and supplies and be resistant to anything up to heavy machine gun fire. Hand to hand combat with such a soldier would be one-sided—over in seconds."

"I see what you mean."

They ate and chatted for the next twenty minutes. Chet Strauss had just confessed that he believed he was a serious target of some foreign regime bent on hijacking him for military secrets. She saw this as a lousy forecast as far as a future relationship was concerned. If it were true, how could one adjust to such a cloak and dagger existence? She knew that any relationship would be complex, with a certain amount of emotional expense. This man carried baggage that stretched beyond comprehension.

Chet finished his plate, reached for his coffee cup. "This is nonsense. I'd love to hear about your interests. So, tell me, *where in the world* did you come up with the idea of the Aurora universe and your main character?"

"That's a whole new subject, Chet. It would take me a while to explain it all. Let's give it second date. How about a week from now?" *I'm not going to rush this. He needs to know his limitations.*

"You're on."

A week later, date number two arrived as planned. They chose Noel's Seafood again and only switched menu choices. Chet had consumed her thoughts most of the week, almost to the point where she'd neglected some of the simple things, like chores, employee payroll and her swimming lessons. Bibi and Ollie had forgiven her. Luckily, neither had said that she had her head in the clouds. She was pacing the relationship, keeping an interested but cool distance.

They took the same booth they had the previous week. They finished their appetizers, and Chet propped his chin with his palm and gazed across the table. She discovered he had a fine-tuned memory when he started in as though they hadn't missed anything in a week.

"From where we left off," he said, "let's hear your story. That' my first hunger."

The question didn't catch her completely off guard. Yet she was no stranger to being drilled about her work, especially from the media. She would not give Chet the rehearsed answer. Something more intimate would be offered, more personalized. Like the truth.

"You could say that Endura is everything that I'm not," Diane began. "I first envisioned her much the same as she appears today. She's tall and stately, almost Amazonian. This gives her a perspective that allows her to see others from an equal, eye-to-eye vantage point, or in some cases, she gets to look down upon some people." Diane crossed her eyes then stuck her tongue out. "It's my way of getting back at all you tall people."

Chet narrowed his eyes. "What's that force field around her? Where did she get that?"

"That was issue number one. During a deep exploration probe, her ship got too close to an event horizon, where she was "demolecularized". Upon barely escaping the black hole, her atoms reformed, leaving her with that aurora shield, or plasma envelope. She carried that attribute back with her when they landed safely on Earth. She then discovered that the aurora shield had some pretty unique properties. Nothing could penetrate it."

"What did Aurora get in the deal?"

"It provided her with some neat qualities, like added strength and speed. While nothing could get through the force field, it was also true that she had lost the ability to physically mingle with her own kind. She couldn't be touched by human hands without adverse effects. Her sense of touch was lost forever."

"Sounds almost autobiographical."

He wants a deep, inside probe. "Oh, it is. Endura was desensitized to her environment. She lost some basic human traits—physically and emotionally. She saw herself as a freak.

A bit hard on her, but that's the way she saw it. What was left to do other than complete the visage and adopt a new persona? She added a one-piece latex suit to her ensemble, a mask and a hip pouch of sling blades. Shazam! Crime fighter extraordinaire." Diane laughed. "She's a brooding superhero--the number one poster child for race, religion and color equality."

Chet cleared his throat. "What does Endura seek? Does she have anything to look forward to other than a solitary existence?"

Diane looked at him coyly, catching the innuendo. "She only lacks some of the basics that keep her from living the way she wants. I know that she would love to walk in a lush meadow with the grass between her toes. Maybe stroll on the beach without all the curious eyes. She wonders what it would be like to have a cat nuzzle her leg. I think if she had her wish granted, she would prefer not to be so famous. If she could blend back into society, I think happiness and peace would find her again. But it's an impossible dream to fulfill. Nevertheless, she endures. Pardon the pun."

"I notice she goes it alone. Men are quite attracted to her, but she spurns their advances."

"They're always attracted to her for the wrong reasons. Most of them are afraid of the strange outer light, neglecting the inner one, which is always much more accessible."

She watched his facial expression soften, knowing she had reached an inner part of his core. That had been her intent. Her stove was hot. He could always leave if he couldn't stand the heat.

Chet looked at her across the table with a dopey expression. "Well, I like Endura! It sounds like she's made fruit punch out of lemons. I would only remind her that love and understanding is not something beyond her reach, no matter how pessimistic things appear. She's special. I think she requires a special type of love."

Right answer. You don't flinch, either.

Dessert arrived after finishing the main course. The dopey expression had flip-flopped. There was hardly anything not to like about Chet Strauss. They swapped forkfuls, her apple pie for his strawberry shortcake. Diane nearly slipped under the booth while leaning forward, but he caught her, bracing his leg against her limbs under the table. Once she steadied herself, she said, "Thanks. I go rag doll at the most inopportune times."

"I never mind catching dolls," he said, gazing over his fork.

"How many dolls have you caught?"

"Just one so far."

I can't believe this is happening. I'm uncomfortably giddy. It's time to end this date before something really stupid flies out of my mouth.

Nothing had changed much during their third date, which arrived on the third week of their platonic relationship. This time, though, a movie had predated the dinner, a romantic comedy that had both of them in stitches. They laughed at nearly identical scenes, both ending up in happy tears. Diane had been offered an aisle space with enough room for her wheelchair, but Chet insisted on sitting her in his lap through the show. He had a special usher return the wheelchair and run interference for them when the feature had ended and they were ready to leave. Yet something had progressed during those two hours that hadn't surprised her. With hands firmly around her chest, his arm cradled under her breasts and his breath blew hot against her neck. It was first time she felt anything physical stir between them. Could he have cared what he was doing? To throw caution to the wind, she didn't care at all. She had more of a feeling of like for Chet Strauss.

At the end of their meal at their favorite eats, the check arrived via a waiter Diane knew very well. They had performed a ritual for the past two years. Tonight, would not be any different. Although this waiter knew that Diane had an interesting man in tow who had lasted more than a few casual dates.

"Have you heard of that new drug Damnitol?" asked the waiter.

"No," said Diane. "What does it do for you?"

"You take two pills, and the rest of the world can go straight to hell for up to eight full hours."

Diane laughed, slapping the table. "It ain't got anything on Peptobimbo. Two full cups swallowed before a date increases breast size, lowers intelligence and prevents conception."

The waiter gave a loud hoot. They both looked at Diane's dinner guest. Chet cocked an eyebrow, and without missing a beat said, "That's nothing. You can take Dumberol with Peptobimbo and it can result in the enjoyment of country music, gun racks and pickup trucks." He looked around nervously.

The waiter gave Diane a nod. "Not too shabby. A vast improvement over the last one. Now can I get you folks an aperitif to polish off the festivities?"

"I'm good," said Diane.

"Ditto," said Chet, handing the waiter his credit card.

As the waiter excused himself, Chet rounded the table and gently hoisted Diane into the chair. He said, "I have something I'd like to show you. It's never had an audience before. Besides, I think the two of you should meet."

He rolled her out into the parking lot and secured her in

the van. He promised to take it easy with the ride; started up, then drove down the highway. She hadn't the vaguest idea of what he had planned but decided to go along with it. He hadn't shown any signs of being a serial killer up to this point. Contrarily, he had earned some valuable points, demonstrating some refreshing camaraderie—everything she relished and expected.

Chet took a small side street off the highway and then entered a maze of dirt roads amongst some small arroyos. At one point, they passed a sign that read BOLSA CHICA CONSERVANCY AND WETLANDS. She knew they were taking the back road into his property, an area she had never visited before. There were no reflective markers or street lamps. All she could see were some rusted chain link fences clogged with scrub brush. Several dark shapes materialized into broken down oil wells, frozen in ghostly stasis.

They crested a small hill. The van headlights fell onto a distant structure that was partially illuminated by several small flood lamps. A corrugated tin warehouse and a small clapboard building sat off to the side. Chet stopped the van, pulled a device down from the visor and aimed it out the window, stabbing his thumb on it twice. It was a remote.

"Have to shut everything down," he said. "Or else we'll drive into a fireworks display."

She nodded, guessing that he was turning off his security systems. They continued on, Chet rolling the van to the end of the warehouse which was equipped with a large swing door and a smaller entrance door. He operated the remote again. The large access door swung upward, revealing a dark, cavernous maw. He drove into the structure then shut the van off while the door swung shut behind them with an audible clang. Fluorescent lights popped on overhead.

"You've got this place *wired*," said Diane when he lowered

the lift gate to the concrete floor. "I'm impressed. It's like trying to get inside a bank vault."

"It requires quite a few input codes to get in safely. I wrote the program myself. I've got movement sensors on the property 100 yards out, plus split screen security cameras covering every compass direction."

Diane slowly rolled down the length of the hangar-like warehouse. Presses, lathes, grinders and other hardware took up the main floor space. Workbenches defined the perimeter, laden with every hand and power tool known to man. Some of the machines were totally foreign looking. She saw something that looked like a large gun barrel with mirrors on each end. She did recognize two electron microscopes, having seen such devices in labs at college. But she had to stop and read a label on one very peculiar box-like apparatus, having no idea what it was.

GAS CHROMATOGRAPHY-MASS SPECTROMETER

"It's used for forensic metallurgy," Chet explained.

"I imagine it is," she said, a bit overwhelmed by all of it.

Diane motored further down the length of the warehouse floor, passing up several full-sized chalkboards riddled with equations. It looked like certain areas of the warehouse held separate stations involved with the production of different materials. Rolls of fabric sat next to a hot press induction mold. Fifty-gallon barrels held shiny metal rods; the title written across the barrel read TITANIUM STOCK. A large desk arrayed with computer hardware and monitor screens took up the last station.

At first glance, and just off to the side of the computer equipment, Diane gave out a gasp, thinking that another human occupied the warehouse. It was soon revealed that the human likeness was a suit of camouflaged panels strung together over thin tubing and hinged framework. It hung from a tall T-rack. Nothing bulky or obvious. But a graceful, formfitting suit that included thick tread boots, gloves and a gold visor helmet.

Chet stepped up to the suit. "Ms. Nine, meet TACS. My acronym for 'Tactical Armored Combat System.' This is the version I plan to introduce to the DOD."

Diane rolled closer to it. "So, this is what all the fuss is about. Looks like something out of Buck Rogers." She rolled a circle around it, noting a small backpack the size of a thin suitcase. A canister, the size of a thermos bottle, sat under the backpack.

Chet explained, "A compilation of several disciplines—four years of research and development, with six years of production. The armor is an improvement over the Ceradyne boron carbide. I developed tri-hook Velcro fasteners. I did retain the Nomex fiber to make it fireproof. The rest of it is mine, especially the pneumatic piston servos and the mini-compressor."

"How does it move?"

"Don't ask me about the nuclear power drive. I can't even begin to tell you where I found that. Suffice to say, the US Navy is missing a copy of some blueprints. Not stolen. Acquired in the name of research."

"Don't you think this belongs in a more secure facility?"

"And risk some black op agency stealing my patent? I love my country, but I'm not prepared to hand something over to them without due process or a signed contract. I'm ready for a demonstration, but I haven't had the suit on a proper test subject yet."

"Why haven't you tried it on yourself?"

"I need to be an observer. Besides that, I'm too familiar with the applications and systems. This needs testing on the everyday military recruit. All the bugs have to be evaluated while they're being field-tested. Then the tech writers have to write the instruction manuals. It's an elaborate process."

"What's holding you back?"

"The proper test subject."

"Ah, now I get it. You need a pilot for your little cockpit. That's why you were talking about me walking again."

"It's more than that. It's helping me along with my project, but I'm offering something in return. I have the means to duplicate all or part of TACS. I've been working on it for the past three weeks. I only need to complete customizing the frame and retrofit the propulsion feature to work for you. I'll provide you with your own version in exchange for the research."

"Just as long as I don't glow in the dark afterward. When do we start?"

"That's fantastic. I need to take the last fitting measurements and record some data."

"Where do you want me?"

"Now?"

"Why not? It's going to be past my bedtime by the time I get home. I might as well give my roommates something to bitch about."

He pointed to a long stainless-steel table. "I'll need you stretched out on that. Then I can do a last torso scan and record the data. Problem is..." The hint of a small blush appeared on his face. "You're wearing a dress and shoes."

"You're good at taking things apart. Just take away what you don't need. Unless you're shy."

"Not *that* shy."

"Problem solved, then." She couldn't believe she had agreed to it. It was either harmlessly adventurous or reckless. Maybe both.

He had her maneuver her chair next to the table and then placed a cotton pad over its surface. He lifted her gently onto it, holding her on her side. He unzipped the gown and began to work it down her body, shifting her trunk, inching it past her hips. He next removed her shoes and then flattened her on her back, legs straight out and arms at her sides. Next, he rolled a portable halogen lamp next to the table, directing it down on her. Diane closed her eyes against the glare. Chet spoke as he worked.

"I'm running a tape now, getting the precise limb measurements. That's so I know where your joints meet." He left for a moment then returned to place a pair of sunglasses over her face. She opened her eyes, seeing him entering numbers into a calculator. He rolled the combat suit next to the table and began removing the armor pads with hard yanks, which produced ripping sounds. She watched him dismantle the skeleton frame, laying the individual parts on the table.

He held the framework pieces next to her, starting with the legs. "I'm using a scratch awl to mark the frame components, along with some additional points that will allow extra support straps. Normally, any soldier can stand under his own strength. In your situation, the frame will have to be modified for both balance and propulsion. Tricky, but doable."

"How will I keep my balance?"

He scratched his chin. "Gyros and weight sensors. That'll be the hard part."

"Okay. But how am I going to make my legs move? If my legs don't move, the robot parts can't follow. Right?"

He disappeared from sight for a moment. She could hear him tearing through tool chests, upending boxes on tables, causing a calamitous racket. When he arrived at her side, he asked her to hold out her strong hand.

He took the pinky finger on her right hand and depressed it into a glob of putty, molding the pliable substance around her finger. "I've just taken a mold of your digit. I think I have a way for you to operate the lower chassis."

Diane let him prod, lift, stick and poke. She had no clue about everything he was doing. She was literally in Chet Strauss's hands. If there was any possibility that she might walk as a result of the experiment, she vowed that she would give it a chance.

Lying there, she fell into a dreamy, almost comatose state. She found herself walking barefoot over a hill, feeling meadow grass between her toes. A chorus of birdsong drifted on the wind, tickling her ears. Several people were at play in the grass, but as she passed, not one of them looked up to stare at her. It felt so normal that she actually felt out of place. Someone called out her name from behind, and then felt a hand on her shoulder, someone touching her in a friendly gesture. She looked behind her but saw no one. They had disappeared. Then she heard the voice again.

"Diane!"

She opened her eyes, turned her head. A familiar face came into focus. Chet, her date. He looked excited. "Oh, darn," she said. "I fell asleep. Sorry, I wasn't bored, just relaxed."

"It's okay. It made things easier. I've got you completely mapped out. It will take me a couple of days to implement the changes."

"How long have I been asleep?"

He looked at his watch and laughed. "About two hours. Baby is really going to have my ass on a platter."

"It's Bibi."

His eyes landed on a few places of her anatomy. *He's got that dopey expression on his face again*. What was she thinking? Dopey expressions and thoughts were not exclusive tonight, the kind that gave one the shivers in a naughty, reckless sort of way.

Considering it came as a mild shock, it was possible she would regret it. It was too late for that now. The only thing left to do was say it, so she drew a deep breath and let it out. "I know how we can really piss Bibi off," she said huskily. "And it has nothing to do with being late."

He stared down at her for a long moment until a burst of comprehension alighted on his face, indicating he understood the suggestiveness of the comment. He did not hesitate when he propped her up to undo her brassiere. He arched her hips to remove the panties. In the next moment, he was nude on the table. His fit of passion surprised her. She wasn't quite sure what to expect with the lovemaking session. A tiny part of her felt disgust and shame. Another part yearned to discover the passion that had been so absent in her life. Yet another part convinced her that she didn't have to give a damn about what anybody thought or said. The inner turmoil within struggled only briefly.

The *I don't give a damn* won out that night.

4

Diane rolled down the staircase ramp into the living room and stopped to turn the TV off via the remote. She zipped into the foyer, nearly colliding with Bibi, who'd just burst from the kitchen, carrying a large punch bowl filled with Halloween candy. Bibi set the bowl on a serving tray next to the front door and jumbled up the candy pieces. Her personal assistant had dressed for the occasion, wearing a black leotard one-piece suit, a small red cape and a long blonde wig.

Bibi turned around. "I see that you managed to dress yourself. It took you thirty minutes this time. You should have called me."

"I need more practice. It always gets easier." A lingering pause. "What under the stars are you supposed to be?"

Bibi performed a small pirouette then drew her shoulders back, showing the image of a lightning bolt emblazoned across her ample bosom. "I'm one of the Fantastic Four, if it didn't occur to you. I'm Storm, and I come with a warning. Be careful, 'cause I can electrocute your ass."

"Save it for the kids. You'll want to electrocute them before the night is over. Do you think we have enough candy?"

"Just like last year. Only they're getting Snickers this time."

Bibi walked into the kitchen and brought out a stool to place next to her candy station. She flopped on the stool, glanced at her watch. "Looks like your boyfriend pulled a disappearing act. You sure he's coming tonight? Or is he going to put you off another day? It's been six days. He was supposed to call yesterday. I swear all these scientists have trouble keeping a schedule. I don't know why you bother." She snapped her fingers in revelation. "Oh, I know why you bother!"

"Okay, Bibi. You don't have to make it sound X-rated. I'm a grown woman. I knew what I was doing. I don't have any regrets."

"But you gave up your most precious gift to a complete stranger."

"You're not playing fair, Bibi. He's no stranger, and I would do again." Diane held her head back and closed her eyes. "Besides, it was heavenly!"

Bibi's face softened. "Di, you don't have to answer to me. Crap sakes, I wouldn't mind this fat ass gettin' plugged on a regular basis, or at least before the next ice age sets in. I'm just aching for you to be certain about all this. Dude came into your life awful quick—made some promises that don't settle right with me. You've been waiting for this. Damn it, *I've* been waiting for it. Even if it means he's gonna haul you on out of here and out of my life..." She pushed out her bottom lip then crimped her eyes shut. Her voice rose to a whine. "Oh hell, here I go again!"

Diane rolled up to her, taking her hand. "Don't take it so hard, honey. It was bound to happen. I've been looking for somebody I could trust for ten years. I'm not saying this is the right thing, but it's so close, it has me all lightheaded. I just can't help seeing a little bit of Clark Kent in him. I know it's hard for you understand." Diane looked down the hallway and saw Ollie approaching. "Now there's a sight that's sure to cheer you up!"

Ollie walked on tremulous legs across the marble floor, trying to balance on six-inch clogs. He wore white slacks and a vest pepper shot with rhinestones and colored sequins. His eyeglasses were pink, heart-shaped. A top hat sat provocatively on his head.

Bibi wiped her eyes. "Now that's just wrong in so many ways. Dude, you blew it if you were trying for Liberace."

"Don't be crass—you're not even close," said Ollie with a terrible English accent. "I'm Sir Elton John, on my way to a concert with the queen. Besides, I have a real date tonight with a papa bear."

Diane and Bibi erupted in laughter. The doorbell rang. Bibi opened it, her fist in the candy bowl. Chet stood on the porch, dressed in jeans and a T-shirt. He looked apologetic.

"Uh, trick or treat?" he tried. "Sorry I'm late. I should have called."

Bibi stepped aside, giving Diane room to pass. "She's all yours."

Diane rolled out the door. Chet accompanied her with a slow walk to his van. He paused to give her a lingering kiss. Once he had her strapped inside, he took the wheel and pulled out of the driveway. He took a different route to his place this time, entering from the Talbert Avenue side. The ride was swift, a little on the reckless side again. She waited until they drove onto his property before she spoke up.

"I was a little worried," she said, watching him disarm the security system. "I thought you might have gotten cold feet and ditched me."

"It was nothing like that. The alterations took longer than I thought. Just a total retrofit with some new design work."

He looked over his shoulder, smiling at her. "But it's all good news. I *did it*, and it's ready."

"I knew you could do it—I had faith."

They drove into the warehouse. The overhead lights flickered to life, much brighter than Diane had remembered before. When she disembarked from the van, she rolled down the main aisle. Several stations were filled with scattered tools and extra parts, obvious signs that Chet had been hard at work from one end of the shop to the other.

She knew he possessed a talent for producing highly technical components. However, she needed to keep her expectations in check. After all, he had not promised something as simple as fixing her blender. He had told her that complete mobility was in her future. Not a trivial claim.

The process began like it had before, with Chet lifting her up on the table and setting out a few specialized hand tools. Only this time, he had fashioned a backrest for her, allowing her to sit upright to watch the process. There was no need to strip down since the exoskeleton frame would fit over her clothing. He explained that the cotton jumper she was wearing would allow extra padding that would guard against chaffing.

All the suit components were disassembled and laid out on a smaller table, but she could not see the armor pads that she had seen on her first visit. After removing her tennis shoes, he worked her feet into a pair of thick-soled boots, which had small, ball-socket piston joints at the ankles that connected to outside frame supports. He snapped a shin segment of framework into the boot top that reached to the knee joint. The knee-to-hip sections followed. He took great care in aligning them, making sure the knee and hip joints fit precisely. He used several claw-shaped devices that he called "outside calipers" to recheck the measurements. She noticed that he had snapped the lower leg components together like

Lego toys. The fasteners were different, though, resembling small bullet heads that clicked into tiny sockets.

He next held a large butterfly-shaped flange over her hips. He aligned it carefully. She could see that it weighed next to nothing by the way he handled it.

"The pelvic girdle," he said. "Where the center of gravity is most crucial." He snapped the device in with several clicks, lifting her rump to connect the underside portion.

"It seems like you're building it in sections from the toes up," she said.

"If any part suffers structural failure or is damaged, it can be replaced with another snap-in duplicate. Modular construction lends itself to assembly line production."

He leaned her forward to snap in a long-segmented rod into the back of the pelvis. This part functioned as the vertebral column. Only he added two hoops covering the upper part of the torso that looked like rudimentary ribs. From the back of her neck, he attached a cross frame, equipped with two opposing shoulder sockets. He snapped in two rods that ran laterally down the length of her arm, stopping at the elbow position. He did the same with the other. The last frames he attached were the forearm segments, which included the elbow joists and servomotors.

She marveled at how delicate the framework seemed. The thickest piece was the backbone rod, slightly larger in diameter than an empty toilet paper roll. Everything else was thumb-sized in girth, composed of tubing and struts. The servomotors were very small, stationed at every joint of her body.

He shook out a large mat of flexible line, joined together in a peculiar spider web fashion. He laid it over her entire length, from ankles to neck, and began snapping it into the framework.

"This is the pneumatic line harness," he said, "composed

of separate looms that feed the small servomotors. It's carbon-carbon, with braided filament, able to stand extreme pressure."

"It's almost like blood veins," she said. "It looks like I'm turned inside out."

"Well, you are in a fashion. Insects use an exoskeleton arrangement to protect the vital organs. The same process is applied here. Only you have two frameworks—one internal, one external. You're one up on the bug world."

The last process involved securing the framework to her limbs. Starting from the ankles, he took padded straps, equipped with Velcro fasteners, and wove them through the framework around her limbs, pulling them snugly. When he reached the end of her arms, she felt completely encased, as though the frame had now merged with her body.

He walked several yards down the main aisle and unhooked a small chain from the wall. The upper end of the chain looped through a block and tackle arrangement secured to an overhead rail. He walked the apparatus over to her table, holding two piano wire stands that were also attached to the overhead. He hooked each wire into eyehooks in her shoulder frame and then ran the small chain through his hands.

Diane felt herself being lifted up off the table, suspended in a bent-knee crouch—a marionette on strings. He gently pushed her to the edge of the table, guiding her legs over. He gave her a shove, and she cleared the table to float a foot off the ground. He lowered her so that her boots lay flat on the floor, yet he allowed no weight upon them.

So far, she had watched the assembly carefully, making mental notes of how things attached and where they connected. His next procedure gave her no view of his movements, as she felt him attaching something to her back. She asked him about it.

"It's the power pack and brain. It slides into a rail slot on the spine rod. It contains the processor, power cells, compressor/generator, gyroscope and some mercury switches. I'm presently snapping in the connectors into the main loom."

"Oh. How come I didn't see any wires?"

"Most of the electrical conduits are concealed inside the frame parts. They're not wires, but conduit tape. Every frame completes a circuit."

He moved to her front, looked her up and down. "Are you comfortable? Is there anything too tight or restrictive? How's the breathing?"

She waved her arms, finding the movement slightly hampered, but attributed it to the extra joints that had to move in harmony with her own. "It feels comfortable, a little on the snug side." She took a full breath then let it out. "Breathing is okay."

Next, he fitted two pincher components to each hand, securing each to the end of the wrist frame. The small pincher devices followed the profile of the thumb and middle finger, and he strapped them to each via small wraparound fasteners. Then he placed formfitting gloves, equipped with cutouts for the pincer tips, over each hand.

"These are extra strong grabbers that aid in grip and crushing power. They're strictly for military applications, but we might as well include them. Not too practical unless you want to hang from a cliff face indefinitely."

"No helmet?" She remembered seeing it on the table.

"Not yet." He left for a moment and then returned with a small tube that had a buckle strap and connector on the end. He held up her hand and splayed her fingers. Singling out the pinky finger, he pushed the tube over it then secured it to the glove.

"The glove end over the pinky has been cut out." he said. "Wiggle your little finger inside the tube and you'll feel four small touch-sensitive tabs—like tiny key buttons. Down, up, right and left. Those tiny tabs control the entire movement of your legs. By tapping the down sensor, you activate a forward thrust leg movement. Tapping slowly, but repeatedly, initiates a walking rhythm. Fast downward tapping produces a jogging mode, and so on. Try it several times. Get the feel of clicking the sensor by using the strength of the little finger."

Diane worked the digit with small downward tapping motions. She could feel minute clicks, but only if she used just the right pressure.

"The rhythm has to be precisely controlled," he said. "Nothing spastic or out of sync. Now find the left sensor and tap against it. That one turns you left, by swiveling the ankle, knee and hip joints. It provides a 25 percent maximum turn angle for one click, sending a surge for 05 seconds before it returns to normal. Three rapid clicks will give you a 90-degree turn. It's a bit primitive, but with practice, you'll be able to perform smooth, almost unnoticeable transitions. Try the left and right features."

She tried the function and had trouble activating the sensors, missing the clicking sensations. She spent a few minutes on each side, training the finger to hit the right spot every time. "Okay, I think I have it."

"Great. The top sensor sends the "crunch" signal. That means the legs will scissor down, allowing a low crouch, a seated position in a chair, or getting up from a prone or fallen position. That function will be the most difficult for you, since it requires the use of your back, shoulders and arms to aid the maneuver. Work the upper sensor. One click will produce the crunch mode at normal speed. Another click will open you up. Two rapid clicks will crunch you much faster. Two more rapid clicks after that will open you up again, much faster. One click, plus three rapid clicks, produces a vertical leap, and keep in mind, that's from a standing position."

"Gads, it's complicated. I don't know if I can remember it all."

"Here's a quick reference card. Study it until you're blue in the face. Do that now."

She brought the card close to her face, reading the print and diagrams.

"You always have to remember what your body position is at any given moment. You could cross a number of sensor signals or do something out of sequence that causes a train wreck. It will be similar in operation to your joystick control for your chair, but not as easy. Do you understand?"

"I'm sure I can handle it." She took a full thirty minutes to read the card over and over again. "I think I've got it. The small bubble on the power pack—that makes it go hot. The hip one activates the lower half. And I keep the pinky finger in the float position."

She found the hot button and depressed it. She felt a primary surge through the framework, stiffening the suit. She heard a barely audible humming noise.

He nodded. "That's the air loading, filling the lines behind the actuators." He pulled on the chain, lifting her one foot off the floor again. "Now, using the small finger, tap the down key very slowly and observe the reaction."

She did so. Her right leg cycled once, followed by the left. She continued the rhythm one raised step at a time, free-floating, walking through the air. She increased the speed and felt a noticeable tugging sensation, the overhead support wires absorbing the shock. When she reached a certain resonance, her movements became violent, so she had to cease. She wobbled to a stop.

"Try your swivel angles."

She tapped the left control; the suit pivoted. She tried the other side, using different combinations. Rapid turns produced violent reactions, prompting Chet to steady her several times. She tried the crunch, in slow and quick succession, having no problem mastering the maneuver.

Chet slackened the wires to let her full weight upon the floor, but cautioned, "Float the finger—neutral."

She settled on the floor, upright but wavering slightly. But the balance feature was rock-steady. She was the one fighting against it.

"Excellent!" he said. "Okay, the walk tab—down button. Take it slow."

She took her first tentative steps, trying to synchronize her mind with the movements. He released the chain completely. Clop—clop. She could hardly believe she was walking, albeit with aid. The visual perspective brought back a flood of memories from her childhood.

"Oh, my God." she said. "I can't believe I'm doing this!"

"Walk the length of the warehouse. The tether will follow you."

He stayed by her side, spotting her movements. Her boots made heavy slaps on the floor, flat-footed and clumsy. But she was doing it! Her legs were driving her forward, and she marveled at how her knees rose and descended so effortlessly. When she reached the end, he told her to make a 180-degree turn by using the correct taps and clicks. He assured her that the overhead support mechanism would swivel around with her.

"Sorry, but there's no reverse. You can't back-pedal."

She made the complete turn in jerky increments, nearly losing her balance. She recovered by using her upper torso as a counterweight to straighten out. He unhooked her from the wires for the return trip. She panicked at first. He was expecting her to solo. *Am I ready for this?* She held her arms out like a tightrope walker then made the gentle taps.

"Keep your head up," he warned. "You don't have to look

down at your feet. You'll see them in your peripheral vision. That's it. Step up the pace."

She not only stepped up the pace but raised the speed to a brief trot. She tried to stop before she hit the table but went off balance and pitched forward. Chet caught her and they both tumbled to the floor.

"That's okay," he said. "Those things will happen. Now get up under your own power. Remember to assist with your arms and shoulders."

She resumed her stance moments later, using the crunch function, but it took her three tries to perform the maneuver.

She tried to keep the frustration out of her voice. "Looks like this will take a while to master."

"It isn't going to happen all at once. You've only been in the suit for fifty minutes." He took the armor pads off the table and snapped them onto the frame. "These will keep you from getting hurt by providing shock absorption. I'd also like to watch and record the mobility."

"Then let's use the helmet, too."

"Are you sure?"

"Let's go for broke."

He put the tactical helmet on her head. He shoved the visor back, claiming that she didn't need her view obscured. He walked with her around the warehouse, while he recorded her movements with a digital video cam, encouraging her to perform different maneuvers and body poses. At one point, after turning too sharply, she toppled and hit the floor hard. This time, she rose quickly, unharmed. He had her leap once from the crunch position. Her jump took her three feet off the floor, and she landed with a flat-footed thud.

She stopped once to admire her reflection in a stainless-steel refrigerator. The only thing recognizable was her face peeking out of the rectangular opening in the helmet. The rest had transformed into something unrecognizable, but ominously powerful. She felt a strange sense of exhilaration—a freedom as though she had been given a new birth. This was not the same Diane Nine she had known an hour ago.

"You look happy and fulfilled," he said. "I admit to being a bit giddy, myself."

"It's nothing short of a miracle," she gushed. "You said you could make me a duplicate?"

He nodded. "The lower half is all you need. I have the material to make another. I can streamline it, so it fits under an oversized pair of jogging shorts or baggy slacks. I have a spare power pack that I can fit to it, which, by the way, you'll never have to charge."

She stepped up to him, carefully encircling his neck with her arms. She gave him an awkward kiss through the helmet. He tenderly reciprocated, and to her surprise, he wiped a single tear from his cheek. A few of her own happy tears ran.

He brightened. "I have an idea. Let's give it a test run over some urban terrain. You know, see how it performs on different profiles. I can't wait to see how it—"

"You mean outside?"

"I mean in town. It's Halloween. You'll be just another costumed figure running around. We can get away with it."

She didn't argue. She walked straight to the van, opened the passenger door and then hesitated, contemplating the entry.

He paused behind her, watching with interest. Yet he did not help or instruct her. He let her read the card.

She decided on a stooped over, step up, swivel and crunch. It didn't exactly work that way—she bashed her helmet on the headliner and kneed the dashboard. It took her five minutes to seat herself. She buckled up, frustrated at her poor performance. Chet had already loaded the wheelchair and had been watching her from the driver's seat.

He gave her a thumbs up.

She noticed he appeared just as excited about the suit as she was. While he drove off the property, Chet spoke up. "Damn, this looks like it's going to work! I can't see the brass refusing to give it the green light. Everything seems to be working, even with the modifications. In theory, a soldier could return to an aid station with his legs shot out from underneath him." He looked at her for a second. She thought she saw a little lunacy in his eyes.

She hadn't the heart to stop him from talking about the success of the project. He went on and on about how such a tactical fighting suit would save American lives, "bring more boys back home", he'd said, and give the armed forces the upper hand in a terrorist urban conflict. He exhibited bravado when speaking about corporations she had never heard of, like Darpa, Cyberdyne, and Sarcos. He took delight in ridiculing many of his former colleagues and peers, scientists and engineers whom he said had rebuked his theories. Though excited about his breakthrough discovery, she detected a deep bitterness in his attitude.

They drove down the hill on Talbert Avenue. He ceased talking when something caught his attention in the side mirror. He whipped his head to check the other side. Diane looked from her vantage point and picked out a pair of headlights behind the van. When she turned to look at Chet again, then back in the mirror, the headlights had disappeared. He let out a frustrated moan.

"This time I saw something," she said. "A pair of headlights followed then suddenly went out."

"That's what I saw. Here I am jabbering about how wonderful everything is, not paying attention to security. Just to make sure..."

He stopped the van to put it in reverse, which activated the backup lights. Looking through the side mirror, Diane could see the outline of a dark car pulling over to the shoulder.

"That settles it," he said, throwing it in drive. He stepped on the accelerator, peeling rubber over the blacktop. "That screws our outing. I'm sorry I got you into this."

"Stop apologizing. Take us straight to my place. Whoever it is won't get past gate security to follow us onto the property." Then she dared, "You can spend the night and wait for this to blow over."

"Are you sure?"

She glanced at him. "Why not? We can figure out what to do once we get there."

"Your place it is then."

She kept her eye on the side mirror during the trip. She could see the tailing vehicle still behind them, but it had fallen back a good distance, an obvious attempt at hiding. When they reached the security gate to Huntington Harbor, the guard had trouble with Diane proving her identity until she took the helmet off to show her face. Once through, Chet drove straight to the front of her house. Several groups of children still moved in clusters down the sidewalks, hitting up the expensive homes for candy. It looked like they were safe for now. No one would dare follow them into a gated community.

Chet unloaded the wheelchair, while Diane inched out of the seat. This time she exited the vehicle with half the trouble. Suddenly struck with a mischievous idea, she put the helmet back on, knowing that Bibi would answer the door. Chet motored the chair around, making taps on the joystick, while walking next to it.

"Just get in it," she said. "It's much easier to control."

"I think you're right."

And you're an engineer, she thought.

When she stepped up to the front door, Diane used a

single digit to press the doorbell. She heard a "Hold on" before the door swung open to reveal Bibi, who, when she saw what had come to the door, tossed the candy bowl in the air and reared back in terror. She saw Chet sitting in Diane's wheelchair. She stiffened.

"You." Bibi pointed at Chet. "Haul your ass on out of that chair! What do you mean rolling up here in—"

"It's all right," said Diane, flipping the visor back. "Trick or treat, Bibi."

The large woman glared at the suited figure for a moment, then stomped her feet in a tantrum, mashing Snickers bars. "Now why the hell would you want to be doing something like this to me? Damn you for that, and what in the hell have you got yourself wrapped up in?"

"Just calm down." Diane took a few jerky strides into the foyer. She told Chet to run the chair into the house. Once he was inside, Bibi began to gather up the spilled candy, but she did not take her eyes off the TACS.

"This is Chet's invention," said Diane. "It's the full suit, the first prototype. He's going to make me a duplicate of the lower half. Isn't it wonderful?" Diane made a few awkward turning steps to display its angles. She took the helmet off and held it at her side.

Bibi narrowed her eyes. "I suppose so if you want to be an action figure. You won't have to look like that all the time, will you?"

Chet exited the wheelchair. "No, no. She needs only the lower half—the internal framework. It will fit right under some loose clothes."

Bibi's expression changed. "Well, that's all right, then. Maybe."

Chet told her about the suit's functions, particularly how it worked. Bibi listened patiently, up until the point when Chet halted his narration and slapped a hand to his forehead.

"Holy cripes," he said. "I didn't activate my security system at home. It's wide open. I was so busy yapping away that I completely forgot about it!"

Diane turned to him. "Then we'll just go back and close it up."

"It's too risky. You stay here. If I'm not back in one hour, give me a call." He gave her a business card. "If you want out of the suit, just depress those pressure snaps at the joints. Remove the sub-sections one at a time."

"What's too risky?" asked Bibi. "Better do some explaining about that."

Chet glanced at Bibi, but he bent down and grasped Diane by the shoulders. "You have to stay here, Diane. I'll take care of this. But you have to promise me something."

"I'll try."

"I want you to promise me that you won't let the TACS out of your sight for *any* reason. Guard it with your life. It'll be safe here with you."

"I promise," she said. "Nobody takes it away from me or gets their hands on it."

He said, "I *love* you. They'll never take that away from us."

Bibi threw up her hands. "What in the hell is it with all this drama? Who are *they*? What are they going to take away?" Bibi went on with a mini-rant.

Diane was not listening but kissing Chet and seeing him out the door. She stepped back into the house after she heard Chet's van start and leave the property. She blew out a long plaintive breath. "Don't fret, Bibi. It's under control. Let's try to relax. If you want to do something, break me out of this suit. It's starting to cut off some circulation in my arms. I don't even know what it's doing down below."

Bibi asked a dozen questions while she followed Diane up the ramp to the master bedroom. Diane tried to answer them all, mainly to soothe the large woman's fears. When she sat down on her bed, she stretched out, allowing Bibi easy access to the parts. Bibi read the instruction card carefully and began to unsnap the components, starting with the boots and lower legs. Diane reached around her shoulder to turn the master switch off.

"Ollie came home from his party in tears," said Bibi. "Seems he caught his soon-to-be boyfriend hidden in a broom closet, giving somebody else a special delivery package."

"Oh, poor Ollie. How's he taking it?"

"He's locked himself in his bedroom, listening to Barbara Streisand records. He might have taken a couple pounds of candy with him. I figure he's good for at least a week in there."

Diane sighed. "Love's a bitch. Although, the tides have turned in my favor."

"Uh, huh. Maybe so. Isn't he taking some kind of a risk with you running around with this robot machinery for all eyes to see? I thought it was some kind of secret project for the government."

"You see, that's just it. Sometimes he doesn't think. He was so thrilled it worked, I guess he just lost his train of thought. Honestly, I did too. We were planning to go out on the town and try it out. That was until reality set in. I think he's being followed, Bibi. He can't figure out who is chasing him around in the shadows. I saw it tonight. It's got me worried."

"Now that's what I'm talking about. Why do you want any part of that? This man's bringing baggage to the table. You might think he's some boy scout, but he just might be as screwed up as the Science Fiction channel."

Diane smiled, looking wistfully at the ceiling. "Yeah, but he's got that new car smell!"

"Well, you should have kicked his tires first."

"I'm in love with him, Bibi."

"Watch your language around me."

Bibi finished removing the suit. She stacked the parts on the floor next to the bed. She spanked her hands and said, "Damn, I'm good. At least it breaks down easy enough. Hold on and I'll fetch your buggy."

Diane waited for Bibi, occasionally glancing at her watch. Only twenty minutes had passed since Chet had left. Already she found herself agonizing over his absence and what might be happening. When Bibi arrived, she lifted Diane into her chair. They went down to the kitchen, where Bibi made coffee. They kept on semi-alert for kids at the front door. Diane didn't believe any more trick or treaters would arrive, since it was approaching ten o'clock. She had other things on her mind besides candy and kids.

At the one-hour mark, Diane called Chet's number. There was no answer. She sipped her coffee then tried the number fifteen minutes later, letting the phone ring a dozen times. The same result came after twenty more minutes. Frustrated, she let loose with an anguished moan.

Bibi shut the coffee machine off. "I don't have to be told where this is going." She picked up a doughnut from under a glass tray and grabbed some keys off a wall hook. The front door slammed, followed by the noise of an engine starting. Diane rolled to the front door just as Bibi opened it. The large woman retrieved a sweater out of the hall closet, draped it around Diane's shoulders and said, "I know what you're thinking. I won't hear the end of it until we check on Mr. Science Guy. Engine's running."

"Thanks, Bibi. We have to check it out just to be on the safe side."

"Where's everybody going?" asked Ollie, standing in the

middle of the hallway watching the two. His eyes were puffy. His long flannel nightgown had chocolate stains on the front.

"You stay here and sulk," said Bibi, "we're on our way out to check on somebody."

Ollie bit his lip. "But I don't want to be alone right now."

Bibi rolled her eyes. "Then put some slippers on, then get your ass in the van."

Diane entered her custom van via the side door lift. Bibi anchored her chair and took the driver's seat. Ollie sat on the front passenger seat, holding his shoulders against the cold. Once they had driven out of the security gate, Diane supplied directions to Chet's property.

After following several dirt roads and wrong turns, they found the lot. Diane pointed to a large structure just on the fringe of the headlight beams. "There it is. That's Chet's warehouse and bungalow." She could see the warehouse door standing wide open, with bright lights illuminating the interior.

Bibi rolled the van slowly over the oil-soaked ground toward the warehouse. "Does everything look all right from here?"

"I just know that he's locked himself inside both times I've been here. That's his van just inside, with the driver's door open. That part seems odd. But what do I know? It's also strange that no alarms have gone off. He said the whole place was wired against trespassers."

Bibi parked fifty feet away from the opening. They disembarked, hardly making a sound. Diane rolled across the clearing, flanked by her friends. For a moment, she realized how hilarious they must look, sneaking around on private property in the dead of night. But they weren't here to win a fashion show.

Diane pointed to the small, unlit house. Bibi nodded and

headed that way. Diane and Ollie passed through the warehouse entrance, moving silently down the length of the warehouse, passing Chet's empty van. Ollie knelt to check something on the floor.

Diane reached the back of the warehouse, where she had seen the large computer station. She saw the first signs of a disturbance—two chairs knocked over on their sides. The scene revealed more. Several wires lay on the floor, pulled from surge protectors. Three monitors sat on the long computer desk, exactly where she had remembered seeing them on her previous visits. But all the large desktop computers which had been stationed underneath the table were missing.

Bibi's voice echoed hollowly behind her, giving her a start. "Dude's not in the house. It's locked. Nobody's home."

Diane did not want to raise a panic. Somehow, she wished the whole thing was some kind of an elaborate Halloween prank and that Chet Strauss would jump out from behind a filing cabinet and yell, "trick or treat." She really didn't expect that to happen. Not now. Portents of doom were skirting the edge of her mind, manifesting some very ugly scenarios. *Please, God, don't let it be something terrible.*

"This looks like little blood drops on the floor," said Ollie, kneeling with his face very close to the pavement.

"How do you know it's blood?" asked Bibi.

Ollie ran his tongue over his lips, looking irritated. "Because I've seen enough of my own to know."

Diane did not want to hear that. She refused to believe there was blood on the floor in some warehouse out in the middle of nowhere that belonged to a man she had just fallen in love with.

Something else lay on the floor that was out of place. She asked Bibi to pick up the items and show them to her. One was a blue matchbook cover. The other two items were smashed cigarette butts.

Chet Strauss did not smoke.

She tried to read the writing on the matchbook cover. It proved to be impossible through the blur of tears.

5

Agent Eugene Gene took the end of his pencil and pushed two glazed donuts together. He shoved the large bear claw below them and coaxed the jelly-filled donuts to the bottom of that. There. He'd just crafted the perfect woman—thirty-eight-twenty-six-thirty-six. Buxom, sweet and bad for the health—the summation of everything he looked for. He removed the right breast and took a bite from it. He checked his email again. Nothing going on. Yet.

He had another week before he left on vacation. Three glorious weeks. It looked like Hawaii would be his destination, maybe Maui. Some surf, sand and plenty of fruity drinks would be the perfect prescription for what ailed him. No more Middle East countries smelling like dead dogs that could sandblast or broil you the minute you stepped out of your hotel room. Spending the past year in Baghdad, chasing down IEDs had done little for his nerves. Not to mention, his social life, where every female glimpsed on the street consisted of a pair of eyes and hands peeking out of shapeless gunny-sacks. He had forgotten what a nice pair of tanned legs looked like. But he expected to catch up and get fully saturated with some semi-X-rated scenery. Maui it would be!

He heard soft pads behind him, then a breathy voice. "Playing with your food again, Gene?"

He looked over his shoulder, catching sight of a flak vest and a shock of red hair. Cha Cha Susie Delaney, who looked like she'd just come off the firing range, gave him a mischievous grin and made a play for the bear claw. He slapped her hand away. "You're getting too fat for any vigorous field work, Susie. Trust me, you'll thank me later."

"Aren't you the flatterer? The vest *always* makes me look fat. Let me make a prediction: line six is going to light up and you'll have to answer it. I just passed by Harvey's cube. He's squawking with somebody about some military hardware that seems to be over his head. I'll bet he passes the buck off to you because it's too early in the morning for his brain cells to function. STW is not his favorite dish."

"Civilian call?"

"Sounds like it. If I win, I get that bear claw. If I lose, I'll let you take me out to a five-star restaurant and pay for everything."

"You're on." *Did she just chump me?* He shrugged.

They stared at the desk phone for a full two minutes. Gene was just about ready to plop the bear claw back into the doughnut box when line six lit up. Cha Cha Susie smiled and snatched the treat. She made a big show of biting into it in front of him before she left. He punched in the call, adjusted his headset.

"Agent Eugene Gene, how can I help you?"

"Are you sure you want to help me?" asked the female voice. "I've already been rerouted three times in forty-five minutes."

"The agency is just trying to get the correct department for you, ma'am. I'm agent Eugene Gene and go by Gene assigned to the Directorate of Intelligence. My official designation is science, technology and weapons analyst. Now, do I sound like somebody you should be talking to?"

"I guess we'll find that out. My name is Diane Nine and I'm a resident of Huntington Beach, California." Pause. "Do you have to write this down?"

"You're being recorded."

"Great. Anyway, my boyfriend is missing. Last night he went to check up on his property and just vanished within a timeframe of ninety minutes. He told me to call him. He never answered, so I went to check his place out."

This sounded domestic already. Any military hardware connection to it would be a surprise.

"Did you contact your local law enforcement agency, Ms. Nine?"

"That was the first thing I did. After their investigation, they said it looked like a break-in, tied in with the absence of the owner. They said to give it seventy-two hours and then check back if he didn't reappear."

"How do you know this person, Ms. Nine? And how do you spell your last name."

"It's a recent relationship. I guess you could say it's intimate, involving adult commitments. My last name is Nine, like the number."

"This wouldn't be anything resembling a domestic dispute, would it? I'm sorry, I have to ask."

"Not at all. The relationship was very positive and cordial. And I'm not the scorned woman type. This is something different. I'm afraid for his life."

"I need a name and residence for this individual. If possible, a birthplace and job location." He poised a pencil over a stationary pad, intent on getting the vital facts written down.

"Well, he's Chet Strauss. I assume Chet is short for Chester. He's about forty-years old, six-foot three and about 200 pounds. I don't know his birthplace—we never got that far. According to his business card, his address is 71 Snoopy Way, Huntington Beach, California. That's a small dirt road off Talbert Avenue near the library. He owns a small residence and large warehouse located out in the abandoned oil field tract."

"Do you know what he does for a living?"

"He's an engineer and physicist, having worked for NASA and MIT—you know, a real whiz kid. He told me he was linked to some defense contracts and in the process of approaching the government with a project. Oh, and he holds something like forty patents."

"Please hold for a second." Gene waved at one of the junior analysts. He had to throw a doughnut to get his attention. When the agent came over, Gene handed him the small piece of paper and whispered, "Background, deep probe."

"Okay, I'm back, Ms. Nine. Why would you say this man's life was in danger?"

"He's been followed for the past six months, I think he said. He suspects it's a foreign agency, possibly military in origin. I've been with him when he's been followed—tailed, more precisely."

"And the reason for the surveillance?"

"Okay, I'm not making this up, but he's created what he calls a military combat exoskeleton. It has a lightweight titanium chassis, with actuators and motivators, he calls them. It has bulletproofed armor inserts. I swear it looks like something out of Star Wars."

"You've actually seen this hardware?"

"I've actually worn it and tested it. It is fully functional. He was about to introduce it to the Department of Defense and arrange for a demonstration. He used me as a test subject while he documented a trial run with a video camera."

This woman was traipsing down imaginary lane. Her description had a haunting similarity to hundreds of other garage-built projects he had documented over the years. Everything from flying battle tanks to invisibility suits, he'd heard it all. Any semi-talented mechanic with a box of Craftsman tools could knock out a pretty sophisticated high-tech machine in his spare time and call it the next wonder invention of the century. The world was full of wannabe Edison's.

"Do you know what kind of a power source this suit had? Would you liken it to the Hal-5, or Berkeley's Lower Extremity Exoskeleton? Or maybe the XOS version?" He had to trip her up somehow.

"None of those. It was his own design. He said it used a mini-nuclear power cell pack or something like that, something that didn't need charging for a very long time. The whole thing weighed less than fifty pounds. This thing was not a toy that ran off batteries, I guarantee that."

"Did you say 'mini-nuclear power cell' pack? A fusion machine-device?"

"Yes, I did. I remember that he called the suit TACS. That stands for tactical armored combat system."

Gene wrote that down, underlining it three times. He had never run across the acronym before, but it didn't mean it couldn't exist out there in cyberspace or the patent's office. But what really threw him was the 'nuclear power cell' connotation. As far as he knew, there hadn't been a paper written on such an energy device. Especially a portable one. He couldn't imagine somebody running around with high-grade plutonium strapped to their body. For one thing, such substances were nearly impossible to obtain, never mind manufacturing a working model. He went on with his questioning.

"Ms. Nine, I'm curious why you are bringing this to our attention. Obviously, you have personal reasons because someone you care about is missing. Other than that, how do you feel this will impact our department?"

"It's a national security issue! Chet said that any country lucky enough to have this technology would be an unstoppable force. He said everything about urban warfare would be changed forever. It could fall into the wrong hands, like the Middle East, China or North Korea."

Gene noticed the junior agent heading in his direction, so he asked Diane to hold the line.

The junior agent shook his head. "Nothing on a Chet or Chester Strauss from that location possessing anything near that background. I can call DOD and see if they have a file on him or know of his work."

"Okay, do that and get right back with me. Hit up NASA, too."

"Will do."

Gene reconnected with her. "Did this man ever produce identification to you, or had you seen an official document that had his photo on it?"

"Not exactly. He did tell me he'd had a driver's license for over twenty years. I did see him pay for a dinner with an American Gold credit card. He seemed very legit about his identity and background."

"Did this man have a nickname or use a pseudonym?"

"Not that I'm aware of. Just Chet."

"Does he have any friends or family in the area? At least someone who can vouch for his identity?"

There came a long pause. "He seemed to be a loner. Not a lot of social interaction. I know it's not much to go on. I've only known him shy of a month, but I'm sure that something has happened to him!" Her voice wavered. "He's a real sweetheart. He probably never knew what hit him."

All men are sweethearts in the first month, he thought. They always screw up somewhere later down the road in the relationship.

The junior agent waved his arm for attention. He pointed

at the screen and shook his head. Then he swished his finger across his throat, pantomiming the "death" sign.

Gene sighed. "Ms. Nine, according to our preliminary check, we have no such records in our database on the person you've just described. We have no state driver's license issued in that name for the state of California, no place of employment, social security number or criminal record. The Department of Defense turns up nothing—no contracts or associations, no secret clearance, past or present. I don't know what to tell you other than it's possible this man has misled you or his mental capacity is unstable. I wish I had better news."

"Are you certain you've checked him out thoroughly? This man had no reason to lie to me. As God is my witness, I saw what I saw. You've got to check this out!"

"I promise that if we get any more information on this person I'll contact you. Your number's been recorded. I'm afraid we just don't have enough to go on at the moment. If you have additional information on further developments, get in touch with me directly. I'll put you on my contact list."

"Oh, this is just...what am I supposed to do now? Pretend this never happened? Look, I found a matchbook in his warehouse that came from La Casa De Las Madres in the City of Nueva Gerona. I really think that might be an important clue."

"I'm sorry. We need something more solid on this Chester Strauss before the agency expends any resources. You also might need to re-evaluate your info or opinion on this man's background and integrity. I'm sure you understand that matters like—"

The phone line went dead.

Gene kicked back in his chair, stared up at the cork ceiling, particularly at a fluorescent bulb that flickered in seizures. Right now, that bulb reminded him of his nervous system going into spasm mode. He thought he could actually feel a few more of his hairs uproot themselves from his thinning scalp and fall to his lap. He did not need a break. He needed a full-fledged getaway vacation. He needed Maui, condensed and liquefied, loaded into a hypodermic needle then shoved straight into his ass.

He heard the junior agent's voice over his shoulder.

"Somebody whacking our crank?"

"Nah, she was sincere enough. I think she met some gigolo Joe that needed to impress her so he could jump her bones. She only knew him for a month. Sounds like he really went to some lengths to set her up. You know how many wives we get, swearing that their husbands are really secret agents. They call up wondering when their extra benefits and salary are going to start rolling in. They swear they won't break the agency code of secrecy if we just mail the checks."

"Yep. I had a few last month. Dad or boyfriend doesn't feel appreciated enough around the house. After a six-pack of beer, he squares off with his mate. Tells her, 'You'd be surprised if you really knew what I did for a living, only if I told you, I'd have to kill you', type bullshit line."

"Tell me about it."

"Wouldn't be a bad idea if you did some Google on that broad. Seems I remember that name from somewhere. I think she's a host for some children's cartoon network or something. At least the gal I remember was in the public eye. I could be wrong."

Gene watched the junior agent leave and then turned toward his plasma monitor. He seriously wondered if this woman was even worth a mouse click. He had better things to do than dicking around in cyberspace. He checked his email again. Nothing. Well, maybe he would give it a shot, just out of curiosity.

He typed her name into the bar, a strange name, he

thought, and hit the enter key. The result gave him 455,000 hits for the name. The entries profiled a female artist/writer who had a syndicated comic strip in the major newspapers, along with a popular series in the comic book universe. Three websites were listed; one of them was indicated as the "Official Home." A large Wikipedia page was also listed. He clicked on the official home website and read the inventory bar, which listed photos, excerpts, artwork, articles, profiles, interviews, lectures and appearances.

"Ah, I knew it," said the junior agent, walking up to Gene's station, holding a newspaper out in front of him. He splayed it open on the desk. "This one. She's the gal that does Endura of Futura. I knew I'd seen the name somewhere. Pretty popular stuff, especially with the younger set. You should keep up on the funnies."

Gene looked at the small colored panels. "I'm not a funny man; you should know that. Thanks. It *might* be the same one."

Gene page-clicked through the website bio, bringing up a colorful menagerie of cartoon figures, spaceships and galactic panoramas. He found her digital picture. He gazed at the head shot. She was a looker, he decided, and could have been tagged a typical Scandinavian, with white-blond hair and blue eyes. He had a thing for eyebrows. The expression on her face suggested her mugging for the camera, a cross between mischief and silliness. The bio stated that she was a California native and current resident of Huntington Beach. The legend included everything from charity appearances to conference attendances to radio and television spots. He strongly suspected this was the woman he'd just finished talking to, but he had another check in mind. He bookmarked the site and brought up the NCIC database. It didn't take him long to get through her rap sheet.

She didn't have one. Her criminal history was spotless.

He found two parking tickets—that was it. He had hoped to find at least one 72-hour stint at a mental facility but that came up nada. That presented a big problem. He had an obvious celebrity on his hands who had just made a fantastic claim about an alleged disappearance, involving a man who had been working on a high-tech military component. She had contacted local law enforcement officials, and now the offices of the Central Intelligence Agency. If she was looking for publicity, she was going about it the wrong way. In fact, she had everything to lose by making such grandiose claims, chief amongst them, her social standing, fan base and job. High profile people did not make outlandish claims without the intention of backing them up.

It reminded him of the time when a governor swore that he had a terrifying UFO experience and needed to confess the details to the media. His constituents warned him about such publicity and how it could affect his political standing. The governor did not listen, opting to open up that bag of maggots. He never sought reelection for another term because of the negative fallout. The last Gene heard was that the man had accepted a position as a casino manager in Las Vegas.

The crux of the matter involved the invisibility of Chester Strauss. There would have been a record in the database on anyone working for a top-secret facility, especially since the CIA had access to such records. Or was this something deliberately kept from the agency that had entered the black op realm? Was it so new that the information hadn't trickled down yet? Would the director know about it? *Should* he know about it? It had all the hallmarks of national defense and foreign espionage. If the story was true, the risk factors in ignoring the claims were horrendous and subject to far-reaching consequences. Then again, if he had nothing and the whole affair was just a joke, they'd laugh him out of the agency for using up precious resources and manpower.

Gene stared at the picture on the monitor again. He tried to read past the beautiful face—into the soul. Either she had been duped by a conman and fabricated the story to get even, or she had actually told the truth as she had witnessed the events. Overall, he couldn't deny a good feeling about her. She *did* seem sincere. His inner bullshit barometer hadn't gone off.

He began printing out selected pages. He pulled a new vanilla folder out of his desk drawer. Using a black felt-tip pen, he wrote DIANE NINE on the outside cover. When he had the pages printed, he stood up to take a deep breath.

If it warranted a full investigation, the director would send him on his way to California. If he failed to produce a justified reason for the trip, he would be left to his own devices. That meant getting his vacation bumped up. *Adios Maui. Hello California.*

He drew his shoulders back and began a determined march down the aisle. It was in the hands of the agency God now.

6

Diane snapped her cell phone shut, swung her chair around in a reckless arc, nearly clipping Ollie, who had been listening intently to the conversation. Bibi stood at the entrance to her bedroom, leaning on the door jam. Neither wanted to be the first one to ask what happened.

"I would have understood it if he didn't believe me," said Diane, motoring across the carpet and turning around—her interpretation of pacing. "But I got the feeling he knew exactly what I was talking about and ducked the subject on purpose!"

"So, he blew you off," said Ollie. "It's Roswell all over again."

Bibi rolled her eyes. "Now wait just a damn minute. Did it ever occur to you that they don't know anything about this guy because he's not in the system? Stop and think about this. Dude comes swooping into your life making all kinds of fancy promises. Then he suddenly goes poof like a fart in a gust of wind."

Diane stopped her wheelchair, considering Bibi's words. She could have believed the woman, had it not been for her assistant's indomitable need to find fault with her choice of men. Bibi had foiled more than her share of Diane's encounters with eligible dates via subtle forms of sabotage. She suspected that Bibi's fear of sharing Diane's attention or losing her job were the primary reasons for the insecurity. Truly, Bibi's fears of being unemployed were unfounded, but Diane could never seem to convince Bibi that she would never be set adrift or fired.

It was a friendship and cohabitation that went back eight years, about the time Diane's career had just started taking off. Diane had helped Bibi through her last year of nursing school by offering her a room with low rent. To show her loyalty, Bibi had stayed on with her in a type of caregiver arrangement, first monitoring Diane's medical needs, and then later picking up more of the business and domestic matters. To say that Diane would be lost without Bibi was an understatement. They were not only friends, but family. Sisters.

Diane looked at Ollie. "Did you check the print on the matchbook cover and those cigarettes? You might have to do an advanced search."

"Well, I didn't get the chance because I was too busy eavesdropping on your conversation. But my first impression says that maybe this is something the government won't admit to. It's way too 'eyes only.' They might have thought you were a spy, digging for information. You can bet that they would put their hounds on it if something went haywire, though. You should have told the agent that you had the suit. That way the story would be verified."

"He didn't believe what I was telling him. So, I got angry and cut him off." Just thinking about it riled her. "Go check on those items for me, Ollie." She could have peeled her laptop open, but right now her hands were shaking so badly she'd miss the keystrokes.

Ollie scurried out of the room. Bibi stepped up to Diane

and patted her head gently. She spoke softly, almost apologetically.

"Look, honey, this man has worked some kind of bad juju on you. It's got you all tied up in knots. Now as smart as the dude is, don't you think he could get himself out of a tangle if it came down to it?"

"He doesn't have those kinds of smarts, Bibi. I'm not even sure he would know how to defend himself against a bunch of thugs. He was probably outnumbered and surprised. And..." Diane wiped a moist eye. "I really *love* him!"

"Well then, I'm not going to argue the point. If you're sure he's the one you've got your heart set on, then I'm going to be there for you. He ain't such a bad sort. If he's in trouble, maybe we can help."

"Thanks, I need your support and understanding."

Ollie appeared at the doorway a moment later, his head cocked in confusion. He held some papers in his hand. "Okay, guys, rap your heads around this. I had to use a magnifying glass to read the print on the cigarettes. Then I did a thorough search. They are a Guarina brand, made in Camaguey, Cuba. The matchbook comes from the hotel La Casa de las Madres in the city of Nueva Gerona, which we already knew. But check this out—that's on Isla de la Juventud, or Island of Youth, just off the southern tip of the main island of Cuba."

Ollie handed Diane a digital map printout. She looked at it. "Are you sure about this? Cuba?"

"Sweetie, I triple-checked it. No mistake—that's where those items came from."

Diane mused, "It sure makes sense if they wanted to stay under the radar. It's totally out of the way and not under the jurisdiction of the United States. Cuba claims to be a socialist republic, but their hearts beat to the drum of communism."

"You think the damn Cubans nabbed him?" asked Bibi.

Diane shook her head. "I'm just saying it's a great operating base for sympathizers. Any terrorist or communist faction could set up shop there and hardly raise an eyebrow. It's a short hop from the US border by air. Who knows where they're *originally* from?"

Bibi narrowed her eyes. "Diane, I don't like that look in your eyes. Don't you dare say it. You have responsibilities here. Your boss will kill you. Then your agent will resurrect you and kill you again. You can't go traipsing off to some foreign country in search of a boyfriend!"

"We'll not be traipsing anywhere," said Diane.

"That's better."

"We're going on a well-deserved vacation. We'll be flying."

Bibi staggered for a moment and then thrust a palm to her chest. "Oh, lord. Tell me you didn't say that. I don't think my pump muscle could take it."

Diane resumed rolling back and forth across the carpet, her face tight with concentration. "I'll have to notify my publishers and send in a large enough backlog for at least a few weeks. Then reroute the mail to the post office. Ollie, have Brinks Security check on the property every twenty-four hours. I'll give the neighbor the key so Chauncey can water the plants while we're gone. Bibi, you'll have to call my agent and cancel any appearances. In fact, no one can know we've left the country. We can't leave a trail." She stopped abruptly, pivoting the chair around. "Ollie, do you think we'll need overseas shots just to be on the safe side?"

"Uh, I'm not sure if—"

"Okay, we'll get 'em then." She turned on Bibi, speaking quickly. "As a precaution, I'll need to change disguises frequently once there, to stay out of the public eye. So, break out my incognito wigs and sunglasses—you know the ones. Although it's a fat chance anybody will recognize me in Cuba —comics are probably banned there—we still can't take the risk."

"What about airlines?" Bibi wrung her hands.

"I think it's a good idea if we fly charter. That way we can avoid the big airline crowd. Make the arrangements with Frank's charter." She sucked in a deep breath. "It sounds like we'll have to fly to Miami, then into Havana. From there we'll make our way to the island and then get a bead on this Casa Madres hotel, so we can make plans from there." She exchanged looks between the two. "Have I left anything out?"

Bibi waggled her head. "No, I can already feel the backache from packing all this shit. What are you going to do with *that*?" She pointed to the suit parts on the floor, stacked next to the bed.

Diane screwed up her face in thought. The Central Intelligence Agency as much as denied its existence. She knew it was a high-tech breakthrough in military hardware. It was an object the other side wanted for their own gain, Chet had told her. The risk in leaving it behind was obvious. She had no doubt that its location would eventually be discovered by those who were after it. If *they* in fact knew exactly where it was, then it would only be logical to keep it out of their hands by removing it from the premises. The only question was where would it be safe? *I also made a promise*, she remembered. *A promise that can't be broken. It stays with me.*

"It's simple," said Diane. "It goes with us so we can keep it safe. Pack it and stack it deep in my carryall. We'll pad the top with other junk."

"Carry-on?" asked Ollie. "What about security?"

"Frank's Charter," said Diane, "means minimal security if we go in the back door with a priority boarding. He's always done a good job of keeping me out of the crowd glare. He's never questioned my gear."

Bibi looked at her, revelation dawning on her face. "That's the same Frank Coppola that has a crush on you—

the charter we use all the time. Di, you're going to play kissy face with that man so you can sneak your machine onboard."

"That's about the size of it."

"That's the easy part," said Ollie. "What about Cuban Customs? Heck, they strip-search people."

Diane gave him a defiant look. "I've already got a backup plan for that. It's worth the risk. Think positive, Ollie."

Bibi slapped her thighs, looking heavenward. "I guess I better arrange for the passports. We're leaving for Cuba."

Diane wrung her hands. "That's the spirit."

After disembarking from the shuttle van, Diane rolled across the tarmac on her way to the charter hangar owned by Frank Coppola of BreezAir Charter Services. She had a small train of Travelpro luggage hooked behind her wheelchair that looked like a mini locomotive pulling three freight cars and a caboose. A few people gawked at the strange procession from the parking lot a dozen yards away. But their path to the plane was relatively free of curious eyes, and they had avoided the baggage claims area by coming in from the back gate—Frank's "celebrity entrance." The guard had orders to wave them through. Bibi, who had paid in advance for the tickets online, walked a step behind Diane, carrying her favorite luggage case. Ollie brought up the rear, shading himself with an umbrella.

Frank Coppola stepped out of the hangar entrance just as the threesome approached. A man in his fifties, wearing a crew-cut, aviation glasses and a broad smile, Frank held up his arms in dramatic welcome.

"Hi, Frankie," said Diane.

"Man, it's good to see you again, Luscious. Seems like it's been ages."

Diane rolled to a stop, accepting a cheek kiss from her

favorite pilot. "It's good to see you, too. But it's only been about five weeks, Frank. You act like it's been years."

"It's always years in between visits with you." He cocked his head. "That's a new look for you. Red hair this time?"

"It's low-profile time again. Nobody needs to know where I'm vacationing."

"Nothing's changed." He looked toward the hangar, waved his arms frantically. "Get this luggage aboard, guys."

Two teenagers dressed in blue overalls ran across the tarmac and began to disengage Diane's luggage train.

"Chop, chop!" said Frank. "Don't weigh it, we're pressed for time." He looked at Diane. "You're the only passengers, so you won't be hurting for room or privacy."

Diane smiled. "Thanks for the priority rush. We really need to get there quickly."

"Don't thank me yet. Since I'm taking the big Citation Sovereign, we'll layover for fuel at Dallas-Fort Worth, then straight into Miami. From there it's just a few minutes airtime to Havana. But I'm afraid that's as far as I can take you, judging from the track-line of the weather system coming up from the south."

"That bad, huh?"

"Looks like the beginning of a hurricane and they've already named her. If it veers off, I'll take you on to Siguanea or Rafael Cabrera on Juventud. But it doesn't look good. You picked the worst time to head down into the Caribbean."

Diane wasn't expecting that. Like a fool, she hadn't consulted the weather service for that latitude. "Just take us into Havana. We'll shuttle across the island and board a boat or ferry."

"Glad you understand. I hope you have your passports and I.D. in order. Remember about fruits, pornography, combustible ma—"

"We're clean, Frank. Don't worry your head."

He placed his hands on the wheelchair rails, his eyes stern, unblinking. "I don't mean to pry," he whispered, "but you could have picked any destination in the world to have yourself a fun blast. Why Cuba? It's not exactly a safe haven. It sure isn't a prime-time destination for American tourists, even though some parts do cater to the rich."

"Change of pace, Frank. I thought it was about time I saw how the other half lived." She watched his reaction, hoping she hadn't aroused suspicion.

He straightened, blew a sigh. "Just be damn careful." His mood lightened. "All told, I should have you into Havana in about eight or nine hours. So, we better get in the wind before the wind catches up with us."

"I owe you one, love."

They stowed her luggage and had her strapped into a jump seat in record time. The young flight attendant, who Diane knew to be Frank's niece, supplied her with a complimentary blanket and pillow. Music headphones were passed around. Ollie and Bibi took seats down the aisle from her within speaking distance.

After listening to some classical music, Diane fell asleep, dreaming during the first leg of the flight. Images and thoughts of Chet Strauss filled her world with lingering memories. She awoke with a start twice when she heard him calling out for her. His pleas sounded painful, coming from very far away. She called out to him in her mind *I'm coming, Chet, I'll find you!*

She awoke at the midway point, the fuel stop in Texas. She had a brief lunch and then napped again for the second leg.

Diane awoke when they landed in Miami. The jet was fueled, inspected then taxied for the short leg to Havana. They lifted into the sky on schedule. Fully rested, Diane ordered some coffee, intent on staying awake for the last leg.

She had no window to gaze out of. She could only imagine that they were passing over foamy swirls in an azure sea, crystal-clear reefs and the tiny white specks of sailing vessels. She could see Ollie and Bibi sitting together, and noticed they looked pensive, even though they had dressed for the occasion in festive shorts and colorful tops. She desperately needed their support, even though things seemed hasty and emotionally charged. She wasn't asking them to read her heart. She needed them to trust her judgment. It wasn't like this was the first time she had fallen in love.

There had been one young man three years ago who had given her quite the romantic ride. He'd introduced her to the delights of physical and emotional passion, yet they hadn't fully consummated their bond. The relationship blossomed for a while. But his priorities soon came to the fore. She lost him to an Ivy League university, where he ultimately graduated, not only in the academic sense but also to someone else. It had been her first real sense of loss, heartache and rejection. *That's not going to happen this time,* she thought. *He really does love and cares for me. I saw it. I felt it.*

An overhead speaker broke her train of thought.

"This is Captain Crash speaking; we will be arriving shortly at José Marti International Airport. We'll be experiencing some mild wind turbulence on our decent. The sky is cloudy and the outside air temperature is eighty-four degrees. We hope that you have enjoyed your flight with BreezAir Charter. Make sure your seat belts are fastened, and please return your tables to their upright position. God, I love saying that!"

Diane laughed. Her two companions didn't think it was funny.

When they landed in Havana, Frank secured Diane's luggage train to her chair then gave her precise directions to customs.

"Sorry I can't take you all the way," he said. "It's confirmed there's a large hurricane headed for the eastern tip of Cuba. By the time we got there I'd be catching the fringe of it. It just isn't safe. My professional advice is to stay out of the air."

"I understand. We'll be just fine."

"Call me when you need a pickup. Give me twenty-four hours' notice."

"Will do. It'll be a couple of weeks."

He hugged her then gave her a lecture about Cuban society. He shut up when she promised him dinner and a movie when they met up next.

The three had their passports ready when they reached Customs and baggage inspection. A female inspector waved Diane around the walk-through detector and readied a wand but then hesitated. Diane had the distinct feeling this employee was new, a bit nervous to clear a wheelchair-bound passenger. Bibi began to unhitch the bag train so the custom officials could inspect the contents. Buckles were unsnapped, zippers pulled, pouches opened. Ollie held back in the crowd as he had been told to do from prearrangement by Diane.

The inspector dropped to her knees and held a mirror under the wheelchair. Then she made a slow circuit around Diane, pausing to examine something. She moved to the large carryall bag strapped to the back of the wheelchair. She lifted the Velcro flap, looked inside.

"What is this, Señora?" she asked in passable English.

If you don't look too closely, you won't discover it's a military combat exoskeleton. But it came out, "That's my Invertomatic machine. It lets me hang upside down to increase circulation and straighten my spine." Diane leaned her head down, stuck her tongue out, while making a face. Trying to simulate an upside-down position taxed her acting abilities.

"Que?"

Bibi jumped in. "As a physical therapist, I highly recommend it. You should think about getting one yourself, seeing as how you are on your feet all day."

The inspector pulled out a penlight and shined it down at the opening of the carryall bag. She frowned. "It looks like an engine down there or something." She unsnapped her two-way radio and spoke into it. Diane assumed she was requesting supervisor assistance.

This is going south fast, thought Diane. She gave Bibi a subtle nod. The large woman retrieved a thick stack of papers from her personal bag and presented them to the young inspector, explaining that they were doctor's and therapist's reports that required Diane to own such a device. The young girl pushed the papers away, giving the two a grim smile. She pointed across the floor at two approaching men.

A supervisor and security guard stepped up to Diane and asked the inspector about the problem. The inspector pointed to the bag. "I do not know what that is in there."

The supervisor peeked inside. Diane explained what the object was again, telling the airport personnel that it was nothing more than a new-age gymnastic apparatus and she always took it with her on all her flights because her doctor and therapist had ordered her to use the machine regularly.

Bibi thrust the paperwork at the man. "This is the prognosis report for Ms. Nine's affliction. There are also twenty-five testimonials regarding the effectiveness of the Invertomatic." She stressed, "*Doctor's orders.*"

The supervisor thumbed through the stack of paperwork, then frowned. His expression read *I'm not going to read all of this; it's probably American propaganda*. He looked at the line of waiting disembarkation passengers, who were beginning to stack up in a nasty clog. There were more than a few mumbles and curses coming from the anxious crowd. Regardless, he bent over and patted the side of the large container.

The accompanying security guard took a long look inside the carryall then reached inside. Diane knew that the situation was deteriorating. The time for plan B had arrived. She gave Ollie several exaggerated winks, who'd been standing in the crowd, watching the shakedown. Ollie put a small cup to his mouth, set it down and thrust his hands in his pocket. He forced his way through the crowd. Just before he reached the wheelchair, he stumbled and flung his hands out in dramatic fashion. He hit Diane's shoulder a glancing blow and then opened his mouth wide, issuing a stream of orange slurry that sprayed into the back of the carryall. The three airport personnel lurched backward, narrowly missing the flying chunks. Ollie fell to his knees, holding up a pen and paper.

"I'm so *sorry,* Ms. Nine," Ollie wailed. "I just wanted an autograph, but I was so nervo—"

"No autographs today!" exclaimed Bibi.

Diane flicked a piece of Beefaroni from her sleeve and looked up at the supervisor. "I'm sorry, this happens all the time with the fans."

The supervisor tightened his jaw, looking at the mess on the carrier. Some of the splatter had landed on the tops of his shoes. The security guard pulled a hanky and knelt in an attempt to clean the shoes, but the supervisor chopped his hand down. "Alto!" he said. He waved Diane through, with the words, "Apologies for the delay. Welcome to Cuba." He then turned on the other two and spoke rapid-fire Spanish.

Diane waited for Bibi to assemble and organize the luggage. When it was attached to the wheelchair, they passed through the departure gate and onto the main terminal floor. Bibi ran ahead to disappear into the crowd, explaining that she had to find an exchange. Ollie took the long way around and caught up with Diane.

Diane glanced at Ollie, who was still wiping his face with a napkin. "That was perfect," she said. "For a minute I thought we were toast. Did you catch what he said afterward?" Ollie had told her once that he knew just enough Spanish to get him into trouble.

"I understood enough of it. He said something about your purse being filled with tourist dollars, so the hell with it."

She kept her voice low. "Thank God they were squeamish."

When Diane and Ollie reached a phone in the airport lobby, Bibi met up with them, claiming that she had exchanged dollars for pesos. Right now, they needed a bus service to get them to the south end of Cuba, where they could arrange transportation to Isla de la Juventud. Ollie made the call.

After a few moments, Ollie hung up the phone. "Okay, I got a wheelchair-access shuttle van for hire. It should take us to the coast of Pinar del Rio."

"That'll do us," said Diane.

When they stepped outside of the lobby onto the street, Diane looked around. The architecture appeared to be a hodgepodge of baroque, new art deco and old colonial. Two smells predominated—fried tortillas and pipe tobacco smoke. What was most amazing were the cars driving up and down the street. Many European makes were in evidence, but the majority of the models were American, straight out of the '50s and '60s. All of them gleamed in pristine condition, waxed to bedazzlement, with new chrome, immaculate whitewalls and treated rag tops. The drivers sat bolt-upright with their shoulders back, obviously proud of their rides.

Like an insect swarm bursting from a hive, a small knot of children surrounded the threesome, offering shoeshines, flowers, plastic toys, cigarettes and other flotsam for sale.

Ollie flung his arms about. "Shoo, you little urchins! We don't need anything today."

"Don't feed them," said Bibi. "They'll only come back for more."

"Don't be ridiculous." Diane passed out some small bills. The children squealed with delight and then ran down the street waving the bills for all eyes to see. "Americanos!" they yelled.

"Now they're going to bring reinforcements," said Ollie.

Before another crowd of children approached, their shuttle arrived with a screeching halt at the curb. The driver opened a large swing door on the side and slid a ramp down. Diane rolled up into the bed of the shuttle, while Bibi and Ollie boarded their luggage and secured the chair. The driver pulled away from the curb with a sudden burst of speed, leaving several pursuing children in his wake.

The driver said, "Welcome to Cuba" in perfect English. "Where would you like to visit?"

"We need to go to Pinar del Rio," said Diane, "and take a ferry or boat to Isla de la Juventud. How did you know we spoke English?"

"Ha! Only Americans would dress as you have and give dollars to orphan children. There is a small port facility in Pinar del Rio. They have the new hydrofoil boats there that can make the crossing very swiftly. It costs a few pesos more, but it is well worth it. They also have accommodations for the handicapped."

At least he didn't say "lame" or "crippled," Diane thought. "That's exactly where we need to go."

Diane brought a few books to read but didn't feel like absorbing herself in someone else's story right now. She glanced out the window, hardly watching the scenery go by. Chet Strauss consumed her thoughts again. He'd had a mystical, mesmerizing effect on her the first minute he'd picked her up in his strong arms. She'd felt his heart beating through his ribcage, knocking against hers. She had lost herself in the pools of those brown eyes, succumbed to the warmth of his easy smile. He had made love to her with complete abandon, unconcerned that half of her being was unable to respond in like fashion. He had kissed her long, passionately like a love-struck troubadour straight out of the pages of some romance novel.

What more could she ask from a man who seemed to have everything? A quick wit, sense of humor and heightened intelligence were not inborn traits picked up in a random gene pool. He was self-sufficient, even having a profound appreciation for the arts. It was as though he had been meant for her all along—a heaven-sent gift. Nothing could convince her that she wasn't doing the right thing. It had been such a long time since the love bug had given her a nip. She would not deny those feelings.

Law enforcement had been dubious about her claims, unwilling to believe what she had told them. She could understand the local cop's reluctance to become involved in what they thought might be a domestic issue. She could also find it believable that the CIA would denounce such a story about a secret project. If anything, she had alerted the agency to a civilian's knowledge of the project, raising their antenna. Which meant what? That they would come after her for breaching national security measures and lock her up in some gulag? Let them try it. She'd warned them, told them the truth. Let it be on their heads from here on out.

She allowed herself a look out the window again. A small sugarcane field passed by along with a few tin and lumber houses. They were on a small two-lane blacktop road that led up into the foothills. Pine trees lined both sides of the road. Past the treetops, she could see some tall peaks amongst some foggy clouds. She wondered if they would be following a mountain pass to gain the plateau on the other side. The brochure had described both islands as being heavily forested.

A large panel truck passed them on the shoulder, kicking up a tornado of dust. The shuttle driver stiffened in his seat and yanked the wheel, swerving the van. Ollie spilled a game of solitaire on the floor, while Bibi toppled into the aisle. The driver drove the heel of his hand on the horn, swearing Spanish expletives out of the window.

Diane watched the mystery vehicle pull up ahead of the shuttle. It kicked up a hail of gravel that pinged off the grill and window screen.

Bibi resumed her seat and cinched the belt across her lap. "What the hell kind of maniac runs a handicapped shuttle off the road?"

Diane looked out the front window with a terrifying sense of calamity. Her feelings were justified, for in the next moment, the back end of the truck loomed huge, filling the front windshield of the shuttle. She knew it had slammed its brakes on. She got out the word "brace" before the shuttle driver applied the brakes, sending them into a skid.

The shuttle hit the truck off angle, more of a glancing blow than a full-on impact. Diane's body thrust forward, not violently, but with enough momentum to jar her against her chair restraint. Thankfully, Bibi and Ollie had belted up, negating their being thrown from their seats.

The back door of the mystery truck swung open through a pall of dust, vomiting out several men who were dressed in tourist clothes. They dashed to the shuttle, carrying long-clip pistols. The shuttle driver lurched from his seat in an attempt to latch the service door, but one of the intruders got his hands on it, sliding it open. The others rushed in and quickly subdued the driver, taping him into his seat, and then pulling a sack over his head.

An Asian man, with a birthmark over his left eye, nimbly leapt down the aisle and held a gun to the side of Diane's head, while he yanked open the flap to her chair carrier. "It's here," he said to the others in a calm voice.

Diane did a headcount of the intruders, noting five men and one woman. The female looked Anglo, sporting red hair and hazel eyes. Three men were Middle Eastern in appearance. The other two were Asians, small in stature and more animated, especially the gun wielder who now moved to the front of her chair and eyed her from head to foot. Although Diane could not see Bibi behind her, she heard her words ring off the van walls.

"Who the hell are all these mud-colored people?"

Ollie said, "This is an outrage! This is a private shuttle service!"

Mr. Birthmark stepped up to Ollie, clenching his fist. "You shut up, little fruitcake man. You speak when spoken to."

Diane held up her hands in submission. "Stop it! You don't need all this cloak and dagger shit. Just tell me which one is Agent Eugene Gene."

The intruders exchanged perplexed glances. One of them activated the lift control. The hazel-eyed woman released the tie-downs on Diane's chair. Another man pitched their luggage out of the side door onto the dirt. Yanked to their feet, Ollie and Bibi were marched out of the van.

"You, too." said Birthmark to Diane. "Move your machine out."

Diane didn't have to be told that these people were not members of the Central Intelligence Agency. Nor were they hooligans intent on robbing tourists. They'd checked her carryall bag in the first minutes after forcing themselves aboard. Birthmark had said, "*It's here.*" This smacked of a terrorist hijacking. She had no choice but to obey their commands. Guns were an irrefutable persuader.

She maneuvered her chair onto the ramp, allowing herself

to be lowered. Once on the shoulder of the road, she watched one of the group inject the shuttle driver with a small hypodermic needle and remove the tape from him. They left him slumped over the steering wheel.

Birthmark ordered her to move to the back of the large panel truck, which she did. Two men took a hold of her chair and hefted it into the truck bed. They threw her luggage in and then herded Ollie and Bibi inside. Once the rear panel door closed, the truck engine revved to life. In a moment, they sped off at a fast pace. A tiny interior light flicked on, illuminating the truck bed interior. Several sleeping bags and packs took up one corner. Two laptop computers sat on the floor, held there by bungee cords. Three ice chests and a Coleman stove took up another corner. A port-a-potty sat bolted to the floor. In the confines of the interior, the little toilet gave off the pungent odor of human waste.

Diane looked at her friends. They were terrified. It was the first time she had ever seen them stunned to silence. Unless they were storing up venom for an outburst. Right now, her own hands were shaking like sticks. Someone had to act as the spokesperson. Better that she speak up than let a dangerous silence remain.

"Who are you people? What do you want with us?"

Birthmark answered, "You don't need to know anything. You just need to cooperate and go along for the ride."

Diane looked hard at the spokesman. She couldn't decide if he was Japanese, Chinese or some other Asian lineage. He spoke impeccable English, aside from clipping the words at the end. She thought the best ploy in this situation was to surrender—admit defeat—bargain their way out.

She tried, "You're welcome to anything we have. We have currency and valuables. Enough for all of you. You don't need to do this, whoever you are."

Her plea pulled guffaws from all. The female seemed especially delighted, cackling loudly over the others. She offered her thoughts. "You should tell the capitalist bitch that such negotiation doesn't work in this country, Cho. They have nothing to give that we have not already taken."

Birthmark, now revealed to be Cho through a slip of the tongue, swished his arm violently at the red-haired woman. Her eyes dropped to her lap.

Diane caught the heavy accent of the woman as being Ukrainian or Russian in origin. She was certain Ollie had picked up on it, too, since he had always been good at discerning dialects or ethnicity. The other three had remained quiet, and though clean-shaven, there were Middle Eastern traits in their features. A mixed bag of nuts. Which led to the conclusion that they might be dealing with the same group who had kidnapped her boyfriend!

"So, what have you done with Chet Strauss?" Diane asked. "You're not fooling anyone. You were the same people who had him under surveillance in the States. I saw you following us."

"You don't know what you saw," said Cho. "It's all a fantasy in your head, like your cartoons."

"Then you should know," said Ollie, "that Diane is known all over the world because of her so called 'cartoons,' and she's bound to be recognized. This is flat-out kidnapping. You guys are going to be so hosed for this. It's a federal offense."

"Your federal homeland security is worthless here," said Cho. "You are too far removed from your country to be of interest to anyone. Accidents happen abroad every day. Consider yourselves just another one."

Bibi balled her fists. "You gotta have some kind of stones to terrorize a woman with disabilities. If you want that military suit, why don't you just take it and leave us alone? I don't care if you want to GI Joe-your-ass all over the place. You haven't got any business disrupting the lives of decent folks or sticking needles in shuttle drivers!"

One of the Middle Eastern men flared up. "You quiet your mouth, you insolent pig!"

Bibi reared up. "Don't you speak to me like that, you camel-humping mutha fucker!"

Cho broke open a satchel and pulled out a length of duct tape. He handed it to one of the men, who proceeded to wrap Bibi's mouth. The large black woman put up a struggle but received a chop to the back of her neck.

"Don't hurt her!" Diane screamed.

"Anyone else?" asked Cho, wiggling the tape.

"You might as well do me," said Ollie, "because I'm not going quietly into the good night."

Cho obliged the request and wrapped Ollie's face mummy-like. He then held the roll under Diane's chin, shaking it with menace. "How about you?"

Diane shook her head, not wanting the same treatment. She needed her verbal skills to communicate with these thugs. Pandering to their misguided egos might be the only way to extract information from them. Pushing them too far could mean dire consequences for the three. She had no idea what they had done to the driver and had no wish to suffer the same fate. Being dead or unconscious had zero advantages in a fight-back scenario.

"I won't give you any trouble," said Diane. "I want your assurance that you won't harm my friends. I'll cooperate, if that is what you want me to do." *In other words, I'll give what I feel like giving you until I can figure a way out of this mess.*

"That's better," said Cho. "You should always respect the higher authority when you have no bargaining power. You will not be gagged if you remain civil."

Diane put on the submissive captive look. "You never

answered my question about Chester Strauss. I'm concerned about him—more than concerned. He's special to me."

Cho sat down, crossing his legs. "The man you speak of is in our custody. He is unharmed."

"Then you do have him?"

"For now. Until we no longer require his services."

"Do you mind if I ask where you're taking us?"

"To an undisclosed location where the tactical suit can be evaluated and tested."

"But why Cuba?"

"We find that the territory of Cuba serves as a neutral municipality for our activities. Our socialist views are also shared by the government, giving us free-reign and impunity."

"That tells me you're not privateers."

"We are a triad, the tentacles of larger collaborative powers. You don't think we could have tracked you without resources, do you?"

"My government will eventually catch up to you for your theft of top-secret military hardware. They'll spare no expense to find you. And it won't be long before the media is alerted to my disappearance. I've been spotted at the airport lobbies. I've left boarding pass records. How are you going to avoid all of this detection and get away with it?"

Cho grinned. "Spare me your feeble logic. You really think you have it all figured out. Your government has no idea of what you are carrying on the back of your chair. Your disappearance begins with the last location of the shuttle. From there on, you have vanished."

"What happens when the shuttle driver wakes up after that injection you gave him?"

Cho laughed. "He won't wake up. We put him down like a dog. The chemicals in his system are non-traceable. It will take a lab weeks to discover the reason for his death. By that time, we will have arrived at home with the prize in hand."

Diane swallowed dryly. They had killed the shuttle driver to cover their tracks. She didn't think her or her friend's lives were worth spit now. Her mind raced in code-red mode, wondering how quickly they would be disposed of. They had the combat suit. So, what was stopping them from causing three more deaths?

Diane looked at her friends, wondering if she would ever see them again. She blamed herself for subjecting them to this theater of horrors. If she could have just taken it all back.

7

After an undetermined time of ceaseless jostling and suffocating humidity in the confines of the truck bed, the truck came to a halt. Diane awoke in small increments, having spent a good time of the journey alert, but passing out to exhaustion. Having no idea how many hours had passed, since her watch was missing from her wrist, Diane rubbed her eyes groggily then looked around. The terrorists were just getting to their feet, stretching, yawning. She was relieved to see that Ollie and Bibi had had their tape gags removed. Both were fully conscious. Diane asked them if they were all right. Ollie nodded but made a little moaning sound when he touched his sore lips where the tape had been yanked from his face.

"Thank the Almighty you nodded off the last twenty minutes of the ride," said Bibi, "so you didn't have to see me piss in that bucket."

"I saw you," said Ollie, trying to lighten the mood.

Bibi squinted at him. "You don't count."

Diane couldn't believe her friend's spirits were up, considering the circumstances. She voiced her regret for their predicament. "I just wanted to say that I'm sorry for getting you two into this. I wasn't thinking about anything but my selfish desires."

"You didn't kidnap us," said Bibi. "How were you supposed to know? By the way, that bitch stole your Rolex while you were passed out." She pointed to the redheaded woman.

One of the men rolled the loading door open. Even the weak light outside caused Diane to wince against the glare. She could smell salt air and hear the cries of gulls. The rush of waves crashed in the distance. *A shoreline.*

"Everybody out," Cho ordered.

Once again, they lifted Diane off the truck bed. She now sat in a gravel clearing on a small bluff that overlooked a half-moon cove. A white yacht bobbed next to a stone pier. A large white stucco home that looked like a Spanish Hacienda sat on a flattop promontory. It sported multiple levels and balconies. A tiny red flag waved on a cupola high on the roof. The structure was surrounded by tall palms. Whether it was state-owned or a private residence was not determinable. The property screamed *opulence*.

"Where are we?" asked Diane.

"Not that it makes any difference," said Cho, "we're about 15 miles west of Pinar del Rio on a private estate. Now get moving."

"Where to?"

Somebody kicked Diane's wheelchair. "Get down to the dock, lame bitch!"

She rolled down, while the others gathered up the luggage behind her. Cho walked slightly ahead of her down the incline, leading the way. He looked back every so often to check her progress. Reaching the bottom, she rolled out onto the small pier, ending up at the transom of the boat. A deck-hand appeared and laid a plank down, bridging the boat rail and pier foundation. They ordered Diane to cross the gap.

She rolled across cautiously and then was lowered to the aft deck of the boat by muscle power. Ollie and Bibi were ushered across, along with the luggage. The lines were cast off. They motored out of the cove, hitting some chop. Instead of following the coastline, the boat steamed out into the open ocean. Diane noticed the sun sat low and pink in the west. In the distance, the sky looked sick, filled with charcoal-colored clouds. Some wind gusts pelted her face, threatening to blow her wig off. She tried to bring her mental compass to bear.

They're heading to Juventud Island. That's the only explanation for their course.

Cho pointed to the rear salon. "Inside, you three."

They had little choice but to obey. Once inside the teak-paneled salon, Cho and his men poured themselves drinks then sat down on sectional couches. A few of them began to thumb through magazines, while two others broke open a deck of cards.

Bibi held Diane's hand and bent down to look into her eyes. "You okay, doll? This is a piss poor way to spend a vacation."

"I'm fine. I'm more worried about you two." She spoke from the corner of her mouth. "I think we're headed to Juventud Island, our original destination."

Bibi nodded and then straightened up. She projected her voice. "I don't know whether you people are going to shoot us or toss us overboard, but I think we'll cheat you out of your fun if we starve to death first."

Cho flicked his wrist. The red-haired woman walked through a forward companionway. The rattling sound of dishes and pots reached them, presumably from the galley. She appeared fifteen minutes later with bowls of chili, French bread, carrots sticks and a pitcher of fruit juice. Ollie sat on the floor next to Diane, while Bibi sat on a divan on her other side. Somehow, their proximity to her lessened the threat, providing a small measure of comfort. They were still three mice under the glare of several cats. They ate in silence, watching their captors. Cho seemed amused by their feeble attempt at camaraderie.

"So y'all are planning on taking over the world," said Bibi. "You think you can just throw on that robot gear and become a superpower? Either that or you want to fence it off to the highest bidder so somebody else can pimp it out."

"Such military hardware can level the playing field when a million-foot soldiers are wearing it," said Cho. "It's no guarantee of superpower status, but it is a step up the rung for those desirous of catching up in the military defense arena. Supplied to the infantry of several allies, the force can be an overwhelming deterrent. Ground war is an essential part of offensive or defensive maneuvers. One can always invade a country, and by shear air power and armament, obliterate the objective's tactical defenses. The foot soldier remains the necessary element that must root out and destroy the very core of the enemy—soldier against soldier. You call it 'mop-up.' We call it tradition."

"You come up against the United States," said Bibi, "you'll get *your* ass mopped."

"What we may lack in a technological sense, we make up for with countless infantrymen, willing to swarm into the ranks of an invader. Armed with such military combat suits, like the one you have hidden in your chair pack, even a small third-world nation stands a fighting chance to protect themselves against imperialist oppression."

"What makes you think you'll win?" said Ollie.

"Your best example of this lesson was your Vietnam War. There you were forced to meet the enemy on the ground without all of your exotic weapons and tactics. You lost the war because you never gained the advantage."

"We didn't lose sight of our ideals," said Diane. "The

ideals of freedom from oppression and communist regimes. Nations that would dictate the way society lives, breathes and behaves—those were the things we stood for—fought against. Whenever some communist dictatorship crossed the boundaries to conquer a democratic republic, we were there. We'll always be there."

"You want to monopolize the world," spat Cho, "with your culture and free enterprise. You would stop at nothing to convert those who have no desire to follow your lead into a capitalist's future, where the common man sleeps in the gutter and the fat tycoons become more prosperous with each passing day."

"We're a charitable nation," said Diane.

"You are elitists. You claim to care for the masses, yet you have no health care for them. Your own population has lost faith in your political system. You are awash with anarchy and turmoil, filled with disloyalty because your own citizens speak out against your leaders, disgracing them in the media."

Diane clenched her teeth. "Such is the cost in the pursuit of personal rights and freedoms. Speaking of which, you have none. Your dictatorial regime suppresses creativity, imagination and personal freedom. You hold your own society at gunpoint, daring anyone to veer from the party line. That allows you to implement illegal search and seizures, torture, with trumped up charges that lead to cruel and unusual punishments and executions."

"Why do you even listen to her?" asked the red-haired female. "She does not even speak for her own people. She is from the rich caste. She makes her living scribbling ridiculous cartoons in funny papers. She is out of touch with reality."

"Because she has a God-given right to express her opinion," said Ollie. "It's called freedom of speech where we come from."

One of the Middle Eastern men glared at Ollie. "You

would be flogged within an inch of your life for opening your mouth to express any ideology in my country, little queer, fag man."

"You've just proven my point," said Diane. "No tolerance or basic humanity whatsoever. Now tell me who the elitists are?"

Cho snickered. "Maybe you are, for having a Negro and homosexual deviant as slaves in your employment. How ironic that you should speak of personal freedoms or equality when you are the worst example of such a lifestyle."

Ollie and Bibi shifted uneasily on the floor. Diane tried to quell her temper before she spoke. "They were friends of mine before they joined my household. Their enlistment to help me was voluntary. We have no slavery in the arrangement. You just wish that was true."

The boat hit a large swell, lifting them up momentarily, before dropping the hull with a thud. The engines revved, the boat made a perceptible swerve. Diane suspected they had reached blue water and were now fighting some heavy swells.

Bibi said, "You have what you want. Why don't you just cut us loose? We can't do anything to you."

"You'll provide us with insurance," said Cho. "We cannot have you running around with the knowledge you have of us. We'll decide when your usefulness is no longer needed. For now, you remain our guests. The condition is not negotiable."

Diane took a sip of fruit juice but studied the faces of her kidnappers over the rim of the glass. She couldn't determine their individual ethnicity with any accuracy, although she could make a more precise a stab at it. Cho had to be North Korean. She guessed the woman to be Russian. The Middle Eastern men were harder to discern race-wise. They could be Afghans, Pakistanis, Arabs, Iraqis, or even Iranians. Without a doubt, they were a triad representing three socialist-communist governments, all very well organized. She did not know if they were the same individuals who had spied on Chet Strauss in the States or were just another arm of the operation. What an operation it was—a full-tilt espionage contingent with plenty of manpower, planning and resources. She knew for certain that they had contact with Chet Strauss because they knew too many personal details about the three of them.

"I suppose it's asking too much to divulge your names," said Diane. "Be nice to know who we're dealing with."

"You already know my last name," said Cho. "She is Tatiana. She will assist with your womanly needs. You do not need to know the rest, other than to obey their commands."

Diane looked at her Rolex strapped on Tatiana's wrist. "I don't need her to help me. I prefer my own people. Which reminds me, I would like to relieve myself. But I want my helpmate's assistance."

Cho raised his arm to point. "Straight forward on the port side. Tatiana will escort you."

"I said I don't want her help," said Diane and grasped Bibi's hand. She rolled down the narrow corridor and found the small head. Once inside, Bibi positioned Diane on the stool. Both managed to occupy the cramped interior. Diane locked the door against entry. She kept her voice hushed to a whisper.

"We seem to be dealing with three different governments. Cho is the spokesman—the highest ranking. I'm sure we're headed for Juventud Island. They must have some hidden base of operations there."

"Yeah, I figured that much," said Bibi. "I suppose we're going to the same place they have Chet."

"No doubt. Now listen, I don't know what they plan on doing with us once they get us there. If we're separated for any reason, try to make it to Casa de las Madres any way you can. If you find a phone, alert the United States Authorities—

maybe the Department of Defense or NSA. Explain the situation."

"That's a big 'if', girl. What if these kooks waste our asses? I can't get that out of my head. I'm just a nigger to them." Bibi sniffled. Diane could see the woman's hands shaking.

"You can't think like that. We have to stay together and protect each other. I'll see if I can work on their sympathies, what little they have. We sure can't fight our way out of this. So, hang in there. Whatever you do, try not to insult them. Just play along."

"Okay, but if they—"

Several loud slaps came from the door, followed by the voice of Tatiana. "Stop conspiring in there and get out!"

Bibi unlatched the lock. The door swung open. The Russian woman gave them the thumbs out gesture, her eyes cold and menacing. They exited the head and entered the salon. Diane noticed that Ollie was sitting outside on the aft deck, curled up with his back against the transom. Spray washed over the rail, wetting his face. He looked so tiny and frightened in the failing light. She heard a few of the kidnappers suppressing laughter, knowing immediately that they had terrorized the small man.

Diane rolled out onto the pitching deck, pulling up next to Ollie. She held her hand out. He took it, rose to his feet.

"Are you okay?"

"I guess," he said, holding on to the rail. "Once I get past the image of being dressed in feathers and castrated in public."

Once back in the salon, Diane shook her fist at the men, forgetting her compliance rules. "You must be really proud of yourselves. So help me God, if I had legs I'd be in your faces right now. You're a pack of wild animals!"

Outside, the wind howled and the sea rose. The ship moaned under the onslaught of wave sets striking its hull. It seemed like Poseidon had risen from the depths to swirl his mighty trident in the waters.

Yet it was another God that rose up out of the southeast that would quake the hearts of mankind.

The private yacht weighed anchor next to a small jetty on the north shore of Juventud Island late in the evening. A small launch tied up to the yacht to offload the passengers, who were then ferried across a small inlet into a protected cove. During the move onto the shoreline, Diane nearly toppled into the shallow water due to careless hands, but they managed to transport her wheelchair into a small clearing. A large panel truck, similar to the last, waited for them with its engine running. Herded into the back, the loading door slammed. Once again, they braced for another journey to an unknown destination. As the truck powered up a steep incline, Cho snapped a dome light on then settled back for the ride.

With no way to judge their direction or miles traveled, Diane felt at a loss for approximating their location. She noticed that none of the kidnappers carried radio sets to communicate with any outside agency. She wondered the reason for it, suspecting that they might not want to broadcast any frequencies that might be picked up by other sources other than their own. They could also have made the transport much swifter by utilizing a plane or helicopter. Then again, maybe they had no desire to be detected on commercial radar or reveal their location to airport authorities. So far, they had coordinated their moves with exact military precision.

Diane knew they had picked Juventud specifically for its isolation. The tourist brochure said that it was a principality covering 2,500 square kilometers with a population of 85,000 residents. Pine forests covered almost the entire island, a topography that could easily hide any clandestine operation. The question was how they would spirit the combat suit off the island to get it to their ultimate destination.

Amused, Cho studied Diane with eyes that were mere slits in the weak dome light. His face had a yellowish, diseased pallor. "You look like you are plotting something, Ms. Nine. Rest assured there is nothing you can do to escape your confinement. It would be prudent for you to ease your mind —conform. A good soldier always obeys."

"Maybe I should call you colonel," said Diane, "or is it captain? They wouldn't have sent anyone with less rank than that. You seem to have a proper education, probably from one of our own Ivy Leagues. How ironic that they would pick you for an espionage mission, dealing with an enemy that can't even put up a fight or defend themselves. You've missed your moment of glory—your soldier-to-soldier confrontation."

"Whatever the task or mission, a good soldier always obeys," said Cho. "I hold the rank of colonel. I'll live to see ample glory and confrontation as a result of what I've done today. I expect full honors from my country, with the assurance that I will have command of a new Special Forces regiment. Therein lies the glory, the accomplishment, Ms. Nine. The fruits of my labor will achieve the rewards—the end result. A good soldier is also patient."

"I see. The payoff comes when you use this technology, the end result being a rampage. With the combined forces of two other nations, it sounds like your agenda would be nothing short of world domination. Strike hard. Strike fast. Strike first."

"It seems your left hemisphere functions as well as the right." Cho gave a short sarcastic laugh.

"I have my moments of logic and deductive reasoning," Diane quipped. "I don't need intuition to tell me that you're holding people against their will who can't help you further your mission. Keeping us when we can't help your cause is senseless. In fact, we hamper your movements. Where's the economy? I'm sure you can see the logic in that."

"She's trying to twist you into a pretzel doughnut," said Tatiana. "She would say anything to fog your mind and soften your guts. We hold the playing cards—these fools hold nothing."

The truck hit a deep rut. The wheelchair bounced high and came down on one wheel, flipping it over. Diane fell toward the floor, but not before several hands had latched onto her to break the fall. No less than three of the kidnappers had reacted instantly, even before Ollie or Bibi had a chance to move. Cho slapped the wall several times, screaming for the driver to slow down. Once Diane was lifted into her chair, she strapped herself in.

One thing was evident when Diane studied her opposition again. They had her preservation in mind. They had reacted swiftly when seeing her in peril. They would not have rescued Ollie or Bibi so quickly. They would have let them succumb to their injuries and laughed about it. Not her. She could only conclude that they had direct orders to keep her safe. *They're saving me for something—I'm part of their plan—they need me.* Tatiana had been wrong about them holding all the cards. Somehow, Diane had to exploit a weakness.

"As I was saying," began Diane, "we're not needed in your great scheme. I don't care what you do with me, but these two are baggage. Do yourself a favor. Unburden the dead weight. Your superiors will thank you for it."

"You're not going to listen to her demands, comrade," spat Tatiana. "She has nothing to bargain with."

"Let her speak," said Cho.

"Thank you," said Diane. "I beg to differ about the bargaining. First, I'll offer my complete cooperation to assist your goals if you let my friends go. They're useless to you. I can promise you they'll not breathe a word about anything they've seen here, which is next to nothing anyway."

"She is trying to leverage you," said a Middle Eastern man.

Diane locked eyes with Cho. "I give you my word on it. It's a fair deal."

A pall of silence fell over the group. Nothing was heard but the creak of the suspension and an occasional wind gust hitting the side of the truck. All eyes focused on Cho, awaiting some response, but it did not come through words at first. He rapped on the back wall divider three times. A small slit opened. He spoke into it.

"Stop the vehicle."

The truck downshifted to a roll, eventually halting. Cho pointed to the loading door. "Open it up."

There came a moment's hesitation before one of them rose to do his bidding. A man pulled the door up and stood by it. Cho stepped up to opening. He looked coldly at Ollie and Bibi. "Get out. Your lives have been spared."

Ollie rose, his eyes fixed on Diane. "I can't do this. I can't leave you alone!" He looked close to tears.

Bibi got to her feet, speared Cho with a look of defiance. "I'm not going anywhere without this lady."

It happened very fast. Cho stepped up to each one, giving them stark shoves. They tumbled out of the truck and hit the ground with bone-jarring thuds. Diane bit her lip, watching their luggage tossed in the dirt.

Cho jabbed a pistol at the two, dagger-like. "Tell the authorities anything, and I promise you that you will read about your mistress's head floating in the Gulf Stream. One word, you seal her fate. Now go back home where you belong."

Diane got a glimpse of recognition from Bibi before the door rolled down with a loud clang. For a minute, she could not catch her breath, having seen the last of her friend's faces filled with confused terror. Alone and stranded on a desolate island, she agonized over how they would get back to humanity to find shelter. They had been left on a dirt road in the dead of night with foul weather closing in.

The truck lurched. They picked up speed over the ruddy terrain. Diane felt the confines of the truck closing in on her, the eyes of the kidnappers slithering over her like snakes. She was alone now. She didn't really care what they thought about her. She'd accomplished her one-woman mission—to see her friends to safety. Bibi knew exactly what to do—get to the Casa de la Madres hotel anyway she could. Her friends could be at odds with each other at times, but they could also show plenty of resourcefulness when they had a task to perform.

"An equitable trade," said Cho. "Your life for theirs. Know that I will hold you to your promise. Any hint that they have contacted the authorities, and I will personally see that you are dispatched."

"After I've served my usefulness, then what?"

"It will depend on your performance."

Performance?

There was little need to carry on any further conversation. She wheeled her chair around, showing them her back. She tried to relax in spite of the jolting rhythm of the truck. She let her chin drop and then closed her eyes. Ollie and Bibi appeared in her mind's eye. She willed them with all the clairvoyant power she had in her mind to pick up and march on bravely. They would also agonize over Diane's predicament. But for now, they were alive—safe. She allowed a brief image of Chet to inhabit her inner vision. The memory of his kind face was enough to give her some hope.

Diane felt her shoulder rudely shaken, causing her to snap her eyes open. The truck had stopped. They must have reached their destination. She asked for the time. Tatiana took great satisfaction in reading it from Diane's watch.

"It is one in the morning."

Diane needed to know the time. It would approximate how far they'd traveled. She calculated a truck moving at 25 miles per hour over rough terrain for three hours would move 75 miles from the coast, presumably inland. It wasn't much to go on, but she had little else to keep her mind busy with positive thoughts.

The rear door opened. She could see nothing more than pitch-black. The sound of the wind rushing through pine branches and the heady scent of sap alerted her to a new location. Once on the ground, she strained her eyes to pick out objects. At least five different light sources shone from several structures. A large bungalow type building sat in the largest clearing. Five SUVs sat parked side by side under a dim outside lamp—three silver and two black. The forest fringe surrounding the area looked cleaved away as by an ax stroke—an encampment hidden away in a dense forest. With only one access road in, it resembled a Colombian drug fortress.

Someone slapped the back of Diane's head with such force her wig flipped off. "Get moving!"

Biting her lip, she motored her chair forward, following Cho's wavering flashlight beam over the forest floor. Pine needles and small twigs crunched under her wheels. They arrived at the side entrance to a cinder block building with a tin roof. A generator hummed somewhere nearby.

A door opened, spilling light. Cho ordered her inside. She ran the chair up over a lip and onto a dirty concrete floor. The place looked like a small sorting room, equipped with long wooden tables, carpeted with dust and debris. Several smaller rooms led off from the main floor. She reasoned they might be offices or private quarters. Five overhead lamps lit the interior, which attracted scores of moths that pounced off the naked bulbs.

"I'm sure you are more accustomed to the Ritz-Carlton," said Cho, "but for now you will take one of our guest rooms. One of the smaller ones over there." He pointed. "Tatiana will be in the next room over if you need anything. You will find a receptacle and tissue paper inside. Get some sleep. You will need it."

"Where is Chet Strauss? I want to see him. *Alive*."

"All in good time. Do as you are told or you'll see nothing."

She had little choice but to obey and motored into one of the small guest rooms. A dirty Army cot with a thin mattress took up one side of the wall, while a wooden table and chairs took up the other. There were no windows or inside lock mechanism on the door. A waist-high plastic barrel with a lid sat in the furthest corner, while a toilet paper roll protruded from a peg on the wall. Lovely. She could see herself hefting her lily-white ass upon the crap bucket just as someone barged in. She wasn't beyond making the best of the situation, considering her friends were out there somewhere in much worse shape.

She sidled up next to the cot then pulled herself from the chair onto it. She hefted her legs onto the soiled mattress to splay them out. She lay back, closing her eyes, this time trying to wipe all thoughts from her mind. A moment later, she succumbed to complete exhaustion.

Voices squeezed under the door crack, coming from the main room. Diane had no idea how long she had slept but guessed it to be in the late morning hours. The wind howled outside and the flimsy plywood roof rose with the gusts, causing staccato slaps on the tin roof sheets.

Of all times to have a bladder ache.

It took her a full fifteen minutes to urinate in the makeshift head then climb into the wheelchair. Her purse was still inside the side pouch. Taking out the paper money, her passport and other identification documents, she shoved them in her brassier. A tiny color brochure of Juventud Island went into her front pants pocket. Running her fingers at the bottom of the pouch, she found a small aluminum letter opener and a blue matchbook cover. Those were also hidden.

When Cho and two others stepped into her room unannounced, they were dressed in full military uniforms complete with medals and campaign ribbons. Each had an AK 47 combat rifle slung over their shoulders. The only thing missing in their regalia were name tags.

Cho opened up the flap on her chair carrier, checking the contents. He said, "What, no sabotage? You had the time. Why not risk it?"

"Because you said not to. I'd like to get out of this with my life, rejoin my friends and forget this ever happened. I wouldn't mind Chet accompanying me on the way home, either. I gave you my word about cooperating."

"That is very good." He gave her a broad smile, an obvious show of contentment with her disposition. "You'll join us for breakfast?"

"Do I have a choice?"

He bowed, stepped aside, allowing the chair to roll past him out onto the main floor. One of the longest tables had a cloth stretched across it. Bowls, platters and silverware were set. More than two dozen uniformed men and women sat, chatting. Tobacco smoke filled the air like a London fog. Chet was not to be seen anywhere in the sea of military uniforms.

Diane rolled up to the table and studied the newest faces. The same three ethnic profiles were in evidence. The only ones distinguishable were the high-ranking Russian officers, only because of their accent. The Asians were North Koreans. The origin of the Middle Eastern types posed the biggest question.

Cho addressed the table occupants. "I'm honored to announce that the GSA has congratulated us on the acquisition of the hardware and eagerly await the results of the testing and performance data. Comrades, after years of operations we will soon return home to our families." This brought a raucous applause, the noise only eclipsed by the buffeting winds outside. Cho went on. "And it will be none too soon since we have a category five hurricane headed our way. Hopefully, we will be aboard the transport that will have us on our way within 24 hours." Cho sat down.

Two women dressed in camouflage Khaki outfits appeared from a backroom, carrying kettles and trays. They used ladles to fill the bowls with thick, meatless porridge. Several loaves of bread were diced into finger-sized portions and distributed. Three teapots were placed at strategic positions. With no prayers or thanks, the attendees dug in, slurping the mud-colored goulash.

Diane had a difficult time getting past the bland taste of the meal, resigned to taking timid nibbles. Every so often, someone would look at her with a deadpan expression. Chat was kept to a minimum. What little conversation ensued was between the same cultural groups, speaking in their native language. Clearly none of it was meant for their captive guest's ears, but she suspected she might be the topic of some of the comments, if not most of them.

When the meal was finished, the help cleared the table as

quickly as it was set. Cigars were passed around, but most of them were pocketed. The group showed a tense eagerness to get under way. Cho led Diane out of a side door and into the compound. The air above swirled with tornado-like gusts, looking bruised and beaten. Dust and pine needles choked the air, which crackled with electricity.

Cho quickened his pace. "Hurry up to the storage complex."

Diane followed, maneuvering over the ruts, keeping her head down against the wind gusts. The others followed, most of them losing their hats in the wind. When they reached the largest building in the complex, Cho swung the door open and braced it for entry. Diane rolled inside, wiping the grit from her face. After the crowd entered, Cho locked the door.

The front part of the building was devoid of objects, except for posts connected to overhead joist beams. The only accoutrements were some benches, tables and chairs at the front. At the other end of the building, the dim glow of a television set or monitor screen flickered in and out of phase. A tall figure stood motionless next to one of the tables at the far end. Without being told, she moved in that direction, keeping her eyes on the mystery man's face. Then recognition kicked in upon approaching closer.

"Chet? Is that you?"

She sped up. The man turned around. She almost ran him over when she crossed the distance. She held out a pair of trembling arms, tears welling in her eyes. It was Chet, and he was dressed in a grungy lab smock, looking at her with glazed, emotionless eyes.

"It's me—it's Diane!" she said, incredulous he didn't react. She ached to hold him, just to touch him. It looked like he might have been tortured.

Chet stepped around to the back of her wheelchair. The flap opened, hands jostled inside the carrier. It was a strain to see what he was doing. He pulled out several pieces of combat chassis and placed them on the table. He made several more trips before he had emptied the contents. He then organized the pieces, beginning to study each one with a magnifying glass, turning each piece over, fingering the joints and connections. Two tripod-mounted video cameras sat on the floor. Two handheld versions sat nearby on a chair seat. Large barbells sat on a small black rack in the middle of the floor.

"I'm sorry you had to get mixed up in this," Chet said at last.

Diane rolled her chair closer to him and spoke to his back. "I came looking for you after what happened." She reached out to touch the fringe of his smock but stayed her hand. Something was wrong. Chet Strauss could have been a thousand miles away. He looked, felt indifferent. He could have been in shock, she realized. Meanwhile, the officers gathered around the two to stand in a half-moon circle.

"It was all a ruse," Chet said with a tired voice. "You were meant to be here. It was planned."

"What are you saying? *Look* at me, Chet!"

He went on with his inspection. "We had to find a way to get the suit out of the country. You were the best transport vehicle for that problem. Who else could have secreted a nuclear-powered cell pack through airport security? You cluster-fucked them, just like we knew you would. You were a mule."

"But *them*!" She jabbed a finger, indicating the others. "They were stalking you. They chased you because you said they wanted the—"

"It was *staged*." He turned around, facing her. "I got on a flight and left. It only looked like I was in danger. Wake up. Smell the latte."

She began to shiver. "You don't..."

"Love you? Care for you? I only hoped that you would

make it here with the TACS in one piece. You did an excellent job following the clues, acting the part of an amateur sleuth. They decided to pick you up early, not wanting to risk you losing your package to thieves or going down in some freak channel crossing."

"You can't mean any of this, Chet. They made you say this."

"My name's not Chester Strauss. I cooperated fully."

Tatiana chortled behind her. A few of the officers cleared their throats. One of them laughed but covered his mouth to muffle the outburst.

Chet Strauss stood there like some idiotic automaton. Or *whatever* his name was. What was worse, he had said those words with a grin on his face—a grin that she'd grown to love.

Diane fought to force words out of her mouth, but they wouldn't come. She couldn't breathe—could not stop the spinning in her head. It seemed like a panic attack. The only thing to escape her mouth was a shrill scream and it came out like a steam whistle.

8

"Keep your filthy hands off me!" spat Diane as they splayed her on the table. Two of them took an arm each, while another pressed down on her forehead. Cho stood over her. His face took on a red, sweaty gleam. It seemed like his canine teeth had grown like those of a vampire.

"You *will* cooperate," he told her. "Or I will take you within an inch of your life and keep you there until you change your mind."

Diane tried to look at Chet's face as he proceeded to snap the components on her, starting with the boots and lower frame. "How could you do this me?" she begged.

Chet answered with a breathy calm, "You did it to yourself by being the best possible candidate. I'd seen you at the library for months prior to our meeting. You spent most of your time inside. I knew your favorites stacks. I asked around about you. That's when I found out who you were."

"So, you did a deep probe on me."

"Sometimes you spent the morning or afternoon out on the nature trails. I saw what you were doing there. So, I decided to create that accidental meeting. I quickly discovered that you were the perfect test subject for the suit. Your chair had a neat little carrier on the back. It was a simple matter to retrofit the suit to accommodate your special needs. The thrill to walk again was your enticement."

"The matchbook and the blood?"

"Deliberate plants. The matchbook and cigarettes led to this island. The blood droplets on the warehouse floor came from a dead rabbit. I had to spook you into thinking I was kidnapped."

"Yeah, and you went so far as to get me to fall in love with you to do it. All that charm, a false front. Maybe I can understand that I deserved to be chumped. But you know what? You're working for *them*. Or they've bought you. That makes you a traitor to the United States."

He shook his head. "It's called selling to the highest bidder. The Global Socialist Alliance offered me twice what I knew the American Military would for the patent and plans. When the GSA first found me and heard of it, they decided they wanted the first prototype. The condition was that I would not seek any first deals with the US."

"Tell her why," said Cho.

"North Korea, Iran, and Russia decided a mutual pact would be the best way to defend against the imperialist superpower. I was already aligned with the GSA's political analogy, being that my views were far left and socialist. So, it was a no-brainer."

"So, the all mighty buck got you to take that final step over the edge. You are *pathetic.*"

He stopped for a moment and held his prosthetic arm out in front of her face. "There was a little bit more persuasion than that. Oh, I resisted at first. But that's when they broke my arm—compound fracture. It didn't heal right then became infected. It was amputated two weeks later. They used those strong-arm tactics to guarantee my trust."

"Tell her about the consequences," said Cho.

"If I failed to smuggle the suit out of the country and deliver it to them, they would break the other arm, thereby ruining my chances to create the greatest piece of military hardware in history. If I betrayed them to the U.S. government, they said they would take my life, no matter what kind of protective custody I was offered. Believe me, they would have nuked the city I was hidden in rather than let me live with the knowledge I had."

"Well, I'm real broken up over that." She gave him a bitter, sarcastic look. "You should have known what you were getting into with these thugs. Did you think what could happen? I see a first strike in our future. Do you want to be responsible for an all-out war against your own country? Or do you even have a country?"

"It only matters if I'm on the wrong side of the conflict. In this case, I won't be."

The wind picked up outside, slamming against the walls of the building. The overhead lights flickered in seizures.

Cho stepped up to the table and clapped his hands sharply. "You will have to proceed faster. We have bad weather approaching. There will be no postponement of this demonstration."

"I'm moving as fast as a one-armed man can," said Chet, ruffled. "Man your cameras—get ready to document."

The upper torso components snapped into place. They flipped her body over to make the final connections, including the attachment of the armor segments, and then pulled her into a sitting position. Chet activated the 'on' switch, which produced a mild humming noise. A perceptible surge tightened the suit. Chet pulled her legs over the lip of the table. They stuck straight out like steel rods.

He held her shoulder for support. "Now remember how we did this the last time. You are simply going to perform some maneuvers for filming purposes. No funny stuff. Do as you're told."

"Why in the hell did you pick somebody like me to do this?" she said. "I'm not even that good at working the controls. You could have enlisted a non-handicapped subject to do all these tests. I'll just screw it up...and maybe I should."

"It gives me bragging rights to demonstrate the full functionality of the hardware with a paraplegic test subject. It shows just how compatible and easy it is to operate by the worst test subject possible."

The *worst* test subject possible. How apropos of his true, unvarnished feelings for her.

"You can imagine," he went on, "what a healthy, trained soldier could do if someone like you can operate it." He held the helmet in his hand. "Now descend to the floor and walk to the middle of the room."

Cho's group backed away, providing a wide birth. She knew the controls well enough to perform the basic maneuvers he had taught her. The control functions weren't totally foreign. The sooner she got it over with the better. But then what?

Two manned tripod cameras swung in her direction, while two handheld camera operators shuffled across the floor to get the best angles. Mouths gaped openly as she slid off the table and walked to the middle of the floor. Chet stepped up to her and fit the tactical helmet over her head, pulling it down snugly then securing the chinstrap. "Now walk normally to the end of the warehouse, turn and return to this point."

She made the steps with precise cadence. The two cameramen followed on each side, documenting the movements. Reaching the other side, she turned and started back. She reached the starting point, ending up standing next to him.

"That's fine," said Chet. "Tatiana is standing at the other end of the building where you just came from. She is holding a book open. Use the touchpad on the right side of the helmet to activate the magnifier. Read the print on the page she has opened."

A mere flick of a button did the trick. The page zoomed in. She began to recite the first words. "Hapscomb's Texaco sat on number ninety-three just north of Arnette, a puissant four-street burg almost one hundred and ten miles from—"

"That's enough," said Chet. He addressed the onlookers. "Comrades, that is the beginning of the first sentence from an American author's book called *The Stand*. The distance is over 25 meters." He addressed her again. "Same touch panel. The night vision control this time. When the lights are turned off, I want you to count the number of rifles trained on you."

The warehouse faded to black with the click of a breaker.

She found the switch and tapped it. The darkness was replaced with a green phosphorescent glow through the face shield.

"Four rifles are pointing at me."

Cho's voice: "That is correct. Excellent!"

The lights snapped on. She shut the feature off and turned to face Chet, wondering about the next command, barely in emotional control. He pointed to the barbells and told her to perform a dead- lift with them over her head. She bent at the waist, gripped one in each hand then pressed them aloft. The maneuver caused a slight teetering. At that precise moment, she locked eyes with Chet and, for a moment, had the urge to swing one of the barbells down and cave his head in. He must have seen that temptation since he stepped back a few feet.

Chet addressed the crowd. "Those dumbbells weigh 100 pounds apiece. Yet she has effortlessly lifted them over her head. The servos and actuators keep them aloft without her having to expend any energy. The maximum dead-lift weight capability is over 500 pounds—nearly three times the strength of a normal foot soldier."

The test subject let her arms swing down, letting the barbells drop to the floor, cracking the concrete. A few rifles raised in her direction. She remembered that she was encased in bulletproof armor able to withstand small caliber fire. A plan formulated. She had never acted impulsively in her life or shown outright acts of heroism. For the last ten years, she'd lived life vicariously through her alter ego on sketchpads and panels. Endura was everything the comic book artist was not —brave, impulsive, forceful. *What would you do in a situation like this, Endura?*

When a wall panel flexed against a powerful wind gust, the answer came like a biblical revelation.

"You're not paying attention," said Chet. "I want you to use the trot mode over the length of the floor. You do remember how to do that?"

He'd been right. She hadn't been paying attention. To him. The wall flexed violently again. It looked to be made of stucco over plasterboard. The vertical support beams were nearly three-feet apart. It was perfect.

Chet stepped up to her and slapped her shoulder. "I asked you a question! Believe me, you *need* to do this."

Pure reflexes prompted her to pull her arm around in a deft arc, striking Chet in the chest, knocking him to the floor. She pivoted and tapped out a run sequence. Picking up speed, she hit the wall full force, punching a hole through the side of the building. Her forward momentum carried her tumbling forward into a belly flop on the dirt outside. She fumbled with the finger control, trying to jack herself up into a stance, failed twice, but was up on the third. A hail of impacts struck her back armor. They blazed away on full auto! She kicked forward and began a dead run for the tree line.

The sky was a dark mass of roiling debris and dust, the wind howling against the cowl of the helmet. She did not look back but concentrated on the primal urge to get away as far from her pursuers as possible.

She cornered the first tree, then another. Activating the night vision brought up an image of bright green tree trunks and gray forest floor. Shouts and commotion followed behind. Bullets struck the trees. Large chunks of wood splintered, vaporizing pieces that struck the suit. Keeping the body balanced proved difficult, bending into the turns and dodging the largest pines. She stumbled several times nearly going down. *No time to hit the deck now. Get it on!*

She passed through a clearing, turning on more speed. A fallen log hove into view. She tapped for a jump, cleared the log but came down cockeyed and hit the turf hard, belly-skiing across a carpet of dead pine needles. She was up in a few seconds, continuing on.

The forest was a maze of old growth. It got easier picking out a path by looking ahead and planning the direction. A slope on the right materialized into a steep hill. She adjusted her route and then chugged up the steep incline.

Time and distance were lost. The exoskeleton had propelled her at terrific speeds, along with a complete lack of fatigue. Even at full speed, the lungs and heart were tricked into believing it was only a walk in the park. No sweat. No cramps. Unlimited energy with plenty of reserves. There was no reason to look back.

The climb seemed to go on forever, when at last the top was reached after twenty minutes. Looking down, no pursuers followed. The corner of one of the buildings in the clearing below was just visible. Bleary ant-like images moved across the valley floor. They were vehicles leaving the compound. All around, the boughs whipped in a frenzy and the wind screamed.

A smile came to her face, even though her location was a mystery. The enemy was left scrambling below like a bunch of mad hornets.

The atmosphere closed in like clamped teeth. The ozone crackled, giving off an electric smell. If memory served, Juventud lay in the direct path of an approaching hurricane. The only thing keeping her upright and holding her together was the suit. *I have the advantage right now, and I'm going to use it. Try to catch me on human legs, you morons.*

The ridge line of the hill proved to be the easiest and fastest path. Who cared where it led? The first raindrops pelted her helmet like drum rolls.

Thirty minutes later, the wind picked up with a new ferocity. Soon she was bent over, driving against gale force winds and sheets of rain that threatened to slap her down. The terrain became more difficult to negotiate; large rocks and ruts fouled her footing. She lost her balance at one point and went down, requiring her to crawl to a nearby tree trunk to get upright. There was no question but to keep on moving, fighting every inch of the way.

After cresting the ridge line, it descended into an embankment on the other side. She found a canyon that offered shelter from the most violent wind blasts. The rain continued unabated, finding its way between the seams of the armor. Her clothes became soaked. A chill started in the pit of her stomach, rode up her back and into her shoulders. Realizing the suit had no real thermal protection, keeping on the move was the only way to stay warm.

The canyon opened up into a wide ravine. She slowed to a fast walk, skirting some large river boulders. Her fingers began to numb, especially the control finger. She missed her stride several times and stumbled, but remained upright, determined to press on. Staying on her feet seemed a near impossibility. Branches and flying debris became projectiles, delivering a tremendous racket against the suit and helmet. At one point, the wind lifted her high off the ground and set her down like a chess piece.

A lull in the storm came after another hour. The rain stopped as though turned off by a valve. The wind died off to gentle wisps. Either the hurricane had passed or the eye had arrived. Using her visual enhancement showed a small valley that opened up onto a flood plain. A small bend revealed rock outcroppings near a steep embankment. She headed toward an overhang shelf of rocks and squeezed into a small cleft, then pulled some loose bramble in front of the opening in an attempt to conserve some heat. It was a good thing she'd ducked for cover, for in the next five minutes the wind picked up, and the rain began to lash the ground. It had been the eye of the hurricane after all!

She drew her legs up against her chest, trying to fight off the shivers. Safe for now, she thought of Bibi and Ollie. Could they find help in time? Bibi would remember her last instructions to make it to the hotel at all costs. Diane would make it there, too—at all costs. For now, she would wait until the storm passed before heading out again. There was another reason to make it out of this mess alive. The traitor and fraud, Chet Strauss, would pay for everything he had done or would do.

Huddling in the rock shelter brought no passage of time. Sleep came in fits and starts, dependent upon the freezing cold and the crack of thunder. Lightning struck close by numerous times, lighting up the landscape in a skeletal X-ray of black and white. Wetting her lips with some runoff water provided the only moisture. It was a priority to avoid dehydration, but there would be plenty of standing pools of water after the storm ceased. Hunger would be another problem, depending on how far away a food source existed. Though she did not have the urge, there was no mention of how to relieve oneself in the combat suit shy off lying prone and dropping the britches.

Well, Chet, Mr. Brainiac, you didn't figure on a female wearing the suit, did you?

Removing some shrubbery gave her a look outside. The landscape was completely transformed. Trees had snapped at their trunks; branches lay over the ground in pick-up-sticks piles. Standing trees had been scalped of all their foliage. A strong breeze still ruffled some of the naked branches, and the rain had slowed to a drizzle. A few small patches of blue sky had opened up. It meant the worst of the storm had passed, probably headed northwest into the Gulf. Judging by the shadows cast by a few trees, it looked late in the afternoon, maybe four or five. She exited the rock shelter and started off at a fast walk. The ground was soggy, filled with mud puddles and branch litter.

Now, to get my bearings. Cho's boat had brought them to the northern tip of the island. Remembering the little brochure, she pulled it out of her pocket after loosening an armor panel. She studied it for a few moments, noting that Nueva Gerona would have to be east of her location. The sun was setting in the west. She approximated her location, to mentally draw a path east. There had to be a road somewhere, even a path that led to the capital city.

She trudged east with the hope that it was the right direction. After two hours, a path appeared that led through the forest. She followed it, realizing it could have been nothing more than an animal trail. But she halted after hearing a peculiar noise, a humming sound then the grating of pebbles. Walking toward the sounds revealed a narrow gravel road, strewn with branches and twigs. It had obvious tire ruts. The sound was a passing vehicle. After reaching the road, she took cover on the shoulder behind a pile of broken tree limbs and downed telephone poles.

Nothing approached from either direction. The road led from east to west. The only thing to do was to wait for a car to pass. After fifteen minutes, an old pickup truck rolled by its suspension sagging from a load of furniture. Ten minutes later, a bus rumbled down the road, kicking up a rooster tail of mud. One did not just throw out one's thumb, expecting a ride. Not when one looked like some alien robot from another planet. Word would spread about the "armored monstrosity", and very likely bring it to the attention of her pursuers or the local authorities. It was akin to wearing a sandwich board that read *Come and get me, I was last seen here!*

Several more cars passed before a likely candidate approached. An old two-ton stake bed truck rumbled up the road. Barely moving at no more than five miles-per-hour, it carried a tall load covered with a green canvas tarp. Diane braced and just as the truck passed, she broke from cover into a swift trot behind it. It started to pull away. She picked up her pace and reached out, grasping the end of the bed, pulling hard, thrusting up belly first onto the bed. She crawled under a loose flap in the tarp then pulled it over her. *I'm safe*, she thought. The cartons behind her back reeked of produce. Breaking one open caused an avalanche of strawberries that scattered all over the truck bed.

Nothing like hitching a ride on a strawberry truck.

Fond memories of sharing strawberry shortcake with her mother brought back an intense urge to sample the goods. *No telling when I'll get the sugar again*. She indulged, cramming several of the sweet bulbs in her mouth. She tore the carton open further and made a meal out of it. More strawberries ended up in her lap than in her mouth. What the hell. There were no witnesses to the theft or anyone watching the robot monster making a pig out of herself. After eating to the bursting point, another idea came to her in a flash of genius.

She would need some type of disguise after reaching a population center. The truck *had* to be headed to the capital city.

The canvas covering was old, suffering from dry rot. The letter opener made swift work of the rotted fabric; she cut a large rectangular piece from the covering, carved out a ragged circular hole in the middle of the piece and pulled it down over her head. Though the true length could not be tested by standing up, it looked long enough to cover her extremities. It would have to pass for a poor man's serape.

The ride smoothed out when the truck hit a patch of paved road. It picked up speed, dodging litter-strewn obstacles in its path. The sound of cross traffic faded with the Doppler, with the occasional blare of horns. Peeking from her hiding place showed tenement buildings, single-family dwellings and small shops. Many of the structures had no roofs, and most of the windows were blown out. Wind-blown debris clogged the gutters and sidewalks. Huge trees leaned at precarious angles, some of them uprooted and sitting upside down. Disaster area.

After a few turns on surface streets, the truck pulled into a large square festooned with tents and wooden lean-to shacks. Tables sat in rows laden with fresh fruit, vegetables and nuts, while vendors cried out for attention. *The marketplace.* All of the hurricane debris had been swept into massive piles that blocked some of the aisles—a testament to the harried determination of the Cuban people, who were eager to resume their livelihoods regardless of the catastrophe. It was pure irony that devastation laid all around them, but here they were setting up shop as though nothing had happened.

The truck slowed to a crawl amongst the pedestrians. This was the only chance to disembark. She scooted to the edge of the truck bed, removing her helmet, but kept a firm grasp on it. She pushed her legs over the side and jumped, hit the pavement, toppled onto her back, the helmet bouncing several yards away. Several people rushed to her aid in an attempt to offer assistance, but when they got a closer look at what lay on the ground, they backed off.

The monstrosity rose awkwardly to its feet, adjusting the homemade sarape. A young child walked up to the fallen person and smiled, holding the helmet up. Diane took it gratefully and offered a handshake. That was a mistake. The girl took one look at the gloved claw, gave a shriek and ran off.

Diane looked anything but inconspicuous as she tried to find her way out of the marketplace. Her stiff-legged walk through the muddy puddles drew numerous stares. She reached an end stall on a frontage road and approached the proprietor. A smallish woman with long braids falling from underneath a torn straw hat looked at this very strange human being.

"Buenos dios, Señora," Diane tried in her best Spanish. "Uh, donde esta Nueva Gerona?"

The woman gave her a blank look and shook her head. Diane tried again. The woman responded by pointing to the ground.

"Excellente! Donde esta el hotel Casa de las Madres? El Camino Real?"

The woman pointed north down the street.

It was a long walk before arriving at the first largest hotel on El Camino Real, after following the address on the matchbook cover. No one followed her out of curiosity, which was a relief. Those who saw her gave her a wide berth or stepped hurriedly away. A few locals gaped in wonderment. Some rushed into their businesses and homes at the bizarre sight. Thankfully, most of the populace was boarding up broken windows, sweeping trash or surveying the damage to their buildings. Right now, no one seemed too interested in the weird looking stranger amongst them. Especially after what had just occurred. The hurricane had done its damage from one end of the city to the other.

Such a stranger did not need an encounter with the local police right now, which meant cover was a priority. After studying the numbers on the buildings again, she knew she was close. Looking down the sidewalk amongst the pedestrians, her breath caught in her throat. There was no mistaking the sight of Bibi pounding across the pavement in her direction. Hollering for joy would get Bibi's attention, but there was no need. Their paths would intersect at any moment.

Bibi continued down the sidewalk, moving with reckless strides over the muddy debris. But the large woman had her head down, not watching those in front of her. Diane hooked her arm with her assistant's before she passed. Bibi swung around angrily, brandishing an upraised fist, but lowered it when she recognized the face of her friend. Bibi's face made the instant transformation from anger to shock. The two embraced with a body crash.

"Oh my god, I thought I'd lost you, girl!" Bibi squealed. "How in the hell did you get out of that mess?"

"Shusssh! Not so loud. Long story short, I crashed through a wall then hid out in the forest. Where's Ollie? Is he okay?"

"He's trying to find something to eat right now. We're holding up in that Casa Madre dive just like we planned. This island was hit by a hurricane that wasted everything."

"I know. You did fine, Bibi. How on earth did you get here?"

"We just followed a road, lugging' all our gear, until we found a highway. Hitched a ride on a lemon truck just before the storm hit. We ended up right around the corner from here. Then we found the Madre hotel. Got one of the last rooms." She whistled. "That was one hell of a tornado—blew us clean off the highway a few times." Bibi pushed her hands into Diane's stomach. "Damn, you're wearing that thing."

"What the hell did you think? Never mind. Take me to your room. We have to pack and get our knees in the breeze. Those thugs will be after us. This might be the first place they look."

Bibi hesitated. "I was on my way to buy a gun at a pawn shop. I was thinking about going to the cops. I'm sorry, but I figured they could organize a raid with some commandos or something."

Diane pulled her to the side, pushing her up against a brick facade. "We can't do that right now. How's it going to sound when some Americans spout off about a foreign military force that's bent on getting their hands on super secret U.S. hardware that *we're* holding? Nobody wants that hot potato. This is still Castro's Cuba. We're not exactly liked by this republic."

"I didn't think of that."

"Did you make any calls to the American authorities?"

"The electricity is down everywhere. Not many cell phones here. Besides, all the towers are down. So where does that leave us?"

Diane looked around. Debris clogged the streets. Electrical lines hung like linguine from poles and rooftops. Two cars were upended in the street. People were still trying to clear paths so they could enter buildings. This was not the place to devise a plan. "Right now, I have to get changed out. I'll explain the rest later. Get me into your room."

Bibi led the way up the street. They walked past five large buildings, until they arrived at a six-story Spanish Colonial that carried the name Casa de las Madres across its only intact glass window. Bibi opened the frosted glass door that had a huge pane broken out of it. They entered a smoke-filled lobby, occupied by a hoard of hurricane victims, most of them crammed on soggy sofas and flimsy chairs. The carpet squished under foot where the rainwater had surged into the building. Sheets of wallpaper hung, stripped from the walls.

Several lobby occupants watched the couple cross the muddy floor. One man held a checker piece in midair as he looked at Diane's mechanical boots. A woman behind the lobby desk glared at the two, clenching her fists.

"My guest," said Bibi. "Invitado, okay? More pesos, okay. Lots of dollars."

The lobby clerk shook her head in disgust. She gave the couple a dismissive wave, indicating her begrudged approval. Bibi led the way upstairs, and turning around said, "It's just one flight up, number two-eleven."

Diane had not climbed stairs with the suit before, so when she activated the leg lifts, she planted her feet unusually hard on the steps, sending a tremor through the staircase and banister. The act brought scores of looks and curious expressions. When they reached the second floor, Bibi unlocked the door to the room then ushered her inside.

Diane let out the breath she had been holding. "Man, that was freaky." She looked at the small room. Their luggage containers sat upright stacked against the wall. She pulled the serape over her head then let it drop to the floor.

Bibi opened up the suitcases. "Where do we start?"

Diane eased herself into a sitting position on the bed. "We start by getting me out of the upper half of this suit. Unsnap the power pack on the back—it has to go into the frame slides on my front. Then remove everything from the waist up, except the left glove and lead wire. Secure the power pack on my stomach then connect the lead wire to it. The pack has a manual 'on' switch." Diane flipped the shoulder switch off. She instantly fell on her back. "Damn it. I forgot about that. Prop my back up with a suitcase."

Bibi retrieved the largest carrier from the floor and

propped her friend up into a sitting position. She added two pillows for reinforcement.

"That's better. Get started."

While Bibi fumbled awkwardly with the suit, Diane filled her in on the events that lead to her escape. She told her about the Global Socialist Alliance, along with the role that Chet Strauss played in the operation, explaining his role as a traitor and how Diane had been used to smuggle the suit out of the country. In conclusion: "I'm sorry I didn't listen to you. I thought it was love, Bibi. That's how sure I was."

"Well, I knew the dude was funky as hell, but I never saw anything worse than a mind fuck. I knew you were lonely, Di. Can't fault you for that. But this is another ballgame altogether. Sounds like we're up to our necks in communists." She gave a hoarse growl. "Damn, I thought they were gangsters, not full-on foreign terrorists."

"They're after this prototype suit. They won't stop until they get their hands on it."

"I say we toss the thing away and get on the first flight out of here."

"That's just it. We can't leave it here to be found by them or this government. They want to start a war, Bibi—a first-strike slug-fest with the United States. They want to put millions of soldiers in these for a major invasion."

"Let the commies come knocking. We'll kick their asses six ways to Sunday. This shit is too heavy duty for us, Diane. Let somebody else handle it down the line."

"Yeah, who do you propose? The CIA? Military Intelligence? Cops? You know how well that went over."

"Exactly. It won't even be an issue until it's in their faces, so it's their own fault for not listening in the first place." Bibi unsnapped the large chest piece and started on the arms.

"We're talking about the security of our country," Diane went on. "Bibi, you're not seeing the whole ugly picture.

This technology belongs with us, only because we won't abuse it. We're looking at a huge military complex that has world domination on its mind. You hand this over to them and you might as well kiss-off democracy for good. And that means all your personal freedoms. I would have thought you'd had enough of the slavery issue in your people's history."

"Don't bring that into the argument. Let's say we do get out of here with the suit. What makes you think our government is going to believe one word of this?"

"Why don't we concentrate on getting out of here first? It doesn't look like we're going to be able to leave this island by conventional means in the next day or so."

"Why do you say that?" Bibi finished removing all the upper components, having laid all of the pieces on the bed. She left the glove attached, along with the finger controller and lead wire.

"Because that hurricane tore up everything. They'll have to clear the airports for safety before any planes take to the air. Politics." Diane positioned the power pack over her lower abdomen and held it there. "Use those tie straps to secure this around me. That large tape wire jacks into the top of the hip joint."

"Of course, it does," Bibi mumbled. "It's like some frickin' Transformer toy. I've never seen so many gadgets and whatnots in all my life. You sure this is gonna work when we're finished?"

"It did when Chet had it hooked up. I don't have a wheelchair anymore, so it'd better work."

The door swung open. Diane and Bibi turned with a start. Ollie stood in the opening, holding an armful of groceries. When he saw Diane, he dropped the load on the floor and flung himself at her feet. His lips trembled, and tears sprang from his eyes.

"Oh, my god," he blubbered, "I didn't think I'd ever see you again!" He buried his head in her lap.

Diane stroked his thinning hair. "It's okay now, Ollie. We're together again. You have to be tough and ready because we have a lot to do."

Ollie looked up into her face, smiling bitterly. "I just couldn't stand that you were out there all alone and nobody would know how to take care of you, and that they were disrespecting you, and maybe they were going to...going to do something to you. But that's all better now because you're here with us. Did they hurt you? Did they lay their stinking hands on—"

"I'm fine, Ollie. I escaped and jumped on a fruit truck." She recounted her last twenty-four hours to him. When she finished, she could see that he'd sobered up emotionally. He asked what he could do to help.

Bibi said, "You can help me get this suit rigged. And pick up our chow. It's all over the floor."

They ate salmon sandwiches while they worked. Diane orchestrated the assembly, double-checking, making sure the connections fit properly. They stored all the armor segments and extra frame parts in a luggage container. They discarded some of their personal items to make room, mostly shoes and heavy coats. Diane gave power to the half-suit when they finished. She experimented with a few maneuvers. It worked fine. She had one more request. "I need baggy clothes to cover the frame, but I didn't pack any."

Bibi said, "And you're looking at my fat ass when you say that? Name your bling."

Ollie cut up a bed sheet and used it as fat padding, while Bibi fitted Diane out in her largest cotton slacks and long-sleeve cotton warm-up jacket. With the addition of an extra brunette wig and bulbous sunglasses, the ensemble was complete. Diane looked like a pregnant, arthritic tourist who had no shame or fashion sense, which mirrored the appearance of just about every other American tourist in Cuba.

Bibi and Ollie grabbed the largest suitcases, while Diane hefted two smaller ones. They trudged down the stairs. Bibi checked them out at the desk, handing over the hotel key, and left a large tip. Curious eyes followed them out onto the sidewalk. The threesome began a swift stride down the street, attempting to distance them from the hotel. They stopped after two blocks then ducked into an alley. Diane pulled her friends into a huddle.

"Ollie, break out that computer map and find us a small port city. The smaller the better. If nothing comes up, we'll have to ask a cabbie. They're going to be watching the major airports, even the smaller charter businesses. But like I said, I doubt if anything is going to be able to fly off this island. They might know that. The commercial ferries and hydrofoils are a bust because they'll be watching those, too. We need a small charter boat to take us across the Gulf. Maybe to Corpus Christi or Rockport. Somewhere out of the way but definitely in the States."

"You said you counted a couple dozen of them at the compound," said Bibi. "Do you think there's more than that on this island? What if they have a whole army?"

"I don't think they have a militia. I counted five SUVs in their encampment. That would mean they had twenty-five to thirty people, tops. That's not very many to spread over this island to hunt down three people. So, we've got more than enough chance to stay out of sight."

"Yeah, but look at us," said Ollie. "A handicapped female, a fat black woman and a little gay guy. We should have worn neon signs." He went back to studying his map.

"Okay, maybe so." Diane frowned. "Just keep your eyes peeled for any new black or silver SUVs. Those vehicles will stick out amongst these jalopies. Let's make sure we spot them before they're on to us."

Ollie ran his finger along the map. "We've got two choices that I can see. Siguarea and Coccodrillo. They look like small coastal cities. Which one?"

"Which is the most remote?" asked Diane.

"Coccodrillo is at the extreme southern tip of the island."

"That's the one."

Bibi stepped out to the curb and hailed the only cab on the street. An old Chevy with faded orange paint, pulled up. With the help of the driver, they loaded the luggage in the trunk and piled in. It took Diane a moment to position herself in the front seat, using a twist-pull motion to get in. Her awkwardness did not go without the driver's notice. He asked her about their destination in perfect English.

"Coccodrillo," said Diane, not offering anymore.

"All the way to Coccodrillo?"

"Yes, all the way."

"Okay, good for me, then!" He threw a lever on the dash and stepped on the gas.

"No translation necessary," said Ollie. "It means it's a long ride, so he's going to make a lot of cab fare."

"Only Americans spend so much money in my country," said the driver, pulling the cab up onto the sidewalk to avoid a broken light pole and a crumpled metal sign.

"How did you know we were Americans?" asked Diane.

"It is the way you speak, dress and carry yourselves. I can always tell these things."

The cabbie drove through the city streets at reckless speeds. Instead of slowing for obstacles, like pieces of sheet metal, tree branches and broken signs, he drove over them. Pedestrians fared no better, having to leap out of the way at times. When he reached the highway on the outskirts of town, he opened it up further. The cab left a blue-white trail of oil smoke in its wake, and it sounded as if every nut and bolt in its chassis were coming loose.

The cabbie looked at the floorboard on Diane's side. "What's wrong with your feet? Can't you walk good?"

Not that it was any of his business, she said, "I had an accident and I'm wearing braces to keep my legs straight. It's hard to walk sometimes."

"My mother was a crippled woman," the cabby lamented. "She had crooked legs, but she was good to the children. We had twelve in our family. She died of an infection on the legs."

"I'm very sorry to hear that. I'm sure she was a wonderful mother."

The cabbie took the empathy as an invitation to spill his guts. He began a long story about his early family life, his career and the present political situation in Cuba. He talked about the hurricane and how it was the worst disaster to ever hit the island. Diane tried not to listen and stared out the window, watching lumberyards, orchards and shattered roadside stands pass by. Right now, thoughts of escaping and getting back home preoccupied the mind. How far of a head start did they have? Would getting off the island pose a major problem? What would they do if they were spotted? Who could they trust and what might happen if they were caught?

An hour into the ride, the cab driver pulled onto a gravel road, then drove up a heavily forested incline. He had to exit the vehicle to remove fallen timber from the road several times. After thirty minutes, Ollie tapped Diane on the back and spoke over her shoulder, informing her that they were not headed in the right compass direction for Coccodrillo. She spoke to the driver over the loud cassette music. "Why didn't you continue on the main highway? You're traveling west when we have to go south."

"It is only a shortcut," said the driver, thumping his fingers on the steering wheel in time to the music.

Diane did not like the look of the detour. “We don’t mind the longer drive. It’s more money for you, right?”

The driver pulled slowly to the edge of the road and turned the engine off. He thrust his hand down the front of his pants and pulled out a two-inch .38 revolver. He pointed it at Diane's midriff and spoke with a grin, showing a large gold tooth. “Yes, it will be more money for me. Now step outside and empty your pockets.”

Bibi moaned. “Ain’t this a mutha fuckin’ bitch!”

9

The driver held them at gunpoint a dozen feet from the cab, while they went through their pockets. They handed over currency and change. Diane made up a story about why she didn't have a purse. The driver ordered her to hand over her costume earrings and sunglasses. Bibi had to relinquish her purse, three jade rings and two tiny diamond studs.

"I've got my pecker pierced," said Ollie sarcastically. "I suppose you would like that bauble, too!" He tossed his wallet at the man's feet.

Diane clutched Ollie's wrist in a fierce grip, the sign to hush up. They didn't need another outburst. One did not anger a thief who held you at gunpoint. There was no logic in it.

Diane would appeal to any vestige of decency in this man. "I hope you'll leave us out here unharmed with our luggage."

"You should turn around right now and start walking into the forest," said the cabby.

"You can't be serious," said Bibi. "How can you leave us out here with nothing? All of our clothing—our personal belongings are in those cases."

"Such things have a market value where I come from.

There are many people on this island who could use such clothing and nice things. Most people here cannot even afford a cell phone. Some have never seen one before. You take for granted what others wish for in their dreams. You can always get more nice things."

"That's not fair," said Ollie. "You're leaving us out here to die. Look at this woman who can barely stand before you. You can't strand such a soul out in the wilderness and tell me you have a conscience."

The driver jabbed the gun at them. "You have your lives. You should be lucky I don't take that from you."

Diane made a few awkward steps toward the man. "You went out of your way to tell me how loving your mother was to your brothers and sisters, even when she was in such pain. I have the same type of pain. One of my carriers contains my medicine and extra braces. You wouldn't have left your own mother out here in such a condition, would you? At least let me walk in dignity with a feeling of hope. Or would you have me fall on the ground and wallow in the mud? What would your mother have said about such a thing?"

The driver pointed the gun at Diane, his hand shaking. "Why do you think you deserve special privileges?"

"Because just like your mother, I don't have any advantage. Maybe one day I'll be a mother and have many children. Children that will need my care."

The driver stepped to the trunk of the car, but not before giving her a dramatic eye roll. He opened the lid. "Okay, which bag do you want?"

"The large bag that looks like a giant backpack," said Diane, knowing that he had just given in to her request.

The driver unsnapped the lid on the pack, looked inside. "No guns in here?"

"No," said Diane. "No guns, I promise. Only my medical gear and supplies."

"Why do you have the football helmet?"

"I fall down a lot. It's to protect my head."

The driver lifted the pack over the lip of the trunk, letting it fall to ground. He slammed the trunk lid, cornered the car and slipped into the driver's seat. He pulled away from them. Instead of making a U-turn, he drove up the narrow dirt road until the vehicle disappeared from sight.

No one moved for a few minutes, until Bibi grasped the handle strap on the pack. "I wish you would have pleaded the case for the pack that had the groceries."

Diane looked at her in surprise. "I didn't want to push our luck. I'm glad to get what we did. We could have ended up with nothing."

"Excuse me," said Bibi, "but I hate to tell you we did end up with nothing. I lost all my credit cards and the money you gave me to hold."

Diane patted her chest. "He didn't get everything. I've got a stash in my bra. It's plenty to tide us over. What we need to do is get back down to the highway then on our way to Coccodrillo. Right, Ollie?"

"That's the way south."

They started off at a slow, measured pace. They would have to conserve energy if they were to reach the highway in halfway decent shape. Fortunately, the road led downhill, making their progress easier. Diane had plenty of reserve walking power, where her friends did not. She set the pace by their speed.

They took turns hauling the heavy pack, taking rest stops frequently. Diane made the longest hauls with the pack since she had the added power in her step. She only had to trade off when her carrying arm gave out.

The pelvic and leg framework began to chaff her skin during the journey. Ignoring the pain did little good. She wanted a hot bath so bad it made her woozy just thinking about it. None of them had any desire to be stuck out under the stars in the outback of Juventud Island. It had only been a few days ago that she was at home, secure in the fact that she'd had a new boyfriend (so she thought), a wonderful career and a beautiful house. She had swapped it all to be assaulted by a hurricane, robbed and land smack in the wilderness of a foreign country, wearing a machine from her waist down. Not to mention, foreign terrorists were bent on catching them. From paradise to purgatory—it was a piss-poor tradeoff.

"What do we do once we get down to the highway?" asked Ollie. "We'll be visible to traffic. Our GSA friends might be cruising the route, looking for us."

"We'll just have to stay off the highway and hoof it south."

"A ride would be a whole lot better," said Bibi.

"Yeah," said Ollie. "Like the last one we just had. I swear to all that is holy and decent, I don't trust anybody in this country. We've got 'tourist' and 'sucker' written all over us."

"I ain't walking to this Coco city," said Bibi. "This body wasn't designed for long distance out in the open. It's like bitch-slapping' my heart. I'm planting' my ass on upholstery, riding rubber over the road."

Ollie sniffed. "How are you going to do that without throwing your thumb out? It could take hours to get a ride. This whole country's been trashed. People aren't in their right minds."

Bibi huffed, "Screw hours. I figure on throwing something else out. Besides, you have to know how to pick your ride. You just don't let anybody suck you into their car. And in case you haven't noticed, I'm more of the right color here. You folks are a few shades off the spectrum for dealing with these sorts. I can pass for Jamaican. Ollie, you look like you came straight down from Nome, Alaska. I'd roll your ass, myself."

"She's got a point," said Diane. "I'd hate to look in a mirror right now. Bibi, if you have a way to cop a ride then good on you. We'll have to stay tucked away."

Bibi nodded. "That's a fact."

They made it down to the highway in two hours. Diane and Ollie moved off to the side to take cover behind the largest tree trunk they could find. Most of the scrub and needles had been blown from the shrubs and trees due to the passing hurricane. Their view of the highway came through a jumble of naked branches. They watched Bibi trudge down to the edge of the highway. Diane was curious about the large woman's plan for flagging down a safe ride.

Several vehicles roared down the highway, headed north. Many of them dragged trailers, filled with household goods. Other cars had personal items strapped to their roofs. There were only a few southbound vehicles, but Bibi let all of them pass without making a move.

"What do you think she's doing?" asked Ollie. "She doesn't seem into it."

"She's watching the approaching traffic. She's just holding her head down a little, trying not to show desperation."

"Yeah, but we *are* desperate. And what's up with all these cars packed with goods heading north? It looks like a mass exodus."

"I don't know, Ollie."

They watched for another fifteen minutes. A box van and three more cars passed. Suddenly Bibi straightened up, laying her hands upon her chest. In the next instant, she unbuttoned her blouse and yanked it open, exposing two enormous breasts. An approaching pickup truck locked up its brakes and went into a side slip, before coming to a complete halt.

The driver pulled over to the shoulder, while rolling down a window. Bibi trotted to the vehicle. She leaned into the open window, indulging the driver in conversation.

"What sluttery," said Ollie.

"Don't be so quick to judge," said Diane. "She's using what she has to good advantage. It reminds me of the saying, 'never ask a woman what she would do to feed her children.' You don't want to or need to know. I would have done the same thing except that I have too little to stop for."

Bibi turned around and signaled them with a frantic wave of her hand—a definite invitation.

Diane walked through the tree cover, Ollie following with the heavy pack. When they approached the truck, the driver eyed them, a silly grin plastered across his face. The man's eyes were swollen, bloodshot. He pointed to the truck bed. "Aqui esta." He pulled Bibi into the cab next to him and laughed uproariously. "Tetas grandes—muy bonita!"

Diane and Ollie hauled themselves into the truck bed, sandwiching the pack between them. The truck pulled onto the highway. The rear window being absent from the cab, Diane could hear the shenanigans going on between the two.

Bibi goaded the man. "Yeah, you like these big guns, don't you? You old slimy bastard. That's it, take a handful, you chump-ass loser."

The truck began to weave. The speed increased and then decreased. All the while, the driver continued to grope his passenger, while slurring his Spanish.

Ollie cupped his voice toward Diane. "This guy is completely saturated. He's liable to drive us right off the road."

"He's probably never driven a sober day in his life. So, I think we might be safe. Do me a favor and put your head back to listen in. You might catch some of the lingo. It could help us."

Ollie nodded. He put his back up against the cab near the opening.

The driver babbled on, driving with one hand, using the other to fondle Bibi. The large woman nodded her head agreeably, feigning comprehension. Diane could hear her say things like "Yeah, you betcha" and "You don't say so?"

Diane reached under her top and pulled out her stash. She had her driver's license, a thick wad of pesos, social security card, and two credit cards, one of them an American Express. It would be enough to hire a charter pilot to get them off the island, hopefully onto the shores of the United States. Unless something else went south. She could not bear another setback. While she thought about it, she tucked the items back into her brazier then slumped down in the truck bed. *No sense in making myself out a target.*

Diane could just see over the lip of the tailgate to spot approaching vehicles. Anything that looked like a new black or silver SUV would set off warning bells. Only a few cars had passed them, rapidly overtaking the truck. A new worry presented itself. The erratic swerving of the truck could bring the police down on them. Then what would they do? How would they explain their predicament of being on foot, stranded in the middle of the island? And what about the suit?

Diane nudged Ollie. "Do me a favor—distract me from my thoughts. Do you understand anything that guy is saying?"

"Bits and pieces. Most of it is about how he'd love to suck her drums, or cha chas. He says that his two wives won't mind if she spends the night. He keeps asking her if she's married and if she's a voodoo woman. Then there was something about how he makes a lot of money hauling trash or scrap. That's why he's going to Coccodrillo, to pick up Hurricane scrap, because the place was really trashed. That's what I've heard so far."

"Poor Bibi. She can't understand a word he's saying. As long as he's keeps hitting on her we've got wheels under us."

"Oh, no doubt we'll cruise right into Coccodrillo the way he's going at it. I just hope she doesn't perform any other services while he's at the wheel."

Diane burst into laughter. She knew that Bibi had the man right where she wanted him. There was no higher honor than taking one for the team.

After an hour on the road, the truck slowed. Diane turned to look through the rear window. A steady stream of oncoming traffic moved at a slow rate of speed toward them. Horns blared. People shouted from their windows. Someone threw a tomato that hit the inside panel of the truck bed with a wet splatter. The driver gave them the finger and shouted obscenities.

"What's going on?" asked Ollie. "Where are all these people going?"

"I don't know. Maybe they're leaving the city. They're all packed up like they're moving house."

A woman from a passing car yelled, "Emisora de radio! Emisora de radio! Idiota!"

Diane strained to see the disturbance. "What's she saying, Ollie?"

"I think she said, 'radio station, you idiot'."

"How am I supposed to know?"

"No, I didn't mean *you're* an idiot. They're telling our driver to turn on his radio because he's an idiot. It must mean that a major broadcasting network is up and running. Probably an emergency broadcast."

Diane could clearly see the dashboard of the truck. Precisely where one would have expected to see a small radio there was none, only a rectangular cutout. The dash was only equipped with an old eight-track cassette player. Furthermore, an external antenna was missing.

More oncoming cars passed, their drivers continuing to shout out warnings. The driver rolled up his window to shut out the noise. They drove slowly down a gentle slope. That's when Diane saw what all the commotion was about. Bulldozers and small lifting cranes blocked the main intersections of the city. Countless other utility vehicles were either parked or in motion, slowly driving through the devastation. Emergency crews were on foot, sifting through debris or shoring up partially collapsed buildings. Telephone poles were snapped at midline, the heavy gauge wire lying over the landscape like black snakes. Entire roofs were missing from the largest buildings and structures. Tiles and slats lay strewn over the landscape like an explosion of confetti. The city of Coccodrillo did not exist anymore.

Four men in Khaki uniforms, and sporting semiautomatic weapons, stood at the bottom of the hill in front of a barricade made out of building debris and fallen timber. Three cars were pulled over to the shoulder. Armed men interrogated the vehicle occupants. Roadblock. When the driver saw this, he cursed loud enough to be heard down the hill. Two officers approached at a trot with weapons held at the shoulder. They barked orders to the driver. Bibi fumbled to refasten her blouse, while Diane and Ollie hunkered down. Diane had a feeling this would not go well, as she listened to the conversational tone between the armed men and the driver. It grew heated at one point and there came a sound like that of a boot heel hitting the truck. She hoped Ollie could understand the exchange. A moment later, one of the armed men stepped to the rear of the truck. He first glared at Diane, then at Ollie.

"Quien esta aqui?" demanded the officer.

"Touristas," said Ollie, and then held a conversation with

the officer in his best Spanish. The exchange went on for an uncomfortably long time. Diane feared their pack would be inspected or confiscated. From the conversation, it almost sounded to her like Ollie was interrogating the officer. When the dialogue was finished, Ollie gestured his thanks, ending with "Muchas gracias, senior." To which was replied, "Si Dios quiere." The officer met with the other, and together they walked back down the hill.

Bibi stuck her head partially through the window. "What the hell was that all about?"

Ollie took a breath but addressed the driver first with a few words. The driver acknowledged with a nod. Ollie then went on to explain. "I just told the driver to wait a moment until we can figure out what we're going to do. According to those officers, who are army regulars, Coccodrillo has been evacuated in accordance with their martial law. Hurricane Marla totally flattened the city, tearing down most of the infrastructure, making it unsafe. Because of the looting and health hazards, the residents have been ordered to relocate to disaster centers that are stationed 30 miles up the road."

"What the hell does that mean for us?" said Bibi.

"They're building a tent city equipped with lodging, stocked with food provisions and fresh water. No one is allowed back into their homes until the all clear is given. The militia is currently going through the city to evict the most stubborn shop owners, who've refused to leave their businesses. Long story short, we're not allowed in and are ordered to report to one of the aid stations."

Diane cocked her head. "Can't we get around to the docks?"

"That's what I'm saying—there are no more docks. Most of the watercrafts are damaged—either beached or broken up or sunk. Two piers were destroyed. The cruise ships and ferries were diverted two days ago. Even the small airstrip is rendered useless due to the damage."

Bibi's brow wrinkled. "Damn, dude. We can't go back the way we came. We might run smack into those terrorists. We haven't got time to be camping out in an aid station."

"We haven't got a choice." Ollie's face reddened. "There's only one alternative. Army dude said that just a little ways up the road there's some smaller encampments occupied by residents that don't want to be that far from their homes in case they're called back early. He says they're organizing their own little groups. He thinks they might have enough supplies to remain self-sufficient for a while."

"Where are these little encampments?" asked Diane.

"About two kilometers up the highway—a dirt road that leads west into the hills."

Diane knew they expected her to make a decision. They couldn't backtrack up the highway, running the risk of meeting up with the terrorists. The bad guys might look for the threesome in such a large encampment, since she had escaped from them on foot.

"Okay, we go to one of the small encampments to lay low," said Diane. "At least we'll be isolated from the main groups. Ollie, tell the driver to drop us off there, if he would be so kind. Just out of curiosity, where is *he* headed?"

Ollie relayed the request and questioned the driver then received an answer. "He said that he'll drop us off. He's planning to sneak into the city so he can pick up his scrap whether they like it or not. He says his wives will beat him if he comes home without any profits."

"He should be bitch-slapped for general purposes," said Bibi.

The driver pulled the truck around then headed up the highway. Ollie spoke to him in Spanish. In a very short time, they came to a dirt road that led west. The driver made the turn, downshifting the truck to accommodate an uphill grade. Diane could see freshly broken branches and brush piled on the fringe of the road, along with deep tire furrows in the mud that showed evidence of recent traffic.

A horn sounded ahead of them. The driver pulled over to the shoulder, allowing a Volkswagen to pass that was driving at an excessive rate of speed.

"We must be in the right area," said Diane. "By rights, there should be no traffic around here."

Those feelings were confirmed when a flash of color peeked through the forest maze showing it was one of the small encampments they were looking for. Dozens of people milled about in a small clearing. Some of them unloaded packages or unloaded goods from vehicles. A few teenagers drove stakes into the ground, securing large tents.

Diane slapped the side panel of the truck. "Stop!"

The driver pulled over. Diane and Ollie exited the bed, removing the pack. The driver offered Bibi a sloppy kiss, but she pushed him away. "Don't press your luck, Poncho. No more freebies."

They watched the truck swing a U-turn and then swerve down the hill. Diane led the way to the small camp, following some recent tire impressions. Before they saw them, two dogs rushed forth and barked at the trio. Viewing the newcomers as intruders, the dogs stood their ground, displaying sharp canines.

"Remain perfectly still," said Ollie. "We'll have to wait for the owners to get them to stand down."

The racket alerted the camp occupants. One woman and two men walked in their direction. They called the dogs off when they reached within a measured distance of the threesome. A woman called out to them in Spanish. Her tone dripped with accusation.

Ollie exchanged brief words with her. An older man spoke up next.

"I speak English. What do you want here?"

Diane said, "Thank you for the English. I'm Diane Nine. These are my friends, Ollie and Bibi. We don't mean to intrude. We're temporarily displaced—refugees from the hurricane. We don't have any place to go until Coccodrillo is opened up."

The old man wore baggy white shorts under a green smock top. He eyed the three, spending a long time studying Diane's boots and her control hand. He asked, "Where is your transportation?"

"We were dropped off," said Diane. "We're on foot." She heard a baby cry in the distance.

"These people are from the shanty on the north side," said the old man. "They have next to nothing to share with outsiders. As a group, they didn't have the petrol to make it to the evacuation center. I'm a neighbor from the same community. It's obvious you're not. What do you have to offer the group in exchange for assistance?" His focus fell on the large pack.

"Not very much, I'm afraid. I do have some pesos. This carrier contains my spare braces. I'm paraplegic and cannot walk without the hardware. To answer your question: we can gather wood, serve, and collect items. We won't give you any trouble."

"We're stranded," Ollie blurted. "We were robbed not too far from here. That's why we don't have any personal belongings."

"No handouts expected, kind sir," said Bibi.

The man gave his head a disapproving shake. "You're American tourists. Fortunately for you that is all that happened. The Cuban Brothers have even less tolerance for Americans than Fidel. Your newest president isn't helping matters, what with all the sanctions. And your Guantanamo Bay is an insult to human rights and justice."

"I don't mean to make this into a political debate," said Diane. "We're looking for some type of cover, a little sanctuary."

"Indeed," said Ollie. "If you have one shred of decency, sir, you'll at least find lodging for Diane. She's handicapped and without her wheelchair."

Bibi held her head back, while closing her eyes. "What is that godly smell? You folks cooking?"

The man sighed. "Stew—red beans and rice. I'll regret this, but I suppose you can share a meal with us. No guarantees. You'll have to be voted in by the others to take up residence. Follow me."

The man headed toward the camp. A small dark woman collared the dogs and followed him. Diane walked into the clearing of a meager campsite. She stopped to take in the sights. Their transportation amounted to four vehicles, two trucks and two older cars. She counted around 50 individuals out in the open. At least twenty of them were children under the age of ten. She estimated there to be six infants in the arms or on the backs of their mothers. Nearly all the people wore tattered, unwashed clothes, evidence of extreme poverty. Most of the faces were sallow, haggard ridden. Two large kettles sat on stone fire rings, their bottoms glowing orange from small kindling fires. A woman with a long-torn skirt stirred the brew. She looked askance at the three strangers with contempt.

The old man picked up three wooden bowels, then motioned for them to approach. "Well don't stand there like stumps, come over here and pull up a rock."

Diane and her friends took seats near the kettles. Each was given a bowl of stew. The female host gave them a bread heel apiece, followed by three tins of water. Bibi drank straight from her bowl, finishing it quickly. She asked for seconds. Diane could have slapped her.

Ollie eyed the old man. "Who are you, sir?"

"I'm Russell Blackthorn," said the old man. "Canadian by birth, but resident and citizen of Cuba for the past forty-two years. My parents brought me here on vacation when I was ten. I swore I would come back one day to visit or take up permanent lodging. I arrived in Havana when I turned twenty-one. I studied medicine here and became a doctor. That's about all you need to know about me, since the rest of my life is rather boilerplate. However, the three of *you* have my curiosity off the charts. I wonder if you might fill me in."

Ollie began by describing his association with Diane and the details about his employment. He explained that he served as her physical therapist, trainer and masseuse. He admitted to his sexual orientation, without being asked and then spoke a bit about his political affiliations. He ended by saying that he was generally happy with his life but hadn't met the right "bear" yet.

When it was Bibi's turn, she began by talking about her vocational nursing background, tying it in with her employment to Diane. She listed the responsibilities required to be a personal assistant. Shc had no views on politics or religion but did give him an account of her early family life and upbringing, including snippets on how hard it was for an African American female in today' society. Russell showed a pronounced interest in her story and asked her to elaborate on some of her personal experiences in detail. Bibi obliged, but ended her story with a rant about Cuba, outlining her displeasure of being robbed by a taxicab driver in broad daylight. Russell sympathized but did not appear shocked by the incident.

Diane didn't think starting from the beginning would hurt, so she began with, "I fell out of a tree house when I was little," and went on from there. When it came to describing her family, she spoke regretfully about the painful memories.

"My father was unemployed at the time of my accident. Naturally, there was no insurance, so the bills mounted. He took to drinking and snitching my mother's prescription drugs to ease the pain. The creditors came down hard on him. When he did find substantial employment, they garnished his wages. Dad didn't last long after that and disappeared about six months later."

"Where did he go?" asked Russell.

"We received four letters from him in the next two years. They were all postmarked from different countries. We never saw him again. I struck out on my own when I was eighteen. Later, I began making a little income from graphic design work and comic freelancing, so I was able to shoulder most of the debt. I eventually paid off all the medical bills and set mother up in her own condominium. I bought my dream house much later. Mom died of ovarian cancer two years ago."

Russell swatted a fly. "But how did you ever carve out an occupation within such a household of turmoil, combined with the affliction that struck you down?"

Leaving nothing out, she recapped her many operations, along with the painful recoveries. However, her eyes lit up when she described her joy at discovering graphic freelancing and art while glued to a wheelchair.

"Fantasy art was my great escape—my ticket to salvation," she said. "I was confined—immobile from the accident. I had always been active for a little girl, so I began to get frustrated and antsy. I needed an outlet for the sake of my sanity. I began doodling, which turned into full-scale renderings in charcoal and watercolor."

"Where did you get the materials for all this?"

"My mother gave me what supplies she could borrow or

buy on special discounts with her welfare checks. I became obsessed with the medium of comic books and graphic novels. Combined with my love for science fiction and fantasy literature, I married the two and began writing and illustrating my own little chapbooks, which were clumsy attempts at first."

"Did you seek out any education for your craft?" asked Russell. "Or were you one of the naturally talented?"

"Hardly a natural. I joined an on-line art institute and began taking regular classes. When I thought my work showed merit, I began sending the material to the most lucrative publication markets, the big franchise slicks, some of the video game companies. The local papers did feature stories on me and displayed my work. I think my popularity-slash acceptance grew partially from my physical condition. They never failed to photograph me without the wheelchair in frame. So, you could say that my handicap actually worked in my favor. To this day I don't know if that's good or bad. But I have been told that I'm a talented artist. I take solace in that."

"She's an original, all right." said Ollie. "Talk about overcoming obstacles."

"Seems to me I've heard of you in the news," said Russell, "only I can't remember when that was. A few years back, I believe. Sorry I haven't seen your work, but outside reading and entertainment is hard to come by here unless I get it straight from the tourists."

A young boy stepped up to Russell, handing him a glass jar filled with water. The man sniffed it and held it up to the light, studying its contents. He handed it back with some instructions in Spanish. The young boy gave him a pert bow then trotted off.

"I just checked a sample of the creek water," said Russell. "I told the boy to have the lot of it boiled before consumption."

"They seem to respect your opinion," said Diane. "Are you their spokesman or leader?" She took a few more bites of the stew, savoring the taste.

"A benefactor. A deliverer, perhaps. These people have very little in the way of professional services or care. I've tried to provide some help or comfort along the way. Advice and knowledge is cheap. I offer it up if I can provide a relevant solution. Most of their problems are easily solved because they are so basic. Their needs are few when they have little aspiration or hope. I try to provide some of the easiest necessities. They never ask for anything more than I am able or willing to give. It's a symbiotic relationship."

"What do you get out of it?" asked Bibi. "You some kind of Robin Hood?"

"I don't steal, if that is what you mean, Ms. Bibi. I donate my time, some expertise, some medical assistance and a little emotional comfort. Not to say that I'm without recompense." He gave a wheezy laugh. It was the first time Diane saw him smile since their meeting.

He went on, "I can't tell you how many britches I've had sewn, sweaters knitted, shoes resoled. I've never had to cook my own meals. Oh, and live chickens. I don't know what it is with my little community, but they've always blessed me with more than enough of the blasted creatures."

"A whole bunch of chickens?" Bibi cocked her head.

"Such a number at one point that I hadn't the yard space to contain them. They give what they can afford, or what they consider valuable. Some of them are absolute masters with the textile craft, basket weaving, and ceramic artistry. I should stress that my arrangements with them are cooperative and mutual. They are not, in any way, a clinical case study for me, in case that was your next question. They are my dearest friends."

Diane found Russell's association with his small community endearing, almost heroic in scope. She would not have expected to see such a thing if not for hearing or seeing it in person. Not that it was impossible. It was just that Cuba had not given her many impressions of humanitarianism or compassion. Then again, she hadn't been in the country long enough to see such benevolence.

Diane had a few questions about current matters that needed answering. "Do you have any idea how long before you're allowed back into the city?"

"This happens all the time," said Russell, packing a tobacco pipe. "Five to seven days, to restore power and import water, is a fast recovery. We've had a number of those. This one? Marla? Two weeks, maybe more before the first occupants are allowed back in for restoration work. The brick buildings always fair the best. The clapboard and wooden framed structures are always flattened, which means complete rebuilding. The owners of those dwellings are, of course, the poor, the people you see around you now." He gave fire to the pipe then blew a nauseous cloud.

Diane chewed her lips, thinking about immediate needs. "Will these people make it through the time period without suffering?"

"There is always suffering here, an unavoidable byproduct of a nation that does not have the proper infrastructure to care for all its citizens. Conditions here will begin to deteriorate within a week. Our limited vehicles could only carry enough supplies for that duration. I packed what medical supplies and drugs I had on hand, but even those will not be enough, since we're likely to be visited by other small groups that are in need. Most of them had to hike out of the city proper, their backs laden with bulk staples and water containers. We don't expect any relief soon, not for this bunch."

Bibi looked down at her empty bowl. "Damned if I don't

feel like hogzilla right now. Why did you have to ask him that, Diane?"

"It's not the adults I'm worried about," said Russell. "The infants will need whole milk and formula. That's impossible without refrigeration. Powdered milk would do in a pinch. We'll need aspirin, Tylenol, dressings, antiseptics, inhalers, antibiotics, insulin for the diabetics, morphine and other prescription medicines. It's a logistical nightmare. We've always managed to bring a few shovels, though. That's something we've never forgotten."

"Why do you need shovels out here?" asked Ollie, setting his bowl down.

Diane gave Ollie a cross look.

"Oh, my. I'm so sorry."

"Death is life," said Russell. "There's no apology necessary. A mile to the west of here is another encampment, then another and another. Death never discriminates. We all share in it. The irony is that it is the first time that I would welcome the aid and resources of your country, even though I hate them for their conduct in the foreign arena. The United States does have a track record for aiding its citizens in times of natural disaster. Katrina comes to mind. If only we could be so fortunate."

"Katrina was bumbled," said Bibi.

"Nevertheless, lives were saved." He took another draw on the pipe then looked at Diane's ankles. "You know, I pride myself on keeping up with the most recent prosthesis and limb braces, due to an extensive career. The medical journals I've read do not have anything in production that approaches the sophistication of the device you are wearing. It appears to use robotic telepresence. Is that correct? Would you mind telling me where you obtained it? Perhaps the name of the manufacturer?"

Diane tried not to falter. "It's actually a prototype from

an independent manufacturer. Strauss Industries. If that helps."

"Most peculiar. I've never heard of Strauss Industries. If not for the jerky movements and the exposed framework, I would have missed it completely. How could something like this not be in production when it seems to work so well?" He pointed his pipe stem at the finger controller. "Very unique. I would like to look at it when you have some free time."

Diane nodded. "That's if we have some free time."

Russell grinned. "What kind of a host would I be if I were to turn you away this evening? I think we can accommodate you for a night. The community will still have to put it to a vote. Extra mouths are a liability here." He stood up and pointed to a large green tent. "You're welcome to use my little hovel. It will afford you some privacy—at least a haven for sound sleep."

"That would be wonderful," said Diane. "It'll give us a chance to discuss how we can contribute to the effort."

"Amen," said Bibi.

"The latrine is over behind that large scrub patch," said Russell. "It's primitive but functional. I'll have some extra blankets sent your way. If you need anything else, I'll be out here with the others. Just give me a good kick. I'm a heavy sleeper." He paused. "If things don't work out with the vote, I'll drive you to one of the large evacuation centers. Good evening, it was nice to meet you."

Diane watched their host walk away and merge with a small group who were in the process of erecting a surplus tent. The other community members were engaged in various tasks, putting the finishing touches on their tiny campsite. They seemed well organized, a bit slow, methodical, but determined to set up a proper bivouac. The children seemed especially well mannered as they ran around taking orders from the adults.

Bibi stood up. "What are we waiting for? It ain't the MGM Grand, but these bones won't know the difference."

When Diane tried to get up, she missed the proper maneuver and fell over on her side. She allowed Bibi to help her to a stance. They walked the short distance to the tent, a four-person Coleman, equipped with a cloth floor and mosquito netting. Ollie led the way in, hefting the large pack. A few moments later, a teenage girl presented them with extra blankets, some candles and one small feather pillow. Diane thanked her then eased down in into a sitting position. She motioned her friends into a huddle, keeping her voice down. Outside, the failing light of dusk approached.

"It's plain that we have to earn our keep if we're going to stay with this group. He plans on taking us to another evacuation center if we're voted out. That would put us at risk of being discovered. We can't allow that to happen."

"What are you proposing?" asked Ollie. "We're out of our element here. What could we do to help these people?"

"You heard it yourself. These people are going to need medical supplies, formula and whole milk. Basic stuff for the kids. Everyone will need to eat and drink for at least a few weeks. That means bulk foodstuffs—rice, flour, corn."

"You'd need a truck or mules to move all that," said Bibi. "And besides, you could only find those things in the city. They have armed goons down there protecting that stuff. Shit, they might even be taking the goods for themselves."

"I'm the truck," said Diane. "You're the mules. Don't you see? Look, what's to keep me from suiting up and paying Coccodrillo a little visit? It's only a mile away down the hill. You follow me to the outskirts. I go in on a little night raid, force some doors open and cop the goods. I bring the supplies to a staging ground where you guys pick them up then ferry the load back to the camp."

"You're crazy," said Bibi. "They'll nab your ass or hose you with gunfire."

"Not if I see them first. I've got night, infrared, and binocular vision in the helmet. I'll be blacked out, wearing dark armor, and I can outrun any pursuer. I can lift or drag three times a normal load. With multiple trips, we can buy these folks some time as well as winning their hearts and minds."

Bibi frowned. "Yeah, but how are you going to keep these people from seeing you in that getup? If they do, they might shoot their mouths off. That'll bring the man down on us."

"Somehow I don't think that will happen."

"When do you want to try this?" asked Ollie, his eyes wide in the fading light.

"We're not going to *try* it. We are going to *do it*. Tonight."

Bibi made a moaning sound.

10

Bibi had a hard time holding the candle still while Ollie snapped the components together. He missed several connections and miss-routed the main loom twice, requiring him to start over. Trying to keep the noise factor down made them nervous, even though Diane knew it to be in the early AM hours. They still ran the risk of awakening someone in the camp. They were getting off to a shaky start for something intended to be a stealth mission.

Ollie finished and assisted Diane to her feet. She put the helmet on and tapped the touch-buttons to activate the night vision mode. It made her two friends look like two green, luminescent ghosts. At least it still functioned properly. She took the helmet off and wedged it in the crook of her arm. Looking at her friend's expectant faces, she said, "We have to sneak out of here without being seen. Ollie, see if the coast is clear."

When he returned, he gave her the high sign then held the tent flap for her. She eased out, trying not to stumble. She walked with light steps through the clearing, carefully sneaking across the forest floor. Ollie and Bibi followed behind. A twig snapped underfoot. Thankfully someone snored loud enough to mask the noise.

When Diane made it to the end of the clearing, she picked up her pace. She pulled the helmet over her head, tapping for night vision. Ollie and Bibi trudged after her a few breaths behind. A hundred yards in, the forest thickened, with a profusion of medium-growth trees and tall shrubs. The downward slope was rife with rain gullies, threatening any misstep. An occasional snag of undergrowth blocked the way, forcing an alternative route. The only natural light came from a sliver of moon peeking behind some wispy clouds.

Breaking from the heaviest cover, the city panorama came into view. Scattered pinpricks of light dotted the landscape, comprised of vehicle headlights and utility lamps lit by generators. She could not see any human activity through the helmet display mode, until she tapped in the magnified infrared setting. Tiny rice-sized objects showed minute increments of movement—humans. There were not many in plain sight, since she knew the buildings could obscure dozens.

Diane walked carefully down the slope which led to a plowed field cordoned off by a barbed wire fence. It took only a few pincher movements to clip the wire strands one by one. They walked through the field, passing a flattened pile of lumber, which at one time had been a small ranch house. They reached a windbreak of gaunt eucalyptus trees, their branches stripped bare. The first destroyed city structures were evident at the bottom of the hill.

"This is as far as you go," Diane told the two. "Stay near the cover of these trees. Wait for me to return. I'll be back."

"What if you get busted?" asked Bibi. "What do we do then?"

"I'm not going to get caught. But if you see me running back in this direction without a load, run like hell back up to the camp."

"Good luck," said Ollie.

Diane crossed the field at a quick pace and made it to the first rubble piles. Choosing the path of least resistance, she found a litter-strewn blacktop street and followed it. Trash-cans, lumber, metal, broken glass, roof tiles, and other structural debris lay about in helter skelter disarray. Trees were snapped at their bases, some of them lying over cars that had been overturned. She did find one useful item in the rubble which she picked up—a large soggy grain sack.

She continued farther into the city, keeping alert for anything that moved. The landscape looked haunted, completely devoid of life. A few birds flew overhead, looking like orange specters. Most of the largest buildings remained intact, but their doors and windows had been blown out, leaving gaping holes. Nearly every building had lost its roof.

She crept past a large hotel. The front of the structure was faceless, the walls and plaster having been blown away, showing the skeletal framework. Cornering the building, she saw a couch bobbing in the muddy waters of a swimming pool. She heard what sounded like gunshots in the distance, but it could have been something else.

She turned onto a street that looked like a business row and tried to read the Spanish writing on the signs. Some of the words seemed familiar. Others made no sense at all. But something looked very familiar across the street—large block letters written on a swing sign that hung by one chain.

FARMACIA.

She crossed the street and stepped through a jagged opening in the plate glass. Wet packages and small boxes littered the floor space. She made her way behind a counter, then into an anteroom that was crowded with high ceiling shelves. The shelves were filled with hundreds of containers of prescription medicines, pills and liquid formulas. Thankfully, most of the packages contained the manufacturer's English brand names for the prescription drugs. The helmet magnifier made reading the print up close clear and legible. She hurriedly swept the best choices into the sack, moving from aisle to aisle. After finishing, she passed through the opening and crept down the sidewalk, watching for more storefront signs.

A truck pulled around a corner, heading her way. It moved very slowly over the trash-laden street. A directional searchlight shone from the roof of the vehicle, lighting up the building facades.

Diane backed into a wall, frozen in place.

A half dozen armed soldiers stood in the back of the truck, holding onto grab rails. As the driver picked his course down the street, their heads turned, following the searchlight beam that splashed on the building walls from one side of the street to the other.

Armed patrol.

Diane remained perfectly still as the truck rumbled by. The beam passed just over her head then swung back to the other side of the street. A few men had looked in her direction but had seen nothing. First appearances, they looked sloppy —disorganized. Their behavior became clear a moment later when one of them passed a bottle around.

They're drunk off their asses. Probably stolen liquor.

One of the men almost fell from the truck bed, which roused the others to shrill with laughter. The other men pushed him playfully, causing him to nosedive over the rail onto the pavement. He hit the ground with an audible *thwack.* The truck stopped. A few men dismounted and picked up the unconscious man. They threw him in the truck like a sack of potatoes. More laughter. The truck continued on.

Diane exhaled and picked up the grain sack then moved down the street. Staying close to the buildings was the best defense against detection. A snarl of high-tension wires lay across the street. Whether they were live or not was not known.

Another three hundred feet down the street brought her close to something that smelled very bad. A few more steps brought her to a sign that read MERCADO. The market door was made of glass, but the top pane was broken out. She reached over it to unlock the bottom half then stepped in. The odor of spoiled meat hit like a hammer blow.

It was a General store. She went to the canned good section and loaded up on beans, corn and peas—easy pickings. Next came bottled water, sacks of whole grain rice, powdered milk, bags of almonds, figs and dried apricots. She was tempted to grab fruit juices, but the sack load already felt heavy. She could carry it, but it could burst at the seams if any more weight was added. She picked out a small hand basket that provided necessities. She topped it off with combs, brushes, towels, mouth wash and toilet tissue. The load was maxed. It was time to head out.

She crept across the street, the sack slung over a shoulder. She missed her footing a few times, finding it hard to work the finger control and keep a grip on the bulky load. She had to adjust her balance, forcing a forward lean to compensate for the load. A misstep would cause a spill, alerting anyone within earshot.

She chose a narrow alley away from the major streets and then crossed another alley a dozen yards away. The path was strewn with broken lumber. It required careful, well-placed steps to cross it. The sack snagged several times on sharp objects, nearly tearing it open.

She emerged from the alley, nearly colliding with a soldier who was walking down the sidewalk.

They both froze.

They looked at each other for a minute. The soldier looked shocked—his eyes wide, unblinking. His weapon lay over his shoulder. He made no move to pull it.

Diane could think of nothing else to do but give him a weak nod, then walk past him onto the street and across to the next sidewalk. A small side road opened up before her and she took it, increasing the pace. The bullet she expected in her back never came. Looking back would arouse suspicion. As far as she knew, the soldier was still rooted to the same spot.

She passed through a broken gate that opened onto a plowed field. The furrows lay nearly flat, as though a giant hand had pressed them down. She tapped for a trot. The soggy earth threatened to mire her boots. She left deep prints in the sod behind her. Prints that might be followed. The shaky magnified image of the windbreak trees on the hill came into view; the place where Ollie and Bibi waited hunkered down in the row of trees. It was only a quarter of a mile away, but it could have been a million miles.

She squeezed through a wooden fence, crossed another small field and then cornered a long chain-link fence. A curious object came into focus halfway up the hill. She tapped for infrared. A large, live object that registered a hotspot stood two dozen yards away. It looked like a small pony, or even a very large dog. Whatever it was, it appeared unconcerned with her presence, since it had its head titled very low to the ground. Was it eating? Creeping closer she found it to be a fat goat feeding on a small patch of soggy grass. A *female* goat, with bloated utters. A long rope trailed from its neck across the ground.

Diane walked to the tail end of the rope and brought a boot down on it. After setting her load down, she grasped the rope and reeled the animal in, tying the rope off on her waist. She loaded up. Making headway again, the goat trailed behind docilely, occasionally letting out a bleat. At the top of the slope, two ghost-like images scampered down the hill. Ollie and Bibi had disobeyed instructions to stay under cover. Warding them off would have done little good, so she knelt in a crouch and waited for them.

Ollie reached her first, dropping to his knees. His voice came out with a wheeze. "We thought you could use some help." He looked past her shoulder. "And we thought that was a dangerous animal stalking you."

"Keep your voice down," Diane whispered. "It's a goat—I have it tethered." Ollie took the un-tethered end.

Bibi fell down in the dirt then crawled on her hands and knees until she could look up at Diane. "Damn, girl. What are you doing with a sheep?"

Diane covered Bibi's mouth with her hand. "Keep the noise down. It's a *goat*. We're taking it back with us. Take this hand basket. Let's move out. We're in the open."

They hiked up the slope until they reached the tree line. They spent a few moments dividing the loads—Diane kept the heavy sack, Ollie the basket while Bibi took the goat rope. They started up the slope. Once they reached the outskirts of the camp, they slowed their pace. It was nearly impossible to transverse the ground without stepping on something that snapped or creaked. They entered the clearing.

Sleeping bodies lay about the campsite in indistinct lumps, some snoring loudly, others shifting under their blankets. One of the sleepers roused from slumber with a coughing fit that lasted for two minutes. They felt sure the whole camp would awake to the disturbance. The stricken sleeper looked in their direction for a moment and then covered up but continued to hack and wheeze. When the noise abated, the three made a break for it and scurried inside their tent, pulling the goat in behind them. Ollie helped remove Diane's helmet and then lit a candle.

Bibi's face dripped sweat in the candlelight. "What are we going to do about him, Di?" She pointed at the goat. "He can't stay in here; he'll step all over our faces."

"It's a she. Ollie can tie her up to a tent peg outside. You can help me unload. Then we can lay the produce and packages on the ground in front of the tent. We'll let the folks wake up to it."

"Just like Christmas," Ollie whispered. "I'll bet they'll be surprised. From the looks of it you got away with a nice little cache. Have any trouble?"

"I was spotted by a soldier. I think he went into shock when he saw me—didn't know quite what he was seeing. He might have been dead drunk or on drugs. It was hard to tell."

"So long as the dude didn't follow you," said Bibi, "or saw where you were going."

"He didn't bother. Like I said, he was paralyzed. Now, if you don't mind, let's get our care package ready."

Diane awoke to the hum of voices just outside the tent. The goat bleated several times. Someone said, "*El donde la amabilidad.*"

Ollie sat up, rubbing his eyes. "It translates to 'the milk of human kindness.' It looks like they found the party goods."

Diane groped for her finger controller and slipped it on and then reared up into a sitting position. She reached over and wiggled Bibi's big toe. The large woman moaned several times then spoke sleepily. "And I was having such a pimped-out dream. Some hot little cabana boy was giving me a massage on a sandy white beach in Bermuda."

"Would you settle for a rubdown from a little fag in the weeds?" asked Ollie.

"I said it was a dream. Not a nightmare."

Diane tucked her top exoskeleton parts under her blanket. Shaking her hair out, Diane found it filthy and snarled. Her skin was oily under the dirty garments. Her breath smelled like dirty midgets had been walking over her tongue all night. She couldn't remember her last bowel movement, which translated to a serious blockage. Having lost her diuretics and medicines, tougher times were ahead. Her friends were no better off—Ollie had horrendous blisters. Bibi's inner thighs were riddled with chaff sores. If they ever got out of this they would need a battery of psychiatrists and a trauma center to set things right.

Diane pushed the tent flap aside. "Let's meet the masses." She reared up awkwardly and stepped out into a large knot of people who sat or knelt on the ground, busy examining the items. Russell stood a few yards off, looking down upon the goods laid out on the blanket. When his eyes met hers, his facial expression softened. The corner of his mouth turned up in a small, but perceptible smile.

The minute the small crowd had seen Diane, their eyes fell on her with admiration, mixed with a bit of wonder. A small female already had a plastic bottle under the goat, busily yanking the udders. A few children placed a small pile of grass at the animal's feet and took turns stroking the goat's head. When Bibi and Ollie appeared, hands went together in a small applause. Several "thank yous" were offered, along with a "Viva America".

"Yep, just like Christmas," said Ollie, puffing out his chest.

"I don't know how you did it," Russell began, "but I believe we owe you our sincere thanks. That's quite a shopping list." He coughed hoarsely, his face turning pink. "Sorry, I seem to have picked up a little bug."

There was no question that Russell might have been the

coughing man last night and had seen them trying to sneak into camp.

"I'm sure we have something that will take care of that," said Diane. "Compliments of one of the pharmacies. Since there is no refrigeration for milk, I thought the goat might fill in as a replacement. We would have made a bigger haul, but it was all I could carry."

Russell looked surprised. "You transported this by yourself?"

"Well, not all of it. Bibi and Ollie did the heavy lifting. The goat came along on its own."

Russell seemed appreciative but concerned. "You could have been killed. The city is swarming with security police and soldiers, not to mention laborers, who would turn you in at the drop of a hat. I'm surprised you made it out."

Diane stepped closer to him to keep her voice down. "It was worth the risk. I'm not totally dense. I didn't do it for sympathy. We needed shelter—a place to lay our heads without the threat of harm. There seems to be a lot of that in this country, especially against us. We're just trying to get back home."

Russell relaxed somewhat. "In that case, you have a home with us for as long as you need. We appreciate the effort you put forth in acquiring thc itcms. Only do me a favor, if you have a mind to duplicate the stunt—tell me first. I might have some ideas of my own. I do know the city well enough to keep the danger level to a minimum."

"Agreed. I wonder if you wouldn't mind directing us to that creek. We're pretty ripe."

"Follow the path to the west. It will lead to the base of a small hill. Try not to contaminate the flow too severely. There are others downstream that need the water. I'll have Consuelo give you some towels." He looked at the ground. "It looks like you brought the soap and shampoo."

Supplied with a basket of hygiene items, Diane and her friends followed a twisting path through the trees, until they reached a creek that flowed through a rocky gorge. The breadth of the creek was dammed with fallen logs and small rocks forming a shallow wading pool. Large flat stones sat on the creek bank to serve as seating benches and washing platforms. At the moment, the area was devoid of bathers, perfect for a private dip.

There was nothing quick about getting Diane out of the lower framework. Ollie and Bibi double-teamed to get the chore done.

"A real clean place for a community pool," said Ollie, unsnapping the leg components.

"They might live in squalor," said Diane, "but they're environmentally conscientious. It's the only source of clean water around. We should go easy on the soap. There's no telling how many refugee camps are downstream."

"Yeah, that means no peeing in the pool, Ollie," said Bibi.

"I'm so filthy right now," said Ollie, "that I wouldn't mind bathing in a pool of piss. I'd come out a lot cleaner than I am now."

When Diane was free of the framework and clothes, Ollie and Bibi lifted her into the water and propped her back up against a rock shelf. They joined her, passing the soap and shampoo between them. They had one toothbrush to share. Diane opted to be the last to use it. It didn't matter. The running water over her body was so engrossing that someone could have threatened her with death, and she would have agreed to it with the provision that she die in the water. She used a dab of shampoo which frothed her hair. The water was cool, just enough to raise goose bumps.

"I get to use more soap because I have more surface area," said Bibi.

"Yeah, and it's all tits," said Ollie.

Diane sighed. "You two should stop. This is marvelous. Enjoy the moment."

After finishing with a good scrub, Ollie gave Diane a thorough body massage. For the first time in days, she could feel her skin come back to life with a delightful tingle. Considering the circumstances, she felt like she was in heaven, given the opportunity to savor every minute of it. Reality would come calling soon enough. That meant escaping the island, somehow finding safe passage to get them back to the States. The recent hurricane damage to the transportation system would hamper those efforts. Cho and the Global Socialist Alliance would take care of the rest of the negatives, relentlessly pursuing the owner of the combat suit. The odds seemed stacked against them with no way out. It would have been so easy to write her way out of the scene like she had done so many times in the Aurora comic book series.

Bibi yawned. "What's next in our game plan? Besides pulling off raids on that little crib below."

Diane considered it. "Nothing I have is original. We have two options of escape: we sail out or fly out. Provided we find a hub that's open to that, we still have to deal with Cho and his little band of merry men. We don't know how well their organization is connected up to the populace. They might have infiltrated the government to gain their cooperation. They could put the word out with a price on our heads."

Ollie slapped the water angrily. "This is a big island. They couldn't have spies at *every* dock and airstrip. I'll lay you odds some high-profile Americans used private aircraft or charters to fly here. They'll be stranded like us. If we're going to get out of here, it'll be our own countrymen who take us out."

Diane toweled her hair. "You're still talking about major airstrips, or even private strips. Cho will be watching the big commuter airports, even the smaller ones. How are we going to find American celebrities? That's the reason they vacation here—to get lost—to hide away from it all. Like I said, all those jerks have to do is visit every facility they can and offer a reward to anyone who spots us. Hell, if they're satellite capable, they can call ahead and take care of business over the phone, in which case if they've already done that, we're screwed."

Bibi spoke around the toothbrush. "Let's get a cell phone and try home again. Call your publisher or agent. Have them contact the suits at the CIA or FBI. Somebody has to listen. Somebody has to figure out that we're in trouble. Doesn't your agent have a Learjet or something?"

"It's a prop Cessna. Where is he going to land to make the pickup? We'd have to rendezvous with him right down to the minute to make the jump out of here. Even if he was convinced, we'd been robbed and stranded, he would tell me to go to the nearest police station for protection, file a report, and then make arrangements to get off the island."

"This place is like Oz," said Ollie. "Lions and tigers and bears. There's no one we can trust."

Bibi washed out the toothbrush and passed it to Diane. "What about the old dude? He's connected up here. Maybe he knows somebody who can get us out of here without raising alarm bells."

"You mean Russell," said Diane. "Don't you think he has his hands full with a camp filled with refugees? How much are we going to tell him? If we lay down the whole story, what's to say he won't rat us out? We haven't even known this group for 24 hours. They really don't have any reason to help Americans."

"Yeah, well we didn't really have any need to help them out either," said Ollie, "but we did when we hauled all those goods up here. I'd say Russell owes us beyond some shelter or food. At least we can propose a deal and see where it leads.

Bribery can be a very effective negotiating tool. Right now, they need us more than we need them."

"I wouldn't go that far," said Diane. "We don't need to be on the road out there by ourselves. At least here, we have a small base away from mainstream traffic. But you bring up a good point about Russell. He's trusted in the community, so he probably knows every pilot and fisherman on the island—at least this end of it."

They got out of the water and took turns toweling each other dry. After Diane was snapped back into her framework and clothed, they started down the path.

They took their time on the stroll back. For the first time, they spoke about the trees and landscape. There was much to admire about the environment, in spite of the hurricane damage. Even with the destruction, they commented about the striking beauty of the wilderness.

When they neared the camp, they heard raised voices. It sounded like someone was crying, judging from the high-pitched whine. The three approached warily. They had no idea what they were walking into, but something was off.

They stepped into the clearing. A dozen individuals stood in a tight group, looking down upon the ground. Russell was on his knees attending to two people: a man and a woman who lay supine. At first glance it looked like an accident of some kind. A fight. Two women were inspecting a small girl's face, titling the child's head from side to side. Nearly all of the people jabbered in emotionally charged Spanish, cutting into each other's words. At least three tents that Diane had seen standing erect lay collapsed on the ground, including her own. Foodstuffs and items lay scattered about the camp as though they had been thrown and trampled. A few babies cried inconsolably.

Some of the people turned to look as Diane approached, cursing under their breath at the sight of her. Russell did not look up, being too involved in wrapping the head of one of prone victims with gauze. A few more insults flew.

"What are they saying?" Diane asked from the corner of her mouth.

"Not quite sure," said Ollie, "but it sounds like 'you've brought the devil down on us', or something in that vein."

"Just lovely," said Bibi. "There go our brownie points."

11

Risking rude behavior by not asking what had happened in the encampment, Diane set out for the collapsed tent to check on a very specific item. Ollie and Bibi followed a few steps behind.

"See if we still have it, Ollie," said Diane.

She watched the small man crawl under the canvas and waited for his reply. She heard his muffled voice a moment later.

"It's still here wrapped up in the blanket."

Diane let out a brcathy sigh. "Good. Reset the tent, would you? I'll be back in a minute."

A moment later, Diane and Bibi were standing over Russell, watching him attend to the second victim of an obvious attack. One would have thought that the man and woman on the ground had traded blows with each other. If it could only have been that simple.

Diane felt like collapsing internally, fearful of the condemnation that was sure to come. It had been only a stroke of luck that she had been at the creek and not in the camp, exposed to the confrontation meant for her.

"I think you owe us an explanation," said Russell,

refusing to look up. The man looked barely in control of his temper.

"What happened?" Diane asked.

"What happened? Look around you. It doesn't take a genius to see that we were attacked. Two men. Two men with combat rifles jumped from a vehicle and accosted the group. One of them spoke broken Spanish, but they were both foreigners. They demanded to know the whereabouts of three Americans that fit your descriptions. We told them nothing. So, they proceeded to use their rifle butts to force the information. These two adults took the brunt of the attack. They even slapped one of the children several times. Suspecting we were hiding something, they raided the camp, ransacking the tents and vehicles—looking for something. Satisfied that we knew nothing, they left as quickly as they came."

Bibi said, "Awe, shit."

"I was at the latrine when they came," said Russell. "The interrogation was over when I arrived on the scene. When I tried to give aid to the stricken, one of the men thrust a rifle in my face."

An apology seemed so fruitless. Innocent people had landed in harm's way because of the three strangers. Trouble had followed them like some hungry mongrel. If not for the timing of the incident, the threesome would have been dealt more than physical blows. They would have lost their lives.

Diane waited for Russell to stand up before she offered to speak. When he finished with the bandaging, he pushed himself up, looking at her for the first time.

"I owe you an explanation," said Diane. "I hope you don't mind if it's private. I don't know how many here understand English, but it's not meant for other ears."

He nodded. She led him to the tent. Ollie had just straightened out the frame and thrown the flap back. Diane took a seat inside. Russell sat across from her. Bibi and Ollie sat down at the entrance, looking somber.

Diane uncovered the blanket to show the pieces of the suit. She explained, "It all began when I met a man named Chet Strauss." She told him how she had first met the man who introduced her to the combat exoskeleton, along with his plans for selling it to the U.S. military. She left nothing out, including her brief romance, the staged kidnapping, then her eventual trip to Cuba to find the missing engineer-slash-boyfriend. She tried to describe the triad organization that had set her up. Russell showed little or no emotion during the story, but kept his eyes pinned on hers. When she finished, he closed his eyes like he was lost in thought. He finally spoke, with a voice tinged with sadness.

"I never thought things could get any worse than they are, but I can see how mistaken I was. I know now that I was not seeing things last night when I glimpsed what I could have sworn to be a robot standing in the clearing. Of course, that was you, fully outfitted. I've never heard of the Global Socialist Alliance, but from what I've seen of them so far, it hasn't been positive. I've never aligned myself to any government, including my own, but I have even less sympathy for your country's military chauvinism, so it is no wonder this faction has seen fit to use Cuba as a base of operations."

"What do you think we should do?" said Ollie.

"You could not be in a worse locale as far as your safety is concerned. I would suggest you bargain with these hooligans—give up the apparatus. At least you might live to return to your country."

"We can't do that," said Diane, the defiance heavy in her voice. "This can't be allowed to get into the wrong hands."

"Why should that determination be up to you? Because of your ridiculous notion of patriotism for a country that in all probability deserves to be overrun and conquered for its own crimes against humanity? Whose hands are the more tainted in this scenario?"

"I don't want to get into a discussion with you about social mores, attitudes or correctness. This doesn't even involve Cuba, past the fact that it is being used as staging grounds for the theft. This project was conceived and built in the United States, with probably stolen parts. It belongs there for that reason alone."

"I won't dispute ownership of the device. I only question its true, intended purpose. Most assuredly, it was designed to wage war on a mass scale. In the hands of what lesser evil does it belong? That is the question for the rest of the world to consider."

The issue was falling into a deep morality rut. Was there any way to salvage a point, wondering if it would do any good at all? Diane persisted, "I think the difference is the motivation of the owner. My country has always assumed a defensive posture, coming to the aid of those who cannot defend themselves against tyranny or oppression. We're not known for first strike blitzkriegs against third-world countries."

"Just sticking your military might where it doesn't belong —global cops," said Russell.

"The Global Socialist Alliance makes no bones about the fact that they intend to put it into immediate use against us." This discussion was becoming more and more one-sided. "They're hopped up for a third world war. They feel that this technology will give them an edge. *They* are the aggressor here."

Russell fingered one of the suit pieces. "Be that as it may, the fact is you've brought this problem into our camp, risking the lives of people who know nothing about high-tech warfare."

"Why don't we just haul our asses on out of here," said Bibi. "It's plain we're not wanted."

"It's not a question of want," said Russell. "The question is do we need you here to complicate an already difficult situation. And I never said anything about turning you out to fend for yourselves. That would be quite a hypocritical gesture. Fortunately for you, the majority of the camp occupants still hold you in high regard. You have only upset the friends and relatives of those who were attacked."

"Now what?" asked Bibi.

"I'll discuss the matter with the refugees. I'll try to explain your side of it, but I can't guarantee a favorable outcome."

Diane stared at him, wondering why he had digressed. "Why the change of heart? We're willing to leave."

"I'm not thinking with my heart. It's logic that tips the decision to keep you on. Your adversaries have swept this camp and come up empty. As far as they know you're not here, which means you must be hiding at some other encampment. That works in your favor."

"Yeah," said Ollie, "provided they don't come back for a second look, or we're ratted out."

"There are no rats in this population," Russell said flatly. "If you're allowed to remain, you will receive the protection afforded any other person. Additionally, I need to know if you were spotted in the city last night. If so, you could initiate a search from the security police, adding another pursuer to your list of enemies."

Diane explained the incident about the guard spotting her. She added, "He didn't follow me, so I'm sure he had no idea what direction I was headed. I took a long way around to return to the camp." She tapped the helmet. "Believe me; I could have seen anything tailing me by just looking over my shoulder."

Russell pushed to his feet and stepped between Ollie and Bibi. "I'll be back with a decision," he said over his shoulder.

At least they had a democracy, even if it was a small one.

Still, it couldn't keep hearts from sinking and expecting a negative outcome.

"We are *so* toast," said Ollie. "These people have enough problems on their hands without being asked to be human shields for three foreigners."

Some raised voices were heard through the tent opening, evidence that Russell had proposed the problem to the crowd. There followed a rabble of discussion, but this time the voices were more subdued. Ten minutes later, Russell returned with the news. His facial expression looked mildly pleasant.

"You're voted into the community. There are really no hard feelings. They're appreciative of the efforts you've made to bring fresh stock and supplies. But we are all of the opinion that you should have some alternate plan of defense or escape should it happen again. We can only do so much. We're not equipped to fend off high caliber weapons."

Diane exhaled. "That's a relief. Thank you for the accommodation and understanding. Is there anything we can do for the injured?"

"It's taken care of. Ironically, some of your supplies were used to treat the injuries. I would like to know what your long-range plans are. Eventually we'll get the all clear to reenter the city but that might take as long as three weeks."

"We don't really have three weeks," said Diane. "That's too much time on the island for them to find us. What we need is a source of transportation, some type of boat or ferry, or even a private pilot that can get us back to the states. The sooner the better. You wouldn't know of someone like—"

"I do, but it's unlikely they'd be in one of the smaller camps. They might be relocated at one of the major aid stations up the highway. I'll send a messenger to make the contacts."

"It would have to be a subtle inquiry. We don't want to raise the antennae of the terrorists."

"Understood. I'll do what I can. In the meantime, relax. You're safe for now." He paused. "If you decide to make any more daring trips into the city, you'll want to find a street named Republicano Nuevo. It's on the extreme west side. It has a variety of smaller shops that aren't so close to the main district. Easier in and out."

"I'll remember it."

That night when she sneaked out with Ollie and Bibi, she remembered the name of the street and found it easily. She found the west side. Most of the shop front windows and doors were missing. She had no trouble entering six specialty shops that carried everything from textiles to hammers and nails. She made it back safely with three loads. Once again, they arrayed the stolen booty on a large blanket at the front of her tent.

The next morning, she awoke to the exited voices of the refugees. She went out to meet them, reveling in their delight. Ollie and Bibi handed out sewing kits and boxes filled with colorful spools of thread, to the adult women. Diane took special delight when she told Bibi to retrieve a special sack from the tent that was filled with small toys, which she handed out to the smallest onlookers.

Russell appeared a moment later, a look of astonishment on his face. Shaking his head, he said, "I don't know how you do it, but we're liable to end up being the most prosperous refugee camp on the island. You seem to have taken my advice."

"Oh, I did. Your tip was right on the money, or product, more precisely. I even hit a hardware store, although I don't know what I'm going to do with the tools."

"We'll find something to do with them, I'm sure. The toys are a nice touch. They bring hope to the little ones."

A small girl with nappy hair stood before Diane with her hand tentatively stretched out. Her eyes were the size of silver dollars. Diane let a little mermaid doll fall gently into her palm. A tiny fist clenched over it, and in the next moment the small waif ran off squealing, holding the prize high in the air. The next recipient was a boy, hobbled by a crooked spine. Diane found him a small tin fire truck, which he excitedly grabbed, then fell to the ground, running the wheels of the toy into the dirt. By the time she had emptied the toy sack, she'd heard the words *Gracias, Señora* more times than she could count. Surprisingly, a few thanked her in perfect English.

Bibi handed out perfume, soaps, and small washrags to the adult females, who stood in an orderly line. "Now that's for you so you can smell just right for the man of your dreams," she told one of the women. "And this one will pimp you up and make you irresistible," she told another. "Don't forget to scrub behind those ears and down there in those nether regions, girl." Bibi looked at Diane. "You should put razors on the menu. Some of these women have legs like a Bigfoot."

"That's normal for them," said Diane. "It's the same way with some European women."

"Yah? Well, it's a hot bed for fleas and lice, if you ask me."

Diane chuckled. "No one's asking you, Bibi. Carry on."

Ollie sat Indian style, with dozens of tobacco sacks and rolling papers on his lap. The adult males stood in a crooked line, several of them licking their lips in anticipation. Ollie soon went through the line of adult males, handing out the items, but he held some supplies in reserve.

"This is extra stash," Ollie told them. "Otherwise, you'd smoke it all up in a couple of days. And remember, no gambling or fighting over weed. We'll have another cigarette day if you all behave yourselves." He caught himself clumsily and then translated the Spanish version. The men nodded, backing away. Matches snapped. Soon the encampment sat under a thick pall of blue-white tobacco smoke. A few of the smokers bent over and coughed hoarsely, having taken in too much on their first pulls.

Diane tossed Russell a small, wrapped package, which he deftly caught. When he opened it, his eyebrows shot up. "Aldabo Crema Cognac. I won't even ask."

"Purely for medicinal purposes, of course," said Diane.

"Oh, entirely. I wouldn't think of actually drinking it." He looked away for a moment. "I'll send someone to make that inquiry for you. It shouldn't take more than a day or so to get some news. Are you going out again tonight?"

"Yeah, it's a great spot. No traffic, just like you said."

Diane caught his very subtle wink before he walked off. She didn't care what he used the cognac for, but she believed that he'd earned the right to tip a few back, considering the responsibility he'd shouldered in trying to run a camp that would otherwise be in turmoil without him. The other matter did matter; that he could find someone willing to provide them safe transport off the island.

Diane felt a tap on her shoulder. A small boy held out a fistful of green stalks, a small flower peeking up from it. She accepted the offer and smoothed his cheek. A few more children honored her with gifts, including a frog, for which she gave thanks for but turned it loose.

A few minutes later, the trio was served breakfast where they sat. The newcomers partook of the poor man's stew. A few adults hovered over them, giving the impression that all they had to do was ask for anything and it would be granted.

Ollie slurped loudly, showing his approval. "I could really

get used to this in a third-rate vacation sort of way. Primitive, but refreshing."

Bibi snorted. "Say that again? You're telling us you don't miss your instant messaging, Google fu, and CGI movies? No way. You're headed for some serious withdrawals if this goes on any longer."

Ollie pointed a piece of bread at Bibi. "You are totally ignorant of my machismo side."

"I didn't know you had one."

"I've seen just as many John Wayne movies as anyone, and I've always had an irresistible urge to buy motocross tickets. The Boy Scouts had the most influence on me. They taught me how to make a fire with a twig and a piece of string, and how if I didn't drink too much of my own pee I wouldn't die of thirst. I graduated star-eagle with about ninety merit badges, or something."

Bibi blinked. "Color me white and about to flop in a dead faint at your feet."

"You say that now."

Diane knew that all was well when best friends exchanged barbs. It would make everything so much simpler. Ollie had been right in one respect, that in another place and time this existence could have been a refreshing reprieve, an escape from all the foibles and responsibility of metropolitan life. Anyone could get used to it and even enjoy the inconvenience of living with nature in the raw. It would have to be amongst the right company, though. The refugees were a gentle, accommodating sort. They had no great expectations other than the most basic amenities—to eat, sleep, work in peace and raise their children. It was no surprise how Russell had warmed to them, acting the part of the mother hen with his brood of chicks. Had she been a doctor and living in a city with people embedded in squalor, she might have devoted her energies to the people who needed help just like Russell had done.

Bibi threw a pebble at Diane. "Hey, you! You look like you're about ready to bust a vein in your head. What's on your mind?"

"I was just thinking about things—really nothing."

"You should be thinking about how we're going to protect ourselves if those bangers come rolling in here again to bust our balls."

Diane prepared to tell her just how hopeless their chances were in dealing with an armed force when an idea struck her. Her comic book heroine, Endura, although she had great physical strength and stamina, always had to rely on various props to use as weapons against her foes. The Amazonian was forever devising traps, explosive devices and projectiles to fend off the bad guys. Never armed with nothing more than hand weapons, Endura always made use of common items found in her environment. She could spit nuts and bolts with bullet-like velocity and accuracy. Once, she had torn apart a wrought iron fence to fashion spears. She could hurl a bowling ball with enough force to knock down a wall. Even after being cornered in a junkyard, she had thrown tires like Frisbees at her enemies.

Diane rose to her feet. "I just had an epiphany."

"Maybe some of that medicine you brought back will take care of it," said Bibi.

"No, I mean I have an *idea*. What would Endura do in a case like this? How does she deal with villains?"

"She uses her brains," said Ollie. "She's innovative. But how is that going to help? Oh, I get it. You've got the suit, so you make that work to your advantage."

"Exactly." Diane felt pumped. "I'm not defenseless. I've only used the suit to run away. I've never taken advantage of its full potential."

Bibi wobbled to her feet, spilling her soup bowl from her lap. "Grab your tits and get hold of your wits, woman. Running away is the only thing that suit is good for. You don't have any firepower. If you go head-on with them, they'll just burn you down."

Diane wasn't listening, but on her way to find Russell. After searching the encampment, she was directed to the latrine where she found him straddling a ditch.

She spoke to his back while he relieved himself. "I need to talk to you about a strategy I have."

"I'm a little busy at the moment," he said, the side of his face flushed.

"That's okay, go ahead. I need to know how loyal your community is—if they can keep a secret. That means no communication, not even a whisper to another refugee camp. It has to be a total blackout, even if we have to cut ourselves off from the outside completely. No trade, no visiting, no gossip, and no second- or third-party messages to friends or relatives. Can that be done?"

Russell wiggled once then zipped up. He turned around. "I suppose it could be. It's rather extreme since there's always contact going on back and forth. You're talking about complete isolation. For how long and why?"

"For as long as I am here."

"Are you expecting company again?"

"I just need to be ready if it happens. I won't allow them to harm these people. I'm ready to make a stand."

He walked slowly back toward the camp, shoulder to shoulder with her. "No one really blames you for what happened," he said. "It was a tense moment. Tempers flared, emotions boiled over. I think the best thing for you to do is to stay low for now. At least until my runner comes back with the news that we've found you transportation."

They stood over his blanket a moment later. She sat down with him, glanced at his belongings. His possessions were sparse: a small backpack, a medical bag and a dozen paperback books sat next to a rolled-up comforter. She vowed that the next item on her hit list would be half a dozen tents. Rain was inevitable in this latitude. A sudden squall was a major possibility.

"Now what's this about a community pledge or secrecy?" he asked.

"I need to practice some defensive moves in the suit. That means wearing it out in the open, but within the confines of the camp. Naturally, I'm going to be seen, so I need some assurance that I won't be ratted out."

"I know each of these people personally and can account for their integrity. Although we have a few thieves, adulterers, and alcoholics in the population, I don't think it will be too much of a problem. I'm wondering why you're choosing to reveal yourself now. I was hoping to have you out of here once word gets back."

"That might take days, which could lead to another visit between now and then. I won't have the time to prepare once I'm on the road trying to escape."

"Well, I can probably guarantee you a 'see, hear, and speak no evil', as long as you don't carry things to extremes. I'll have to post sentries on the compass points to watch for strangers, just to keep them out of the area. Mind you, you can't keep something up like this indefinitely. I would advise you to do whatever you need to do quickly."

"That's all I'm asking. You don't think I'll frighten them, do you?"

"Well, you didn't frighten me that night. Of course, I wasn't quite sure what I was seeing. If anything, you'll draw their curiosity."

"Then we have a deal?"

"I suppose so. I'll explain it to them the best I can. I can propose some kind of an oath for them to obey."

Diane proffered a hand, which he shook. She joined Bibi and Ollie, telling them of her plans and Russell's participation. Bibi looked doubtful. Ollie appeared galvanized, ready for action.

"So now we scavenger hunt," said Diane. "Anything that can be used as a weapon— something that can be thrown with lethal results."

They began to pick at the items on the spread, but it was the hardware items that drew the most attention. Diane set aside eight small packs of nails, along with a box of nuts and bolts. Three medium sized hammers went in the pile. Then she saw something that caught her eye—two six-pack boxes of circular saw blades. She put them with the other items.

"You do know that these dudes will bust a cap in your head if they have the chance," said Bibi. "I say fight fire with fire. Next trip down, sneak up on one of those bastards and knock him out. Take his gun."

"Three problems with that," said Diane. "I'm not a killer, Bibi. You know that. It doesn't mean I'm against putting a bad hurt on them. Secondly, I don't know how well I can manage to shoot a rifle when I'm in the gear. I have the added finger controller that would get in the way. Even Chet said that it would take some training to perfect it under normal circumstances. Thirdly, you're talking about bringing the heat down on us. Those guards know about the camps up here, so they would assume it was a refugee who rolled one of them for his gun."

"I still wouldn't mind having a piece to even the odds," said Bibi.

"I don't want you involved in any fight," Diane stressed. "You and Ollie clear out of here at the first sign of trouble."

"Damned if I will!" said Bibi, then grabbed a bottle of

rubbing alcohol. She got up and pumped thick legs across the clearing.

Diane called out, "Where are you going?"

"To the creek, where I can clean up these sores on my legs!"

Ollie picked up a leather drawstring pouch. "Don't worry about her. She's just steamed because she feels helpless." He shook the pouch. "This would make a good bucket for a sling. You could use nails, nuts and bolts for ammo."

"That sounds fine."

Diane worried about her friend. Bibi seldom displayed any real signs of a temper or frustration. She always laughed off the stress or used her trademark sarcasm. She'd seldom raised her voice in anger, especially to Diane. But when Bibi set her mind to something it was impossible to derail her or stop her from acting out her wishes. This was one of those times.

12

Russell called the group together during the mid-day lunch. After the last morsel had been eaten and the children had quieted down, he addressed the listeners with a speech. Ollie translated for Diane. The words were both compelling and profound. Especially the part about their duty to protect one of their own. Russell detailed the importance of loyalty to the group, along with the need for every man, woman, and child to keep secrets locked away in their hearts. No one was to breathe a word about Diane and her friends. Whatever they saw in the camp would stay there. In conclusion, he had them place hands over their hearts to declare loyalty and servitude to those in their care. Anyone found in violation would be ordered to leave the group. All of them agreed with the conditions. Russell thanked them for their collective pledge. The group dispersed and went about their chores, leaving Diane and Ollie standing in the clearing.

"Do you think that qualifies for a sip of cognac?" asked Russell.

Diane smiled. "I think it more that qualifies. Indulge away."

"Of course, I had to remind them that although you are

not Cuban patriots, those men who terrorized us were even less so. I know they understand the difference. You do what you need to do."

Diane didn't waste any time hurrying to her tent and pulling out the suit pieces. They had already collected their prototype weapons, so it was only a matter of testing her theories. Ollie snapped her into the components, fumbling with the more difficult assembly procedures.

"Where's Bibi when we need her?" asked Ollie. "She hasn't been around since breakfast. She's not the type to miss a meal."

"Still licking her wounds, I guess. She's probably still at the creek. You can always fetch her back here. That's if you're having trouble with the suit."

"I don't need Bibi to know how this goes together. It's nothing more than a big erector set."

It took twenty minutes, but Ollie had her finally suited up and ready for her debut. She pulled the helmet over her head, snapping it into place and then stepped out through the tent flap into the midday sun. Ollie picked up a basket and followed her in a slow walk across the clearing. The non-reaction came as a surprise. Most of the people just glanced in her direction, showing little emotion before looking away. No lingering stares or sharp intakes of breath. The children offered longer gazes but dutifully turned away from the sight of her.

"See no evil," said Ollie.

"Apparently."

They found a large, stunted pine tree on the fringe of the camp. It had a thick trunk base, ideally suited for a backstop. Ollie tacked a paper target to the tree, then loaded the homemade sling with some pebbles he had gathered. The pebbles would serve as the projectiles since they had no desire to lose the real ammo to practice throws. The other items were retrievable.

Ollie handed the loaded sling to her. "Try an underhand rotation. Remember that most of the momentum comes from the elbow and wrist. The release is all in the timing of the swing. Just get good rotations going for a few minutes. You want to feel the inertia."

"Maybe you should be doing this."

"I've got the physics for it, not the physical."

She wound the sling around in a gentle arc, feeling the centrifugal force. Then she picked up the speed, holding the rhythm for a minute.

"You're going to release just after the downward pass."

She waited then let fly. The pebbles struck the dirt.

"Too soon. Try again."

She did. The next batch flew high into the branches. Another try but this time Ollie called out the release point. She sent the load directly into the tree, the pebbles hitting with a cracking echo. Remembering exactly what she had done, she fired off another load that hit the tree low. Ollie said it was still a good hit because it would have struck the legs of an opponent, not unlike a shotgun pattern. Pleased with herself, she continued firing one load after another, hitting the target four out of five times in what Ollie called the "kill zone." Practice resumed until they ran out of pebbles.

Diane tried the hammers next. Ollie positioned her twenty feet away from the tree. He showed her the proper throwing posture. She cocked her arm and threw. The hammer missed the tree completely. She tried again, this time using the crosshairs inside the helmet to reference the aiming point. The hammer struck the tree a glancing blow. The next found its mark dead center. Ollie retrieved the hammers, allowing another salvo.

She spent an hour on the hammer throw. By the time she finished the session, the paper silhouette was shredded. The tree trunk ended up riddled with deep, splintered gouges. They took a break.

"Not bad," said Ollie. "I figure that twenty feet from the target is a normal combat distance."

"The hardest part is getting the finger pressure right through the gloves. The mechanical fingers are hard to position, too."

"It's a sensitivity thing. Adjust for it the best you can."

"I'm just wondering how I'll hold up against direct gunfire. I mean if it comes to that. I took some hits when I escaped, which nearly knocked me for a loop."

"Worst case scenario—they knock you down—you get back up. The rounds won't penetrate the armor; you already know that. You have to keep your cool. Concentrate on what you have to do. No panic. I know that's easier said than done, but it's all in the head—psychological. Convince yourself that you *are* indestructible."

She looked at the haggled marks on the tree. "I wonder if that kills."

"Don't even think about it. Put 'em down. With what I've seen so far, you hit them with any of this and that's exactly where they're going—down and out."

They resumed practice. Ollie suggested she next try the iron tent pegs he had gathered. They had a lighter feel than the hammers. She began to find their accurate mark after tossing them rapidly overhand in succession. She went through several volleys until achieving a tight grouping. The next experiment involved circular saw blades. At over seven inches in diameter, Diane tested their weight on her hand. Experimentation with the finger positioning was needed. Her first attempts were disappointing, the slick metal slipping from her grasp, sending the blades way off the mark. She tried the sidearm whip, but it resulted in the blades flying offline deep into the forest, where Ollie had trouble retrieving them.

"Use the overhead pitch," Ollie suggested. "That way you only have to worry about elevation."

She tried his method and started hitting the tree. The blades whistled through the air, striking the wood with such force they stuck fast. Ollie had to dig a few out with a knife blade. When she threw her second batch of twelve blades, eight of them hit their target within a one-foot radius. Her next batch produced even better results, with 10 blades embedded in the tree.

Ollie slapped his thighs in jubilation. "That's it! You've got it going on with the blades." He walked to the tree and began removing them. "Here's another thing I noticed," he said over his shoulder. "There's no lag or hang time with the blades—much more velocity than the other stuff. If you're on the receiving end of one of these babies, you can't see it coming at you edge on. It's possible to step out of the way of a thrown hammer. But these, you'd have to be hawk-eyed to dodge them."

"Then that's what we want."

"You betcha."

She practiced throwing the saw blades for another two hours, perfecting the maneuver until she was hitting the target with 100 percent accuracy. She tried throwing from seated and keeling positions, perfecting the maneuver. Ollie begged off, complaining of exhaustion from extricating the blades from the tree.

"We'll try another session before evening," said Ollie. "I really think you're in the zone. I'll see if I can't make some kind of an ammo belt and pouches to hold the inventory."

"Why not? Batman has his utility belt. Come to think of it, so does Endura."

"Endura's belt isn't such a bad model to follow."

Ollie packed the projectiles into the hand basket. They walked slowly back to camp. Once again, upon their approach, the refugees averted their eyes. Mothers pulled their children in around their legs, placing their hands over their faces. It gave Diane the uncomfortable feeling that the community felt shame or outright fear upon the sight of her. It was not the feeling she wanted to instill in the people who had become friends.

"Ollie, tell them not to be afraid or ashamed. It's okay to look. There's no punishment."

Ollie translated the message to the small crowd. He repeated the words slowly a second time. Still no reaction. From the other end of the camp, Russell looked up from attending to one of his patients and said, "To avoid the issue is their way of dealing with it. Out of sight—out of mind."

Diane removed the helmet. "It's a bit extreme. I would appreciate it if they would relax a bit. They might listen to you."

Russell clapped his hands for attention and addressed the crowd. He used only a few words and then went back to work. The crowd turned their heads toward Diane, smiles showing on their faces. Some of the children jumped about, expressing joy.

"What did he say, Ollie?" Diane asked.

"He said, 'Superman is a friend' and not to be afraid of him."

"Oh, that'll do it every time—just mention Endura's competition."

They arrived at their tent. Diane thought it strange that Bibi hadn't returned from the creek or come looking for her. She told Ollie to check the creek area just to make sure Bibi hadn't decided to take a nap there.

Diane headed off to check the rest of the encampment.

She picked up some small admirers on the way, who reached out to touch the suit. She had a dreadful thought when she reached the latrine. Bibi might have fallen in the narrow ditch and become wedged. She could see that no such thing had happened when she arrived there. When she turned around, three children almost bumped into her.

"Have you seen the big lady, Bibi?" she asked the kids, holding her hands out in front of her, simulating a large belly.

The children laughed. One of them said, "Santee Cross!"

"No, no. Uh, el Negro grande?"

They shook their heads.

"You guys are no help."

Diane retraced her steps back to camp. She saw Ollie weaving his way through the trees. The expression on his face did not relay good news. Before he got to her, he shook his head in the negative.

No reason to press him about a thorough search of the creek. She's not there.

He looked winded, obvious signs that he'd covered ground.

"Do you think something has happened?" she asked.

"There's no reason to worry about it. I'm going to hunt down something I can use for an ammo belt. Unless you want me to help you out of the suit."

It was not good news. Ollie should have told her he was worried sick about Bibi and that they should continue the search for her. After all, no friends should go missing without other friends trying to find them. Diane relented, though, not wanting to raise a panic when there might be a simple explanation for Bibi's absence.

"Okay, you go ahead. I'll stay in the suit and hang out around the tent."

Diane turned away, fearful she would lose her temper

with the little man. His nonchalant attitude irritated her. She marched to the tent and threw the flap back. She pitched her helmet through the opening. She heard a distinct smack.

"Damn it to hell!" Bibi's voice wailed.

Diane peeked inside. Bibi sat on the tent floor, rubbing her forehead. "Where the hell have you been?" Pause. "Sorry about the helmet."

"You don't need to throw down on me. I just felt like walking around. I've had a lot on my mind lately."

"Bibi, you know what we're up against. For all I knew you could have been snatched up, or worse."

"Maybe we should be looking a lot closer to home for trouble."

"What do you mean by that?"

Bibi glared at her. "I don't trust them. None of them. I don't feel safe here."

Here we go again. "Don't start, Bibi. These are the first people who've shown us any trust at all. We're fine if we lay low with them. Russell's going to get us out of here."

"You're so damn sure about that."

"Your paranoia is working overtime again, Bibi."

"Like it did with Chet Strauss—that kind of overtime?"

"I don't even want to talk about this right now. You hear me? Enough is enough. We don't have any options except to rely on this community. Otherwise, we'd be out there right now—big fat targets for you know who." Diane stared her down, showing she was not about to budge on her point.

Bibi picked at a fingernail. "So, it looks like you've been practicing in the suit. How'd it go?"

"Thank you. It went great." She told her about the session they had out in the woods. Bibi seemed mildly intrigued. It puzzled Diane that her friend appeared distant or changed somehow. She wondered if an apology might be in order, but before she could offer one, Bibi stood up and left the tent. That left Diane stuck in the suit.

"Oh, the hell with it." She flopped on the comforter. She stared up at the ceiling of the tent before her eyes grew heavy. She removed the finger control and shut the power pack off. Some time passed before her thoughts gave way, allowing a sleepy shroud to overwhelm her.

She awoke when someone wiggled her arm. Her eyes adjusted slowly to the dim light of evening.

"Sorry to bother you," said Ollie. "You were sleeping so soundly. I brought you some supper. Or I can take it back if you don't feel like it right now."

"No, that's fine." She slipped her control finger on, then activated the suit power. She sat upright, accepting the small food platter filled with corncob quarters and rice. She ate half the meal before spotting the leather utility belt at her side. The belt had small wire baskets, loops and pouches attached to the main waist strap. Ollie had outdone himself in the craftsmanship department.

"That's totally clever, Ollie. It looks like it will hold everything."

"I loaded it up. It's a bit heavy but that shouldn't be a problem. The blades slide right into the wire baskets for easy access."

Diane finished the meal and exited the tent, nearly stepping over some children who had been loitering nearby. She greeted them affectionately, accepting a gift from one that was an action figure of Batman. One small boy rapped his knuckles on her armored shin and then backed away. It was fine as long as the attention didn't degenerate into perverse worship.

Ollie followed, carrying the empty supper platters. "Another trip into the city tonight?"

"Yeah, I was thinking about it. Even if we're out of here

sooner than expected, they could use the supplies. Where's our black goddess?"

"She took off right after supper. She's beginning to worry me."

"I was hoping you'd say something like that. We won't need her tonight. She can have a break—work out her issues. She's probably mad at me."

"You're not going this early, are you?"

"Don't see why not—it's dark."

Ollie disappeared inside the tent and reappeared a moment later. He had the fully loaded weapons belt stretched between his hands. He encircled it around her waist, pulled it tight, tying it off with a wire. "There. You're loaded for bear."

Diane felt the bulk of it. "I hope this doesn't get in my way."

"It's the other dangerous things that might get in your way that I'm afraid of. It stays." He ducked in the tent again to retrieve her helmet.

Diane picked up two large canvas potato sacks at the side of the tent. They walked across the clearing together. Russell stood near his sleeping area. He gave her the thumbs up gesture. She nodded but offered no words. A few refugees followed some distance behind, but Ollie spoke a few Spanish words to shoo them off.

When they reached the windbreak trees, Diane donned her helmet and adjusted the view for night vision. She checked the other functions, finding them operative. She turned to Ollie. "Just stay put like last time. I shouldn't be more than an hour or so."

"Consider me tucked away."

She headed down the slope, this time taking a wide sweeping arc to come in from a different direction. She crossed the breadth of the large field. A broken fence line offered cover to trek the rest of the distance down to the fringe of the city. Reaching a dirt road on the edge of the market district, she adjusted the visor magnifier. Her breath caught in her throat. Dozens of human figures filled the night vision mode. The infrared picked them up as well. They were scattered in and around the backsides of the shops, some of them partially obscured. Others were in full view. Their positions suggested that it was not some random dispersal. She approached as close as she dared and watched them for a full fifteen minutes. None of the personnel moved from their positions. They were fixed—stationed.

It could have been an unlucky coincidence. Then again, it might have been a deliberate stakeout. She could have walked right into it. There was no traffic at all in that zone the previous night. Russell had indicated the street as being the safest entrance point.

When she panned away from the shops, she picked up hot spots in the infrared, including half a dozen large vehicles that gave off thermal signals. Clearly, a much larger security force had been deployed in the city—three times larger than anything before.

She made a cautious but hurried trek back up to the ridge line. Upon reaching the windbreak trees, she found Ollie hunkered down behind a mangled shrub, his eyes wide.

"It's no good," she said. "The place is swarming with guards and soldiers—more than I've ever seen." She helped him to his feet. "What wrong with you?"

Ollie shivered. "I dunno. I heard the wind shrieking through the trees. It sounded like high-pitched voices. I freaked. Glad you're back. Maybe next time."

"There might not be a next time."

Diane led the way back to camp. Ollie kept a grip on the back of her belt, following in her steps. Aside from their footfalls, the only noise that penetrated the night air came from a few crickets and some wind hissing through the tops of the trees. An odor from the slight breeze arose from the latrine, evidence that they were close to camp. Yet as they approached, they could not hear any voices or see any activity in the clearing, not even a dog. The refracted light of oil lamps and candles were also missing. She dialed up the helmet magnification in infrared and performed a complete scan of the area. She froze.

"Now what's wrong?" Ollie whispered.

"You stay here. Something's not right—the camp's vacant."

She stepped through the last of the tree cover to enter the clearing. No children. No adults. Empty blankets. Deserted tents. The only thing that stood out was a heat signature on the cooking coals and a vehicle parked on the other side of the clearing near the narrow entrance road. A proper make on the car was not recognizable, since it faced her head-on. Incipient panic filled her thoughts—an intense gut feeling that she had just walked into a trap. Before she could turn around and run from the scene, several beams of white light stabbed her, pinning her to the spot. *Flashlights*. Several human heat signatures stepped out from behind the largest trees on the camp perimeter.

A male voice spoke with a broken Russian accent. "You should be pleased to bring the suit off at this time and step away. You will not make the resistance."

She counted three-armed men—one dead ahead, two at her sides. They were all farther than twenty feet away. She stepped toward the spokesman, to close the distance. "And what if I don't?" she asked. "What are you going to do about it?" Her hand slid to her belt.

"Then it will not go pleasant. Surrender now and the pain will not come."

"You'll just have to give me a moment to take it off."

With a stark move, she pulled and flung a blade, hitting

the one facing her in the groin. He yelped and doubled over, dropping his weapon. She took three steps and ducked down in a fast crunch, placing herself directly between the other two, who now had her lined up in crossfire. The armed men hesitated just long enough to allow her to reach for a hammer and cock her arm. The hammer flew as the shots rang out, striking one of them in the shoulder, disabling him. She sensed several bullets impacts on her legs. The other gunmen ran sideways and let out a fully automatic burst, raking her across the breast plates. She nearly went down but turned around to face the man squarely. Big mistake. The explosions from the rifle barrel threw out huge bursts of light, obscuring her target. The bullets hit her square in the chest, throwing her off balance. She kicked the finger control and ran in the direction of the vehicle. Bullets twanged off her back; one hit the top of her helmet, snapping her head sideways.

Diane almost ran into the SUV, catching her leg on the fender. She put the mass of metal between her and the armed man, who now advanced on her and took precise aim. The front windshield splintered with a round, then the side window blew out. The metal doorpost was hit next, splaying it open like a flower. She realized the gunman was firing straight through the vehicle in the hopes of hitting her. She lobbed a hammer over the roof, but it went wild. He continued to walk toward the rear of the SUV, while pulling the trigger rapidly. She wondered if he would ever run out of bullets. There came a lull when she heard the metallic sounds of a clip being exchanged. She had to move now!

Cornering the vehicle, she ran straight for the gunman. The man slapped a fresh clip in the breech then jacked the slide. She reached him just as he raised the weapon to waist level. She hit him with a shoulder block. He spun once then collapsed on the ground. She turned and kicked him in the face, nearly taking his head off. Lights out.

It wasn't over.

The man, who had been hit with the hammer, rose to his feet and sighted his weapon on her. She pulled the blades from her belt and flung them hard, one after another. She saw bright flashes, momentarily blinding her. She braced herself against the impacts, fearful she would go down at any moment. The gunfire abated. She heard a plaintiff moan. She saw the man drop to the dirt and lay still. Checking her pouch, she found she had five blades left.

She heard a plea for help. It came from the man she had hit in the groin. He lay on the ground curled up in a fetal position. She walked up to him and kicked the rifle away from his reach.

"Where are the refugees?" she demanded. "What have you done with the people?"

"I don't know what you say," he gasped.

She took her helmet off and spoke in a clear, demanding voice. "Where are the hostages? What have you done with them?"

A twig snapped. Diane swung around, looking into the trees. Ollie appeared, crouching low and moving across the clearing. He had a rock in his hand. "Did you get them all?" he asked.

"I think so," she said. The prone man got a kick in the ribs. "Where are the rest of them?"

Diane heard Ollie drop the rock then mutter, "Oh, no. We're screwed."

She swiveled her head. Thirty feet away, a fourth gunman approached them. He had his rifle pointed at Diane's face. She could do nothing but stand there awaiting the inevitable head shot. *That's what I get for taking the helmet off!*

"I have the drop on you, as they say," said the gunman. "Step away from my comrade. I do not wish to splash him with your blood."

Diane saw movement from the corner of her eye, a dark phantom shape in the trees.

Ollie said, "Oh, my God."

The mysterious figure burst forth from cover. Then all hell broke loose.

13

Diane fell on her face and hugged the dirt. Ollie dove to the ground a millisecond after, using the injured man as a shield. The terrorist gunman wheeled around, his face contorted in surprise. The flash of bright gunshots erupted from the tree line. The gunman had no time to react to the surprise attack, taking multiple hits in the torso. His hands flailed like a string-yanked marionette before he fell in a heap.

Diane chanced a look. It came as a total shock to see Bibi standing there. The large woman stepped across the clearing and stood over the lifeless form. "Eat that, bitch!" she said, then pointed a semiautomatic pistol at the other prone man. She pulled the trigger several times, but it clicked on an empty chamber. "Son-of-a-bitch!" Bibi walked to each man and yanked their handheld radios from their belts. She brought down a heavy foot on each, cracking them to pieces.

Diane got to her feet and stared at the large woman, whose clothes were soaked from head to foot. The desire to say something was overpowering but the words would not come. It was just as well; Bibi did all the talking.

"Four of 'em came busting out of the SUV and caught the camp by surprise. Three of them stayed behind to ambush you. The other...*that* one..." She pointed to the bullet-riddled body. "Ran us up to the creek and held us there so he could keep watch on us. I slipped into the water and went upstream. Then I came out and wove through the woods to get back here. I knew something was going down, so I figured I'd try to stop it."

Diane found her tongue. "Where'd you get that gun?"

"I'll tell you later. Right now, I'm going back to the creek to fetch Russell. He's got some explaining to do." Bibi picked up one of the rifles. She trudged off into the darkness.

Ollie picked up one of the rifles and headed toward the SUV. "I'm going to give us some light then check on these other guys," he said, his hands visibly shaking.

Diane waited for the headlights of the SUV to illuminate the clearing. When they clicked on, she knelt down and studied the man who had the groin wound. Seeing that he wasn't bleeding profusely, she said, "You'll live. Unfortunately." She checked him for extra weapons and found only a hunting knife, which she slipped in her belt. "Where are the rest of your terrorist friends?"

"We were the first to arrive," the man gasped. "The others...on their way."

She waited for five minutes before Bibi and the group showed up, threading their way through the trees. Mothers clutched traumatized children to their bosoms. The adult males held their heads down, not for fear of stumbling in the dark, but from the shame of their inability to protect their families. The last person to enter the clearing was Russell, who had Bibi's rifle planted at the back of his head. Nearly all the refugees went to their tents and sleeping mats. No one cried out in anger or surprise. The only sounds came from the wounded men on the ground who pleaded for medical attention.

Bibi prodded Russell in Diane's direction, until she had

him stopped nearly in her face. Bibi nudged him hard with the rifle barrel. "You want to tell girlfriend about the conversation you had with your buds?"

Russell hung his head, eyes averted.

"I didn't think so," said Bibi, raising her voice. "The minute these thugs rushed into camp, they asked about you. Dude said that if you didn't show up, then it happened down there. Then he said that if anything went wrong on that end, they could put the pinch on you when you arrived back at camp. He didn't think I heard any of it."

"Let me guess," said Diane. "That messenger you sent was told to look for the terrorists, and if he found them, he was to make a deal in exchange for my whereabouts, then lead them back here. Those weren't all guards down in the city. Now everyone is looking for us. Which means—"

"Which means we have to get out of here right now," said Bibi. "You grab supplies. I'll herd these assholes together."

Ollie had heard the conversation. "Let's take the SUV. They don't need it now." He jumped on a third handheld radio, smashing it into splinters.

Diane resisted the urge to slam a fist into Russell's face, which would take precious seconds. Instead, she shoved him hard, and he landed on his ass. She hurried to the tent, gathered up their personal items and brought them back to the clearing. She yelled at Ollie to find the keys to the SUV and then hurried to the small supply area near Russell's mat. She packed as many supplies as she could stuff in a sack and took the load to the SUV. She brushed the glass off the seats and checked the interior of the vehicle. She found the rear compartment loaded with ammo boxes and a few sacks that contained groceries and bottled water.

Ollie arrived at her side, breathing hard. He tossed the rifles onto the rear seat floorboard. "None of these Bozos have the keys."

She looked at the console. "Forget it. They're in the ignition." She yelled out, "Bibi, hurry up! Pick up my helmet on the way."

Ollie jumped behind the driver's seat, starting the engine. It took Diane two tries to get into the passenger seat, getting her legs unstuck. Ollie toggled the electric seats back, allowing her clearance. He pulled the vehicle around facing the dirt road. He snapped the dome light on. "Okay, at least we have a dash compass. Uh, West? Yeah, we'll go west."

"What's out west?"

"I have no idea."

"What's taking her so long?" Diane demanded.

Ollie looked in the rearview mirror. "It's hard to say, but it looks like she's tying them up."

"Lay on the horn."

Ollie did so. "There, she's on her way."

Bibi arrived at the vehicle and jumped in the back seat, slamming the door. "Hit it!" She passed Diane's helmet over the backrest. "I wasn't about to let those bastards get to their feet and run around. One of them isn't ever going to get to his feet again."

"Thanks for saving our lives," said Diane. "I knew something was up when I got close to the city. An ambush was waiting for me."

Ollie spun the tires, making a left on the small dirt road. The vehicle hit several ruts, swerving, but Ollie kept his foot on it and switched to high beams. Once he had it straightened out, he said, "I don't even know where the hell I'm going. All I can think of is the west end of the island because I remember the brochure didn't show much out there."

Diane found a map in the glove compartment and opened it up. The legends and names were in Spanish, but it contained a geographic rendering of the entire island. Most of the prominent landmarks and cities were featured. Tiny red lines represented unpaved roads, but they were hard to see with the vibration of the vehicle. She said, "I think the road we're on heads west toward a main highway. The highway ends in a peninsula called Punta Frances. We'll be boxed in."

"Boxed in means it's dangerous," said Ollie. "They won't expect us to go there."

Diane nodded. "Yeah, well it looks like some kind of a resort. Could be roadblocks or guards, and you know what that means."

Ollie yanked the wheel, throwing them into a skid. He recovered. "It's too late to retrace our path—they'll be coming up from the main highway. You know what? They're going to broil us alive. Wait till they find out what we did to those guys."

Bibi slapped the backrest, making Ollie jump. "Where the hell have you been, homeboy? They've been lookin' to tag us since day one. You think this is going to make any difference?"

"I'm just thinking about the guy that you nailed."

Diane thought about that, too. Bibi had killed a man. Though they had all been caught up in a moment of adrenalin rush, a life had been taken. When the shock wore off, Bibi would suffer an emotional crash. Diane was certain of it, from knowing the personality of the woman who had always used nothing more lethal than blunt sarcasm to inflict harm. On the other hand, if Bibi hadn't acted, they could have all been killed and buried in shallow graves. Bibi's suspicious nature was justified.

"It's a miracle you had that gun," said Diane, meaning it to be a question.

"Wasn't hard to get," said Bibi. "I put some rubbing alcohol in a bottle then went down into the city. Found a guard who looked bored, so I offered myself up. He got busy with the alcohol before he did with me. Dumb bastard's face turned purple before he knew what he was swilling. After he got sick and puked, he passed out. I just lifted the piece off him then came straight back up to camp. I had to practice firing the gun in the woods without using the ammo. I hid it in my waistband while I was in camp. Sorry, girl, you just pissed me off with all that passive shit. I had a bad feeling all along about that Russell guy. He just seemed too eager to help us, which got my hair up."

Diane turned in her seat. "Remind me to listen to you next time."

"Wasn't your fault. That's the way you are and everything. Besides, you were the first to warn us about trusting him. I'm the only one that has to pay for what I did. I'm never gonna make it off this island alive."

Diane raised her voice. "We're in this together. We'll make it off the island if we have to fight off the whole god-damned country."

Ollie drove the SUV over a rise and down into a forested grove. He slowed the vehicle, craning his neck to see through the broken windshield. An intersection lay dead ahead. "Looks like we've picked up that main highway. Do we take it to gain some distance, or do we go off road?"

"I say take the damn thing," said Bibi. "We need the distance right now."

"Go for it," Diane agreed. "If we're riding into hell we might as well get there fast."

Ollie turned onto the highway and hit the gas. They could see distant headlights, both ahead and behind them. Diane looked out of the shattered window, trying to focus on the scenery. Mounds of trash and broken limbs lay in piles along the shoulder. Advertising signs were either blown over, flattened, or snapped from their support posts. They passed by a panel van flipped on its side that had its side torn out. Ollie slowed down to pass a road crew, who were loading broken timber onto a flat bed. A flagman waved them around.

"No roadblocks or barriers so far," said Ollie. "It doesn't mean we won't hit one further on."

"That's the chance we have to take," said Diane. "We'd better switch out rides first chance we get. The one we're using is hot as a furnace—Cho and his goons will be looking for it."

They ran into a roadblock after another 20 minutes. Three-armed guards stood abreast, spanning the width of the highway. An impassable concrete barrier stood behind them. A hastily rendered sign, written in Spanish, stretched across a wooden frame.

Ollie said, "The sign says that Varadero and Punta Frances are closed to traffic by order of the government. We have to turn back."

"Just double-back a few hundred yards, so we can go around it," said Bibi.

"I'm on it."

Ollie pulled around, drove up the road a measured distance and then entered the forest. He switched to four-wheel drive, fighting the wheel to maneuver between the trees. They hit some culverts and ditches right away. Ollie swore under his breath, straining to see through the spider-cracked glass, fighting to stay on a level track. The SUV bucked so violently their heads hit the roof. Huge fallen limbs blocked the forward progress, prompting Ollie to skirt the obstructions and find alternate routes. It was the most jarring ride Diane had ever experienced. She feared that they would bog down permanently.

"I'm trying to stay on a western course," said Ollie. "Make sure you're buckled up!"

The headlights illuminated a rise in the landscape. Ollie downshifted to climb the grade, spinning the tires in muddy pine needles. When they topped the rise, the vehicle tipped forward and began an uncontrollable skid down the hill. A fender struck a tree and spun the SUV around. The driver's side wheels caught in a ditch. The vehicle hove up then flipped over.

"Hang on!" Diane yelled.

The car tumbled with a calamitous roar. For a moment, everything went out of focus. Side over side, the SUV gained momentum falling down the slope until it struck a tree, where it wedged in an upright position. Diane brushed the glass off her, trying to get a look around the cab. Ollie had disappeared inside an airbag. Diane's bag hadn't deployed, but her belt had held her firmly in place. Bibi fought with a seat belt restraint in the back seat that had wrapped around her neck. The large woman extricated herself amidst a string of curses.

Ollie punctured the airbag. "I can't believe that just happened."

"Damn you, Ollie." Bibi swore. "Can't you get down a hill without falling down it? The rifles missed me, but I know damn well an ammo box can hit me in the face."

"It was a matter of physics when we lost traction," said Ollie.

"I'd like to bust you over your head with your physics and put *you* in traction."

Diane slapped the dashboard. "Shut up, both of you. Listen to that sound."

Outside the faint sound of a shore break reached their ears, waves lapping over a sandy beach. The scent of moist, salty air filled the cab. A gull's cry carried on the breeze. They had reached the coast.

They exited the crashed vehicle and stepped through the brush, following the rhythmic sound of the waves. Bibi limped behind, carrying one of the loaded AK 47s at her hip. Passing over a bluff, their feet found the first hint of a sand dune. With the dim light of the moon overhead, Diane could just make out the berm line, the sudsy white foam of breakers. She could not see for any distance down the coast due to the darkness but imagined there had to be structures somewhere. Ollie confirmed that this part of the peninsula was occupied, due to its location.

"This is prime time real estate," he said. "If we follow the shoreline left, we're sure to run into habitations. I'm not sure about the other way."

"We'll check out the right side for now," said Diane. "We don't want the commercial district of a port city."

They began the trek. They didn't make it more than 500 feet before a dilapidated structure that spanned the entire breath of the beach, blocked their progress. Broken lumber, plaster and pieces of furniture sat in mountainous piles. The skeleton of a two-story building leaned at an odd angle behind the broken trash.

"What is this place?" asked Ollie.

Bibi replied, "You mean, what *was* this place."

Having not brought her helmet, and kicking herself for it, Diane said, "it looks like a small seaside hotel, complete with a pier and boat dock. Or what's left of one. All the boats look like they're beached. You can see the masts from here. This might be a good place to duck for cover. It looks abandoned."

They made it back to the vehicle and picked up the strewn supplies. Diane used her helmet to find most of the items that had been thrown clear of the vehicle. The women ferried the items down to the obstruction, then began to clear a path through the rubble. Ollie stayed behind to hide the vehicle under the brush.

Diane tossed lumber aside, while Bibi held a small flashlight she'd scrounged from the SUV. "I don't know what the sense is of laying up in this busted up place," said Bibi. "It's not going to get us off the island."

Diane threw a roof beam over the pile. "Your pessimism

isn't going to get us off this island. What do you suggest we do, drive to the airport and buy our tickets across the counter? In case you haven't noticed, we left three injured and one dead back there. To say their friends are going to be pissed is an understatement. We need to ditch ourselves in real good and then come up with a solid plan."

"Hop-scotching all over this island isn't a good plan. We need to get *off* it."

"That's why we're going to settle in here for now. It's part of the plan."

"Last time I checked, my ears worked fine. Lay your plan out."

"I'll know enough when the sun comes up. If it looks good for my idea, we'll try it."

Diane slung a huge plank board to the side and kicked some ceramic tiles out of the way. It opened up the last part of the clog. They picked up the load and carried it through. Diane and Bibi stumbled several times, picking their way through the flotsam. When they reached the front entrance doors of the shattered hotel, they had to pull a broken glass panel out of the door frame. They set their load down just outside the entrance.

Diane stepped into the lobby, which looked like it had been carpet-bombed. Furniture sat in broken heaps; papers and notebooks lay scattered in soggy clumps; torn drapes hung from snags caught up on splintered ceiling timbers. Their boots slogged through four inches of mud, evidence that a tidal surge had inundated the entire first floor. A broken spindle-rail staircase led up to the second floor, where the upper hallway showed sheets of wallpaper hanging from the walls like the shed skin of an animal.

Bibi panned the flashlight around. "Holy shove it up my butt and break it off. This place is trashed beyond belief. Looks like a tidal wave hit it."

Ollie appeared at the doorway, holding a BIC lighter, an ammo can and several blankets. "You were expecting a cushy five-star with all the amenities? We were lucky to find this place." He piled the blankets and the ammo can on the lobby counter and stepped around it, disappearing through a side door. A moment later, his voice rang out from a distant hallway. "I think I found the manager's room. It looks okay."

The women hauled their loads in and stacked them on the counter. They followed the path Ollie had taken. They ended up in a small hallway. They passed a large hotel kitchen and serving area then mounted two steps to an open door. When they entered, Diane looked around. It was a living room, remarkably intact. Three doors led off from the main room—a small kitchen, bedroom, and a bathroom. The place looked almost pristine. More importantly, Diane could not smell any gas resulting from a broken line.

They moved their belongings inside the room in less than twenty minutes. Ollie placed three lit candles in the living room. Ollie and Bibi sat on a sofa, watching the eerie candlelight flicker against the walls. A mute television set sat across from them, looking like a mocking one-eyed monster.

"Well, it beats camping out," said Ollie, "and whoever the owner-manager was, they had enough forethought to fill the bathtub with water. They must have read that in an emergency manual."

Diane gave a weary sigh. "I just hope all the occupants made it out. I think the whole second story roof is missing. That's what I was hacking through out there on the ground."

Ollie cracked his knuckles. "Why don't you let me get you out of that suit? You look like hell."

"Right now, Ollie, it would take a lot of energy to get more comfortable. I'm afraid I just don't have it. Leave it for tomorrow. Maybe you can figure out a way to help me go potty. 'Kay?" She collapsed on the damp sofa.

"That's a deal."

Diane looked at Bibi. The large woman sat slump-shouldered, staring at her lap. With painful slow motion, Bibi pulled the pistol from her waistband and looked at it for a long while. She pitched it across the room, where it clunked on the floor. Then she began to cry.

Diane, knowing the shock had finally worn off, clicked her power off and pulled Bibi into her arms. She spoke soothing words. "It's okay, honey. You were caught up in the moment. We would have done the same thing. You're a very good and loving person, and you've already been forgiven. Diane's here...it's okay now."

The two women fell asleep in each other's arms.

The early morning sun brought the true devastation of the hotel property into focus. Some of the largest boats lay on their sides, while the shallow draft vessels sat upright. A few had smashed against the stone breakwater ending up in slivers on the shore. Two small powerboats had flipped over and lay on the sand like beached whales. There were twenty-one boats in all; none of them were afloat in the surf or tied securely to what was left of the pier, which was a jumble of broken jackstraws waving in the lazy surf. Diane couldn't decide which boat looked to be the best candidate after puzzling over the configurations. She had no more knowledge of boats and seamanship than quantum mechanics.

"We need something we can pull back into the water," she said, trying to negotiate her way through the wreckage. "It should probably be a sailboat, since we don't know if the engines will work in the other ones. What about these with the big fin on the bottom?"

Ollie appeared from around a busted hull and looked at

the boat Diane studied. “I only know enough to tell you that those are fixed keel sailboats. You’ll never drag them into the water because those things are filled with thousands of pounds of lead or something. Our best bet is one of the smaller sailboats that have the other kind. I think they’re called centerboards or something. You can crank those up into the hull.”

Diane stepped over a pier piling. “How big does it have to be so it’s safe?”

“I wouldn’t take anything out there less than fifteen feet in length,” said Ollie. “Of course, it depends on where we’re going. If you’re going for the US coast, the larger the better. The Gulf can get pretty rough out there. I wouldn’t take one of these little day sailors—they’re more fit for bays and coastal waters.”

Bibi shook a piece of seaweed from her shoe and looked at Diane. “So, that was your plan. The painful truth is that we don’t have any experience of cruising around in the drink, whatsoever. It would be just our luck to tip over and go straight to David Jones.”

“I wouldn’t be too hasty,” said Ollie. “We could make it to mainland Cuba without too much trouble. Granted, the conditions would have to be right. We can find a good compass on one of these wrecks. Then all we have to do is sail north.”

“Sail all the way?” asked Diane.

“Sail is the best choice. We can’t afford to break down. None of us are mechanics. The gasoline might have become contaminated in all this weather. The SUV has gas, but I don’t know how much it’ll take to get us to our destination. Too many variables. Our best bet is a small auxiliary engine like an outboard and a full sail rig.”

Ollie walked past Diane to stand on the edge of the berm line. He examined a yellow sailboat that sat near the water in an upright position. He hopped inside of it and began opening up deck hatches. He disappeared for a moment inside the small cabin then reappeared. He gazed upward at the mast.

Diane stepped up to the boat. The logo on the hull read *Catalina Capri 22*. She had no idea what that meant, but supposed Ollie did, because he looked pleased with its size and lines.

"This is the one," said the small man. "Not too big—not too small. The sails are stowed in the locker. The auxiliary battery is still onboard. It has a mount for a small outboard, which we'll have to find. It has room enough for our supplies and us. It's also the closest boat to the water, so we shouldn't have too much trouble launching it."

Diane stepped around to the rear of the boat and put her shoulder against the transom. Using the suit's power, she shoved hard, digging her boots into the sand. The rear of the boat lifted for a moment then settled.

"We'll have to do this the smart way," Ollie advised. "I don't think you have enough driving force to move her. We can lay some round posts down so she'll roll, then winch her into the water."

"I was just testing," said Diane. "I didn't think it was going to work. How soon do you think we can be ready?"

"If we push it, six to eight hours. I'll rig a windless up to that pier piling out there and hook up some line. I can lay the posts, mount an engine, tank some gas, rig the sails and then sit back and relax while you two load everything we need."

"Push it?" asked Bibi. "Seems like that's all we're doing is pushing it. Why split from here when we finally have a crash pad?"

Now she's changing her mind about leaving, thought Diane. "Because we can't risk it. So far, everybody on this island has stabbed us in the back. I'm not waiting around for another jab."

Ten minutes later, Diane entered the hotel to gather up supplies. She filled plastic water bottles, scrounged can goods from the hotel kitchen and hunted down plastic apparel to be used as foul weather gear. Bibi was in charge of the weapons and ammo, making sure to wrap them in waterproof material. Diane struck gold when she found several prescription drugs stowed in a lower cabinet behind the check-in counter. The drug inventory consisted of Nembutal, Percocet, Darvon and Tylenol. She stashed the bottles in a small plastic lunch box. She found a navigational chart of the island, indicating the reefs, shoals and diving areas. She carried the items out to the boat and handed them to Ollie, who packed them securely aboard the little Catalina.

Diane made one last sweep of the upper floor of the hotel, looking for anything they might use for their trip. Most of the roof was missing from the upper floor, along with several walls. Furniture, and even the carpet had been sucked out of the rooms. She found one room that had collapsed in on itself. Inside she smelled the unmistakable odor of decomposition. Sifting through the debris, she found the bloated bodies of a woman and child locked in a *rigor mortis* embrace. She gently removed them from the wreckage and then carried them one by one outside.

She found a gravel-strewn path at the back of the hotel and buried the bodies, using a shovel she found in a brick shed. She said a few words in prayer over them, idly wondering who they were. She doubted that their friends or relatives even knew of their demise. The heartfelt moment brought tears to her eyes. She slapped them from her cheeks, angered that such a thing had happened.

"Hurricanes don't discriminate," said Bibi from behind her back, having approached with quiet steps. "There are probably more of them around here. I've been smelling death all morning. But that was a nice thing you did, honey."

Dianne tried to smile but she didn't have the heart for it. They'd had their fair share of pain and terror, but the islanders certainly weren't immune to the misery. It seemed that the hurricane had picked its own route of destruction across the island. Some parts were untouched, while others had been obliterated. Overall, the death toll had to be astronomical.

Diane threw the shovel down and walked with Bibi to the shoreline. Ollie waved at them from the water, having just tied off a block and tackle arrangement on a broken pier strut. He sloshed up to the beach, uncoiling a spool of nylon from his arm. He then took up the slack. The line ran through the pulley system and back to the boat where it was attached to a bow cleat. By pulling hard on the line in a shoreward direction, the boat was supposed to roll down the wooden piling ramp and enter the water. At least that was the theory behind it, Ollie had explained.

Bibi set a toolbox down next to the boat. "I found this near a shed out back. You might be able to use them to fix something."

"Thanks. I could use a pair of pliers," said Ollie. "I need to pull the battery out of the SUV so we have an extra for cabin lights. No generator, you know. All I could find was a five-horsepower outboard. It starts on the first pull. Plenty of gas, too. I packed all the supplies you brought, except for those water containers. Oh, yeah, you might want to toss out those soggy berth mattresses." He fingered a blister on his hand. "So, it looks like we might be pulling out of here pretty soon." He picked up the toolbox and walked down the beach.

Diane helped Bibi over the rail then handed the water bottles to her one at a time. Bibi placed them in the bench locker, fastened it shut and then squeezed inside the small cabin. She came out a moment later, dragging the sopping mattresses. Diane flung them onto the beach.

Bibi pointed to some orange vests half buried in the sand. "I didn't see any of those life jackets onboard. Maybe we should stock up on some."

Diane picked up several life preservers around the tide line. She handed them to Bibi, who stowed them in the cabin. The large woman sat down on the transom bench, rubbing her face. "I don't mind telling you that my butthole is all puckered up on account of this. I was hoping there was some other way to get us out of here, but I don't know where I got that notion. I'm afraid of dark water."

Diane gave her a sympathetic smile. "God's hand is not likely to come out of the heavens and scoop us out of here, Bibi. But he can guide us. The only thing we have to worry about is Ollie's sailing skills. We should double up on the prayers for both."

Ollie stumbled over the flotsam, carrying a battery. He handed the battery to Diane then jumped aboard to take the hand-off and place it on the rear deck. After he used a bungee cord to secure it, he turned to the two women and said, "I thought I'd try the radio in the vehicle before I removed the battery. One of the government radio stations was running on an emergency channel. Among the obvious news, the word is out that a killer maquina extraterrestre is on the loose. A reward has been offered. We're toast, folks."

"What do those words mean?" asked Diane.

"It translates to 'alien machine', if you can believe that. Apparently, you're some kind of terminator robot bent on wiping out the population. I'll bet it was the refugees who thought that one up to lay down a false lead."

"Thank you for that bit of news," said Bibi disgustedly. "If anybody wants me, I'll be in the fuselage having nightmares because we have a price on our heads." She squeezed through the cabin door and slammed it shut.

Ollie picked up the towline and jumped inside the boat. Diane tried to scissor a leg up over the rail but kicked the boat. With a few undignified maneuvers, she climbed aboard. Ollie instructed her on how they were going to brace then pull the line in hand-over-hand. They took their positions.

As they pulled in tandem, the boat inched forward across the pole ramp. They increased the speed of the pull, gaining more momentum. The bow reached the water; the first waves slapped against the hull. They pulled harder, faster. The boat dipped once and then bobbed. Soon they were riding in the swells.

"I just knew it would work." Ollie pulled the rope on the tiny outboard. The engine burbled to life. Next, he cut the towline loose from the bow. He came back, gunned the engine, and steered the small craft through the waves.

Bibi's head appeared from a small topside hatch. She looked around. "Dear Lord, we're floating. How did that happen?"

Ollie beamed. "Compliments of your captain. Fasten your seat belts and put your tables in the upright position. We're on our way!"

Bibi ducked down, slamming the hatch. Diane burst out with nervous laughter, not sure if she was actually happy that they were finally on their way or whether they'd just embarked on a one-way ticket to the bottom of the ocean. Nevertheless, she looked at Ollie proudly, wishing she could high-five him at the moment for a job well done. At least one of them knew how to sail a damn boat. She felt certain she would learn the skill before too long.

Ollie called her to the tiller. "Just hold this handle straight," said Ollie. "It acts like a rudder and steers the boat. Keep the throttle twisted. Yep, that's the speed we want."

Diane did as she was told, sitting on the transom bench. Ollie pulled the lid off a bench hatch and jumbled up the insides, mumbling to himself. He tried another hatch, digging deeper into its innards. Before long, the deck was scattered with all manner of items.

"What are you looking for?" Diane asked, ready to help if he needed it.

"I just had it a few minutes ago," he said over his shoulder.

"Had what?"

"The instruction manual."

14

Gene had found Diane's charter service easily enough by using some good old-fashioned gumshoe tricks. Frank Coppola, from the charter service, had been more than forthcoming with information, but could only give Gene an approximate destination. Gene had flown American Airlines to Miami. From there he'd taken a flight to Havana, transferred to a smaller airline and flown the last leg to Nueva Gerona in terrible weather. Finding La Casa De Las Madre had also been easy because that was the name she'd dropped, but that's where the trail ended. Cold. He wasn't even sure, after interrogating the lobby clerk, if Diane had ever showed up and rented a room under her real name. He thought he'd lost her for good.

The only thing that gave Gene any hope was the clerk's admission that two Americans had rented a room just recently and that someone resembling Diane's appearance had accompanied one of them up to the room. Although this woman had walked—she had not been wheelchair-bound. That threw him. On the plus side, they had been the only Americans registered at the hotel in the past week. On the downside, the clerk could not supply the names of the occupants because they were so badly scribbled on the receipt. They'd paid in cash. The clerk described the renter as a large black woman.

It was a heads or tails toss. Either he had found evidence of Diane's presence, or he had stumbled upon a bizarre coincidence.

Just to make sure, he asked the lobby clerk to describe the guest who had been in the company of the large black woman.

"She very pretty white woman. She wear a wig, but I know she have white hair. She walk like...like...." She demonstrated a stiff-gated strut across the floor, holding her arms out.

"Thank you very much," said Gene. He gave her a generous tip for the information and then walked across the lobby. He took a seat on a courtesy chair, ready to plan his next move. There were only a few people in the lobby. A couple sat in front of a small black and white TV, while two others swapped moves on a chessboard. The hotel, rigged by an emergency generator, made the TV screen give off annoying flickers.

The quiet of the lobby would also allow him some privacy while going over his notes. He removed the vanilla folder from his briefcase and thumbed through the printout. He had copied every blog, article and interview he could find on her. He needed to find any friends or associates that might have accompanied her on the trip. He suspected she had an agent and publisher but ruled out the possibility of them traveling with her. He needed someone closer—a best friend, or even an assistant.

It took Gene twenty minutes to find what he was looking for. It was an interview article, where Diane explained how she'd managed to keep up such a prodigious output of work while taking care of day-to-day life chores. She gave credit to

"Bibi" and "Ollie", who she described as her *live-in helpmate loves*, without whom her existence would be impossible.

Gene underlined the names and scratched his chin. To him, *live-in helpmates* fit the bill of very intimate friends who would be the most likely people to travel with her. Especially if they performed the functions of personal assistants. One male, one female. But no mention of color or ethnicity. Who was the black gal?

He seriously contemplated his sanity at this point. Oh, he'd received his vacation time easily enough, a full three weeks with pay. But Maui never looked like this. Walking straight into a hurricane- ravished foreign country was not his idea of a premium getaway vacation. Nearly all the land line communications were down or in repair status. Transportation was sparse at best. Most of the roads were impassable. He doubted if anyone here kept accurate receipts and records that he could trace to find his missing people. Only some parts of the island had restored electricity. He wondered if a bloodhound would serve his purpose better.

The couple watching the TV burst out laughing, breaking his concentration. It was a local newscast. Gene listened to a few words, understanding the Spanish perfectly. He almost felt like laughing out loud at the reporter, but the more he listened the more intrigued he became. The reporter went on to describe the recent homicide of a foreign national that involved mysterious circumstances, with an additional claim that three others were seriously injured in the confrontation. What really pricked his ears was the humorous description of the suspect seen in the area of the assault. The reporter announced that refugees declared that a *maquina extraterrestre* was responsible for the attack—more to the point, a hideous robot monster had taken on an armed squad of men and beaten them into submission.

Gene got up to stand in front of the screen so he could see

the area of the attack. From what he could determine, the place looked like a campground populated with tents and camping supplies. Several people stood in the background, waving at the camera. A few held up signs that begged for emergency assistance. When the newscaster signed off, he gave his location as just outside of Coccodrillo.

Gene sat down again and opened his briefcase. He pulled out a map of the island and ran his finger over the city names. Then he found it. Coccodrillo, a small port city located on the far side of the island. It was a long shot. But right now, it was the only shot he had.

He slammed his briefcase shut, picked up his gear and headed out the door. He hailed the first taxi he saw. He told the driver to take him directly to Coccodrillo.

As they drove down the small street, the driver stared at him through the rearview mirror. A grin broke out over his face showing a prominent gold tooth. Gene could smell alcohol in the cab. He hoped he hadn't made a mistake catching a ride with this man.

"An American," said the cabdriver. "You will like Cuba."

Gene didn't trust the shit-eating grin. He pulled his briefcase and overnight bag tight into his lap. "How can you tell I'm an American?"

"Oh, I can always tell these things. It is the way you dress, the way you speak and the way you carry yourself."

"Then you're very perceptive."

The cabdriver laughed boozily. "Yes, I can always tell these things."

15

After several tries, Ollie managed to raise the main sail. Diane remembered to sit down before the boom swung around after the sail had filled with air. She only knew about the precaution after having read the instructions to Ollie. Between the two of them, they'd learned the most important aspects of proper sailing techniques—how to catch wind and point the boat.

After they reached a mile offshore, Ollie steered the boat in a northerly direction, holding the tiller firm. He watched the compass that he had screwed to the rail. Diane did her best to read the navigational chart, trying to interpret the symbols and numbers. She had to be on the lookout for reefs and shoals which indicated shallow water. The boat had no electronic instruments aboard. Ollie had told her beforehand that they would be sailing by the seat of their pants, nineteenth century style. What she did not understand and asked aloud is why they were not venturing farther out in the ocean if their intention was to make a dash straight for the U.S. coast. He offered his excuse for the maneuver.

"Better to keep the coastline in sight in case of an emergency. I feel safer with a frame of reference. It's the long way around the bay, but better to be on the safe side."

"I suppose the extra time isn't going to matter," said Diane. "But what happens when it turns dark? There goes any visual aid."

"I suppose there will be some lights on the island by which to navigate. But I'm not going to risk it. We'll anchor when it gets dark and then wait for sunrise."

It made sense. Why risk running into something in the dark? Ramming into an obstruction in the dead of night had no appeal to her. Besides, Chet Strauss had never mentioned anything about the buoyancy of the suit, whether in full or half-worn mode. Strapped within the suit, and even wearing a life vest, it was possible she could sink like a cannon ball.

As a precaution, she asked Ollie to help her into another vest. He strapped one to her back. She eased back against the rail, now satisfied that she had done everything possible to protect herself.

The cabin hatch opened with a slap. Bibi looked at the two, her eyes crossed. "This sucks major time. My heads spinning and I can't..." She crawled out on the deck, threw her head over the rail, and expelled her guts. Diane wanted to comfort her but the risk of tipping the boat was too great. She could only watch Bibi suffer through the ordeal.

Ollie hunched his shoulders. "Even the fish gotta eat."

Bibi wiped some spittle from her mouth. "Yeah, and they like little gay men who taste like huckleberries."

Ollie had the grace to keep his mouth shut. Diane looked out over the water, not knowing why she was scanning the horizon. It was just a feeling that came over her, like the times when she thought somebody had been watching her from afar. Then the reason for that feeling became clear. The prow of a very large ship appeared from behind the promontory of the bay, headed in the direction of the peninsula. It was so unexpected she thought she might be hallucinating.

Diane pointed to the large vessel. "Will you look at that!"

Ollie jerked his head in the direction, putting a palm over his forehead. "My gosh, that looks like a liner." He swung the tiller hard over. The tiny sailboat sliced through the waves in a new direction. "But it's so damn far off, and she's *really* steaming."

Bibi leaned over the rail, staring. "We might get picked up if it's a friendly cruise ship. Maybe it's Carnival!"

Diane could not make out any markings on the ship. The sun glared off its side obscuring the profile. She scrambled for her helmet and put it on. She could see it clearly once she had the magnification up. She picked out a huge red cross on its hull.

Diane said, "It's the American Red Cross" and began waving her arms.

Ollie fell on his knees and tore through the bench lockers, tossing items on the deck. He ripped a plastic container open, revealing a large pistol and cartridges. He snapped one of the cartridges in the gun and held it overhead, pulling the trigger. With a hiss, the tiny rocket shot skyward. He loaded again, shot another one.

Bibi waved her arms, screaming at the top of her lungs. Frustrated, she pulled her breasts out and swung them like great beacons. "C'mon now, I know you can see *these* babies!" she yelled.

"They're big enough targets," said Ollie, firing another shot in the air.

Diane couldn't think of anything else to do other than waving her arms and holler with all her volume. The ship continued on its course, cutting through the waves like a titan that would not be deterred from its mission. She'd never had such a feeling of helplessness, watching their proverbial ticket to freedom steam off in the distance, completely unaware of the little sailboat that bobbed like a tiny cork so many miles away. Surely, they would have known that distress rockets meant someone was in danger. Wasn't there an international law that required a large vessel to assist another in an emergency?

"We're over here!" Ollie cried. He fired the last of the cartridges.

A small piece of ash alighted on the deck. Diane looked up, did a double take. The sail near the top of the mast had caught on fire. Ollie looked up, squealed, dropping the pistol on the deck. For an incoherent moment chaos reigned, causing a collision of bodies on the small deck. Hands flailed, warnings were shouted. Ollie ripped a tiny fire extinguisher from the cabin wall and shot a plume into the air that was carried away by the ocean breeze. Diane leaned over the rail to spank the water upwards, but the effort was futile.

Ollie raked the extinguisher up and down wildly. "They might see us burning then render assistance."

"How about we send up a flaming Ollie," Bibi screamed, then went for the man's neck with a chokehold.

The two went down in a tangle on the deck. The tiller swung, heeling the boat off course. Diane fell on them and yanked them apart, shoving each one in opposite directions. "Stop it, the both of you!"

"He's trying to kill us." said Bibi.

Ollie shoved his back up against the transom, winded from warding off the blows. "I was trying to save us, unlike you who was making a spectacle of yourself."

"Just let me hit him once, Di."

The top half of the sail burned free of the support line then fell over on itself. It smoldered for a while, finally falling in cinders to the deck and into the water. What remained resembled a tattered flag billowing uselessly in the breeze, accompanied by the pungent smell of burnt Dacron. The boat fell off the wind and began to bob in the swells. Ollie started the engine and straightened the craft, putting them back on a course parallel with the coastline. Diane helped to take down what remained of the tattered sail.

"Don't we have a spare?" asked Diane.

Ollie shook his head. "No, that was the first thing I checked. Not even a spinnaker. I wasn't expecting anything like this. We're under engine power from here on out unless we beach and try to salvage another one. Even then, I can't guarantee that we'll find a duplicate or anything that will fit. We'll lose time—risk exposure, too."

Diane looked at the fuel cans bungee-tied to the deck. "How far do you think we can go?"

"Well, we have to use full throttle to push this tug. With twenty-five gallons, I'm sure we could make the Cuba mainland. As far as reaching the States, I'm not sure anymore. You break down or run out of gas in the Gulf, you're asking for a world of hurt."

"I don't want to hear anymore," said Bibi. "I say we land this boat at the nearest port and take our chances. I don't trust you at the wheel, anyway."

Diane really didn't know what to do or what decision to make at this point. For now, they were off the island, safe from capture or death. But they ran the risk of not making it to their destination. Their options were narrow at best, nonexistent at worst. They stood the chance of rescue from the U.S. Coastguard, provided they could make it into the Gulf where such a vessel would patrol. She knew it was up to her to call out their next move. She did not make it without apprehension, considering how badly her past decisions had landed them in trouble.

"We'll go on," said Diane. "I think our chances are better out here. At least we know we're out of their clutches."

Bibi mumbled, "Why am I not surprised? Seems we're hosed either way." She squeezed into the cabin and slammed the hatch.

They motored on. Ollie kept the boat on a steady course, following the coastline. They ate a small dinner of canned beans.

Hours later, the sun dipped below the horizon with a blaze of pink and red. Ollie spoke about anchoring for the night. Diane had a better idea, suggesting he try her helmet on to aid with night vision. After he put the helmet on and adjusted the magnification, he confirmed that he could pilot the vessel with the shoreline clearly visible. The only question now regarded his stamina. Diane promised to take over the duties when he became tired.

Sometime after midnight, Ollie relinquished the steering tiller to Diane. He curled up on the deck under a blanket, so he would be close by in case she needed him. Bibi remained in the cabin, which left Diane alone with the sea and her thoughts. Using the helmet, she could see the vague outline of the coast dotted with the occasional flickers of light, which she guessed were vehicles or small encampments. The hull of the craft pitched and rolled with a steady rhythm, occasionally dipping into a deep trough. Waves slapped the hull, the sound keeping her alert. After a while her body began to sway with the rhythm of the waves. It was almost like waltzing to music.

She couldn't have been more than three hours into her shift when the rhythm of the sea changed. A stout breeze picked up, pelting spray against her back. The boat began to dip with a more violent energy, the bow plunging under the larger swells. The wind whistled over the naked mast. At times the propeller lifted out of the water to spin with a high-pitched whine.

A loud thump came from the cabin. Bibi swung the

hatch open and yelled through a spray of salt water. "What's going on?" She stepped out, grabbing the rail for support.

Ollie awoke, throwing off his blanket. He rose to his feet and got a hold of the boom to steady himself. "When the hell did this start up?"

"About ten minutes ago," said Diane, fighting with the tiller. "I can't believe we've got another hurricane on us."

Ollie took the tiller from Diane. "Hurricane, no. Squall, yes." He reached out. "Give me that helmet."

Diane helped him get it over his head. He looked toward the shoreline and brought the boat around in that direction. He ordered the women to crouch low and grip the rails. Wind gusts threatened to throw them to the deck. Waves capped with white froth slew over the cabin top, lashing their faces. It all seemed so surreal. Diane fought to bring her mind to heel. This was not the time to lose it. She had to trust Ollie with every fiber of her being. Their lives depended upon his skill.

Ollie yelled into the maelstrom, "I'll need you to crank the centerboard up when I tell you to!"

Diane made her way into the small cabin. She had to fight with the suit controls, attempting to get herself in the correct position. Bibi followed her in and used her outstretched hands to brace herself in the cabin against the rocking motion. Outside the tiny motor had taken on a high-pitched whine, beginning to sputter. Then the craft began lifting vertically with the huge swells, nose-diving like a porpoise.

"Crank her up!" Ollie yelled.

Diane spun the crank, careful not to apply too much pressure. She didn't need to break the handle.

"Crank her down when I tell you."

"Gotcha!"

Diane waited for the command. The boat plowed into the waves. The hull bottomed out twice, then lifted high and came down with a thud on a sandbar. Another wave shoved the craft forward, propelling it atop a crest. When the boat dropped it hit hard, sending a nauseous vibration through the hull.

"Crank it down now!"

Diane cranked with furious pulls. The boat twisted sideways, bottoming out a last time. It held fast. Then all movement ceased, except for a rocking motion. The cabin sat tilted at a crazy angle, but Diane could tell they were no longer afloat—Ollie had run them up on the shoreline, beaching the craft.

Bibi blew out a jittery breath. "He crashed us on purpose?"

Ollie entered the cabin, soaking wet. "I ran us aground—ditched it. Believe me, I didn't have a choice." He took the handle and forced a few more revolutions out of it. "I'm setting the keel in the sand. It'll keep us from being swept out in the back surge."

Bibi sat down heavily. "Now what do we do?"

Ollie swiped the water from his face. "We stay buttoned up—ride out the weather. No sense in going outside."

Just then the wind slapped the hull with a ferocious gust. The first raindrops fell on the cabin roof. Soon the noise turned into a roar, drowning out their words. They wrapped themselves in blankets to form a human knot. There was nothing left to do but ride it out as Ollie had suggested. They fell asleep to the sound of the driving rain and the screech of the wind.

Diane felt the sunshine on her cheek before she saw it. Bibi stood outside the cabin door looking back in. There was no sound of the storm or sway of the boat, only the gentle lapping of waves. Somewhere a gull screeched. Diane threw the covers off her and stepped out of the cabin.

"Your highness stole your helmet and went traipsing off down the beach," said Bibi. "I couldn't stop him. He's feeling all macho right now."

"That's okay. He's earned it." Diane truly meant that, too. Ollie seldom stuck his neck out when it came to physical prowess or confrontation. But after last night, he'd shown the initiative to get them out of harm's way, using a courage she hadn't seen before.

"You know, Bibi, it wouldn't hurt to give credit where credit is due. Ollie is still a man who has that male instinct to protect those around him. That includes you and me. Right now, he's probably checking out the territory to make sure it's safe."

"Yo, Diane. He *crashed* us."

"He *saved our lives.*"

They had a quick standup breakfast of canned beans and stale tortillas before they hiked down the beach in search of Ollie. It was easy to follow the single set of footprints in the sand since the beach had been wiped smooth from the surge. The tide line was loaded with driftwood, plastic shards, branches and bits of broken boats. Diane could not see any habitations, docks or piers, in either direction.

They followed the footprints past a small grove of palms that led to a flood pool. After a few minutes, they spotted Ollie, who was walking in their direction from the interior of the island. He had a map to his face, carrying the helmet at his side. To Diane, he looked terribly thin and fatigued. But when he looked at her his eyes were full of hope.

"Good morning, ladies. I've been scouting. From the profile of the shoreline, I can see that we're on the extreme west side of the island. By dead reckoning, the city of Riviera is due east of here, straight across the interior. It's not an easy go. The marsh starts about 300 yards in. It then gives way to tundra. The Los Idios River runs down from that direction. We can follow its course."

"Why are you telling us this?" asked Bibi.

"I thought you might want to pack it in to the city. It's a fly speck on the brochure."

Bibi snorted. "You mean you want us to go back into civilization again so we can risk being spotted?"

"I'm saying that there are eighty-six thousand people on this island and that Riviera looks pretty small—maybe a populace of two hundred or so, tops. Keeping to ourselves, we might be able to blend in without drawing any attention. Let's face it. We're not in very good shape to stay out in the wild. Me, I can manage it for a while."

"Why all the concern?" said Bibi.

"I'm thinking about you two. Diane needs some therapy—she's way off her maintenance. You could use a hot bath and a soft bed. At least we might be able to get a message out by phone. It's worth a try. I'm not going to lie—it's a risk."

Ollie's words cut to the core. Their immediate priority was survival. The boat had sustained too much damage to be functional. There was no replacement in sight. A water escape was out of the question. He was suggesting that they might merge into a small community, allowing them to gain back their strength. It sounded completely logical, once they considered the consequences. They would risk discovery unless no one suspected them of anything abnormal. There was Bibi to think of, too. She'd suffered the worst; her biggest enemies were her weight and lack of physical stamina. She probably had one more push left in her before she collapsed. There were no hospitals out in the wilderness.

"I think we should go to Riviera," said Diane, "because we're out of options." She turned to Bibi and gave her an arched brow.

"I need the path of least resistance," said Bibi. "That includes the easiest way out of here. I could use some downtime and a meal, heaven knows it."

They returned to the boat and packed their supplies. Diane chose the largest tote carrier, filling it with the heaviest objects, including the weapons, ammo, and canned foods. She tossed one of the rifles in the sand since they had no need for more than three. Ollie and Bibi divvied up the other supplies, strapping loaded packs to their backs.

Ollie started out in the lead, walking them into the interior. They traveled south through a thick bog until they reached the Los Indios River. They topped off their water bottles then headed upstream, following the bank of the watercourse. They concentrated on walking on the high riverbank that kept them out of the swamp.

Diane had never seen such a landscape before, except in the pages of National Geographic. A type of Spanish moss hung from gnarled eucalyptus trees. The area smelled of mud and rotted vegetation. The heat was mild, but the humidity soaked their clothes. A strange type of mangrove root seemed to leap out at their ankles, threatening to trip their every step. The place looked bizarrely primeval-- something out of the Jurassic. The only comfort came from the sound of the small river next to their path.

After what Ollie estimated to be a ten-mile hike, they stopped to rest near a small, sandy patch of earth next to a bend in the river. Ollie and Bibi, drenched in sweat, sat down. They had to ring the moisture from their clothes. Diane did not like the way Bibi looked. She suggested she lay down to relax.

Bibi mopped her brow. "I'm all right, just a bit short of breath. It ain't easy walking through this mud hole."

"There are no roads or paths out here," said Ollie. "I'd order one up if I could."

Diane pulled the sticky hair back from her face and looked up the river. "How far do you think it is, Ollie?"

"There's no mile markers on the map. I'd guess it's thirty miles or more. I'm sorry." He looked at Bibi with sympathetic eyes.

"Don't feel sorry for me," said the large woman. "If I get out of this alive, I'll end up looking like a runway model after a bout of bulimia. So maybe that's a good thing. But I'm really feeling it in my thighs and ankles."

Ollie nodded. "I'll try to keep the pace down. The trail is easier on the impacted earth next to the river. But this whole damn island is soaked to the max. If it's any consolation, that means our terrorist friends are getting bogged down on the mud roads, too. The whole island is a disaster area. I'll bet that most of the emergency resources have been allotted to the main island."

"I think I understand what you're saying, Ollie." Diane rung her hair out.

"Right. Juventud Island can go to hell for all they care. You could say that having mainline communication down works in our favor."

"You can see me jumping for joy," Bibi said, her voice edged with sarcasm.

They were on their way after fifteen minutes. Diane held Bibi's hand, assisting her over the roughest terrain. As they entered the first stands of pine, they heard birds chirping high up in the branches. Other than the avian life, Diane could see no ground-dwelling animals except for something that looked like an opossum that scampered up a tree trunk. The desolation gave her a feeling of uneasiness.

After five hours of steady march, they made it to a rock spill, where a few large boulders formed a natural niche. Ollie estimated they had traveled over fifteen miles, probably more. They threw their packs down and set out a tarp under the shadow of the largest boulder. The small river lay just over a rise. Its sound came to them in a caressing burble. They removed their shoes and took turns cleaning each other's sores and tending to blisters. The sun would be down soon. None of them felt like another push. Not at night in this outback region.

Ollie gathered up some small branches, built a small pyramid with sticks and put a flame to it. It took him several tries, nearly expelling the full contents of a lighter just to start a flame, since the wood was so water-soaked. He gathered a new batch of tinder and shoved it close to the flames to dry. It wasn't long before Bibi had curled up under a blanket and fallen asleep. Her every breath came with a distressed wheeze.

"She's exhausted," Ollie said in a hushed voice. "I've got the pace as slow as we can move."

"It's not your fault. This place makes the Amazon look like a picnic grounds." Just as she said that a centipede scurried across her thigh, prompting her to jerk.

Diane let out a huffy breath. "It wasn't too long ago that we were safe in the house; I was scribbling away on some new storyline, and you were plastering pixels all over your precious computer screen. Bibi was eating everything that wasn't good for her and sleeping between clean sheets."

The frustration hit her. "Oh, damn it all anyway. I wish I could take it all back. What the hell was I thinking? That somebody could actually love me for me? What kind of hog swill was I swallowing?"

"It's never one thing that happens." Ollie snapped a twig and tossed it on the fire. "It's always a series of minor events that compound, which leads to a domino effect that becomes unstoppable. Before you know it, you have a major catastrophe staring you in the face. This is our lot and we're stuck with it. Following someone because you thought they were in danger was an honorable reaction. Don't bemoan the circumstances. No regrets. You didn't twist our arms."

"Thanks for saying that. The worst part of it all is that it turned into a national security issue. I'm the worst possible candidate for a burden like that. Maybe somehow, we'll get out of this. But right now, I'm wearing the future technology of modern warfare. Whose side gets the prize when it's all said and done? I'm just a pawn."

"I think you were the right choice. Why? Because it bothers you so much. You've looked at the bigger picture and understand it. It's not an easy burden, being in possession of a device that could change history. Truth be told, you've taught me a few things about the importance of patriotism. There were times when I wanted to steal that suit from you and bury it. Bibi and I talked about it. But after the incident at the campground, I changed my mind. I promise you that these dick wads won't get their hands on that suit on my watch."

She needed to hear that, too. She knew more than anyone else what the combat exoskeleton was capable of. The implications were staggering. Its power supply was inexhaustible. It was bullet proof against small arms fire. The strength assist was phenomenal. Alone, just the tactical helmet was a step up in anything the military currently possessed. And this was only the prototype. Military applications aside, the innovations it promised the handicapped audience were incalculable. The fact that a paraplegic could walk and function in the lower half of the suit had been positively proven. Perhaps with additional tweaks, the quadriplegic population could benefit from its design. Who knew how many lives could be enriched with its further development? Those were truly worthy ideals that justified its preservation.

"It is a *good* thing, Ollie. It's the right thing to do."

He gave her a broad smile then tossed some more wood on the fire. They spoke into the evening until their heads bobbed and they'd run out of topics. Diane clicked the power switch off and fell on her back. She drifted off to sleep, thinking about what it would be like to have a man snuggled up next to her, someone she could trust—a man who really cared about her and loved her. Then she thought how silly that was because she already had a little hero in her midst. Ollie.

They started out at first light. Diane took Bibi's load, slinging it over her back. She knew that before too long the large woman would succumb to lameness.

After five miles, Bibi acquired a pronounced limp. Diane had to assist her. Their pace slowed. They took several breaks. When they found the shore of a small lake, Ollie redirected their route to follow its shoreline east. After a mile, they left the shoreline to continue inland. At one point, Bibi gave a shudder and slumped in Diane's arms.

Before Diane could react, the large woman fell heavily to the ground on her back. Bibi looked upward, her eyes glazed. "It's all over for this fat-ass broad," she huffed. "Feel me, you guys need to head on out. I'm packing it in."

"We're not leaving you," said Diane. "So help me, I'll carry you out of here if I have to."

Bibi licked her lips. "I don't care how strong you think you are with that suit. You can't haul two hundred and fifty pounds of lard on your back. So, give it up."

"We can *drag* two-hundred and fifty pounds of lard," said Ollie. He dug into his pack, pulling out a small Buck knife. He walked off between the trees.

Diane patted Bibi's forehead with a wet handkerchief. "Just relax right now. Leave it up to us. You haven't done anything to be ashamed of."

Diane held Bibi in her arms until Ollie arrived twenty minutes later, carrying two stout limbs. He tossed them to the ground and retrieved a tarp from one of the packs. Using some small lengths of string and some shoelace, he began to fashion an object that Diane instantly recognized as an Indian litter. When he finished the chore, they gently rolled Bibi onto it, and taking a hand each on the handles started off again. They dragged their friend over the forest floor.

They hadn't trekked more than a few miles before they saw their first signs of life. Ollie saw them first, pointing out two children who were crouched by a rain pool. They were throwing sticks in the water. When they saw the two approaching with the litter they backed away then ran east.

"We've got to be close to a settlement," said Ollie. "Unless those kids were lost."

Diane shook her head. "No, they made a straight beeline out of here. I think we scared the crap out them." Then she paused, realizing that the full suit might have frightened them off. She did have the helmet clipped to her belt, exposing her face. *The kids had to see me as human.*

"I've got to put something over this suit," said Diane.

Ollie helped Diane don some extra-large clothes. They would hide the dark body armor. Finished dressing, she picked her litter handle up and began in lockstep with Ollie again. He gave her his opinion on the new look.

"You kind of look like a transgendered football linebacker. I think you were less scary before the change."

She smiled, knowing it was a dig. "If anybody asks, we'll just tell 'em I'm a freak who escaped from a local circus."

They followed a small worn path in the woods. Diane heard a car horn in the distance, then a sound that resembled chopping wood. After a few minutes, they passed a rusted junk car half-buried in the earth. She could make out the corners of some wooden structures just between the clefts of some trees ahead. Buildings. She called a halt. They set the litter down gently.

Diane took a knee next to Bibi and patted the sleeping woman's cheek. "Time to wake up, sweetheart. We made it. But you're going to have to walk this one in."

Bibi opened her eyes. She had Diane repeat the request. Bibi rolled off the litter and staggered to her feet. Diane put an arm around her. They took labored steps down the path. They arrived at the rear end of a row of buildings that were in various stages of disrepair. Bisected by a deeply rutted dirt road, sat another string of small buildings equally damaged, some completely stripped of their siding and roofs. A few tents and Quonset huts sat on the periphery of the small main street. People emerged or entered from the temporary abodes, carrying hand tools and wood. Ollie had been right about the city being a flyspeck on the map. Only it wasn't a city, but a very old village or settlement. A few people sat on horseback, shooting the breeze from their saddles. Riviera could have passed for a tiny Tombstone in the American West, circa 1885. If they *were* in Riviera.

"Let's show some dignity whilst we mosey on in," said Ollie. "We don't have to worry about them outclassing us in appearance. They're as trashed as we are."

They stepped around the first building on the edge of the town, then onto a wooden boardwalk. They walked past a shop that had blown-out windows and a door hanging from one hinge. A sawing noise came from somewhere inside the back of a shop. A dozen residents sat on chairs, drinking, playing cards and smoking at the end of the boardwalk. An old Ford truck rolled down the main street, its bed loaded with potatoes. The driver wore a broad-brimmed straw hat. He spit a stream of tobacco juice out his window after eyeing the three.

The boards creaked under their feet, drawing the attention of the seated residents, who paused to gaze at the newcomers.

"My ankles are buckling," warned Bibi. "I don't think I'm going to make it."

Diane gritted her teeth. "Hold on, honey. We'll get you indoors."

"I'll take care of this," said Ollie, setting his pack down. He walked ahead, to meet with the seated residents. He performed a curt bow. Diane heard him speak Spanish. During the exchange, an old woman pointed across the street at a three-story brick building. Ollie bowed cordially then retraced his steps back to women.

"It's a miracle," he said. "This is Riviera, all right. That brick building across the street is one of the few structures that didn't suffer any damage."

"Whoopty frickin' doo," said Bibi, "and hooray for their building codes, but what has that got to do with us? I'm *dying* here."

Ollie slung his pack over his shoulder. "It's also the only hotel within forty miles. They have a vacancy. And I'm glad to see you're feeling better, you fat fart."

Bibi clenched her teeth. "My life is bleeding away as we speak. Get me there."

They stepped Bibi off the porch and, holding as much of her up as they could, led her to the other side of the street. Diane remembered about her stashed currency. She dug under her clothes to retrieve it. She handed it to Ollie with an order for him to make the arrangements while she waited outside the door.

It was a long wait. Diane could feel dozens of eyes on her from across the street. Yet when she looked toward those curious faces, they turned away, feigning disinterest. Two sets of eyes did not turn away. They belonged to two children, who crept down the street and stopped a few yards from where Diane stood. They spoke rapid Spanish to each other. Then in a flash, they ran down the street to disappear behind a large junk pile.

Diane could have sworn they were the same children who had spotted them in the woods. She suddenly felt sick inside, wondering if Bibi had seen their reaction. But the large woman had only been staring at the hotel entrance. Which left Diane alone with the terrible thought that Riviera might be a lot more hostile than they bargained for.

16

Gene had no idea of his location. He only concentrated on putting one foot in front of the other, headed in the direction he thought might be south. It was hard to distinguish compass directions since the sun was directly overhead at its zenith. He'd have to wait an hour before he took his bearings to be certain.

The cab ride had lasted two hours before it ended in stark terror. The route to Coccodrillo had been suspect from the beginning, which should have raised every red flag in the bad taxi-driving book. Gene had expected a straight shot on a major highway that led to the southern city of Coccodrillo. But from the very onset of the trip the cabby had taken every side road and country lane that caught his fancy. That alone should have raised the hackles on a cautious tourist. Yet Gene had kept his mouth shut, trying to enjoy the ride. Big mistake. When the driver pulled over, claiming to have engine trouble, Gene believed it. When the hood was popped open and the driver told him that he thought the carburetor was acting up, Gene believed it. But when the driver pulled a gun out, getting the drop on him and demanded his valuables, Gene couldn't believe it.

Items stolen: one wallet with all his currency and personal identification, one office briefcase, one overnight bag, one two-inch Smith & Wesson .38 revolver with a shoulder holster, one academy ring, an extra set of keys and one expensive digital cell phone that was useless anyway.

The agent had gotten away with his life, plus the clothes on his back. He could not have been stranded in a more desolate, God-forsaken landscape. It reminded him of a place he had visited once in Arizona called Paradise Valley. Only this place had no similarity to a lush pine forest. The trees were ratty, wind-scalped and there was not a paved road or habitation in sight. What concerned him most was water. The cabdriver had refused to leave him a single drop of the precious liquid. The humidity in the air had to be at least 80 percent or better. After four hours on foot, he estimated he had already lost at least a gallon of body fluid. Of course, every gnat, mosquito, and fly in the territory had been alerted to his stinking, sweaty face and had now formed a permanent black cloud over his head.

Try explaining this one to the agency. Don't even think about contacting the field office and begging them to get you out of this.

They would slap him with a psyche review faster than hotshot Cha Cha Susie Delaney could draw her Glock and punch a bull's-eye. It was bad enough that he'd lost his personal service revolver. But losing all his agency identification neared the apocalyptic. Not to mention, everything in his briefcase contained sensitive files on Diane Nine. Given the fact that she had been telling the truth all along about a sinister terrorist organization, he had inadvertently put her at risk of discovery.

He had really peeled one off this time, he reminded himself again.

He walked another hour before he looked overhead to gauge the angle of the sun. "Rises in the east and sets in the west," he murmured. He positioned his body relative to the west, the direction of the setting sun. North was off his right shoulder. East lay to his rear. His left shoulder pointed south. The road he was standing on was oriented southwest. That wasn't too far off his track, which was the general direction of Coccodrillo. Unless he was jacked around!

Screw it. I'm committed.

He pushed on, unbuttoning his shirt down the front. The insects dive-bombed him without mercy. He couldn't tell what kind of road was under his feet or where it led. It could have been a fire road for all he knew. He hoped to run into a passerby that would give him directions.

Before long, he reached a T-intersection and stopped to look around. A wider road led south. A smaller one led west. A lone telephone pole caught his eye, and then another. The poles followed the south road as far as he could see. That had to be a good sign. He quickened his pace. *Follow the poles.*

He didn't get more than 500 yards before he heard a peculiar sound behind him. He turned to see a horse-drawn cart rolling in his direction. The driver sat slumped in the seat, a sombrero pulled down over his face. At first, he thought the driver was dead at the reins, for the man exhibited no signs of life. As the creaking cart approached, he could see the man's chest rise in fits. An unlabeled bottle sat perched upright between his legs.

Gene hoped his Spanish would be clear enough to be understood. He waited until the cart was nearly on top of him before he clapped his hands sharply. The driver started, spilling the contents of the bottle over his legs. The small horse back-pedaled.

"Dios mío!" cried the driver. "Qué?"

Gene sighed, relieved. "Please, I need your help!" he said in Spanish.

The horse stared stupidly at him. The driver belched.

17

Diane wanted to stay in the claw-foot tub to luxuriate all day long, but she felt sorry for Ollie who had already made his sixth trip with pales of hot water that he'd had to heat on a potbelly stove in the hotel hallway. She'd been the last to bathe, insisting that the others take turns first. Bibi lay on the top bed mattress, snuggled up in a hotel blanket, blissfully in the clutches of REM sleep. Her ankles and knees were swollen and discolored. The box spring mattress was reserved for Diane. Ollie insisted on taking the half sofa. There wasn't much else in the room, except for a table, two chairs and one chest of drawers. Air conditioning consisted of an open window. The small town had no electricity. The residents had told Ollie that it would not be forthcoming until the larger cities had been taken care of, like Nueva Gerona, La Fe and Santa Ana.

"How's my little oyster?" asked Ollie from across the room. "Ready for me to manhandle you out of there?"

"I hate to leave it, but if I don't get out of here, I'll turn into a mermaid. Now there's an idea. I'd truly have a functional lower half that I wouldn't have to strap on."

He lifted her from the bath and placed her on the

mattress. After he toweled her off, he began to apply ointment to some of her worst chaffing sores. "I'd like you better if you stay landlocked," he said. "I can't swim that well, so it would be hard to interact with a mermaid."

She swooned under his attentive hands. "And here I thought you were an expert swimmer from all our therapy pool sessions. You didn't flinch once out there in the ocean."

He started snapping on the lower half of her suit. "The pools at the spas were always waist deep, if you remember correctly. As far as the ocean, I faked it." He glanced at Bibi. "And that should be our little secret."

"Your secret is safe with me. Incidentally, I think I had better go full suit. Just a precaution."

"Or a premonition?"

"You could say that. Remember the kids that spotted us then hightailed it out of the forest?"

"Yeah."

"They gave me the serious once over while you were signing for our room. I'm pretty sure it was the same kids. They pointed at me then took off like screaming chimps."

"You're right to be concerned. I wouldn't trust a newborn baby in this country."

Ollie finished with the suit, then helped her into the oversized clothes. It made little sense to wear the helmet, so she left it in the corner of the room.

Looking out from the second story window upon the street below, Diane could see scores of people involved in carpentry activity. Some hauled lumber, while others boarded up broken windows. A few walked the length of the street, raking and shoveling piles of debris into selected areas. The efforts looked lackadaisical, evidence of a community that knew the insurmountable odds of restoring a town to its once functional glory. Only Diane had doubts as to whether this habitation ever had a glory day in its existence. She felt sorry for the people who had to call it home.

"I'm going to check out the scenery," said Ollie from the doorway. "We need to find out how soon telephone communication is going to be set up. I thought I might offer up a cover story for our presence. No sense in letting their imaginations go wild."

"Yeah, tell them we're a bunch of Scandinavian retards on a backpacking trip who got caught in the hurricane."

Ollie laughed. "Leave out the Scandinavian part, and it's the truth."

She watched him leave then turned towards the sleeping form of Bibi. She contemplated sitting down next to her to monitor her condition, but from what she could see, the heavy woman seemed to be completely relaxed and breathing normally. What the heck, she thought. Why couldn't she stick her nose where it didn't belong? Hiding away was likely to draw more attention than intended. *Let 'em have a good look at the crippled freak.*

Diane left the room and descended the stairs with awkward, clunking steps. She clumped through the tiny lobby, drawing a few stares from some seated patrons. She stopped to pick up a complementary magazine, thumbed through it, glancing at the pictures. She stepped outside and sat down on a redwood bench, opening the magazine up on her lap. As expected, she did not go without notice. A small crowd on the opposite side of the street turned heads in her direction, giving her a good stare. They spoke to each other behind cupped hands, bobbing their heads. Ollie stood next to another group of three people, engaging them in conversation, but their line of sight was also directed at her.

I can stare, too, and keep it up all day.

Suddenly the crowd of onlookers turned in unison to look down the street. A small-horse-drawn cart with crooked wheels and an annoying creak rolled over the rutted ground. Its driver sat bent over, his elbows resting on his thighs. His eyes looked sad and tired, as though he had been on the road for days. But it wasn't the driver that drew the attention of the populace. It was the man who leapt from the back of the cart bed when it slowed to a stop.

The man looked cosmopolitan, wearing black slacks, a blue cashmere blazer and a dark blue sports jacket. He had curly black hair that framed a pleasant enough face, only the jaw was drawn tight, which gave him a grim expression. Diane couldn't see his eyes as he walked toward the hotel, since he had his head down, watching his footfalls over the uneven ruts. He glanced at her when he stepped up on the boardwalk, then paused.

She got a good look at him. Caucasian—Blue eyes.

"Mornin'," he said. "I suppose this is the hotel."

She couldn't decide if it was a question or a statement. "You would suppose right. Although I have to warn you, there are no vacancies. I got the last room." *Perfect English. He could be American.* Then again, he could be someone else disguised as an American. Then why come rolling into town on a hay cart? Her mind fought between precaution and courtesy. Still, she would let him do the talking.

He sat down on the bench an arm's length away and dropped his head in his hands. After massaging his face for a while, he glanced at her and then looked away. Then, his head snapped back. He gave her a long, hard stare. Without warning, he burst out with a maniacal laugh.

She scooted away from him, poised to run in case she had to. The island had thrown every possible surprise at her. Why not chuck a stark-raving lunatic in her lap for good measure?

"I'm sorry," he said, his face relaxing. He groped inside his jacket pocket. "I just realized that the person I've been looking for is sitting right next to me. I'm Gene." His hand came away from his jacket empty. He stomped a foot. "Ah, crap! I forgot about the wallet. Anyway, I'm Gene, and *you've got to* be Diane Nine. I kept staring at your picture on the flight, so I know I'm not mistaken." He pulled back, gazed at her from head to foot. "But what the hell happened to you?"

Diane rose up awkwardly in a defensive stance. "I don't know any Gene. And I don't know how you got my name right, but—"

"Don't panic." He leaned toward her, licking his lips. "Look, I talked to you about a missing person's case that involved some high-tech hardware. I work for the Central Intelligence Agency as a Science, Technology and Weapons Analyst."

"I need some identification."

"That's just it. I don't have any. I got jacked by a cabdriver and dumped on the road miles from here. The son-of-a-bitch took everything I had. Look, you told me about Chester Strauss and how you thought he was kidnapped by a foreign faction because he had a military combat exoskeleton. You have a therapist and trainer, named Oliver. Your assistant and nurse is a woman named Bibi. You're a celebrity cartoon artist who works for—"

"Okay, okay. That's enough." She stepped closer to him, her heart hammering. "I thought you didn't believe me. What are you doing here? How? Better yet where are the rest of your people?"

"Slow down." He glanced down the street. "At first, I thought you were a crackpot. Then I gave it some thought and realized that if you were even halfway telling the truth, somebody had to re-interview you in person. I tried contacting you again, but you had disappeared. Your home address was vacant. I had a dossier on you, so I just followed the breadcrumbs. I say, I, because I'm the only one who thought your claim merited investigation. Call me an idiot for doing so, since it's been my prerogative more than once to follow some damn mysterious lead. Although it looks like...." He gazed at her legs. "It looks like I was on to something. Are you wearing that hardware underneath?"

"Yeah. It's the safest place for it."

He took her by the elbow. "You need to get inside. Take me to your room so we can hash this out."

They walked into the hotel, passing the front desk. The manager eyed them suspiciously and said, "No monkey fooling around here" in broken English.

"It's okay," said Diane. "He's my brother."

"No monkey fooling with the brother."

Gene mumbled under his breath when they mounted the stairs. "This country blows. MS-13 and the Crypts have nothing on this place."

"Tell me about it."

They entered the room. Diane locked the door, giving Bibi a quick glance. The large woman snored, still asleep. They took seats on the box spring mattress. Gene looked at the corner of the room, spotting the helmet. "I still can't believe it. It's true. Mind if I...."

She stayed his hand, knowing that he wanted to touch the suit. She peeled off the over-sized blouse then turned to give him a front profile.

He hissed through his lips, reached out to finger the armored chest panels. "Holy moly, do me sidewise and then some," he gasped. "Is that the mini-fusion reactor?"

"Yes, the small pack-like object on the back. I can fit it to the front or rear."

"But how are you managing to...I mean, you're crip—"

"I'm paraplegic. He designed this finger controller—it has touch sensors on the inside. That's how I'm able to operate the lower half."

His eyes widened. "Damn. Must have some kind of gyro-sensors or a gaggle of attitude controllers. Strange that he's using compressed air. Or is that a hydraulic tank?"

"Look, I'm sorry, but I don't know too much about all the technical functions. I just know that it works really well for what it is. That's why the other side wants it so badly."

He gave her dopey smile. "Forgive me. It's the nerd taking over. You were saying about the 'other' side—what kind of contact have you made with them?"

"All the worst kind. You're not going to believe it."

"Try me. I've come a long way to listen, and I caught some pretty strange news on a local channel that sounded like it was you and your assistants."

She didn't tell the story, as much as she vomited it out. She relayed the events with a lot of anger in her voice. When speaking of Chet, she displayed more emotion than she wished to, but she made it clear that it had all started with his betrayal of her trust. She emphasized how organized and armed their opponents were, stressing that they had no compunctions about killing anybody who got in their way. She admitted that the threesome's current survival was due to luck and timing. When she explained the details of the fight in the camp that resulted in injuries and death, she watched his expression turn grave. She paused when telling him of Bibi's heroics, and how they had come close to losing their lives. He didn't encourage her to go on after that, but she ended the tale with their botched sailing venture and trek across the tundra. When she finished, he sat quietly for a long time, digesting everything she had told him. When he finally commented, his voice was soft and emphatic.

"That's the most heart-wrenching story I've ever heard, considering the storyteller is still alive to recount it. My incident doesn't even compare to what you went through." He looked at Bibi. "The biggest snag is that I didn't tell anyone where I was going. I took my vacation time to get out here, thinking that if I presented your evidence to the director, I'd be laughed out of his office. Now I wish I would have at least left a message of my plans."

"You can't be blamed for disbelieving. It was hard for me to wrap my brain around it. I was seduced. I was seduced because I thought I was in love. Besides being lame, I was blind."

He told her his story about how he'd followed her leads, ending up at the hotel in Nueva Gerona, then how he had seen the newscast that described a strange robot monster on the loose, which ultimately sent him off to Coccodrillo. When he recounted the robbery at the hands of the cabdriver, she looked at him in shock.

"Unbelievable," she said. "That sounds like the same guy who mugged us. Something about the 'I could tell you were Americans' remark."

They laughed, which caused Bibi to moan under the covers. It was the shot of humor Diane needed right now, considering how glum the circumstances were.

"So, it looks like the answer to this problem is a phone and a good ear," said Diane. "Somebody who could get us off this island."

"Agreed. I had my cell phone filched, not that it would have done any good on this island, even if I had a tower to ping off of. Most of the major landlines are down. I spied a service truck and a small crew pulled over to the side of the road on my way here."

"Then at least something's being done?"

"The dumb bastards were sitting in the dirt, drinking and playing cards. Who is to say these people even know how to re-string high-tension wires and replace poles and transformers? Nueva Gerona is partially hooked up. It could be weeks before these outer settlements get any service."

"That's what we figured—to wait it out until phone service was restored."

"That probably won't stop this Global Socialist Alliance from squawking to their people. Especially if they're as sophisticated as you say they are. How big was that boat they ferried you on?"

"About forty or fifty feet, I guess. I think it was a private yacht. They might have stolen it or chartered it. I don't know."

"That's not big enough to have the range it needs to cross a lot of ocean, unless they island-hopped. Do you think they flew in?"

"There wasn't any mention of planes or pilots."

"You said they had very large rubber boats with big outboard engines."

"Yes, I saw two at their base—the compound. They were on trailers, covered with tarps."

"Probably Zodiacs. It sounds like they might transfer to a larger craft, which means there might be one waiting offshore for a pickup."

"What has that got to do with us?"

"Nothing. It's the bigger picture. Sorry, I'm thinking way too far ahead. The fact remains, they're as stranded as we are and have no intention of leaving without that suit. You said there might be about twenty or more of them, all armed."

"Could be thirty. Who knows how many friends or sympathizers they have."

"They *are* in a socially friendly environment. One that's hostile to us. They sure picked the right location for their skullduggery. What I would do for a Special Forces insertion team right now." He rubbed his face again; the veins stood out on his neck like rope.

"Don't take it so hard. You didn't expect any of this either."

"That's just it," he said through his hands. "I *should* have known. I let a cabdriver get the drop on me. The only thing I have to defend us with is a toenail clipper."

"I wouldn't exactly say that." She pointed to the largest carryall pack. "Take a look inside that. I was saving that for last."

He opened up the pack, pulled a rifle out by the barrel and shouldered it. "A fixed stock Kalashnikov, seven-six-two," he gasped. "Where did you get this?"

"We picked them off the enemy at the camp after the fight. We have two more just like it, with about 500 bullets. We tossed a spare."

The doorknob jostled, followed by urgent knocking. Diane opened the door to Ollie, who upon seeing Gene, reared his hands up defensively.

"It's all right, he's a friend," said Diane. "This is agent Eugene Gene of the C.I.A. You might say he just rolled into town."

Ollie dropped his hands. "Whew, for a minute I thought it was somebody else. Thank God the cavalry is here." Pause. "But how the hell did you get here?"

"I'm not a field agent," said Gene. "I'm an analyst. There's a big difference. I'm afraid the cavalry didn't make it this time. I came here alone and followed your trail."

Bibi threw the comforter off her face and yawned. "Then you're just another mouth to feed." She moaned. "I swear we attract the most worthless souls on the planet."

Gene slapped the rifle stock. "Worthless? I can handle one of these better than any of you. Gulf War veteran."

"Oh, that makes it all better," said Bibi, and pushed herself up on an elbow. "Whew-wee...my bones hurt so bad I can hear my marrow screaming. I think I need a trauma surgeon."

Diane broke out some bottled water and smoked jerky. Gene indulged, drinking a full bottle.

Diane spoke over her shoulder while she dug for more food. "What did you find out, Ollie?"

Ollie sat on the floor. "Well, the population here is about 140 souls. Most of them work for a lumber mill twenty miles up the road. The mill is inoperative, with about half the population working on it to restore the main structure. They're all waiting for electricity to be restored. No surprise there. The government provides repair services as the demand dictates, which means they are low priority and don't expect to be connected up for at least 12 more days. Nobody wants to drive their vehicles much, since gas is rationed and none of the station pumps are working."

Diane nodded. "Did you plant those seeds we were talking about?"

"Yeah. We're crazy Scandinavian backpackers who got lost in the woods during the hurricane. I'm pretty sure they'll swallow it. Stories and tall tales seem to be one of their most precious pastimes. They almost had me believing in the Chupacabra."

"Then we don't have to be afraid of anything," said Diane.

Ollie looked at his lap. "All except the robot monster that was seen in the woods by the children. They told me I was lucky to escape its laser gaze."

Diane's hand froze on a can opener key.

Ollie went on. "They said it probably dropped out of a UFO, because they've seen a lot of them in the area lately."

Diane snapped the can opener key and threw it against the wall. "Damn it all to hell. That story's grown legs and walked. Why did I think for one minute that we were safe?" She turned to Gene. "You're a good shot. Put me out of my misery. *Please.*"

Gene set the rifle on the floor. "I don't think it's the time to unravel right now. Maybe I can get a ride into Nueva Gerona to make that call. I'll need some currency, or something to barter in exchange for transportation."

"And then what?" Bibi asked. "You leave us, and right after that the bad guys swarm us because some kids blabbed about some robot monster wanderin' around in the forest. They don't have to look any further than to find three crazy Americans hiding in this hotel. Game over."

Gene looked at Bibi, his eyes narrowing.

"I'll go," Ollie said, his eyes unblinking.

"Yeah, that'll work," said Bibi. "You're going to pose as an agent and convince the CIA of all this stuff going down. Get real."

"He might have something there," said Gene. "He doesn't have to pose. He can represent me. I have a code name and identification number that's privy to the agency. They'll know there's a connection. He'll have to be convincing, relaying enough facts that can express the urgency—a national security issue. He'll have to stress that we'll need an insertion team for immediate evac."

Diane frowned. "Do you think they'll believe secondhand information?"

Ollie looked at Gene. "I know where I can get a digital cell phone. I can't get a call out with it because the towers are down in this area, but what if I took a picture of Diane in the full suit, and then upload it to the agency from Nueva Gerona? I can spill my guts."

"That would be the proof we need. I can supply you with the upload links and fax numbers."

For the first time, Bibi was speechless. Diane saw the logic in the plan. Ollie stood tensed in the middle of the floor, waiting for group confirmation.

Gene stroked his chin thoughtfully and said, "Okay, we

can send him on his way, but we'll need a contingency plan in case we're ambushed. If we're forced to exit under fire or overwhelming numbers, the rescue party will have to know which way we're headed. I vote for slipping out the back then heading across the interior toward Nueva Gerona."

"I can't feel my legs anymore," said Bibi. "I'm in no condition to march across anymore real estate."

Diane nodded. "She's right. We're stuck here for the time being. We can't carry her sixty or seventy miles."

Gene was unperturbed. "With any luck, we'll have a couple of days for you to recover. I'll set up our transportation, but I'll also need some bartering goods."

"We're paid up for a week here," said Diane. "But you're talking about giving up everything we have, including what little money I have left."

Gene looked at each one of them in turn. "You'll need to trust me on this. I think I can fend off an attack. If not, I know I can get us out of here in a pinch."

No one said anything until Ollie spoke up. "Then it's settled. No time like now to get my knees in the breeze. There's an old Volkswagen out there. I'll find the owner. He can stash me in the trunk and make it to Nueva Gerona on pennies of gas. I'll be right back."

Ollie left but returned five minutes later. He held a digital cell phone in his hand. "Just swiped it off the manager's desk while her back was turned. Get rigged up Diane. Don't forget to say cheese."

Diane pulled the rest of her clothes off and donned the helmet. Ollie got her in frame and snapped two digital photos. He also took one of Eugene Gene. "Perfect," he said. "Now for the goods. Let's hurry."

Bibi's face softened, as did her voice. "You dumb little fool." She shook her head. "Check my pack. It's got drugs and a bottle of booze that I stole back from that Russell dude—

use it to rent your car. Don't take the Percocet or Darvon. I need my drugs."

Ollie dug into the bag and came out with the items. Diane handed him some currency then gave him an affectionate kiss on the cheek, along with a lingering hug.

Gene penned a note with all the contact information on it and handed it to him, with the instructions to read it precisely as written to his contact. He added, "God's speed, Oliver. We're counting on you."

Ollie slung his small bag over his shoulder. "I'll get them here for you. I won't leave you out here alone." He gave them a snappy salute, opened the door, and stepped out.

Diane listened to Ollie's footsteps fade down the hallway. She crossed the room to gaze out the window. She watched Ollie emerge from the hotel entrance and walk across the street. He looked so small, so vulnerable, she thought. He'd taken on such a major task, doing so without any qualms or regrets. She prayed that he would make it to the city without running into harm's way. She'd never forgive herself if something happened to him.

"Well, that leaves me," said Gene. "I'm going to think about that contingency plan and see if I can buy our way into the hearts and minds of these folks." He left the room, closing the door behind him.

Diane turned away from the window. She locked eyes with Bibi. The large woman had her eyes fixed on the closed door. "I never meant to be so mean to him," said Bibi. "I really hope he knows that." A fat tear rolled from her cheek and plopped on the mattress.

"He knows it, sweetie."

The third day of their stay at the hotel went without incident. They'd huddled inside, taking turns watching the street below from the window. Bibi was on the mend but still complaining about strains and cramps. Diane watched Gene fashion homemade hand grenades out of bullet powder, nails, and yards of duct tape. He'd already ruined Diane's brassier by trying to fashion it into a slingshot, until he gave up and exchanged the material for an old car tire inner tube, stretched between the crook of a tree branch.

He pulled back on the pouch, letting it go with a snap. "What do you think? These fuses will stay lit, provided the wind velocity doesn't snuff them out."

"It's a waste of good ammunition if you ask me," said Bibi, propped on a chair by the window. She carefully dripped some oil into the breach of a rifle, while glancing every so often at the street below.

Diane smiled. "It better work. It cost me a bra."

Gene lined up eight homemade bombs then swept the empty shells into the corner of the room.

"I wonder if the little guy made it," said Bibi. "He should have been there by now to get the message through."

Gene mopped up the excess gunpowder on the floor with a wet towel. "Sounds about right. Provided he made it without mishap."

Without mishap, Diane thought. The terrorists could have been monitoring the road, pulling over suspect vehicles. They would have found Ollie easily enough, and either killed him outright or tortured him for Diane's whereabouts. Both options gave her a nauseous shudder. *No, he's made it to the city and called. I know Ollie. He's smart enough to stay hidden. He always follows through on an assignment. It's mission accomplished. Help is on the way.*

They had a quick lunch, checked and repacked their gear. Diane took her shift at the window. Bibi, now complaining of a groin pull, took some pain medication. Diane watched the activity below. It hadn't changed much. The same characters sat on their benches and stools, drinking and playing cards, while a select few hauled lumber, removed and stacked debris. A few residents wandered around looking busy or bothered others with meaningless conversations.

A few vehicles passed down the small main street, including a few tractors and pickup trucks. Two horse-drawn wagons stacked with personal belongings rolled into town. The hotel occupants were quiet, including the children. Diane suspected that the manager would toss anyone out who caused the slightest problem or made excessive noise. After all, she probably had a waiting list a mile long for those wanting to stay in the only undamaged structure in Riviera.

It was late in the afternoon when Diane spied a black SUV skid to a stop in the middle of the street. The driver and passenger doors both opened, disgorging two men in fatigues. The driver immediately stepped amongst the crowd and engaged them in conversation. Both men had rifles slung over their shoulders.

Diane rubbed her eyes hard, unwilling to believe what she was seeing. She saw the locals' point in the direction of the hotel.

Diane stood up quickly and moved out of the window frame, throwing her back up against the wall. "We're going to have company," she said, nervously kicking over a can. "They're loaded for bear."

Gene stared at her.

"Then it's on—bring it!" said Bibi, jacking the slide back on an AK-47.

18

Diane's vision came back in stages; her mind wrestled with the whys and how's. A pleasant aroma tickled her nose. It smelled like spicy broth. She blinked a few times. Two enormous faces filled her vision—one black, one white. Interracial angels?

"She's coming around," said Gene.

"I'll bet it was the antibiotics I put under her tongue," said Bibi.

Diane swallowed dryly. "What's that wonderful smell? Barbecued chicken? Oh, my shoulder hurts." Shc noticed she was propped up in a seated position on the hotel lobby sofa. The top half of her suit was missing. Moving her right arm, she could feel tape stretched across her back.

"That was one hell of a charge," said Gene. "You looked like a freight train when you hit that guy."

"Couldn't help it, I just snapped." She remembered the firefight coming back to her in bits and pieces.

Bibi handed her a small plate and plastic fork. "It's seasoned pork and a boiled potato."

"I dressed the wound and taped you up," Gene told her. "The bullet creased a little furrow up your back and nicked your shoulder blade. You could call it a serious superficial wound. I gave you about fifteen stitches with some sewing thread. You're going to be just fine."

Diane took several bites and then caught her breath. "How long have I been out?"

Gene answered, "About three hours. I hate to rush you, but if we don't vacate this property, we can expect more company. I disabled their vehicle. Bibi hid the bodies, except for the two live ones. A family took them in. I guess they felt sorry for them. The manager of the hotel threw a hissy fit and promised that the law was going to hear about what we did to her building. An RPG obliterated the second floor."

Diane took a few more bites and washed it down with a cup of water. She wiped her mouth with the back of her hand. "Naturally. It's always *our* fault." She looked around the lobby. "You better help me into the suit top."

Gene shook his head. "Sorry, it's packed along with everything else. Can you stand up and walk?"

Diane clicked the controller and got to her feet. Taking a few tentative steps, she nodded in the affirmative. The lower half of the suit seemed to be functioning properly. "I'm good to go."

Gene led the women out the front and around the corner of the building. When they reached the rear yard, Diane stopped suddenly. Aghast, she looked at the two saddled horses. The animals were hitched to a clothesline pole. Packs sat neatly strapped upon their backs.

Gene gave her a weak smile. "Except for one AK-47, the deal cost us all the weapons and ammo. That's what the owner wanted in exchange. We have to set the horses free once we reach our destination. They'll return home. They're rentals."

Diane sighed. "I have to give you credit; you seem to

know what you're doing all the way around. Thanks for the medical attention."

Bibi gave Gene a hard look. The man ignored it.

Diane accepted a leg up on the back of the big, gray gelding. She let Gene position her legs since she feared kicking and spooking the horse by using the controller. He next helped Bibi mount a milk crate, got behind her and shoved her atop the brown mare. He strung a lead rope from Bibi's horse to his saddle horn and then mounted Diane's horse. He pulled her arms around his waist and gave a deft kick. Before Diane knew it, they were headed into the backwoods at a steady stride.

After disabling the finger controller, she laced her fingers around Gene and leaned into his back. She could smell the muskiness of his neck—feel the soft curls of his hair on her face. It seemed so strange that this man would show up in her life under such incredible circumstances. He'd believed in her after all—even came looking for her. He'd actually risked his life to protect her and her friends. What a peculiar, wonderful man, she thought. Yet those feelings frightened her. *I don't have any feelings left to give. I'll never risk it again.*

Gene turned his head. "If you begin to feel any pain or discomfort just holler. I'll change out that dressing after we put some miles under us."

He was considerate, too. Damn it. "Don't mind me. You set the pace. I'm more concerned about Bibi."

"She'll be all right. I have her tethered. All she has to do is balance in the saddle."

"Thank God Almighty 'cause I can't steer one of these things, anyway," said Bibi.

They merged into the forest at a slow canter. The jostling took some getting used to, but Gene obviously didn't want to push them any faster for fear of throwing a rider. He seemed to know precisely which direction to go, which perplexed

Diane at first until she noticed he had Ollie's boat compass taped to the front of his saddle. Using the horses had been a genius move. They could transverse the toughest obstacles and terrain. It would be unlikely a chase team would pursue them, unless they were on horseback. Most importantly, they would avoid the main road that bisected the island.

Considering the many locations in the island interior she had been in, the scenery never changed much from the endless stands of pine, saplings and fern undergrowth. Though beautiful at times, it was getting downright annoying seeing the same landscape, as though it had been xeroxed. Had she visited the island under different circumstances, her feelings might have been different—not so cynical.

"Whatever prompted you to join the agency?" Diane asked. She still knew hardly anything about the man she had her arms around, the same man who had probably seen her topless while she was unconscious.

"I guess it was when I took the Boy Scout Oath and decided to follow the scout laws. It was my first brush with redneck conservatism. When I made Eagle and wore my uniform to high school, the kids nearly tore my head off. They settled for stripping me and defiling my uniform. Those people represented my first introduction to criminal behavior. I thought law enforcement was the next logical step after that little episode."

"What a terrible experience for you."

"Since I was a WASP-nerd, with a clean record, it seemed appropriate. After high school, I enrolled in college, studied criminal justice and earned a degree. Instead of trying out for the police academy, which was the next logical step, I decided to enlist in the Army and spent four years with a tank crew. Read all the Tom Clancy books during my enlistment. Hence my pre-occupation with things that go boom or ker-thump. The Gulf War came along and went. Got discharged. From there I ended up at FMC working defense contracts. Put my application in as a suit for the Central Intelligence Agency, passed the tests, and walla! I'm coming up on my six-year pin with the agency. Wouldn't trade it for the world. Although sometimes I think a field position would have been more exciting. Still no regrets."

"Lots of Eastwood and Wayne movies, I'll bet."

"I've got a condo stacked to the rafters with them. Love the guys. I used to try walking with John's swagger. My friends thought I had a permanent condition of hemorrhoids. I eventually cut it out and settled for being just old, boring me."

"Sounds like wish fulfillment—trying to make things better in an impossible world. I know about the 'old boring me' lifestyle. I couldn't ever seem to make a difference. I wanted too so badly. Endura has handled that part of my life. I hate her sometimes—she's courageous, always makes the right decisions and, ultimately, makes a difference. Her powers of persuasion are radical at times, with her headlong dives into the fray. But that's the way her mind works—like a gun that goes off—you hear it and see the flash—then it's over before you know it. Me, I'll slap fight with a plan or idea before I act. I'm also not a very good judge of character."

Why did she feel like revealing so much to this man?

"Sounds like you see Endura as a role model. Your mother?"

"No, mom's not even alive."

"I'm sorry for your loss."

"Endura is the fantasy character I created. She's not real—only in my head."

"I'm an idiot. I forgot about that. You won't hold it against me if I say I've never read the strip?"

She laughed. "You weren't required to know. Kind of refreshing, actually. She gives out more autographs than I do.

The fans are always asking me what *Endura* is going to do next." She gulped. "Are you mari...anyone special in your life?"

Bibi called out, "That is some spooky territory you're traveling over right now, sister. If you catch my fly ball?"

"Thanks, Bibi, I'm not wearing a mitt right now."

"Enter at your own risk then."

Gene cocked his head. "I'm not hooked up with anyone right now, if that's what you're asking. Not to say that I haven't been on the lookout for some long-legged, tight-rear-end librarian type." He cringed. "Wow, that came out wrong."

"I damn well knew it!" said the large woman.

"Enough, Bibi!" Then to Gene, "Don't apologize. I'm the odd one out. I'm new for most people. As far as the other, I would expect someone like you to have a wife and two-point-five kids. You know, the typical conservative household with a picket fence and window box full of rhododendrons."

"Well, the right one just hasn't come along, I guess. Maybe I'm expecting too much."

"Don't' lower your standards on our account," growled Bibi.

Gene whispered, "She's very protective of you, isn't she?"

Diane took a heaving breath. "Insufferably so. She trusts Endura, but not Diane Louise Nine."

"Maybe I should let out about fifty more feet of tether line."

They both laughed.

"I heard that!"

They rode on. Gene led them on a zigzag course, like a destroyer escort in the Atlantic, sometimes doubling back over his trail. He made frequent stops to demand silence, before starting up again. Diane did not question his motives for doing these things but deferred to his judgment.

They passed over several small creeks late in the afternoon, allowing them to top up their water bottles. Gene led the horses upstream. They began a long climb up a rise.

At one point Diane fell asleep against Gene's back and awoke hours later, just as the sun sank in the west, casting a pink and gray hue over the treetops.

Gene looked at the sky then called a halt. Diane slid from the horse with his assistance. Bibi needed help, and when on the ground, she found it difficult to stand up. Now she complained of lower back pain and "jammed hips."

They sat on a ground cloth with their backs up against the packs. Gene knifed open some canned goods, offering up a small meal of cream corn and tomato slices. Bibi took several pain pills before eating her portion. Hitched to a tree trunk, the horses nibbled lazily at some wild grass. Diane ate slowly. Her digestion had been acting up again, giving her severe bouts of stomach cramps.

Gene looked thoughtful, after taking several mouthfuls. "I figure a day for him to make it to a phone. A couple of days to assemble a strike team. Maybe another day for arrival. Hell, without any snags it could happen tomorrow. The problem will be convincing the Department of Defense to throw in their muscle. Sometimes military chain of command decisions can sabotage an operation. I wouldn't be surprised if the okay had to come straight from the Pentagon."

Diane wiped her mouth. "Let's say they do act quickly. How will they locate us?"

"I wrote down what I thought our general course would be if we were not at Riviera. Riviera will be their first stop by default. They'll work backward northeast in a grid search pattern and try to pick us up that way. They'll know we're not on any of the main roads. I told them to watch for a red road flare, which I'll use if I spot a search craft overhead. I packed six flares."

Diane nodded. "That's why you've been watching the sky and listening. What do you think they'll send?"

"If it was up to me, I'd send an R-Q-1 Predator drone with satellite data links. It can pick the date off a dime at ten thousand feet. They could transport and set up a ground control station, launch, and have that baby sweeping the area for us in record time. On the other hand, they could send in one or more assault helicopters or even a search and rescue variant."

"Will they send enough firepower?"

"I would love to see a couple of squads—Rangers or Seals. But what do I know? In a perfect world we'd have it all. Whoever makes those decisions will weigh all the pros and cons. Penetrating foreign airspace is a bitch."

"What if they don't show up?" asked Bibi, just finishing her meal. "Maybe we're not important enough to get our asses hauled out of here."

Diane knew that part of Bibi's cynicism toward Gene revolved around jealousy. He had been the one to treat her wound, which insulted the nurse in Bibi. Diane would have a gentle talk with her later.

Gene remained nonplussed. "At the very least, they have an agent in peril. That's me. The other claims are espionage, terrorist activities, kidnapping, attempted murder, and God knows what other international laws have been broken. I can't give you a definite contact or extraction time. From the damage and casualties we inflicted in Riviera, you can bet that this GSA will come hell-bent looking for us with a search and destroy mission. Keep in mind that we don't need to reach Nueva Gerona. We're looking for the first operational landline phone we can find, or working sat tower."

Diane cocked an eyebrow. "From what you know about them from me, do you think these guys are some independent group that fabricated all of this Global Socialist Alliance stuff?"

"You mean a radical splinter group? I don't think so. They're too well organized and funded. I'm convinced they're the front-line force of a larger command structure that probably originates from one of those foreign countries. If this new alliance has any credibility to it, our government will want to pull out all stops to sniff it out. We're talking about combined axis powers with the capability of attacking the United States and its allies. A serious global third war threat."

"What's the best scenario for us?" asked Diane.

"Hypothetically? Okay, the message gets through. Then immediate confirmation and action. Resources and troops hot-footing it straight out of Guantanamo. With that scenario, we could see a rescue today or tomorrow."

Diane smiled. "Now that's the kind of vision I could sleep on."

"Speaking of such," said Bibi, resting her head on Diane's thigh.

Gene rose up, made a trip to his packhorse and pulled out their only rifle. He rejoined Diane but remained standing. "I'm going to walk the perimeter for a while. Sorry, no fires. Try to get some shuteye." He stepped off into the shadows, the mush of his footfalls fading into the night.

Diane hugged Bibi. Their eyelids closed at the same time.

They were up at first light. Gene changed Diane's dressing then handed out rice cakes so they could eat on the move. They saddled up and headed out. After two hours, they passed over a shallow rock-strewn part of the Loma la Canada River, topped a rise and entered a small dry wash. Diane watched the skies, allowing Gene to concentrate on the path ahead. She suspected he had stayed awake all night, but he showed no signs of fatigue. He offered no complaints. Bibi trailed behind, slumped in the saddle from a restless night's sleep. Diane wondered if the medication the large woman had been taking was responsible for her lethargy.

Gene reigned in suddenly, frozen in the saddle. He scanned the horizon, turning his head in an effort to fine-tune his ears for sound. Diane could see or hear nothing.

Diane increased her hug on him. "What is it, Gene?"

"Could be another bee or fly again. It throws me off every time they buzz around me."

Then Diane heard it, a far-off humming noise. It sounded like a high-pitched airplane engine.

Gene jumped from the saddle. He opened up the rear pack and pulled out a flare. Diane almost lost her balance, craning her head to look up at the sky. She couldn't imagine that rescue forces had been sent in this early.

"You two are blowing smoke," Bibi grumbled. "It's too early for help."

"Don't underestimate your government," said Gene.

As if on cue, a svelte craft banked sharply, appearing out of the sun and diving low over the treetops. It ran the length of the wash and then took a sweeping turn. It swooped down over them. Diane thought that it resembled a huge kit glider or a big model plane. It was nimble, making graceful turns and dives. Gene popped a flare and waved it a few times. He ran several yards to toss it in a large clearing. The craft made one more low-level pass over their heads, waggling its wings before it disappeared from view.

"That had to be a predator!" said Diane.

"Right," said Gene. "We've been made. It just recorded our GPS coordinates. We can expect company soon."

Bibi said, "Dude, that was awesome. Are we really going home?"

"We'll be home soon enough, but I don't think this is over yet. They'll need to debrief us first."

"I'll take my clothes off for anybody," said Bibi. "Just as long as I can go home and never come back to this hellhole."

Gene pulled the horses in together and then helped both women off the horses. Gene untied the packs and dropped them to the ground. He tied the horses to a fallen log, explaining that setting them loose now would be premature lest something unforeseen happened. Much to Diane's relief, he did not say they would be forgotten or stranded.

Diane harbored no doubts about their rescue. So far, the agent had been right about the chain of events. Ollie had made contact. The authorities had reacted swiftly to the information. A search craft had been sent out. Their tiny group had been found. A Las Vegas bookie would not have bet against such odds.

"Is there anything we should do to prepare?" asked Diane, feeling more hopeful than she had in days.

Gene looked at her, and then at the packs. "What say we get you into full gear? I think they wouldn't mind seeing the physical proof of what set this mission off. I know it sure motivated me."

Bibi held her hand out like a stop sign. "I'll do it. You're likely to bust something up."

Diane frowned. "Are you sure you're up to it, Bibi?"

"Honey, I got my second wind the moment that toy plane flew over us and said howdy."

Gene watched as Bibi snapped the components together, fitting them precisely into their sockets and jacks. She explained how and where everything fit together. He hovered over her, watching her every move. Diane found it amusing how animated he became watching the procedure, although it defined his personality completely. *Another tech nerd*, she thought. It gave her uncomfortable flashbacks of Chet Strauss.

It took fifteen minutes to get her into the full suit, including the helmet. Not long after, they heard the approach of a helicopter. The rotor wash came with a deep thumping noise. Diane could almost feel the air sucked from her lungs when the behemoth appeared overhead. Gene sent the horses on their way with rump swats and then directed the women away from the landing area.

The HH-60g Pave Hawk helicopter dropped dramatically, delivering a tornado-like maelstrom of pebbles and leaves. Four soldiers jumped from the loading door and approached the three. One of them yelled out to Gene above the engine noise.

"Agent Eugene Gene?"

"Affirmative!"

"Captain Dodds, Para Rescue. If we can get you to board immediately, please." Captain Dodds gave Diane a double-take and then motioned for one of his men to pick up the packs, and another to assist Bibi who swooned into one of the soldier's arms.

Diane made it to the chopper under her own steam. Strong hands pulled her aboard into the cabin. She saw two more soldiers and one woman. The woman, dressed in black slacks and wearing a flak jacket, gave Gene a bone-crushing hug the second he entered. The engine soared in pitch with a jet-like whine. The craft lifted, spun one hundred and eighty degrees, and flew over the treetops, catching pine branches in its skids. Diane held onto a bulkhead strap, trying to keep her balance.

Dodds crouched next to Diane, cupping his voice. "We're glad to have you aboard, soldier. We saved an engineer's seat for you up front. If you'll come with me."

Diane pulled the helmet off and shook her platinum

blonde hair out. Dodds reared back, apologized for the misidentification. He thumbed through a small notepad and nodded. "Ah, Diane Nine. That's what I get for not reading my dispatch. Like I said, we have—"

"If it's all the same, I'd like to stay here with the others," Diane cut in. "You're not going to lose me or the suit. But I have to ask, what happens next?"

"We're taking you straight to Gitmo for medical aid, debriefing and security."

"What about Ollie? I mean, Oliver? He was the one who got the message through to you."

"We had a little bird pick him up just outside of Nueva Gerona. He's safe and on his way to the base."

"That's a relief. But you have a bigger problem here and you'll need my help with it. These terrorists have a base in the interior. I know what it looks like because I was held captive there for a while."

Dodds shook his head. "My orders were to evac you, get you to safety and secure the prototype hardware."

Diane stiffened. "I'm telling you that the inventor of this suit is with them. He's a traitor. Granted, the triad wanted this suit firsthand because they could develop it faster. The problem is with Chester Strauss; he probably has the blueprints in his possession, and even if he didn't, he could reproduce this suit from memory. I don't think you want this technology in the hands of combined foreign powers. Strauss and his terrorist sponsors are probably stuck on this island. Now is the time to round them up or put them down."

"I'm afraid she's right," said Gene. "She can identify these enemy combatants, and provided we capture and detain them, she is the only one who can provide testimony for the prosecution."

Dodds was losing the battle. It showed on his face. "With all due respect, we've got four other rotor craft deployed in grid search patterns all over this island. We're sure to find them and root them out."

"When?" demanded Bibi. "Next week? Hell no, fool! Diane can bring you right in on top of those jokers. We've been doing pretty damn good at kicking their asses up till now."

Dodds cringed. "I'll have to get approval on this. Don't get your hopes up." He duck-walked to the cockpit and picked up a headset.

Diane held the helmet firmly in her lap. She looked across at the woman who sat next to Gene. The unknown female sat *very* close to him, speaking directly into his face with an inch of room between them. Diane guessed her to be a close acquaintance, or even a colleague, judging from her dress and disposition. Her red bangs framed a pert, attractive face. She seemed a little thick around the middle, but it could have been a vest. Though she had them crossed, it was plain to see the woman had long legs.

Gene noticed Diane's intense gaze at the woman and said, "Forgive my rudeness. This is Cha Cha Susie Delaney. She's a field agent for Central Intelligence. I was just asking her how she got approval to join the team."

Cha Cha Susie?

"I'm glad to meet you," Diane proffered a hand – a useless gesture in the jostling craft. She wondered who Cha Cha had killed or threatened to end up flying a rescue mission, ending up in Gene's lap a thousand miles from home.

"When the director asked for a volunteer, I jumped at the chance," said Susie. "The minute I heard Gene was in trouble, well, instinct took over."

"He's very lucky to have such friends," said Diane, giving her a grim smile.

Bibi glared at Diane. "I'm not going to say a thing or beat

it into your head over and over again as many times as it takes. Uh, uh. I won't do that."

Diane ignored the comment, turning her concentration toward the cockpit. Dodds had just put down the headset. He spoke into the ear of the pilot and turned, threading his way back to the cabin area.

"We just got the okay for a search and identify sweep," said Dodds for all to hear. "That means a 'spotter' capacity only. We'll stay airborne for as long as fuel remains. Ms. Nine will serve as the spotter. We're looking for the bad guy's base camp. Failing to locate it, we'll be vectored back to Guantanamo."

No one said anything. Dodds maneuvered Diane closer to the gun hatch, buckling her waist belt to a security strap. He projected his voice, asking her questions that pertained to the location of the base camp. She told him what she knew of the kidnapping route, although it was limited in detail. He seemed satisfied with the information and made another quick trip to the cockpit. In response, the chopper changed its direction and took on a new course. At her side once again, Dodds told her that their starting point would begin on the north coast of the island then continue inland, bisecting the landmass.

Once they reached the coast, Diane donned the helmet and dialed up the magnification. She studied the small thread-like roads that twisted through the inland forest, knowing that one of them lead to a small encampment of sheds and buildings. She remembered the configuration of the structures, positive that she could recognize them from the air.

The first pass over the island did not alert her to anything familiar. The chopper turned for another pass. Dodds stayed at her side, encouraging her efforts. Gene joined in the visual survey from the other side of the door, offering another pair of eyes through binoculars. Diane hoped she hadn't aroused needless hopes. She *needed* to find the combatants. Though she would love to see Chet Strauss prosecuted for his traitorous acts, the most important issue involved the future threat of the Global Socialist Alliance. An effort to stop them at this juncture had to be made now. No one knew that more than her.

"Anything yet?" Dodds asked over the rotor noise.

Diane shook her head, adjusting the helmet controls, bringing the landscape into wide-field and then narrow view. Ten minutes into their second run and just as they neared the middle of the island, something caught her eye, just as Dodds said that they were short on fuel.

"There's a small patch down there," she said. "Can you circle around and go lower?"

Dodds ordered the pilot to drop.

Below, a small winding road led to a clearing. As they descended, Diane could make out the shapes of the buildings that looked like tiny dominoes. Parts of the buildings were broken and scattered. Then she saw the tops of three SUVs—two black and one silver. Two large blue tarps were plainly visible, covering what she remembered to be the large rubber boats.

"That's it!" she yelled. "That's where they held me!"

Dodds rushed to the cockpit and donned the headset. The Pave Hawk began a slow spiraling descent over the encampment. Diane could see tiny figures emerge from the buildings like excited ants. Small flashes erupted from the group, and in the next seconds, she heard what sounded like pebbles rattling in a can. *They're shooting at us!*

Two more explosions of light leapt from the ground, climbing in dizzy spirals that left smoke contrails. Diane flinched, instinctively pulling back from the door.

"RPGs!" yelled Gene. "Hit the deck!"

19

A horrendous clang was followed by a thump-whoosh. The helicopter lurched. Then it shuddered violently. The pilot's frantic voice filled the cabin while he wrestled with the stick.

"Mayday, mayday, mayday! Red Rider has taken hostile fire and we are going down. Coordinates are...grid one-one-nine, Section C-five. I repeat, we are...."

The craft began an uncontrolled clockwise spin, losing altitude fast. Billowing smoke entered the cabin, and with it came the toxic smell of aviation fuel. Diane caught glimpses of the earth looming upwards—the landscape, a dizzying whirlpool of green and brown. She thought that a crash at this speed would not be survivable. She braced hard.

The fuselage hit the upper most branches of the trees first, providing a temporary cushion until the weight won out and snapped them. The cabin titled crazily, threatening to throw the occupants out of the door. Then the blades hit, sheering off massive limbs and clumps of foliage. The rotor assembly snapped free. The spinning blades cut swaths through the trees, producing lethal projectiles flying in every direction.

The fuselage somersaulted once, then slammed onto the

forest floor, accompanied by the frightened cries of the occupants. Diane's safety harness snapped. The inertia pitched her out of the door and onto the pile of tangled branches. She ended upside down, her legs caught in kicking spasms. She relieved the pressure on her finger controller, then fought to extricate herself. Several moans escaped from inside the twisted wreckage. The cargo door had swung partially shut and jammed. Overhead, the bare rotor shaft hummed to a halt—the damaged engine hissed with crackling heat, sending off a geyser of steam and fuel vapor.

The smell of fuel was overpowering. "Bibi, can you hear me?" Diane dropped to the forest floor and managed to get up. She tossed broken tree limbs away and gripped the door. She wrenched it open with a powerful yank. Bodies lay helter-skelter on top of each other; a few hands and legs moved within the mass. Diane pulled the closest person out of the door, and then the next. The two pilots crawled on their knees across the wreckage to assist in freeing the others. Bibi squirmed out of the tangle. Diane hefted her through the door. Gene and Cha Cha Susie followed shortly after, sporting cuts and bruises.

Captain Dodds doused the outside of the fuselage with an extinguisher. He ordered everyone to keep their distance from the craft.

Bibi slumped to her knees, holding onto a broken branch for support. "Somebody have mercy. A minute ago, I was headed home. Now I'm on this stinking island again. And with a broken back, I think. Ohhh..."

The most serious injury belonged to Bibi, who had a possible spine fracture. Gene had a cut on his forehead. The copilot had sustained a broken arm. The rest of the passengers suffered various other injuries, but shock and bewilderment predominated. Diane checked her suit to see if anything was disconnected or broken, but just as she looked up from her inspection, she spied figures dodging through the trees in their direction.

"You'd better gather your weapons," Diane warned. "We've got company."

Two soldiers scrambled back into the twisted craft. Cha Cha Susie, who had lost her rifle in the crash, yanked a Beretta from a shoulder holster and leapt out of the wreckage.

Dodds yelled, "Everybody take cover on the other side of the chopper!"

Diane bodily carried Bibi around to the other side of the helicopter. The other soldiers gathered there, checking for extra clips and taking up firing positions. The first shots rang out. Multiple pings sounded off the fuselage. Then small arms fire erupted in a barrage. Everyone ducked low or flattened themselves out on the forest floor. Bullets slapped the metal, sending ricochets in every direction.

The sound of a cursing voice from the other side of the chopper reached Diane's ears. She realized that one of their group was missing. The female agent.

Diane looked over the top of the downed chopper. She saw Cha Cha Susie kneeling in the clearing, returning fire, while clods of earth erupted around her. Diane broke from cover, reaching her with a burst of speed, just as the agent took a hit to the knee, vaporizing the flesh and pants material. Cha Cha Susie wailed. Diane caught the woman before she fell. She used her body armor to shield the agent and carried her around the corner of the downed craft, placing her on the ground. One of the Para Rescue team members began to fashion a tourniquet.

Gene moved to the extreme end of the crumpled tail and began placing precise shots, keeping the opposition from advancing. Two paratroopers fired from around the nose section. Dodds fired over the top of the fuselage.

Gene screamed, "Get the guy with the rocket launcher before he gets one off!"

Diane looked at Cha Cha Susie. "Where's your pistol?"

The agent grimaced. "I dropped it out there."

Diane grabbed a clip from Cha Cha Susie's vest pouch and ran to the nose of the craft. She peeked around the edge. Most of the combatants hid behind the largest trees. The one that held the RPG tube knelt behind a huge shrub and had just raised the tube to his shoulder. In the next moment, a flash erupted from the weapon, sending a wobbling missile in their direction. The airborne grenade hissed over their heads, exploding behind them in the forest, shaking the ground and sending down a shower of twigs and leaves.

Diane couldn't wait for him to reload. She raced from cover into the opening. She found the pistol lying where the agent had dropped it, picked it up and bolted for the RPG wielder. All hell seemed to break loose when now all the fire was directed at her. She concentrated on the finger control, keeping her steps in swift rhythm. She fired the pistol on the run, expending the last three rounds in the clip. The RPG-armed man fumbled with another load, his face frantic. He dropped the tube, turned and began to run, just as Diane caught him around the legs with a dive.

They tumbled to the ground, but he was up again before she could get to her feet. Crossfire from his comrades, and meant for her, riddled him. He collapsed in a heap on the ground. She made a frantic crawl for the weapon and crushed the RPG tube with her pincer claws. Up once again, she made a beeline for the downed chopper, bullets striking every part of her suit.

Gene ran into the clearing, offering cover fire. Diane cornered the tail section and sprawled on the earth. Gene was at her side a moment later, dragging her behind the thickest part of the fuselage.

"That was some mad dash," he said, winded. "And I mean mad as in *crazy*. Stay down for now."

Diane gulped for breath, winded from the adrenalin rush more than the run. She shook so badly her finger activated the suit controls. She couldn't get her legs to stop kicking. The other team members were hugging the earth, trying to shield themselves from the pyrotechnic Armageddon.

Holding out against the onslaught seemed one-sided. With Diane and her people outgunned, the enemy would only have to outflank them, or circle around then attack from their exposed rear. Diane's team could run out of ammunition. A direct RPG hit on their position would spell doom.

Bibi crawled across the earth like a dazed centipede, trying to reach Diane's position. Her cheeks glistened wet with tears, the first time Diane had ever seen true terror and hopelessness in her assistant's eyes.

"Are we going to die here?" Bibi asked.

Diane joined hands with the woman, trying to quell her fright. "We're not licked yet. The pilot got the message through. We'll have help soon—I promise."

Dodds projected his voice at Gene. "I'm guessing about twenty guns, but half of them are backing out. Watch your corner for an end-around maneuver."

"Got it covered."

Diane tried to stand but Bibi would not relinquish her grip. She still had Cha Cha Susie's pistol and a fresh clip. She would use it only if they were overrun. Firing blindly over her head made no sense. What did Gene call it? Spraying and praying?

Ten minutes passed. An unexpected lull came to the firefight. Up until now, the broken fuselage had shuddered with a continuous hail of bullets. Now Diane could only hear an occasional crack-ping.

"Can't figure it," said Gene from his position. "I can't see most of them—don't know what they're up to."

"Stay frosty," said Dodds. "They've got something planned."

Five more minutes produced a dead still. With the exchange of gunfire they at least knew where the opposition was located.

Dodds peered over his vantage point, knitting his brows. "Where the hell are they? That last sniper just disappeared."

The soldiers stationed at the nose of the chopper moved to improve their line-of-sight. One of them yelled, "No eyes on them from here. Can't see a living soul."

"It's a trap," said Bibi, raising her voice. "They just want to flush us out and waste us."

"Hush!" Diane urged. "Did you ever think they might have retreated?"

The team members who were able to, stood erect and looked out over the clearing. One of them asked, "How far is that compound from here?"

Dodds answered, "Rough guess, about a quarter of a mile. They might have run out of ammunition."

"All at the same time?" Gene wondered.

Diane popped her head over the tail section. She could see no figures standing amongst or behind the pines, while the thick stand prevented her from seeing further back into the forest. It was inconceivable that the terrorists had given up or retreated when they clearly had the upper hand in the fight. One of their dead comrades, the one she had struggled with, lay on the ground within her magnified field of view. No other trace remained of the terrorists. Then a familiar sound came out of the south—a teeth-rattling thumpity-thumpity-thump, juxtaposed with the whine of turbo-shaft engines.

Diane looked up to see the enormous outline of what looked like a giant wasp. Dodds ran out into the clearing, scissoring his hands over his head. Defying all caution, the helicopter dipped sharply then leveled out. It began a descent into the small clearing, the rotor blades nipping the branches. Sod and needles rose up from the wash in a blinding flurry. Before the craft's skids hit the ground, four troopers bailed from the doors and ran across the clearing. One of the soldiers carried a large plastic med kit. He cornered the downed chopper and administered first aid to Cha Cha Susie. Two others approached Diane, asking if she was injured.

"No, I'm fine. You might help, Bibi, though."

"That prototype is the tits," one of them said to her, his eyes scoping the body armor. "We heard about it from command."

Diane pulled the helmet off. "I'm glad you like it." *This is getting tiring.*

"Sorry, ma'am. No offense."

One of the soldiers stripped a frame off his back and unfolded it into a carrying litter. Bibi looked up into the eyes of a muscular black trooper. She dithered. "I think I might have lost my shoe somewhere, soldier."

The trooper gave her an affectionate pat. "Well, Cinderella, the United States armed forces are here to take care of that problem for you."

Bibi grinned. "Cinderella? Soldier, they done stole my corsage, drank my champagne and busted my glass slipper."

"I'll personally retrieve that slipper for you, ma'am."

Bibi gave him a coquettish eye flutter. "That's the best offer I've had all day."

They gently lifted Bibi onto the frame, then began a swift trot back to the awaiting helicopter. Diane watched them, somewhat in a stupor. Snapping out of her haze, she followed in the wake of the troopers and boarded the helicopter, opting for a seat next to the door. The crush came with getting everyone inside, including the two litters that held the injured women. At least six more troopers had arrived in the rescue craft, a combination of Delta Force and Rangers.

The chopper lifted straight up, banked hard and accelerated, leaving the forest floor of Juventud below.

One of the troopers identified himself as Captain Hicks. He spoke over the noise. "Sorry we were a little late getting to you. We were on a search grid on the east side."

Dodds spoke on behalf of the group. "We just repelled an attack from twenty armed combatants. The same group who dropped our bird. They're equipped with small arms and RPGs. We lost eyes on them just before you arrived."

Diane looked down just as they made a low-level pass over the compound. She now understood the reason for the enemy's retreat. The SUVs and the large boats were gone.

"They've pulled out," Diane shouted. "They used cover fire to escape."

"She's right," said Gene, who also had his eyes trained below. "They're on the run."

"We have orders to medivac you out and secure the prototype," said Hicks. "No deviations."

Dodds pounded his fist on the bulkhead. "Hang the fuckin' orders! The U.S. military was fired upon, resulting in casualties. It's our duty to pursue hostile forces to destination —capture and or destroy."

"And I'm under direct orders," said Hicks, "to avoid an international incident with the Cuban government. It's bad enough that we've crossed into their airspace, but any direct engagement is to be avoided at all costs. This is a black op."

"I want a piece of their ass, sir!" said one of the troopers. "We've blown our cover by leaving a downed bird in their territory. We're committed to finishing this."

Diane listened to the heated exchange with morbid fascination. She had no idea who outranked who in this scenario. There seemed to be no clear-cut definition of one single operational order or command. Of course, nothing had gone by the book, which was the issue at hand. Either it was a stealth extraction of U.S. citizens and a secret prototype, or a full-scale espionage mission. Ah, not to forget door number three, which might be an all-out invasion. *Pick a door.*

Hicks left for the cockpit, squeezing past the mass of bodies. He returned shortly, sporting a face that bespoke of an attitude change akin to a pawnbroker who had been bested in a haggling war. Just then the craft made an abrupt course correction.

"Okay," Hicks boomed, "we're authorized to track hostiles to destination, with the option to engage if fired upon. The pilot is following the access road that led to the compound. The problem will be following their precise exit route once we hit multiple intersections." He unfolded a geodetic survey map and ran a finger over it. "The road leads to a T-intersection. From there it webs out to nine more connected roads and highways."

"They're towing a Zodiac watercraft," said Gene. "It's doubtful they're headed for an inland lake. Eliminate all roads except for those that lead to the coast. This looks like an offshore pickup."

"And out of those," said Diane, "choose the least traveled road."

"What if their intended route isn't on the map?" asked Hicks.

The question caught everyone off guard. The obvious unanswered questions: where were they headed and by what means would they make their escape? Float planes would negate the use of the Zodiacs. The only possible solution would be for them to escape the island via a large commercial vessel. Which made the entire coastline of the island suspect. Most notably, it would have to be an obscure launching point that would afford a quick exit.

Gene rubbed his cheeks. “Narrow it down. Look for a craft larger than fifty feet within thirty miles of the coast, including sailing vessels. Upon finding them, check for remote, accessible beaches in their proximity. That’s the only thing you have to go on. Coordinate your airborne strike force to split up the search areas.”

Hicks nodded. “Sounds like a plan. But we have something else up our sleeve.” Before he divulged what it was, he rushed to the cockpit.

Gene looked at Dodds. “I know you guys were pressed for time, but this is beginning to look like a cluster-fuck. Please tell me that we’re exempt from a need-to-know basis.”

Dodds moved closer to Gene, cupping his voice. “I’m sure it’s going to involve a military spy Sat that we have in geosynchronous orbit over Cuba. Two guided missile frigates are also in route from Guantanamo that are providing refueling and medical backup. It’s called contingency plans, Agent Gene. We’re not as cluster-fucked as you think.”

Gene had no retort for that one, Diane noticed. She looked out the door at the landscape below, watching it pass under them like a big green-brown collage. The roads looked like fallen thread, and the settlements and clearings were mere pimples. Baring miracles, how could anyone locate the precise vehicles they were looking for in such a vast landscape? Unless the satellite could pick them out of the maze, which was doubtful. She wanted so much for this to come to an end. But the pessimism was winning out. Something had to go wrong. Again. Hadn’t she written enough story arcs to know that the climax never came wrapped in glossy paper tied with pretty ribbons?

Gene took her gloved hand, squeezing it. “This will all be over soon,” he consoled. “Before you know it, we’ll be in transit back to civilization, where the real world lives and breathes.”

"Yeah, I never thought I'd miss it so much." *This is a terrible place. I wouldn't even write about it, much less visit it again for any reason.*

Diane looked out the door at the landscape again. A beige ribbon of sand appeared below, scatter-shot with debris, beached watercraft and remnants of buildings and docks. The chopper turned into the wind, dropped in altitude, and followed the coastline north. The pilot reduced the speed. The cockpit crew manned binoculars to scan the area below. She put her helmet on and dialed up full magnification. Gene joined in the search, even though his vision was limited to larger objects.

After thirty minutes, the craft circled for another pass, covering the same search area as before, but it continued south following the gentle curve of the island. Reaching a predetermined fix, it once again reversed its course and flew north. Diane imagined that the other helicopters enlisted in the search were covering other sectors of island coastline.

A commotion of chatter filled the cockpit. The helicopter reversed direction with a violent bank and flew south at a quick pace.

Dodds wormed his way back into the cabin area, squeezing next to the door. He unfolded a map and worked a navigational protractor over it. He licked his lips, a hint of excitement on his face. "We've got a hit on vehicles and a watercraft matching their description fourteen miles west of Playa Larga. That's the south end of the island. Blue Dog picked them up after a Satellite fixed their location. We're headed there now to confirm the sighting."

"Are they in route or in the water?" asked Gene.

"Just preparing to launch – they're on the beach."

Diane flipped her visor up and looked at Hicks. "Please tell me you're not going to get close enough to them to get shot at. They're still armed."

"Ma'am, this is a fully armored gunship, with the latest technology and first-strike capability. We don't plan on sticking our neck out." He looked sideways at Dobbs.

The big gunship passed over the shoreline and flew straight across the edge of the island. Five more minutes brought them above the half-moon shape of a remote beach with a high berm line. The gunship flew in low over the small cove, directly under another circling helicopter that had marked the location by their presence.

Diane glimpsed objects below, surrounded by scurrying figures. Two trailers had backed into the surf line. Tarps had been pulled from the huge Zodiacs. Three SUVs were visible, and at least fifteen terrorists, maybe more. She could swear she could even see Chet Strauss wearing his filthy smock.

"That's them, all right," said Diane. "No mistake."

The helicopter slowed to a hover. The pilot turned the nose of the craft around and dipped slightly, affording them an unencumbered view of the activity below. Diane leaned her head past the edge of the door to see better. The terrorists were well aware of the helicopter above them but were unperturbed and intent on launching the boats.

Gene gazed down. "That's gall. Where do those assholes think they're going? I don't see a ship anywhere."

"No telling," said Dodds. "They've got something in mind. Whatever it is, it won't escape our notice."

Bibi had been following some of the conversation. She rose up from her littler. "Why don't you just make a smokin' black hole out of them and let the crabs pick up the rest?"

"We're not in the business of murder," said Hicks. "We've got the golden egg. We want the goose that laid it."

They stayed in hover mode while another helicopter appeared on the scene. It took up a stationary position. Below, both inflatable boats had just launched and began to beat their way through the waves, leaving frothy smears in their wake. The SUVs and trailers sat on the beach abandoned like unwanted trash. The three hovering military choppers moved slowly, following the progress of the terrorists out to sea. Passing through the surf line, the boats picked up speed. They hydroplaned over the water, their engines straining at full throttle.

The pilot called back, "We've got a headcount of eighteen individuals carrying small arms. No shots fired. We're tracking them to their destination as fuel permits. But we're just about sucking vapor fumes. Nothing on radar out there."

Gene gave the horizon a dismissive wave of his hand. "And that's just it, isn't it? There isn't going to be anything on the radar. No surface ships or boat planes. We're looking for the wrong craft."

"What do you mean?" Dodds and Hicks chorused.

"I'm saying you'd be better off using sonar. We're looking for a submarine."

"Fuel warning light!" cried the pilot for all to hear.

20

They had only been on the landing deck of the guided missile frigate Franklin Pierce for ten minutes for refueling when the commotion started. Bibi and Agent Cha Cha Susie were offloaded and taken straight to medical. Diane and Agent Gene held up the launch, refusing to disembark, thus hampering a major military exercise. The commanding officer had ordered them to the deck, refusing to put non-military personnel in harm's way. Notwithstanding, Diane wore an irreplaceable military prototype that was so important to national security that the United States Government couldn't afford losing it in a major engagement. Meanwhile, a Soviet submarine, found submerged in international waters via sonobuoy contact waited for its comrades to arrive.

"I've come this far through a hurricane, a helicopter crash and bullets," said Diane, "and I'm not about to be locked up in some cabin aboard this ship. I've paid my dues. I'll see this to the end."

"Agreed," said Gene. "The Central Intelligence Agency has a vested interest in this case. I'm a duly appointed representative of that organization. You want me off you'll have to drag me off."

Dobbs looked at the two, dumbfounded.

Hicks threw his arms up in disgust. "I give up. If I had the time, I'd have you sign waivers. Since I don't, strap in. Let's hope to God this doesn't get ugly."

The two officers jumped in. The door slammed. The chopper reared from the deck, spun, and headed off to the south like an angry wasp. The pilot's radio chatter filtered back into the cabin. Diane could understand very little of it, only knowing that they were conversing with other airborne units that were already on the scene.

"What do we do once we get there?" asked Diane.

Hicks answered, "We assess the size and capability of the opposition. Contact has already been made with a submerged vessel. We know it's their intention to pick up the Zodiac crews. They'll have to surface to do that, leaving them vulnerable. We'll attempt to stop the transfer while our frigates converge on the location at flank speed."

"And if you can't stop it?" asked Gene.

"If they submerge and make a run for it, we're prepared for a show of force."

"But you want to avoid that," said Diane.

"Correct. Our primary directive from the beginning of Operation Helen of Troy was rescue. Now it's a capture scenario."

"What's Operation Helen of Troy?" Diane asked.

Hicks looked at her, grinning. "You're Helen of Troy, Ms. Nine. The joint chiefs thought it was appropriate since you launched a...well, you know."

"Oh."

The chopper flew on at top speed. The next sensation came fifteen minutes later with the perceptible downshift of the engine's power and the tilt of the cabin. Hicks announced their arrival, then threw the cabin door open. The pilot maneuvered the craft to offer an unencumbered view below but stood off far enough as to not offer an easy target from an RPG hit or automatic weapons fire.

Diane used the visor magnification to spot the objects. The two large zodiacs were now joined together with a mooring line, bobbing in the rolling swells. Waves broke against their rubber gunwales, showing they were static in the water. Waiting. Another military helicopter hovered in the distance like a gnat. The other chopper was obscured from her line of sight, but she felt certain it remained nearby, also watching the tense drama unfold.

A moment later, a huge bulk erupted from the sea. Breaching like a whale, the sub nosed over and splashed with a huge displacement of water. The tiny Zodiacs rocked like corks. Sheets of water cascaded from the subs conning tower.

Hicks, holding a pair of binoculars, nudged past Diane for a better look. He brought the binoculars to his face and said, "Russian. Nuclear attack sub, Alpha Class. They didn't waste any expense."

Diane shivered. "Then it's dangerous."

"Extremely so."

A hatch popped opened on the rear deck of the sub. Lines were thrown to the inflatable craft. Diane watched a sub crew scurry over the deck, rigging a boarding net—a giant insect gathering in larvae. She couldn't believe the audacity of the terrorists. Surely they knew they were surrounded by hostile aircraft capable of taking them out. Had they no sense or fear? Or did they possess the power to fight off the attack and escape? *Then kill them before they even get a chance to fight back. Blow 'em clean out of the water.*

She felt a bit shocked at the aggressiveness of her feelings. But she *did* want them stopped. She wanted them wiped from existence without mercy. They were death merchants. Their sole purpose was starting a third world war against the U.S. If she had her way, the submarine would be blown to slag, left to forever rust on the bottom of the Atlantic. All hands lost. *Well, just too bad.*

The terrorists swarmed inside the open hatch of the sub within minutes, abandoning the Zodiacs to the drifting currents. The sub's stern erupted in a huge wash. The vessel began to move off, its bow plunging beneath the waves.

"Full down-planes," said Hicks. "Crash dive. They're not wasting any time."

"They're running," said Gene.

"Which means they think we're bluffing," said Hicks.

In response to the sudden movement of the sub, Diane's helicopter turned and flew on a steady track in an eastward direction moving ahead of the sub's intended course. The big chopper picked up speed. The other helicopters broke from their hover to follow in perfect formation. They hadn't flown more than a few miles out when Diane's chopper pulled around and assumed a stationary holding pattern. She noticed another helicopter take up a similar position one hundred yards away. That left a third one out there somewhere. She assumed the three had aligned in a defensive wall, lying directly over the path of the approaching sub.

"We call it Niagara Walls," said Hicks. "Mortar-launched depth charges always gets their attention."

Diane did not know what to expect when she heard the steam whistle noise, followed by the shudder of the helicopter. Seconds later, it seemed like the ocean was lifted into the sky, a straight line of surging water screaming up towards the heavens—an impenetrable curtain of white water. The shock wave hit, giving the helicopter a gentle but firm slap. The sound concussion followed. Diane's eardrums seemed to suck inside her head then pop with a crackle-like snap. On the ocean's surface, the curtain of water reached its maximum altitude. It then fell in a graceful slow-motion plunge. The spectacle resembled a massive waterfall of roiling mist and haze. *Niagara Falls.*

Gene wiped a sweaty sheen from his face. "Jesus, you've blown the ocean up. They're surely dead."

Hicks gave him a mischievous grin. "Not dead. That was the first warning salvo across their bow."

Diane braced, this time knowing what to expect. They experienced a repeat of the first detonation, and it seemed to be larger and more dramatic. This time the wind carried a fine mist from the explosion that drifted into the cabin and gently alighted on her visor. She half expected to see dead fish flopping around—such was the power of the explosive upsurge.

Hicks cracked his knuckles. "Third time's a charm. It's like trying to bulrush the Cowboys offensive line."

The whistling howls filled the air again. Diane watched the ocean lift up from the seabed with a much deeper penetration. A swirling tornado of mud, sand and organic matter burst upwards from the surface in a crazed radial explosion. The shock waves radiated outward, flattening the sea swells. The chopper cabin rocked with a wind blast. When it was over, the sea looked like a brown porridge devoid of any living thing.

The helicopter crabbed sideways, distancing itself from the maelstrom below.

Dodds whooped, clapped his hands. "Well, that dimmed their lights and shook their coffee cups. That was nearly in their laps."

"The last porcupines were set for a seafloor discharge," Hicks explained. "Enough to wreak havoc with their propulsion cavitations."

Five tense minutes passed before Hicks pointed below. "Right on schedule."

The Russian submarine slowly broke the surface, looking like a turd in a filthy toilet. It showed no visible damage, other than an awkward lean of its conning tower. On closer inspection, it was plain that the entire vessel was off-ballast and sitting cockeyed, its systems damaged from the hydrostatic shock. A moment later, tiny figures appeared on the conning tower deck. One of them waved a white piece of material over his head.

Diane let out the breath she had been holding then closed her eyes. It was finally over. The Global Socialist Alliance had been beaten into submission. At least this segment of it. The rest of it lay in the hands of a higher authority—the United States Government.

Diane took off her helmet and smoothed her hair back. Hicks, Dodds, and some troopers gave Diane snappy salutes and approving nods and smiles. She returned a weak, tired smile, not knowing what to say. A high-five or whoop-whoop seemed inappropriate at the moment. She didn't feel like celebrating. She just wanted to be reunited with her friends and strangle them with loving hugs.

Gene broke the silence above the hum of the rotors. "What's next for those guys down there?"

Hicks took that one. "They'll be picked up by one of the frigates and thrown in the brig. Once they reach United States soil, they can expect a trial for espionage, attempted murder, theft, kidnapping and other assorted crimes against our citizens and government. This incident is going to open up an international can of worms, filled with finger-pointing, name-dropping and outrageous claims. Least of which is a violation of territorial sovereignty."

Gene nodded, looking out the door. "Well, at least you got a Russian sub out of the deal."

Hicks chuckled. "It'll be kind of hard to take her in tow when she's sitting on the bottom. They'll scuttle her for sure then destroy any sensitive materials. We expect that, naturally."

Hicks swung the door shut. The chopper banked and headed out.

The ride back to the Franklin Pierce was swift. Small talk filled the cabin; several jokes were offered up, as well as congratulatory back slaps and victory exclamations. Agent Gene bitched about the length of the report he would write upon his arrival at the agency. Dodds and Hicks huddled in conversation regarding the retrieval of the downed chopper on Juventud. Diane just felt relief, especially when the helicopter set down on the landing deck. When the door slid open, she exited the craft with overwhelming joy to be standing on United States property. Another joy assaulted her sight.

Under the aid of crutches, Bibi hobbled across the deck. Diane met her with a crushing embrace, tears spilling freely between them. They lingered in each other's arms for a while as deckhands and officers looked on. The moment waxed dramatic—two star-crossed lovers united after a long absence.

"Why did you have to fly off like that?" Bibi demanded. "Right into danger again. Haven't you had your gut full of it?"

Diane's voice cracked. "I needed to see the end of it. It was personal. We got the bad guys, Bibi. It's a cut, edit and print." She looked around. "Where's our little brave heart? Any news?"

Bibi wiped her eyes; one of her crutches fell to the deck. "I think he's on the other ship. They were going to take him to Guantanamo, but he put up a big hissy fit. I figure they're flying him out here to see us now. It looks like he really saved our asses." She picked up her crutch. "I think I love the little idiot."

They walked to the rail. Diane took a lungful of sea air while she looked out over the ocean. She thought she could see the island, but she might have been mistaken. After all, they were on their way to pick up the sub crew. She would never see the island again. She sensed movement to her left and looked to see who had joined her at the rail.

Gene gave her a sheepish smile and then cast his eyes out over the waves.

Bibi winked at Diane. "Well, I better get back to the infirmary before the nurse knows I split the scene."

Diane gave her a quick hug then turned her attention to Gene. He had one of those silly, nerdy looks on his face again. She furrowed her brows. "What's up with you?"

"Oh, nothing." He blew an exaggerated yawn. "Except that you have the United States Navy standing behind you, hoping that you're not of the mind to jump over this rail because you've been severely battle traumatized."

Diane shook her head. "I'm glad to know somebody values my life. Hasn't seemed like if for almost a week."

"Yeah, well, they don't really give a fig about you. They would hate to see that suit disappear into the drink. They'd like to take possession of it, A-S-A-P. Sorry, but they chose me to give you that news."

"Guh. I figured as much. That's why I'm relishing the moment."

He laughed. "Gotcha! I'm just kidding. You looked so damn melancholy standing here." He screwed up his face. "Relishing what moment?"

She flipped the hair out of her face then looked at him squarely. "I don't think I could make you understand."

"You can try."

She looked out over the water again. "I've really come to know everything about her now—things that I never knew before but could only imagine. I know what it's like to stand as tall as the giants like she's always done. For once in my life, I got the chance to interact with humanity on an equal footing—cross all those boundaries and limitations—to rise to a challenge—change the world—everything that always seemed so normal and easy for her. I never felt such power or purpose, traits that she always possessed."

"I wish I could find all of that for you." His face soured. "Not some dream."

"I learned what real freedom and independence was like—having no need for the assistance from others. I had the ability to run like the wind, to stand, to fight and win. I rode that stallion, forded that river and flew above it all for a fleeting moment in time. I became her and she became me. I stood on God's stage, and for the first time in my life I felt like a hero. It's an empty, soulless loss knowing that you'll never drink that heady wine again. It was, too, just a dream—a lark."

He didn't say anything for a long time. She didn't expect him to understand the connection. But he surprised her with his next words.

"Maybe that Endura gal can do all of those wonderful things. But she was nothing until you gave her life. You're the wellspring from which she flows—all of those ideals and heroics are meaningless without the true creator. It all started with you. It's not going to end there."

She looked down into the waves. "No, it's over."

"I have it on good authority that the government intends to develop a prototype of that suit for the handicapped. No doubt you'll be included in on the design and manufacturing. Besides, I thought you would be relieved to put all this behind you and get back to some hometown comfort."

"Oh, I'm glad the fight's over," she said with surprise on her face. "And I'm really happy that a version of the suit will be produced for people like me. God knows we need it. But... what a hell of a ride it was!"

He laughed. "Even Dorothy had to go back to Kansas. It doesn't mean the world has to go on without knowing your story. Why don't you hand it off to Endura and let her run with it. You could stage it on another planet and change a few names. You could bring it out as a special edition. I might even read that one."

She raised a brow. "I'm shocked that you even know her name."

"You'd be shocked about a lot of things."

"I wonder if I would be shocked about Cha Cha Susie Delaney. How is she, by the way?"

"She'll be all right. Although I think she's headed for a desk job. Her days as a field operative are over. And F-Y-I, I never had any social dealings with Susan other than agency ties."

Embarrassed for probing, her face pinked. "Sorry, I can be pretty direct at times. It's a fatal flaw."

"Did it ever occur to you that I wasn't completely detached from everything that happened?" His eyes stabbed her.

She turned from his gaze. "I thought you were the long-legged, tight-butt, librarian type of guy."

"I think that was some other guy—the one that's still on the island."

He gently turned her face around, leveled his eyes at her again. "Look, I don't need long legs, tight butts, librarians, tactical armored combat suits or capes. I'm not impressed easily, and that takes someone very special. But I'm no prize, either. I'm an agency analyst and that means I speak in code, forget birthdays and suffer bouts of insomnia. But I'm not an idiot. I know what I like."

"So where does that leave us now?" Diane said to the rail.

He moved closer, grazing her shoulder. "I have an awards ceremony coming up—black tie, invitation only. And I really don't have a proper date for the affair. I'd be honored if you would partner-up with me and attend. How 'bout we start there?"

Diane felt that little tingle again. She didn't let it overwhelm her senses this time. Yet, she hadn't screwed a lid over her heart either.

She gave him a sly look. "I'll think about it, Gene. I'll let you know."

When the sub crew was hauled aboard the fantail of the Franklin Pierce and paraded across the deck single file, Diane was waiting for them, sitting in a wheelchair. The commanding officer, Hicks, Dobbs, and agent Gene stood close by waiting for her to identify the key players of the Global Socialist Alliance. Out of the 90 terrorists and sub crew taken aboard, she fingered most of the original group she had seen at the encampment. Primary were the three individuals who she felt most responsible for the mission. They lined the three up before her, so she could get a good look at their faces. Several shipboard photographers, and one recording engineer stood by to document the identities and testimony.

Diane raised an accusing finger. "That man with the birthmark is Colonel Cho. He was the spokesman for the group—the leader. He's North Korean."

She moved the wheelchair closer. "This woman is Tatiana. I think she's a Captain in the Russian Army." Diane rolled up to the woman and gave her a scathing look. Then she grabbed Tatiana's wrist and yanked her Rolex watch from it. "This is my property, you communist bitch. You won't need to count time where you're going."

Tatiana stiffened, red-faced, but held her pose when she saw a few hands unsnap sidearm holsters.

Diane moved in front of the last suspect, her eyes glaring. “I don’t know what this man’s real name is. He went by Chet Strauss. No doubt you’ll find out who he really is and where he comes from. He’s the inventor of the combat exoskeleton, and the person responsible for trying to sell it to the triad, GSA.” She wanted so badly to pour her heart out about all the lies and heartbreak he had caused her. Just thinking of her association with him filled her with embarrassment and deep hatred. She kept her voice steady. “He is a saboteur and a traitor to the United States government. I hope he rots in hell for what he’s done.”

Chet raised his eyes to meet hers, and for the first time, she thought she saw a flicker of honesty in them. He even let that stupid little grin cross his face, while he brushed back a lock of hair. “I’ve got to hand it to you, Diane. The mistake I made was underestimating you. Bravo.”

She gave him the grin right back. “It was your own invention that turned around to bite you back.”

“I suppose it was,” he said in resignation. “What a goddamned irony, eh?”

The three were escorted back into line. The same line that would be strip-searched and confined to the brig within the next hour.

Diane turned her chair around and gave the officers a nod. She got a few thumbs up, but mostly applause.

The commander of the Franklin Pierce stepped in front of her. “Thank you for your testimony, Ms. Nine. Is there anything we can get you?”

Diane blew out a gale force sigh. “Sir, you can get me *home*.”

21

The awards ceremony took place on the south lawn of the White House during a sun-bright afternoon. The lawn swarmed with the requisite contingent of journalists and news photographers, who jockeyed for the best camera angles and viewing stations. The first five rows of foldout chairs held dignitaries, senators, even a few celebrities. The bleachers behind the stage sagged under the weight of White House staff, relatives, friends, and family. The entire roster of Majestic Comics, as well as Diane's agent and president were seated in the front row. Diane knew her peers were there because they'd screamed the loudest when calling out her name. The only people on their feet besides the press were the Secret Service agents and uniformed officers, providing security for the event. The Joint Chiefs of Staff and several high-ranking officers took up two seated rows on the elevated stage directly behind Diane. The whole thing reeked of pomp and circumstance.

Diane would never forgive Gene for duping her into attending the event, not knowing the elaborate ceremony had been arranged for her, Bibi, and Ollie. He'd been told about the probability of the award ceremony while onboard the Franklin Pierce.

While the vice president droned on during the last half of the ceremony speech, Diane had stuck her tongue out at Gene. He laughed upon seeing how miffed she was. She vowed to pay him back with some prank in the not too distant future. For now, she listened to the vice president's closing statements, trying to adjust to the new wheelchair that had been donated by Homeland Security.

"It is a rare occasion," said the vice president, his voice rising, "when such patriotism is demonstrated in the midst of such overwhelming odds and adversity. Ladies and gentlemen, we are reminded of the stalwart force of Spartan soldiers that gave themselves up, heart, body and soul at the battle of Thermopylae...and why is that?" He paused dramatically.

Diane winced, uncomfortable with the comparison.

"Because ladies and gentlemen, these honored guests here with us today knew that to defend and preserve their homeland and secure the safety of their loved ones and families, they were required to exceed the bounds of heroism above and beyond the call of duty. So, for services rendered in the defense of the United States Government and her allies, I proudly bestow this, the Presidential Medal of Freedom, to these brave individuals to whom we owe our sincerest gratitude and appreciation."

A rousing applause followed. Shutters clicked. A few party poppers went off, launching colorful streamers into the air. Diane half-expected a formation of F-16s to do a low flyover, exhausting red, white, and blue contrails, but it didn't happen. For that, she was thankful.

The vice president stepped to Diane's left, presenting Ollie with the medal. The little man looked prim, dazzling in his rented tuxedo and bow tie. When he bowed and lifted his head, Diane thought Ollie's smile would crack his face in half.

Still, his legs looked like noodles, and she prayed that he would not collapse on the platform stage from sheer fright.

Bibi, dressed in an elegant ethnic brown and gold caftan with matching gele head-wrap, fanned her breasts, as the vice president looped the medal around her neck. She kissed the medal and took a deep breath. Her date, the handsome black sergeant whom she had met on the island and who was seated in the first row, gave her the victory sign.

When Diane's turn came, the vice president had to bend over, whereupon he nearly lost his balance. He recovered gracefully, remarking to the crowd how Diane's beauty had nearly bowled him over. This got a standing ovation and a couple "whoop whoops".

Each recipient was offered a microphone and the opportunity to address the crowd or share thoughts.

Ollie said, "I'm just happy to be here, man." He faltered, looking around until his eyes landed on a color guard brandishing the American flag. "Oh, yeah...and these colors don't run!"

Applause. Whistles.

Bibi spoke for ten minutes, her eyes never leaving her handsome soldier escort who hung onto her every word. After she finished, the crowd sat in stupefied silence—but not as the result of a dynamic, profound speech. They simply hadn't understood a single word she'd said.

When Diane's turn came, she held the microphone loosely, gazing at the friendly faces in the crowd. But her eyes shifted between Bibi and Ollie. She cleared her throat, blinked back tears from her eyes. She hoped her voice wouldn't crack when she began.

"Believe me, I'd never do something like that again without friends like these at my side," Diane stated proudly. "I owe them everything. If not for them, well, I wouldn't be here wearing this pretty piece of jewelry—this honorable award. Thanks for all of the attention and love. Bravery does not mean you have to wear a cape or an armored combat suit. Courage and ideals come from within." She pointed to her heart. "God bless America!"

The audience let loose with a deafening cheer. The applause seemed to go on forever.

Five minutes later, Diane ran her chair down onto the lawn amongst the spectators. A small crowd converged on her. She thrust her hand through the mass of flesh and felt it taken in a strong grip. She pulled hard. Gene appeared at her side and knelt down next to her. He shoved back some of the more exuberant fans.

"You look positively radiant," he said, sporting an ear-to-ear smile. "Congratulations. Is there anything I can get you? Besides a big stick."

"How about a real vacation," she said over the din.

"You're on. I'll take you anywhere in the world."

She motioned for him to move closer and he did. She cupped her voice. "I've got my heart set on spending at least a month on Juventud Island. I just love that place."

He pulled back, his eyes filled with terror. "Metal woman—metal brain. You're nuts!"

She coughed out a hysterical cackle. "Gotcha, secret agent man!"

THANK YOU FOR READING

Did you enjoy this book?

We invite you to leave a review at your favorite book site, such as Goodreads, Amazon, Barnes & Noble, etc.

DID YOU KNOW THAT LEAVING A REVIEW...

- Helps other readers find books they may enjoy.
- Gives you a chance to let your voice be heard.
- Gives authors recognition for their hard work.
- Doesn't have to be long. A sentence or two about why you liked the book will do.

ABOUT THE AUTHOR

Chris Stevenson, aka Christy Breedlove, originally born in California, moved to Sylvania, Alabama in 2009. His occupations have included newspaper editor/reporter, astronomer, federal police officer and part time surfer. He has been writing off and on for 36 years, having officially published books beginning in 1988.

Today he writes science fiction, fantasy, paranormal romance, young adult (his specialty), thrillers and horror. He has a total of 13 titles published. He was a finalist in the L. Ron. Hubbard Writers of the Future contest, and took the first-place grand prize in a YA novel writing contest for *The Girl They Sold to the Moon*. Under the Christy Breedlove pen name, he took first place for the best YA book in the N. N. Light Book Awards Contest, and a finalist for the second in the series. Took a 5-Star review and badge in the Reader's Favorite Awards contest, and just recently was awarded the bronze medal for YA horror in the Reader's Favorite International Book Awards Contest. He writes the popular blog, Guerrilla Warfare for Writers (special weapons and tactics), hoping to inform and educate writers all over the world about the high points and pitfalls of publishing.

ALSO BY CHRIS H. STEVENSON

Novels With Melange Books

Force Nine

Novels With Satin Romance

Blackmailed Bride

www.ingramcontent.com/pod-product-compliance
Lightning Source LLC
LaVergne TN
LVHW090553110826
845146LV00001B/114

* 9 7 9 8 8 8 6 5 3 4 6 8 9 *